SANDY HILL

This book is a work of fiction. All characters and
events portrayed in this book are purely fictitious.
Any resemblance to persons living or dead is coincidental.

Contact the author at **tangledthreadsbook@gmail.com**
or visit **www.tangledthreadsbook.com**

ISBN: 978-1461165415

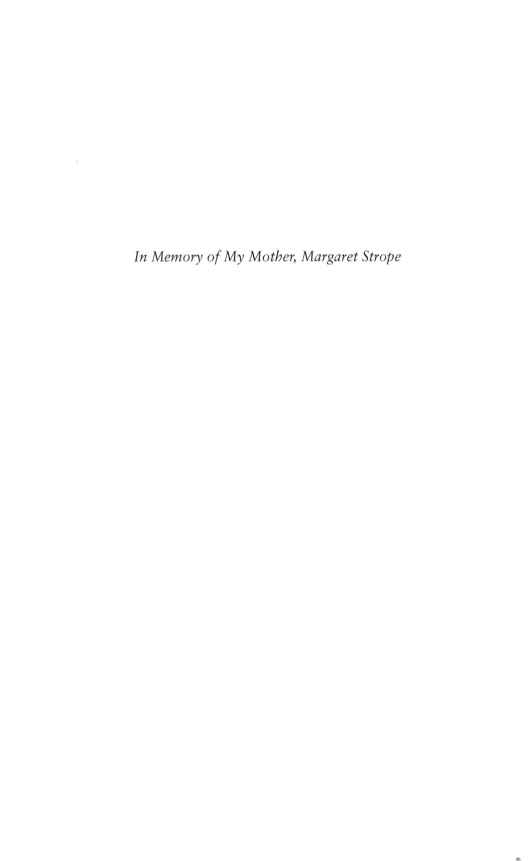

In Memory of My Mother, Margaret Strope

*My thanks to critique group members Paul Barrett,
James Cobble, David Hoag, Adam Lucas, LaTonya Mason,
Ed McKeown, Shontelle McQueen, Nancy Northcott,
Elaine St. Anne, Phyllis St. Clair, Charles Tate,
Barbara Taylor, Maryann Thomas and Kim Wylie.
To consultants James Glenn, Tom Hanchett, Ann Hobgood,
Jason Meyers, Jerrie Nall, Paul Nitsch and Mac Whatley.
Any historical errors are my own. And special thanks to
my husband and fellow writer, Dennis Carrigan.*

Chapter One

March 1957, Whistleton, Virginia

A rest home is a strange place, not that restful and definitely not home. It helps if you think of yourself as an anthropologist. An anthropologist can leave the village anytime she wants. She has a function, something to do. So I pretend I'm an anthropologist, Margaret Mead, perhaps, instead of an 80-year-old woman who walks with a cane. In accordance with my fancy, I've given nicknames to some of my fellow inhabitants of Pleasant Oaks, a place not particularly pleasant despite the staff's best efforts and with any oak trees long gone.

I'd dubbed the manager, Mrs. Atwood, the Witch Doctor. And here she came, hurrying toward me across the day room, her thick heels clacking on the linoleum floor. Around me some of the other residents dozed, played dominoes or stared at the TV set with varying degrees of disinterest.

It was ten o'clock on a rainy March morning. St. Patrick's Day. I'd worn shiny green shamrock earrings in honor of the occasion, along with the black clothing I'd adopted since I came here. A sign of mourning or resistance or fashion? I wasn't sure. The staff had strung rows of paper shamrocks over the doorways in an effort to add some festivity. Lunchtime would bring a cake with green frosting. I gave them credit for trying, but no one else in the dayroom was wearing green.

A soap opera was on TV, the volume cranked up in deference to our deafer residents. The voluptuous Erica had just confessed to Todd that Brad was the father of her baby. Todd wasn't taking it well.

What I really wanted was to play the piano that sat in one corner, which was what I'd been faking when Mrs. Atwood walked up. She'd warned me several times that I mustn't disturb the other residents by actually hitting the keys and making sounds.

God, I missed my own piano. I missed lots of things, but my piano most of all. It had been part of my life for more than 65 years. I'd been here a month, and I was determined not to stay. I'd overcome worse times than these. In the meantime, I'd continue my studies of the natives and play nice — as nice as I could — with the Witch Doctor.

Mrs. Atwood stopped in front of me, frowning slightly. She was a full-figured woman, with a droop at the mouth, a few lines around the eyes to show she must be pushing fifty. Her eyebrows were thin and carefully drawn and her permanented hair was a honey shade with traces of gray at the roots. She wore her usual navy slacks and plain white blouse, like some kind of uniform.

"Delia, must you pretend to play that thing?" she asked.

"Apparently."

She sighed. I was such a burden to her. "You have a visitor," she said.

And just like that, my world changed.

I stared at her. "A visitor?"

I'd rarely had a visitor since my son left me here and hurried back to his home in Los Angeles.

Mrs. Atwood jerked her head toward a tall, slender girl standing in the entrance to the day room. The girl, who looked to be in her late teens, was slightly hunched as if expecting a blow or uncomfortable with her height.

As I approached, she gave me a tentative smile. I smiled back — she didn't deserve to be caught in my dark mood — all the while studying her. First impressions never come again, probably both a loss and a gain.

An immediate point in her favor: She wore a Kelly green sweater, no doubt in honor of the day. It went well with her shiny, straight auburn hair and hazel eyes. Her most striking features were her full lips and wide mouth. It all added up to a certain prettiness, although not great beauty. I had great beauty once, or so I'm told. I look at photos now and wonder who that person was.

I knew what she saw when she looked at me. A tiny woman with wild, shoulder-length white hair and vivid blue eyes that I liked to think still held a spark. I wondered fleetingly what she thought when she saw me banging away at the piano a few minutes ago with my fingers an inch above the keys.

Something about her seemed familiar, but I couldn't place it. She extended her hand. I shifted my cane to my other hand and shook hers, feeling a strong grip and a roughness to her skin. This was someone used to hard work.

"My name is Kate Winton Burris," she said, her voice unexpectedly deep yet with a tremulo of nervousness. "You don't know me."

My heart beat faster at her middle name.

"I'm Delia O'Toole," I said. Maybe her name was coincidence.

We both glanced around at the residents, some of whom were watching the break in the routine. And, of course, Mrs. Atwood was attentive as usual.

"Let's go someplace where we can talk privately," I said.

She nodded as if relieved. We walked down the hall, my cane tapping an uneven rhythm as counterpoint to her light footsteps. As we entered my bedroom, she looked around curiously. A festive patchwork quilt covered the bed, my effort to add color to a room with beige walls and a matching linoleum floor. A rocker sat in one corner with a sunny yellow pillow I'd added for comfort. A few photos perched on the dresser since we weren't allowed to hang anything on the walls. She stared at them as if she wanted to examine them more closely. Good. She had curiosity, and a green sweater to boot. Already I liked her. Or rather, I wanted to like her. But with a name like Winton, who knew what tidings she brought?

The name impelled me past politeness to a direct question. "Are you related to the Wintons of Felthame, North Carolina?" I asked. The Winton name was as bitter as a green persimmon in my mouth, even after all these years.

"Yes. Ruthann Harkey Winton is my grandmother. She sent me."

"Really." Frost coated my response. I reminded myself this girl wasn't to blame for the past and made my next question gentler than the emotions inside me.

"You're three hundred miles from home by my reckoning," I said. "What brings you all the way from Felthame to Virginia?"

"I'm a freshman at Whistleton in the journalism program." It was the small private college five miles away where I'd taught music for years.

"A long way to go to study."

"I guess so." She shifted from one foot to the other.

"What can I do for you?" I asked.

Kate pulled a sealed white envelope from her pocket and held it out. "Grandma sent this to you."

Once, walking along a path on a pleasant day, I stopped short when I saw a copperhead coiled ahead of me. I eyed the envelope with the same wary eye. Irritated at my reaction, I reached for it decisively. Surely, at eighty I was old enough not to let childhood emotions unsettle me.

It was the work of a moment to rip it open and read the contents.

"Do you know what this says?" I asked Kate.

"Not exactly, ma'am." The polite ma'am, the languorous Southern accent I grew up with fell warmly on my ears, an antidote to the letter.

"I know she wants you to come see her, but I don't know the rest. If you're willing to come, I could take you if you can't drive yourself."

"Has your grandmother told you anything about me?"

"Just that you two were girls together in Felthame."

"Indeed we were." I took a deep breath. "This bears thinking about before I can give an answer."

Her glance strayed to the photos. "Excuse me. Is that you?" she asked, pointing to a picture of me wearing a long black gown and seated at a grand piano. It had been snapped when I was perhaps 38, back when my hair was still black.

"Yes," I said. "That was taken at a recital I gave at the college."

"I play the piano some," she blurted out.

"Ah, do you now? Then I guess you saw me playing in the main room." She nodded uncertainly.

"How did you like the piece I was playing? It's Chopin's Waltz in C Sharp Minor. One of the pieces I learned when I was about your age."

She hesitated, visibly searching for an appropriate response. "I've never heard anything like it," she said at last.

I threw back my head and laughed. "Never heard anything like it. Very tactful. I know I wasn't making any noise."

She gave a tiny answering laugh in relief.

"The woman in charge doesn't like the noise," I said. "It interferes with the TV. So I play without touching the keys and hear it in my mind."

I glanced at my gnarled fingers. I wondered whether I could actually play the Chopin piece anymore.

"I like Chopin. I'd love to hear you play sometime," Kate said.

"That's kind of you, but not very likely."

An awkward silence fell. "Well, I'd better go," she said. "Here's my phone number when you're ready to give an answer. Grandma doesn't have a telephone."

I nodded noncommittally. "Let me show you out," I said.

I didn't welcome the news she brought. But it had been pleasant to talk with a young person again, one who appreciated Chopin. This segregation by age was a hardship. For years I'd been surrounded by college students and, in recent years, by children who came to my house for piano lessons.

After Kate left, I went back to my room and sat on the edge of the bed staring at the letter with its shaky scrawl, something a third grader might have done.

"I'm dying," it said. "We have unfinished business. I need you. Please come. Please."

I couldn't imagine Ruthann pleading with anyone, especially not me. And I would have said our business was quite finished, but my internal reaction to Kate's visit told me that wasn't true. Still, to return to the mill village, to see Ruthann — that would be to walk into the lion's den. And I was no Daniel.

My hip ached, and I rubbed it absently. People at the rest home thought the slight limp was related to my recent fall and to my age, but they were partly wrong. It was a lifelong souvenir. Even before what Ruthann called "the accident," there'd been problems between us. They started when we were both twelve. Probably the stage was set before I even met her.

October 1888, a farm near Felthame, North Carolina

I'd just finished gathering eggs and should have been moving on with my morning chores. But the sugar maples on the hill were clamoring to be admired and the sky looked like a bluebird's wing. So I stood in the dirt yard, basket in hand, and breathed it in, trying to remember for when winter came and the trees would be bare.

I heard a sound behind me and turned, smiling, expecting to see Pa back from hunting that big wild hog that had been hanging around the farm. We'd have fresh meat to eat, which would be good, tough as times were.

He staggered out of the woods toward me, blood covering his shirt, and raised one hand in a feeble wave.

"Pa!" I screamed. I dropped the basket and ran toward him. He fell to the ground with a groan and sat dazed, holding his right arm. Through the rip in his shirt, I could see his arm laid open to the bone, the flesh so bloody and torn it made me sick.

"Ma, Naomi, Jewel, Ezra, somebody, help! Help," I yelled, dropping to my knees beside him. Pa's face was white. "Delia," he said. Just the one word.

My two older sisters, Naomi and Jewel, were out in the field. But Ma and my kid brother, Ezra, came out on the porch and looked my way. Then, they pelted across the yard toward us. Everything happened fast after that. Pa was a short, stocky man, full of muscle, but we managed to carry him inside. He fainted along the way.

"That's a blessing," Ma said. "Let's get him on the bed." Blood stained the quilt and I watched it spread with horror. How much blood could you lose and live?

Ma tore off his shirt sleeve and looked at the wound, then reached down, tore off the hem of her petticoat and wrapped it around his arm. "Delia, keep this tight," she said. "First thing, we got to stop this bleeding. Naomi, fetch lye soap and water. This wound is filthy. Jewel, keep Ezra out of the way." Ezra was ten and he'd seen scrapes and bruises before, but none of us had ever seen, ever imagined something as terrible as this.

I pressed for dear life, watching Pa's chest rise and fall, as if just by looking, I could keep him alive.

Eventually, the bleeding stopped and Ma washed the wound. Pa was still unconscious. She grimaced, then sent me for her sewing needle and some thread. "I don't know as these stitches will hold," she said, "but we can't leave it gaping open like that." So Naomi, being the oldest at 15, held Pa's arm still, while Ma sewed it up like a garment. I watched the whole time. It felt like I owed it to Pa. But my eyes kept drifting away and I had to bring them back again. Mainly, I tried not to throw up. The only noise was our breathing. The needle didn't make a sound going in and out of Pa's flesh. Finally, it was over and she bound the arm and leaned back, wiping her hand across her face.

"Let your Pa rest now," she said. Her voice was as hoarse as if she'd been shouting for an hour. "Let's go to the kitchen."

We sat around the table without looking at each other, each in shock.

"We gotta pray," she said. Obediently, we bowed our heads and closed our eyes.

"Dear God, you know my husband is a good man who ain't never done wrong," she began. "Have mercy on him. Heal him and make him whole and strong. If there's anything we can do to help, please let us know. In Jesus name. Amen."

Usually that was it, but this time, we sat silently, praying on our own for a few minutes. I thought I'd prayed hard before, for serious things like rain and a good crop, because the last few years had been hard and I'd heard Ma and Pa talking at night, worried. And I'd prayed for what now seemed trivial things, like that we'd be able to afford a new pair of shoes for me because the holes in the ones I had weren't keeping out the wet and cold. But I'd never really prayed until now. Ma had talked to us about "storming the gates of heaven" with prayer, but I hadn't paid attention. Now we all were storming the gates.

In the next few days, things got better. Pa was able to sit up and get around, although he was weak. He couldn't use his right arm so we pitched in with chores even more. But then the arm got red, with streaks running up it. Soon, he was in bed, either burning up or shivering with chills. Before bed one evening, I tiptoed in to say good night and he looked at me with too-bright eyes.

"Don't worry. Everything will be all right, daughter," he said. But he was breathing too fast and heavy.

"Sure it will," I said.

"I got to go to town for a doctor," Ma said the next morning. "Poultices aren't working." We lived back in a hollow and a trip to town meant riding the mule for fifteen miles.

"Will the doctor come?" I asked. "Do we have money to pay him?"

"I'll make him come," she said. "Do your chores while I'm gone, and pray, pray, pray."

We prayed, did our chores, and took turns at Pa's bedside in case he needed anything. A little after lunchtime, when I was sitting with him, he looked straight at me. "Pa," I said. "I'm here." But he just closed his eyes and seemed to lose consciousness. His breathing slowed, then he gasped and started breathing again. Then he gasped again and his breaths got farther apart.

I patted his face and tried to get him to wake up, but he didn't respond. I ran to the front door. "Ya'll come quick," I yelled. "I'm afraid Pa's going."

They dropped what they were doing and we crowded around Pa's bed. He died within minutes. Jewel threw herself across the bed. Naomi fell to her knees beside Pa. Ezra started to cry. I just stood there, feeling like shattered glass, split into a hundred pieces, everyone of them cutting me up somewhere inside.

And so we buried Pa on a knoll facing the sunrise, because he liked mornings best when the dew was on the grass and the world was fresh and new.

Things continued to happen fast after that, too fast. Two days after the funeral, a man named Joshua Barrett came by offering to buy the farm. He didn't look special, maybe a little fat. He wore overalls like everybody else and rolled a chew of tobacco around in his mouth.

Ma talked to him out in the yard with us beside her.

"Right sorry about your husband," he said, his voice serious. All the while, he was looking around, checking out the field, the barn, the house.

"Thank you kindly," she said. Her eyes were narrow and I could tell she didn't like him.

He glanced at us four children and Ma, all of us skinny and small.

"Mighty hard to work the land without a strong man," he said. "I might could help you out with that."

"Do tell," Ma said. "Imagine that."

It rolled right off him. "Do you mind?" he said. He walked over to our vegetable garden, reached down and sifted dirt through his fingers, then shook his head like he'd never seen such poor soil.

He turned his head to one side and spit on the ground, leaving a wet, brown spot in the dirt. People spit all the time, but this seemed worse, like he was disrespecting Pa somehow. I wanted to smack the man.

Ma folded her arms and made a noise in her throat.

"Beg pardon, Ma'am," he said. After a moment, he went on. "I can make you an offer for the farm. It would give you and the younguns enough money for a fresh start. I hear tell they're hiring mill workers in Felthame. It's a good living. No more worrying about whether it rains or whether insects will eat the crop and such like. I'd take everything off your hands, lock, stock and barrel."

A sour taste rose in my mouth. How could we leave our home?

He looked at us as if he was wondering if we kids should be there for talk about money.

"It concerns them. They stay," Ma said. I stood up straighter to show I was old enough and responsible.

So he named a figure. Ma's mouth tightened. "I'll think on it," she said.

"You do that. Again, I'm sorry for your loss. Send word to Chub Yandle's store. But don't wait too long."

After he left, Ma said he was figuring out how desperate we were. We were pretty desperate. So Ma decided we couldn't go on. We sold the farm, the livestock, most everything except the clothes on our back, and a little furniture to start over in Felthame.

Our last day there, I walked around, saying goodbye to my favorite spots, the creek where we cooled off in summer and my secret place near a little spring. I made my way there and sat on a fallen log surrounded by autumn trees. I let my mind go blank, trying to store everything up in memory, the feel of the moss, the rustle of the leaves, the tiny sound the spring makes if you get quiet enough, the cardinal telling me I was "pretty, pretty." Except my mind wouldn't stay quiet. It kept running around like a spring colt in the pasture. I thought about how I'd miss the mockingbirds greeting me in the morning, and the wind soughing through the loblolly pines. Heck, I'd even miss that old possum that stole our corn. Pa kept threatening to shoot him and make stew out of him. I shied away from that memory and stood up fast. It was almost a relief to go back to the house.

There was one more thing to do before we left, and we all had the same idea. We'd each picked branches of the prettiest maple leaves we could find. We dropped them on Pa's grave until you couldn't see a speck of fresh dirt, then stood in silence.

"We gotta make the best of our new life now," Ma said at last. "Y'all promise me you'll try."

We nodded, but no one said a word.

Mr. Barrett carted our stuff to our new house with his horse and wagon free of charge, which I supposed was decent of him. My brother and sisters glanced back when the wagon rolled away, but Ma and I didn't. I was trying to do what Ma wanted and look forward, even though it felt impossible right then.

So we moved to Felthame where I met Ruthann. That seemed like a small change at the time, compared to what had just happened. But it turned out to be a bigger change than I could ever have imagined.

March 1889, Felthame, North Carolina

Our sixth-grade teacher, Mrs. Allenby, stood at the front of the classroom, "Ray's Intellectual Arithmetic" in her hand. She was giving us math problems out loud. Even though arithmetic was one of my best subjects, it was a bit tricky because you had to do the sums in your head instead of on paper and do them faster than anyone else. Everyone else had dropped out of the contest and now the new girl, Ruthann, and I were tied. This was the final make-or-break question. The winner got three sticks of peppermint candy. Already, I'd mentally taken them home to share with my family.

"If a family uses $3^1/_5$ barrels of flour a month, how much will it use in three months?" Mrs. Allenby asked.

I figured furiously. In my rush to be first, I waved my hand wildly in the air a split second before I was sure of the answer.

Beside me, in the second row, Ruthann Harkey waved her hand, too. My arm was shorter than her long skinny arm and I wanted to be sure the teacher saw it, so I gestured even more wildly and lifted partway out of my seat. Ruthann increased her tempo to match mine.

Ever since she'd arrived three weeks ago, she'd taken a dislike to me, tormenting me when no one else was around. I guess she didn't like to be shown up in school. We both were smart, but what was I supposed to do? Pretend I didn't know the answer so she could get credit?

"Delia," Mrs. Allenby said. "Your hand was up first. Can you tell the class the answer?"

If I missed, Ruthann would have her chance. Ruthann dropped her hand and waited, leaning forward in her seat.

"Nine and three/fifths barrels," I answered, crossing my fingers.

"Correct. Delia is the winner," Mrs. Allenby said. "Well done."

I smiled broadly in acknowledgment.

"You did well, too, Ruthann," she said. "Maybe next time."

I glanced at Ruthann, only to be confronted by an icy stare. I was glad I'd beaten her, even though I'd have to avoid her after school now. It had been worth it to see Mrs. Allenby's approving smile. Mrs. Allenby was ancient and about due for retirement, but I liked her. She made learning, not exactly fun, but interesting. She never rapped our knuckles or made us stand in the corner, but somehow we always wanted to please her. I don't know how she did it.

When school was out, I stood for a few minutes talking with Mattie, my best friend, hoping to outwait Ruthann. Mattie was plump with a sweet smile and friendly nature that made you like her right away. I'd pretty much kept to myself when we first moved to town. So much had changed so fast that I could hardly handle it. But Mattie had sought me out and drawn me in. I purely loved her. After a few minutes, she said, "I got to get home. I have chores to do."

"I know. So do I. Seems like there's always chores."

She went one way, and I started the walk home in the opposite direction. It had rained during the afternoon and the unpaved road was awash in red mud. It made little squishing sounds as I hurried along. But not fast enough. I heard footsteps behind me and glanced back to see Ruthann striding toward me. I could have started running, but her legs were longer and besides it didn't sit right to run from anybody. If Pa were alive, he wouldn't want me doing that. He always said maybe we were poor, but we could hold our heads high with the best of them.

I started humming "Oh Susannah" under my breath. Music made me feel better, even at times like this with Ruthann bearing down on me.

She smiled a fakey smile as she drew abreast. I sent her a fakey smile right back and clutched the sack with my peppermint sticks tighter. She gave a high, prancing kick and mud spattered on my gingham dress. I pressed my lips together in anger. I had two dresses. One was dirty from where she'd tripped me earlier in the week. Now I'd have to wash them both tonight and hope they dried in time for school in the morning. And that would take some scrubbing. Nothing was as hard to get out of clothes as red clay.

"Oops," she said, a word I'd come to hate from her.

"You did that on purpose," I said.

"No, I didn't. It was an accident. Honest."

"Sure it was."

She stepped forward, and with an effort I stood my ground. "Are you calling me a liar?" she asked, putting her face close to mine.

Oh how I wanted to say "Yes, you liar." But I was scared. The way my legs felt I couldn't have run from her even if I wanted to.

"No," I said.

"Good."

"Aren't you going to share your candy?" she asked.

"No," I said again, balling up my fist while my legs shook harder. The sticks were for my brother and sisters and Ma. I'd won them fair and square, and no one was going to take them away if I could help it.

She looked at my expression, then at my fists, gave a half smile and backed off.

"Keep your candy, little baby," she said, and ran on down the road in front of me, spattering more mud as she left. I watched her tall, thin form, my stomach churning with fear, and with anger at her and myself. It seemed as if I should be fighting back, but I wasn't sure how.

I'd tried to be friendly, remembering how it felt to be new. We all brought lunch to school in lard buckets. I noticed she didn't bring anything to eat the first two days. On the third day, when I offered to share my lunch, her face turned red and in a clear, cold voice, she told me that she didn't need charity, and she wasn't hungry anyway. She never had brought lunch yet. Maybe that's why she was so skinny and mean.

After that, things got worse between us. At first it was just at school, but lately anywhere she saw me alone. She was smart, no denying that. And I suppose she could be funny because other kids laughed at things she said, but I never saw that side of her.

One of these days, I thought, as I shook my fist at her retreating back. Big talk, no action. But I couldn't think what else to do. Ma had enough trouble, working at the cotton mill and trying to support us. She'd have a conniption fit if I came home all beat up from fighting. Or, worse than throwing a fit, she'd say she was disappointed in me and tell me there was always a peaceful way to resolve problems if you just looked hard enough. Easy for her to say. She didn't go to school with Ruthann.

When I got home, I brushed off the dried mud, but orange spots still lingered. I tried to put it out of my mind, since I couldn't do anything about it right then, but while I rolled out the biscuits for supper, it kept worrying at me. That was the thing about being bullied by Ruthann. There was that moment when she was there in front of me picking on me, but maybe worse than that was the time afterward when I ran over in my mind all the things I could have said if I'd thought fast enough or dared to. And there was the sick feeling of dread because sooner or later I was going to see her again.

Ezra, my ten-year-old brother, ran in and snatched a piece of raw biscuit dough. "Stop that," I snapped. "You'll spoil your supper." Not that anything could spoil Ezra's appetite, but I wanted to scream at someone.

It was dark when Ma and my sisters got home and I hurried to set the stew on the table before it got cold.

Every night at supper we took turns saying grace, because Ma said we all needed to be comfortable speaking to the Lord. I usually used the same grace and by now the words rolled off my lips by rote, probably not what Ma had in mind.

"Delia," she said, nodding at me to pray and closing her eyes.

"Thank you for this food and all your many blessings," I prayed. "Protect our loved ones and help us to show your love in the world and to each other." Then I added, "And deliver us from evil. Amen."

Ma looked at me when she opened her eyes, but didn't say anything about the unexpected addition to my prayer. We ate in silence except for now and then asking someone to pass food or a comment on the weather.

"Delia, could you please get me some more stew?" Ma asked.

"Yes, ma'am."

The lamp didn't cast much light and I got up from my chair sideways, hoping she wouldn't notice the mud on my skirt. But she notices everything. When I came back and started to sit down, she looked at my dirty skirt and frowned.

"Oh dear. Look at those spots," she said. "You got to be more careful, honey."

That stung me. "But, Ma," I said, "that new girl, Ruthann, kicked mud at me on the way home from school. I don't understand why she doesn't like me. I never did anything to her."

"She shouldn't have done that, but not everybody was raised right. Her ma is dead and her pa gone – somewhere — so she's really lost both parents. And that aunt of hers, well... I shouldn't speak poorly of a neighbor, but they say she's a holy terror, that she can light into Ruthann something awful, which isn't right. Still..."

I sighed inwardly. The next thing out of Ma's mouth would be something to explain why Ruthann's aunt was so ornery. Ma found good in everyone. It was wrong of me, but sometimes I got tired of it. Some people were just mean.

Sure enough, Ma went on. "We have to remember that her aunt has a lot on her, what with Ruthann's ma dying. So now she's raising Ruthann and her brother, and trying to work. I'm sure she wasn't counting on that, her an unmarried lady and all. It must be hard on her."

Vernell, Ruthann's brother, was seven. So far, he seemed cute and sweet. Not like Ruthann.

"I guess," I said.

"Just ignore Ruthann and she'll get tired of teasing you," Ma said.

That was like ignoring the river that powered the mill. Ignore it all you wanted, but it just kept flowing.

"Yes, Ma'am," I said. "I'll try."

Naomi and Jewel had been quiet while Ma and I talked. Ezra paid no attention. Now Naomi and Jewel cast me sympathetic glances. They'd brushed their hair, but lint from the spinning room still clung to it. I quivered inside, seeing myself a few months down the road. School would be out in two months, and I'd turned twelve a week ago. The end of sixth grade was when you were expected to start work at the mill. Ma couldn't put off sending me any longer, much as she might want to.

I looked at Ma, trying to gauge how tired she was after eleven hours at work. She was tiny like me, with the same blue eyes and wild black hair, and she had to stand on a box to reach the machinery. I'd been wanting to ask her my question for a while, but she always seemed exhausted. I guess she never would be rested, so this was as good a time as any. First, I whipped out my surprise. "I won three peppermint sticks at the arithmetic bee today," I said.

She smiled, the weariness falling from her face. "I'm proud of you, honey," she said. Then she gave a little cough. She'd been doing more of that lately.

She leaned over and pulled one of Ezra's shirts from the mending basket. Her hands were always busy. Even at night, sometimes they twitched on top of the quilt as if she was darning or mending.

There were five of us and only three peppermint sticks. I offered Ma one, but she said she wasn't much for sweets. I didn't argue. I cut up the sticks and we kids sucked on them while I asked my big question.

"Mrs. Allenby asked today if I was going on to seventh grade at the school in town. She said I should, with my good grades. I was wondering..." I trailed off when I saw her face.

She jabbed the needle through the shirt, and her mouth quivered. "I'd love to say yes, Delia, but I plum can't. With your Pa passed on, we need the money you'd bring in at the mill. And I haven't got any extra for tuition and books. I'm sorry."

Involuntarily we looked at the head of the table where Pa used to sit. There was no chair, just an empty space, like in our lives. I could almost picture him. Short, trim, with bulging arm and shoulder muscles from farm work. Dark eyes and hair that curled when it rained. I liked thinking of him that way. Not the way it ended up. During the day, I was busy and I'd forget at times, then grief would catch me by surprise, so intense I wanted to run from the room. I was sleeping better, but at times I still had nightmares in vivid color where Pa was bleeding to death and I tried to stanch the blood with my white cotton shift, but I couldn't. The red blood poured out on the wooden floor, buckets of it draining through the cracks in the boards and his life draining out with it.

I shook my head sharply. No point in thinking about Pa's suffering. Better to think about Pa being in Heaven. I hoped they had deer or squirrels there because he purely loved to hunt. But I wasn't sure about Heaven any more. I'd prayed and prayed but God took him anyway. It made me mad at God and scared to be mad at Him, too.

"Delia," Ma said, "You look sad. Are you thinking about your pa?"
I nodded.

"He's in a better place. He's watching over us. He wouldn't want us to be sad."
"No, Ma'am," I said. "I know that."

She sighed and Naomi and Jewel frowned at me for upsetting Ma.
Naomi, at sixteen, liked the mill and was proud of how many sides of

yarn she could handle in the spinning room. "The mill is a good place to work, Delia," she said. "Pretty soon you'll be as good as I am. And you can gossip with the other girls as long as you do your work. You'll learn to ignore the noise and talk over it. And you might even have a little money left over for yourself." She meant after I gave most of my earnings to Ma and we settled up with the company store.

Jewel, who was fourteen, cast a skeptical glance at Naomi. She didn't much care for the mill, but she didn't much care for school either, and what else was there for people like us?

"Naomi just enjoys having Jediah make googoo eyes at her at work," she said. "He's sweet on her."

Naomi blushed but didn't deny it.

"Don't tease your sister," Ma said. "Jediah is a nice boy."

Now that Jediah, a year older at seventeen, was sparking Naomi, I'd overheard Ma warn her to be a good girl and not get in a family way. It was hard not to overhear with only four rooms.

That was another reason I needed to work. We were allowed one room for each mill worker, but if Naomi married and I didn't work in the mill, maybe the company would decide we should move to a house with three rooms. Ezra was old enough to be a doffer now, replacing the full bobbins of thread with empty ones, and that would help. But Ma had asked him to go through sixth grade first. I owed it to the family to help out with the money.

Ma wanted more for us, but it seemed like we were all like rabbits in a hutch with no way out. Ma poked at her food with one hand on her forehead. I pushed my dreams way down, feeling like a bad daughter.

"It's all right, Ma," I said. "I bet I'll like working in the mill."

And so, on a bright May morning when the sun was a pink smudge on the horizon and the air smelled of honeysuckle, Mattie and I walked toward the mill for our first day in the spinning room. Around us, in the faint light, men, women, children flowed toward the mill in a steady stream, laughing and talking as they went. I could barely hear the chirping of birds above the hum that grew ever louder as we neared the mill. The morning star still shone and I made a wish that I'd learn quickly so I could start earning my twenty five cents a day.

Ahead, I could see Ruthann, who had started a week earlier. Ma said she was doing good so far. Her brother, Vernell, trotted along in bare feet, his pudgy hand in hers. With school out and her aunt not wanting to bother with him, it fell to Ruthann to keep an eye on Vernell.

When I walked through the big double doors, I felt excited and apprehensive. But oh how I wished it was the fall and I was walking to my new school instead.

I'd been in the spinning room dozens of times visiting Ma or my sisters, but today I looked at it with fresh eyes. The dim daylight through the high arched windows and the kerosene lamps cast a sickly, yellow glow over the narrow rows of hundreds of spindles, filled with cotton yarn to be wound onto bobbins. Belts stretched upward from the machines like thick umbilical cords. The pine floor was clean, but by day's end it would be covered with lint. And so would I. The floor near the wall would be slippery with tobacco juice spit out by the women who used snuff. Too many didn't use the spittoons. I let out a sigh and squared my shoulders. This was my new home, and it was up to me to make the best of it.

A supervisor sent Mattie in one direction and me in another. With a sinking heart I saw that I'd be tending spindles in the same row as Ruthann. "Good morning," I said as I walked by. She gave a sharp nod but kept staring at her machines. Fine with me. We didn't have to be friends, although it would have been nicer day after day.

I had a general idea of my job from visiting Ma: Move up and down the row watching for the white tufts that signaled snags or potential breaks in the yarn. Piece them up with the special knot Ma had shown me and that I'd practiced at home. I could do this.

The supervisor ran over the basics, then turned to leave. "I'll be back to check on your soon. Ruthann will help you if you have any problems," he said. "She's caught on fast. She seems to have a way with the machines."

Ruthann looked up and smiled at him. "I'll help her, all right," she said, raising her voice above the din.

In the corner, Vernell was playing with another little boy, tossing a ball of yarn back and forth and missing it half the time. His face was scrubbed, his blond hair neatly combed and his clothes ragged but clean. He looked up, displaying bright blue eyes, and I winked at him. He giggled and ducked his head shyly. At least one member of the Harkey family was friendly.

I turned my attention to my work. Your pay depended on how many spindles you could watch at a time. I focused on mine, determined not to make mistakes and to be able to add more spindles — and thus more money — soon. I didn't see Vernell's ball roll my way so when it hit my ankle, I instinctively kicked out, thinking an insect had landed on me. Vernell was reaching for the ball at the same time and I narrowly missed his head.

Ruthann's head whipped around. "How dare you kick my little brother?" she snarled.

"I wasn't kicking him," I said. "The ball startled me. I thought it was a bee or something."

"So you say. Nobody messes with my brother. Got that?"

"Got it," I said. "I would never hurt a child."

"Lots of people can, believe me, and hurt them bad. You can't trust anyone. You got to watch out for yourself." She turned to her spindles with a grim look.

Vernell was watching us with wide eyes. Ruthann smiled at him. "It's all right, sugar. Go back to your game. No one is going to hurt you if I can help it."

He picked up the ball and retreated to the corner.

I suddenly realized I'd neglected my spindles. Three showed signs of breaking. I rushed to the first one just as the supervisor came down the aisle.

"What's this?" he asked, frowning. "You've got to keep a better eye on things, Delia. We'll have to stop these machines now and piece together the ends."

"Yes, sir," I said.

Ruthann smiled.

It was a good thing Ma and our preacher didn't know what I was thinking just then. If what they said in the Bible about inner thoughts being as bad as doing the things, I was Hellbound for sure. My only comfort was that Ruthann would be there, too. Or maybe that is what would make it Hell.

Chapter Two

March 1957, Whistleton, Virginia

Memory and the confines of my room with its view of Pleasant Oak's employee parking lot were beginning to pall. The adjustment to living alone, with no one to share sunrises, to cook for, to linger over dinner with, had been one of the hard things after my husband died. Enough of pity. Everyone had some problem in life. I stood up, ran a comb through my unruly hair and headed for the day room.

Mrs. Atwood walked toward me as I entered.

"Your visitor…" she paused as if hoping I'd fill in the relationship, "…seems very nice."

"Yes," I said. "She does."

"I didn't catch her name…"

"Not to worry. Excuse me."

I looked around. Henry, a short, balding, barrel-shaped man who had arrived at the home three days ago, was talking to Alice, or rather being talked to by Alice, one of the more loquacious residents, who I'd given the nickname Village Crier. She'd spruced up with pink lipstick and a blue top that matched her eyes and blue eye shadow. In a few minutes, a rouge-enhanced woman who'd apparently confused her cheeks with ripe apples drifted toward Henry, holding a paperback book out to him. He looked up, nodded politely and accepted it while Alice scowled at her competitor for the attentions of that rare species in our nursing home, an unattached, still mentally sharp male. I watched the courting rituals like a good anthropologist until Henry caught my eye and winked. Forgetting the proper detachment, I smiled in surprise. He returned to holding court, an answering smile fleeing across his face.

After dinner, I went out on the wide front porch. Boards creaked under my feet. Or maybe it was my bones creaking. It was getting harder to tell the difference.

"Now, don't wander off," Mrs. Atwood said, giving a laugh that failed to soften the admonition.

"Where would I go?" I asked, and closed the door behind me.

I settled into one of the maple rockers, which added more creaking, and watched the dying light of the sun as it sank behind the clouds. This was a mixed time of day. It brought a welcome taste of the natural world but it also meant another restless night of listening to the clicking of nurses' heels in the halls along with the sounds of the nocturnal wanderings of a few residents who apparently harbored vampire blood, since they walked by night and seemed semi-comatose during the day.

After a bit, I realized it could have been midnight for all the attention I was paying to the sunset. What was I feeling, now that Ruthann had surfaced in my life again? Anger? Maybe a little. But that terrible day at the river was far behind me, and I'd learned to go on. Grief? Yes. Some losses never left you. Right now, mainly I felt regret, a regret reaching back to the benefit concert when Ruthann and I were girls. Benefit. Such a positive word. Yet for years I'd thought of it in capital letters: The Benefit. Because that was the moment when the decision I made led to one tragedy after another, like a snowball rolling downhill. Or more like an avalanche burying what might have been.

A figure loomed beside me in the fading light, making me jump.

"Sorry. I didn't mean to startle you, " Henry said. "Mind if I join you? It's a beautiful evening." His admirers were nowhere to be seen.

He was a welcome distraction, just when I needed one. "Feel free," I said, waving toward a nearby rocking chair.

He sat without speaking for several minutes, which I appreciated. Sunset is meant to be a quiet time. The far-off bark of a dog and the long, low whistle of a train drifted toward us on the night air. I breathed deeply, feeling calmer.

Finally, he spoke. "I like your cane," he said, his voice surprisingly deep for a short man. "It's unusual."

I'd laid it across my lap, and the cane's head with its brass figure of a snarling wolf gleamed dully in the lamplight from the windows.

"Thank you," I said. "It's a souvenir of the First World War, from Germany."

"Do you know its history?"

"No," I said. "But I try to imagine the man it belonged to."

"What do you imagine?"

"That he was tall, elderly, near the end of his life but surrounded by family. He dropped it one day walking in a country lane with his dog at his side. After that, he wondered about the person who found it just the way we're wondering about him."

"Maybe he was a viscount with a wolfhound," he said. "Or a baron."

"Who played the accordion," I added, enjoying this brief encounter.

I'd about given up trying to make conversation with the natives, but here I was talking away. Maybe I was bored and, if I cared to admit it, lonely. Henry was a new face, and a friendly one.

The sun disappeared behind the trees and I rose, wishing him a good night.

"I enjoyed our little talk," he said.

"So did I," I said, realizing I meant it.

That night Kate telephoned me at nine o'clock.

"I hope I'm not calling too late," she said.

I laughed. "Not at all. I'm a bit of a night owl." Although night owl now meant eleven o'clock.

"I've been thinking," she said. "Would you like to come over to the college and play one of the practice pianos some day? I could come and get you."

Joy surged through me, followed quickly by wariness. How far had the apple fallen from the Ruthann Winton family tree? Were strings attached? Would she enjoy it, too? Or was this an act of charity? It was hard to be on the receiving end after years of being the one in charge.

"I wouldn't want to put you to any trouble," I said.

"It's no trouble. You'd be doing me a favor. Honest. You could give me a few pointers on my playing."

Put that way, I could accept her offer. Neither one of us would be beholden.

"That's awfully nice of you," I said. "I'd be happy to give as many pointers as you want." My eagerness leaped out before I could stop it. "When would be a good time?"

"Uh, how about Tuesday morning? I could pick you up around eight, if that's not too early." Only two days to wait before I could play again.

"Perfect," I said. "Thank you. Thank you."

That night I dreamed that I tried to play but my fingers had lost their flesh, and my bare bones clattered on the keys. I awoke with a feeling of panic. I'd been playing daily up until a few months ago, before I fell going down the stairs at my house. There was no reason to think I'd lost the ability that quickly. But a few months ago, I'd been living in my own house, too. I'd have said there was no reason to think I'd be in a rest home. It was temporary, I reminded myself. My limp from years earlier, after The Benefit, was permanent, but this new injury would heal.

Two days later, on a sunny morning, Kate drove me over to the college in a battered 1946 black Ford with a motor that sounded alarmingly like someone with asthma. Otherwise, the trip was largely silent. I gazed out the window, enjoying looking at fresh scenery, at trees pregnant with spring green, while Kate concentrated on driving. Perhaps she didn't know what to say to someone my age. I didn't when I was eighteen. I'd been respectful, yes, but old age was a land I couldn't imagine entering.

My attention sharpened as we reached the tree-strewn campus with its winding paths and brick buildings.

"I've only been back once or twice since I retired," I said. "That was fifteen years ago."

"I guess a lot has changed," she said.

She pointed to the new administration building, the student center and the two dorms that had sprung up.

I was pleased to see the music building was the same: a three-story, red brick structure with arched windows and ivy growing up one wall. The strains of a violin drifted through a partly open window, striking me with a nostalgic blow.

The practice rooms were still in the basement, down the familiar stairs covered in the same cracked green tile. But as I stood at the top I realized I couldn't get down the stairs. At least, not easily and not without pain. I glared at them, remembering when steps were just steps, something you hurried up or down, and not an obstacle to work around. Stairs were the main reason I'd agreed to leave my two-story house and go to the nursing home to recuperate. Plus, although I hated to admit it, the fall had made me nervous about being home alone and incapacitated.

I looked down the flight of stairs, thinking of the pianos below, and excitement drained out of me. "This won't work," I told Kate, disciplining my voice to calmness.

"What? Oh, the steps. We can use the elevator. I guess they added it after you left."

The Promised Land opened up again. "Wonderful," I said. "Let's go."

The tiny practice room we entered held a shiny walnut spinet, an oasis to someone dying of thirst. I had never realized how much I relied on music to soothe me, to express my joys, my sorrow.

Kate had been watching my face, which I fear showed a certain naked hunger. Now she gestured to the piano in invitation.

"You first."

I limped over and sat down, flexing my fingers, stretching my arms, warming up the tendons that stood out so visibly on my hands. Now that the moment was here, I felt almost afraid. I hated feeling afraid. I'd done enough of that in childhood with Ruthann. No more.

Sitting up straight with the kind of posture I tried to inculcate in my students, I played a simple C scale. The piano, while the tone wasn't rich, was in tune. I ran through a few more scales, then paused.

I'd thought several times about what I would start with. Wasted effort because, as sometimes happened, music surprised me. I plunged into a piece that hadn't been on my list: Brahms' Rhapsody, Opus 79 No. 2 in G Minor. I played it perhaps badly as far as technique, but gratifyingly for expressing the emotion pent up inside me. My pedaling wasn't crisp and the spacing of chords was less than perfect. I didn't care. I pounded the keys mercilessly in the first section, until even the sound-proofed walls of the practice room could barely absorb the clamor. All the frustration of my fall, the nursing home, the loss of freedom flowed down my arms, through my fingertips and into the piano. When I finished, feeling purified and exhausted, Kate clapped loudly, startling me. Her eyes were bright with excitement.

"That was terrific," she said.

I shook myself back to the present. "I'm glad you liked it."

"Play something else."

No urging was needed. My equilibrium restored, I edged into the second movement of Beethoven's Pathetique sonata, and felt relaxation creep over me. For a moment I closed my eyes as the notes rose up from memory to greet me, my old, reliable friends.

"Thank you for letting me play," I said. I'd rushed parts of the Grave section, but, as I told my students, don't spoil compliments by voicing your own inner critique. Embarrassingly, tears gathered in my eyes. I disliked feeling vulnerable, another emotion I'd vowed to give up. To give me time to recover, I looked around the room. Like all the practice rooms, it offered little except a piano, a bench, a chair for the teacher, bare walls and a mirror where you could watch your technique, especially useful to vocal students.

"Your turn," I said. "Please play a favorite of yours, anything that you like."

She sat beside me on the bench and I slid over, enjoying the familiarity of it all. She flexed her fingers in imitation of what I'd done, then plunged into Chopin's Waltz in C Sharp Minor with a certain verve and definite warmth. I wondered if she'd chosen it because it was the same piece I'd pretended to play at the nursing home. She played a bit too fast near the beginning and too slow in the piu mosso part, but all in all a good effort.

"Very nice," I said. "We can work on your technique, but you play with emotion and that's hard to teach."

"Thank you," she said. She dropped her eyes and her voice was low.

"When I'm playing, it's like a magic carpet. It takes me away. You know?" She looked at me, her face open and vulnerable, the face of someone offering a gift she hopes won't be rebuffed.

"I know," I said. "It's a wonderful feeling."

Then, a little uncomfortable and confused by this moment with Ruthann's granddaughter, I asked briskly, "What's your musical background? How many years of lessons have you had?"

"Five, but I haven't been able to practice as much as I'd like, although I use the practice rooms here when I can. When Mom died, things were tough. But later, Grandma encouraged me to play and said she'd pay for the lessons."

"Oh?" That would be quite a sacrifice for Ruthann. "You're progressing very well then."

"What am I doing wrong?"

"Let's talk about what you're doing right first," I said. If you started with how the students could improve, the criticism crowded out the praise in their minds.

"You're doing well on the arpeggios, which can be difficult. And, as I said, you have good interpretation of the spirit of the waltz."

She nodded.

"Let's hear it again, only more quickly in the piu mosso," I said. "Be sure you start the runs with your fourth finger."

I tutored her for almost an hour, feeling useful again. Then I played several more pieces. I'd have liked to sing a little, but I felt self-conscious about the rasp of age in my once-clear alto.

Ruthann, I recalled, had had a soprano as sweet and clean as spring water. You could hear it soaring out in church or occasionally soft on the evening air when she walked home from the mill.

"Does your grandmother ever sing anymore?" I asked.

"Not that I know of. I kind of remember Grandma singing when I was little. But that was before Mama died and she came to live with us and take care of me while Daddy worked."

"I'm sorry about your mother," I said.

"Thank you. Well, I need to stop so I have time to study. I've got a journalism test coming up."

"Of course. Thank you," I said. "This was truly wonderful."

As we walked out into the bright sunlight toward the parking lot, I realized my leg hurt less than before we started. On the way back to Pleasant Oaks, she seemed to have lost some of her nervousness.

"When did you first start playing the piano?" she asked.

"It was a long time ago. I was thirteen and working in the spinning room at the mill."

"With Grandma?"

"We worked in the same room," I said, a little tartly. Kate had no idea what those days had been like. Nor did she need to know about that, or about the secrets Ruthann and I shared, the deaths between us. Unless something changed, we would take our secrets to the grave, where loved ones lay already, loved ones whose lives we'd changed forever. The thought still hurt across the span of more than fifty years. Did grief ever die? Or did it just find deeper places to hide?

Chapter Three

March 1957, Whistleton, Virginia

The return to the rest home felt like arrival at a well-intentioned prison. It smelled like urine and disinfectant, a smell you got used to until it struck you fresh when you'd been away. Again I vowed to get out of here soon. My leg seemed to be mending from my recent fall. It couldn't be much longer before I could leave.

"Thank you for the lesson," Kate said. "Would you like to do this again? I could pick you up at the same time next week. Are you free then?"

When wasn't I free? And I'd clear the most crowded schedule for another chance to teach, to play the piano. "I'll be ready," I said. "Thanks."

A thought struck me. "You know, Kate, my decision about going back to Felthame won't be affected by anything you do, so don't feel obligated to spend time with me."

"I don't."

She offered to help me inside, but I gestured to the long wheelchair ramp with its iron railing beside the entrance steps, and she nodded. I was grateful she'd offered and doubly grateful she didn't insist on help I didn't want.

Mrs. Atwood spotted me as I entered the lobby.

"Did you have a nice visit?" she asked.

"Very nice."

"You didn't overdo, did you? That would be a mistake."

"No," I said. "I didn't overdo."

I wandered out on the porch, hoping Henry would join me. Maybe he'd been watching for me, because in a few minutes he came out and sat down.

"How was your day?" he asked.

"Any day I get to play the piano is a good one. How about you?"

"A lot of reading. A little hiding." He laughed. "I got a letter from my daughter. Mostly news about the weather, but it's always nice to get mail."

"How many children do you have?"

"Two. One daughter close by and the other teaching in Japan."

So perhaps he'd be having frequent visitors. Sometimes residents whose children rarely visited seemed depressed after they left. Maybe occasional visits were worse than none, upsetting a delicate acceptance of the status quo. More possibilities to investigate in my ongoing study of the place. Maybe I could publish a paper after I left: "The Effects of Intermittent Reinforcement on Emotionally Starved Elderly." I could add it to my study of Alice and "Female Courting Behavior in a Male-Deficient Environment."

"My daughter wanted me to live with her, but she doesn't really have room," he said. "And I'd rather be here than be a burden. I've seen what happens when an ailing parent lives with offspring. Anyway, soon I'll be leaving, going back to my apartment."

I glanced at him, wondering if he was deluding himself. Alice said he had "the sugar in the blood" and was having problems controlling it. She listed some of the dire consequences that could result, like losing a foot, or having a stroke. I couldn't tell by looking how bad things were and I didn't know him well enough to ask.

"At least we're still on the first floor," he said.

The first floor was for those who could maneuver and had some idea who and where they were, although they might flunk knowing that Eisenhower was president. The second floor was for the truly infirm mentally and/or physically.

"Here's to a quick release," I said. I raised an imaginary glass as if in a toast, and took an imaginary sip. After a second, he did the same, smiling at me.

"Mine is Dom Perignon," I said. "A good vintage."

He inclined his head in acknowledgment. "Indeed," he said. "A very good vintage. When I was diagnosed with liver disease, my doctor told me to give up drinking, so this is perfect."

So much for Alice as a source of accurate information.

I gazed out at the lawn, feeling a bit of the sweet melancholy a certain time of evening can evoke.

In a few minutes he said, "You're quiet. I like that."

Poor Alice. She was taking exactly the wrong tack with him.

"Is there any more champagne in the bottle?" he asked.

"All you want," I said. "It seems to be bottomless."

We looked at each other and grinned.

A voice from behind us shattered the mood. "It's getting chilly out here," Mrs. Atwood said. "You'd better come in."

"You made me spill my champagne," I said.

"You've been drinking?" she asked sharply. "That's against the rules."

"Only in our dreams," I said.

Henry smothered another grin.

I wasn't sure why I baited her. I suppose she reminded me a little of Ruthann. But perhaps I should be more careful. I didn't want her reporting to my son that I was losing touch with reality.

It was Tuesday, time for Kate's weekly piano lesson, and she was upset with her difficulties with fingering on a Kuhlau sonatina. The tiny practice room seemed to shrink as her frustration grew.

"Let's take a short break," I said.

She sighed with relief. "It's like my fingers have a mind of their own."

"Everyone feels that way at times," I said. "You're doing fine."

We headed out into a brisk spring day and settled down on a round wooden bench that circled a huge oak.

Kate glanced down and a smile lit her face. "Oh look," she said, "daffodils are starting to come up."

Green shoots were emerging from the base of an oak, a reminder that spring break and my decision about a visit to Felthame weren't far away.

"A few years ago, I helped Grandma plant a bunch of daffodil bulbs in our front yard. It's probably like a field of gold right now," Kate said. "Grandma loves daffodils."

"Does she?" I said. "I'd forgotten that."

"Sometimes she talks to them. She'll say, 'Well, look at you, you pretty thing.'"

"When she was a girl, she talked to the spinning room machines to coax them to behave," I said. "Or maybe order them to behave."

Kate smiled. "That sounds like her."

I realized I knew very little about Kate. "So you want to be a journalist," I said. "What attracts you to journalism?"

"I like to write. And I like to investigate, find out things. Like, sometimes people have secrets they don't want others to know." She glanced at me, then away. "But journalists can bring them out in the open for the public good."

How would Kate feel if she knew what her grandmother had done? All at once, a sense of my own role in what had happened, rolled over me. Not everything was Ruthann's fault. I kept coming back to the decision I'd made so long ago. I was still in my teens, and I'd done the best I could at the time. And yet, as I looked at Kate's fresh face, I thought of the young people who had died because of Ruthann and me. Surely the lives that were better because of both of us meant something too? I'd determined to put our tangled history out of my mind, yet here it came, breaching the surface again and again like some cursed white whale.

"Well," Kate said, "maybe not private secrets. But I still think it's good to shed light in dark corners."

I realized I was having one conversation, laden with inner thoughts about the bitter history between me and Ruthann, while Kate was having another, more open one, in which she answered the questions of her grandmother's childhood friend. Why would Ruthann want her granddaughter anywhere near me?

"Whistleton College is a long way from Felthame," I said.

"True. But we couldn't afford UNC. Then Grandma found out that Whistleton College had a journalism minor and a work-study program, so I could work for sixteen hours a week in the cafeteria to help pay for my education. And I had good grades, so I got a scholarship, and here I am."

Still, I wondered if Ruthann had some hidden reason for wanting Kate close to me.

"Congratulations on the scholarship," I said.

"Thanks. I'm ready to practice now."

I stood and we started back to the music building. "Why don't you play a favorite piece before we tackle the sonatina again?" I suggested as we entered the practice room.

"Maybe the Bach Prelude and Fugue 20 from Book 2," she said tentatively, as if I might criticize her choice.

"A nice selection. That one makes the muscles of my back loosen up for some reason. I find myself smiling when I hit the last note."

She seated herself and began to play. When she finished, I applauded. "Great control on the tempo of the fugue," I said.

A faint pink spread across her cheeks. "Thanks. Do you have any favorites, Mrs. O'Toole?"

"Too many to mention. But I'm still fond of the old gospel hymns I learned when I started playing the piano. It all began in my childhood church on a hot summer day."

July 1889, Felthame, North Carolina

The windows of the church were open, but the faint breeze our family felt walking to Sunday service had failed to find its way inside. We fanned ourselves futilely with our hands while sweat beaded our bodies. The wooden pew seemed harder than usual and I dreaded two hours of sitting through Preacher Robinette's sermons, especially since they tended toward verses about being cast alive into a lake of burning brimstone if we weren't vigilant. I suspected I wasn't vigilant enough, especially considering how I felt about Ruthann. The Good Book said we should pray for those who persecuted us. I'd tried, but I doubted I'd fooled God.

The hymns now, they were wonderful. One of my favorites was "Shall We Gather at the River." I could picture the shining, crystal tide flowing forever by God's throne. I'd probably never make it there, but it was joyous to sing about anyway. Ma thought I sat up front to see better, but really I wanted to hear the voices of the people behind me rolling forward over me when they sang like a field of grass before the wind.

This morning I was impatient for the preacher to finish praying. My head was dutifully bowed, but my eyes were slits as I stared at the big wooden box in the front of the church. It looked like a catalog drawing of a piano, but I'd never seen the real thing.

Ma noticed and nudged me so I closed my eyes. Although I must say how did she know I was looking if her own eyes were properly closed?

Eventually the prayer was over. Thank God.

"Is that a piano?" I whispered to Ma.

"I reckon so. Don't talk in church."

"What does it sound like?"

She shook her head warningly and covered her mouth to suppress her cough.

"I have a wonderful announcement," Preacher Robinette said. "Mrs. Powell, our mill superintendent's wife, has donated her old piano. The Lord loveth a generous spirit. So thank you, Mrs. Powell. Praise God for your loving gift."

"Amen," a few folks called out.

Mrs. Powell, who usually went to her own church, was seated on the first row. She hefted her considerable bulk halfway up, bowed and smiled. She had a pleasant smile, one that looked as if she meant it. She always wore nice clothes, although honestly, she still looked like a cinched-in flour sack. Today she had on a long, pale green dress with lace trimming at the collar and sleeves. I liked to look at pretty clothes and imagine that someday I'd wear things like that. I'd heard grownups say that as a girl Mrs. Powell lived in a big house on a cotton plantation until the Yankees burned it and she "came down in the world."

"And now," Preacher Robinette said, "Mrs. Powell will grace us by playing 'Sweet Hour of Prayer.' Let us all stand and join in."

Mrs. Powell arranged her skirts on the stool with a rustle of stiff fabric, lifted the lid to reveal a row of black and white keys, and struck the first notes. They filled the air and spread out through the church in a blessing of sound. The congregation sang while I leaned forward toward the piano like a flower bending toward the sun.

A month went by, a month in which I worshipped in church, but the piano more than the Almighty, I fear. Every Sunday I watched the minister's wife, Mrs. Robinette, play hymns and tried to memorize the sequence of notes. Today, I was going to sneak back in after church and play the piano myself. My stomach felt fluttery at the thought.

Finally, the service was over, hands shook, goodbyes said. Ma and the rest of the family turned toward home. "I forgot something," I told her. "You all go on. I'll be along shortly."

"We can wait."

"No. that's all right. I... I need to pray on something."

"You're not still pining about having to work in the mill instead of going to school, are you?" Ma asked, her face worried.

"No, no," I said, because what else could I say that wouldn't make her sad? "I just..." A phrase from the morning sermon came to me. "I'm just cravin' a closer walk with the Lord."

I didn't want to tell her I planned to play the piano. It might be on the list of things you shouldn't do.

She looked at me dubiously. "All right. Don't be long."

I hurried down the aisle like a cat heading toward cream, pulled out the piano bench and sat. For a few seconds I waited, my hands in my lap, almost afraid to begin. Sometimes you yearned for things and when you got them, they weren't as good as you thought they'd be. Don't let the piano be like that, I prayed. There. Now I could tell Ma I did pray so it wouldn't be a lie.

Tentatively I pressed on one key, the middle white one. The note was soft and wonderful, I had made this sound. Next I ran my fingers from the bottommost note all the way to the top, then back to the beginning, hitting the white keys, then the black, then every white and black key. For a while, I played around with sounds, seeing what happened if you hit two keys together. Some sounded fine, others were sour.

Finally, I felt ready to try a few of the hymns Mrs. Robinette played. I started with "Amazing Grace" and moved on to "Shall We Gather at the River" until I'd run, haltingly and with plenty of off notes, through all the hymns I could remember.

Then I tried to match the notes of "Amazing Grace" with the notes in the hymn book. That was harder. I kept experimenting and gradually a few recognizable tunes emerged.

A scraping noise behind me made me give a little scream and jerk around. Mrs. Robinette stood there, arms folded. She was a thin woman in her early thirties, who always looked worried and exhausted. And with eight children, no wonder. But today, she wore a puzzled, what-in-the-world-is-going-on look.

"What are you doing?" she asked.

"Trying to play the piano," I said. Now she'd tell me to get out, and that would be the end of it.

"Where did you learn those hymns?"

"I watched you on Sundays," I said. "I love listening to the piano. It just... fills me up somehow."

She gave a little smile, quickly squelched. "I see. But you should ask permission before you do something like this."

The smile encouraged me. "I know, but I want to learn to play so bad."

"Do you?" She came closer and I could see the wrinkles on her face in the sunlight streaming through the church windows.

"Oh yes. More than anything."

She pursed her lips. "I don't know."

God and being in a church must have inspired me because a Bible verse came to me. Mrs. Robinette loved to quote the Bible. "I want to make a joyful noise unto the Lord," I said.

"Psalm 100, Verse 1," she said automatically, then nodded. "Well, I could use a backup, and you seem to have a talent for it. I suppose I could take a few minutes after church for a while to teach you what little I know and we'll see how it goes. How would that be?"

"That sounds wonderful," I said. "Thank you."

Words are so inadequate sometimes.

"Can we start now?" I asked.

She smiled again. "I suppose so. Show me what you know so far."

Before we left, I'd memorized the notes from middle C up to the next C.

"You have a natural feel for this," she said as we walked out into the sunlight. "I'm impressed. How old are you?"

"Twelve."

"Twelve years old." Her voice sounded strange.

"Is something wrong?" I asked. Maybe she thought I was too young to play the piano.

"No, it's just that you remind me of myself at that age. Like you, I lost a parent."

"Pa died last year," I said. "That's why we came to town."

"I heard," she said. "When I was twelve, my mother died. A month later, my pa up and left us." I looked down at the ground, feeling awkward and uneasy. I wanted to say something to comfort her, but I couldn't think what. "The Lord giveth and the Lord taketh away," I blurted out.

She gave me a startled look. "Yes, he does," she said, in a soft voice that sounded like something else was hiding underneath. "He certainly does." She sighed and straightened her shoulders from their normal stoop. "There's another Bible verse I like better. 'Weeping may endure for a night, but joy cometh in the morning.' Isaiah 30, verse 5. Memorize your Bible, Delia. It's been a comfort to me in dark times, and it can be a comfort to you."

"Yes, Ma'am," I said. "And I'll practice in my head what we learned today, too."

She gave a half smile as if I'd said something funny. "You do that."

When I left, I realized from the length of the shadows that we'd been in the church at least an hour. I hurried down the street, hoping Ma hadn't noticed. As if she didn't notice everything to do with us kids.

At home, I sat at the table and ate the plate of food Ma had saved for me.

"What took you so long?" she asked. "It's good to love the Lord, but I was getting concerned." She picked up a stocking and began to mend the hole in the heel.

"I'm sorry. I didn't realize how much time had passed," I said.

"I see." Her voice was dry.

Then I had to confess what had happened because I couldn't very well claim to be praying after church every Sunday. Ma would never believe that.

She laid the stocking down and looked at me. "You lied to me," she said.

"But what if you'd said no. I couldn't bear it."

She studied my face. "All right. I can see it makes you happy, and we need things that make us happy. But mind you don't pester Mrs. Robinette. And, honey, don't lie to me again."

I felt like pond scum. "I won't," I said. "I'm sorry."

I thought about the piano and excitement surged through me again. "Let me show you what I learned today. Pretend this is the piano, see." I drew an imaginary keyboard on the table and reviewed the lesson while she listened, still darning away.

"Your Pa loved music, too," she said, when I was done.

"I remember sitting on the front porch in summer with the fireflies flitting around and Pa playing away on the banjo lively like," I said.

"I do, too. I guess you got your hankering for music from him."

I reached over and hugged her, and she hugged me awkwardly back.

Then she broke into the worse fit of coughing yet. She used to be better on Sundays and Mondays and worse as the work week wore on. Lately, she was wheezing or coughing almost every day.

"Ma," I said, "maybe you should see a doctor."

She just looked at me. Where would the money for that come from?

"Don't worry. I'm fine. Go on now, you'd best wash up that plate before the grease sets."

The next morning, sitting in the outhouse where I could find a little privacy, I hummed the notes I'd learned and imagined where my fingers would go on the keys until Ezra yelled at me to quit taking so long. Walking to the mill later, I moved my fingers in tiny practice movements.

After that, whenever Ma sent me on an errand, I hurried so I could slip into the church and practice. She didn't ask, so I wasn't lying to her. Even at work, notes kept dancing through my mind, helping with the monotony.

In some ways working in the mill was easier than farm work and a lot less smelly. But I was inside from sunrise to sunset. We could stop when we got caught up or machinery broke or bobbins needed changing. I'd learned to talk above the noise, and the other girls — except Ruthann — were friendly. Even she was friendly when other people were around. In private she acted like I'd stuck a sweetgum burr in her bed.

I still missed being outdoors and hearing birds and such. The noise of the machines wasn't the same as birdsong. Or the piano, but then nothing was.

This particular day, I was sweating in the heat, trickles of moisture running down my back and dampening the armholes of my dress. I looked with longing at the huge windows that let light in, but not much air. We weren't allowed to open them very wide, because outside air made the yarn act up. But I was about to keel over from the heat.

I looked around, and Ruthann noticed. We wanted the same thing: fresh air.

"I don't see the boss," she said, peering down the long row and wiping sweat from her eyes.

"OK," I said. "Let me know if you do… Please?"

She nodded and I decided to trust her.

I ran over to lift the window and stick a wooden bobbin under the frame so we could get a trickle of air. The section man wouldn't like that, but he wasn't the one standing in front of that hot machinery all day.

A whiff of breeze blew my way. Ruthann turned toward it, and when she did, she stumbled and fell against one of her machines. She reached out her hand to stop herself, placing her palm flat on the hot metal, then jerked it back with a scream.

"Oh no. Let me see," I said, hurrying over and forgetting all about watching my spindles.

Already her burned palm was red and starting to blister.

"Here." I grabbed the bucket of drinking water that sat at one end of the row and lugged it to her. "Ma always says cold water will make the hurt stop," I said. "Put your hand in here."

She stuck her hand in the water, wetting her sleeves, and gave a sigh of relief. "That is better," she said. "Thanks."

"That looks bad. You ought to get that wrapped up and some salve on it," I said. "Take the afternoon off."

She shook her head. "I can't do that." It was true she wouldn't get paid, but that hand looked like it really hurt. I'd hate to grab thread with a burn like that.

She worked away, wincing frequently. When we got a momentary break, I hurried over to Mattie. "How about if we cover Ruthann's side and ours, too," I said. "There's only three hours left on the shift. We can do it."

"Good idea," she said. "I can't stand to hear her giving out those little yelps of pain."

"You suggest it," I said. Mattie nodded. She had noticed that Ruthann and I barely exchanged a word. Somehow Mattie persuaded her, and Mattie and I stepped lively the rest of the shift, watching for the tufts of white that would alert us to a broken thread to piece up. I felt proud of myself when it was over. The next day, when I showed up for work, Ruthann had two wild roses in her hand. She handed one to Mattie. "I wish it was a daffodil," she said. "That's my favorite flower. It's so bright and happy-looking."

She thrust the other one at me. "Thanks for helping me," she muttered. "I appreciate it. Really."

I stuck the rose in my hair and wore it all day, then laid it on the bedroom dresser that night. By morning, it was wilted and I threw it away.

A few weeks later on another sweltering afternoon, Mattie and I were on the way home at the end of our shift, which was only half a day on Saturdays. My feet were sweaty and aching.

"Let's go cool our feet in the swimming hole," I said. That was a calm, deep spot in the creek, a favorite place for mill workers to soothe their feet.

"I don't know. My mama expects me home," she said. Mattie's mother always expected something of her. Seemed as if Mattie could never satisfy her.

"Just for a few minutes. You need a break."

"OK. I guess so." She gave a little giggle like we were playing hooky.

We heard shouts as we neared the swimming hole and stopped in the shadows to see what was going on. Crystal, Lydia, Peter and Vernell, Ruthann's brother, all eight years old, were there. Crystal and Lydia had made boats from bark and laced a magnolia leaf through a stick to make a sail. They stood ankle deep in the water trying to sail their boats. Peter swung out over the water on a scuppernong vine, hit with a splash and a yell, sending their boats rocking. Crystal's turned bottom side up. I doubted this was the first time from the fact Crystal had her fists on her hips and Lydia looked ready to cry.

"Stop it, you meanies," Crystal yelled.

Peter, clad only in his britches, climbed up on the bank grinning, with mud squishing between his toes.

"You're next," he told Vernell.

"I'm not supposed to get my clothes wet."

"Oh, come on. Your pants will dry on the way back."

Vernell shook his head.

"OK. I'll go again," Peter said. "Watch how far out I get."

Vernell looked at the girls. "Naw, let's go," he said. "Let's not spoil their fun."

Good for him, I thought, impressed he'd stand up for girls in front of another boy. Up to then Vernell had been just Ruthann's baby brother, the one she tried to protect. Now I glimpsed something more in him.

"They're only girls," Peter said. He grabbed the vine, ready to swing out again.

"I know, but let's go." Vernell reached out and took Peter's arm.

"Let go of me," Peter snapped, giving him a shove.

Vernell slid down the bank, mud coating the back of his pants. He dabbed furiously at it in the water, but red clay won't come out that easy.

"I'm sorry," Peter said.

Vernell climbed up on the bank and pulled out his pocket knife. Peter, eyes wide, backed away. "Hey, I was only funnin'."

Beside me, Mattie, who hated fighting, gave a gasp. I stepped forward, ready to put a stop to this. But Vernell just walked over to a nearby bush, studied it and cut off a branch about a foot and a half long and the size of his forefinger. He frowned as he peeled off the bark.

"I'm sorry," Peter said again.

We all knew what he was doing. His aunt would switch him for getting his clothes muddy so he was cutting his own switch, hoping it was not so big it would hurt like the dickens but not so small she'd send him out to cut a bigger one.

"I'll go with you to your aunt's house," Peter said.

Vernell shrugged. "No need."

Peter hesitated. "I'll still go."

They walked toward us, noticing us for the first time. They nodded as they passed.

In the distance, I heard thunder. "Best you get on home," I called to the girls. They scooped up their boats and we walked toward town, separating as we got there. I studied the sky warily and picked up my pace. The streets turned to red mud during a downpour. As I neared our house, I saw Mrs. Robinette on the porch talking to Ma. "Clean yourself up lickety-split, Delia," Ma said. "Mrs. Robinette wants to take you up to see Mrs. Powell."

They both were smiling, but Ma was twisting her hands the way she did when she was nervous. I lifted an eyebrow inquiringly at Ma, but her face didn't give a hint of what was going on.

Ma invited Mrs. Robinette in, apologizing the way folks do for how the house looked, even though it was neat as a pin. She served her sweet tea while I shucked off my apron and tidied my hair.

Ma excused herself and came into the bedroom. "Remember your manners when you see Mrs. Powell," she said.

"Yes, Ma," I said. "Am I in trouble?"

I couldn't think of anything I'd done wrong, except sticking bobbins in the mill window to get some air. And we did cover for Ruthann on her shift. But neither seemed likely to involve a visit to Mrs. Powell, even if her husband was the mill supervisor.

"No," she said. "Best I don't say no more until we see how things fall out."

Mrs. Robinette and I walked quickly up the street. "Excuse me, Ma'am," I said, "but what's going on?"

"Just be polite, and everything will be fine," she said. She seemed nervous, but excited. Just before we arrived, she halted in the middle of the street. "Do you remember how to play 'Never Grow Old?'" she said.

"I think so."

"Good."

We stopped in front of the superintendent's house and she reached out and tucked in a stray strand of my hair.

"You'll do," she said.

The Powells lived in a two-story white frame house with a wide front porch and brick steps leading up to it. Our house was white, too. One-story, though, and set on brick pilings so there was a cool space underneath where our neighbor's dog liked to lie on hot summer days. The houses were painted white by the company and as alike as peas in a pod, except for the superintendent's and store owner's and folks like that.

Big drops of rain began to fall, making dark circles on the brick walk, and we scurried up the steps to the porch. Mrs. Powell greeted us at the door with a smile. Today she wore a dress in two shades of brown in some shiny fabric.

"This is the child I told you about," Mrs. Robinette said.

"Come in, come in," Mrs. Powell said, and led us down a hallway, talking as she went. "So, Delia, Mrs. Robinette tells me you're musically gifted."

"That's nice of her," I said, surprised. "I don't know if I am or not."

"We'll see," she said. "In here, child."

We entered a side room dominated by the biggest piano — actually, the second piano — I'd ever seen. The wood gleamed and it had ornate carvings of flowers and leaves on the front and legs. It was so beautiful.

A lace cloth was draped across the top. In front of the piano sat a carved wooden stool covered with plush red cloth. Mrs. Powell lifted the keyboard lid and ran her fingers lightly over the keys in a way that made me think she loved music, too.

Right above the keys, the word "Chickering" was written in gold letters and underneath it in smaller type, "Boston."

I don't know how my face looked. Probably Ma would have said, "Close your mouth or the flies will get in."

Mrs. Powell and Mrs. Robinette both looked at me and laughed.

"Go ahead. Sit down," Mrs. Powell said.

I sat on the stool, and caressed the keys, not making a sound yet. The creamy ivory felt cool and smooth to the touch.

"Play something, anything that suits you," she said.

I was so stunned by the piano, so unprepared for the whole situation that every tune I knew had run off and hidden somewhere. Then I remembered what Mrs. Robinette had asked on the way over, and memory returned.

I began "Never Grow Old," tentatively, but gained confidence as I went. One or two bottom notes were sour, but I kept going as if everything was fine. When the last note died, I looked up to see the reaction.

"Not perfect, but not bad," Mrs. Powell said. "That's my favorite hymn. An interesting choice." She looked at Mrs. Robinette, who blushed.

"How long have you been playing?" Mrs. Powell asked.

"About three weeks."

"Play something you made up," Mrs. Robinette suggested.

Embarrassed, I realized she must have heard me messing around with my own ideas. They weren't very good. I could imagine the sounds clear as day, but I didn't know how to get them to work right.

I chose a simple tune I'd invented, using some of the exact same notes on the top hand and the bottom, only an octave apart. I liked the mirror effect and felt proud I'd thought of it, even if pride was a sin. The tone of this piano was so much richer, especially in the deep notes, that it sounded pretty good to me.

When I finished, I stared at the keys, afraid to look up this time. Something I'd created seemed more fragile, like the wrong words could spoil everything.

"I see what you mean," Mrs. Powell said to Mrs. Robinette over my head. "I need to think on this."

"I understand," Mrs. Robinette said. "Thank you for your time."

"We have to go now," she told me. I rose reluctantly, caressing the keys one more time.

At the door, Mrs. Robinette thanked Mrs. Powell again, and I did, too.

It had rained while we were inside, one of those brief summer showers, and now the sun was shining. As we walked down the street, dodging puddles, I asked, "Why did you want me to play for her? I mean, I loved the piano, but I don't understand."

"John 21:19. In your patience, possess ye your souls," she said. I couldn't think of a Bible verse that would persuade her to tell me except, "God loveth a cheerful giver," and that didn't seem to quite fit.

When I got home, I told Ma all about it. "What's going on?" I asked.

"Time will tell," she said, sounding like Mrs. Robinette.

I felt excitement creeping up on me because this might mean I would get to play that Chickering piano again. But I tried not to get too excited because then it would be a big letdown if I was wrong. Nonetheless, I thought about it off and on the rest of the day.

The next day was Sunday and after church, Mrs. Robinette asked me and Ma to stay behind while Naomi, Jewel and Ezra went back to the house. We sat in a pew, and in a bit, Mrs. Powell bustled in, wearing a black hat with a big feather and with a gold pin on her ample bosom. We faced her while she stood in the aisle and talked.

"I have spoken with Delia's teacher, and with Mrs. Robinette." Here she nodded at a beaming Mrs. Robinette. "Delia undeniably has musical talent. How much and how willing she is to work hard remains to be seen. However, I am willing to be her patroness. My father always said that those who have much have an obligation to help those who have less."

I looked at Ma, but she was staring at Mrs. Powell like she was that angel the Bible talked about, the one you might entertain unawares.

"I will pay the fee and books for her to go on to seventh grade and teach her what I know about the piano," Mrs. Powell went on. "In return, she will clean my house every Saturday before her lesson. And my husband has generously agreed to let her work part time in the mill so your family won't lose too much of her earnings."

She paused, which gave me time to catch my breath. I felt as if a whole bunch of beautiful music had erupted inside me all at once.

"Is this satisfactory to you, Mrs. Hammett?" Mrs. Powell asked, looking at Ma. Ma's eyes filled up with moisture.

"Yes," she said. "Thank you, Ma'am. I can't tell you what this means to me and to Delia."

"Don't thank me yet," she said. "It rests on Delia's shoulders whether this experiment is a success. Delia, are you willing to work hard?"

"Yes, Ma'am," I said. "Oh yes."

"Very well. This will be for one school term only, then we'll reevaluate."

I wanted to hug her and I suspect Ma did, too, but she wasn't the kind of person you could just up and hug. So I gave her a huge smile and said, "Thank you. I won't disappoint you."

"I hope not."

Then I jumped up and down. I couldn't help it. Everyone laughed, including me.

"I'd forgotten how excited I was when my father bought me my piano," Mrs. Powell said. Her smile faltered for a second. "Of course, it was destroyed when the Yankees... well, no matter. He would be happy to see this."

I felt ready to burst with joy. "Can I play the piano?" I asked.

Mrs. Robinette raised her eyebrows, then smiled. "Now? Of course."

I ran over to the piano and banged out "Amazing Grace" as loud as I could.

"My, what enthusiasm. This bodes well," Mrs. Powell said and swept out of the church.

I slid off the bench, ran over and hugged Ma. She put her arm around me. "Let's go home and share the good news," she said.

This meant I'd be going to the public school in town, the one the mill didn't pay for and couldn't control. I'd heard they had better books and a blackboard and desks instead of benches and slates. It also meant a three-mile walk to town and back every day, but I didn't mind.

But Ma wouldn't have as much income.

"Can you manage as far as money, Ma?" I asked as we walked home. "I don't have to do this."

She stopped to catch her breath, and I slowed my excited pace.

"We'll manage, child," she said. "Put money out of your mind."

"You won't be sorry. I'll study hard and make you proud," I told her.

"You already make me proud."

I couldn't wait to tell Mattie. I ran to her house but her mother said she was picking blackberries. For a split second I thought about going home and wrapping some rags soaked in kerosene around my ankles to keep off the chiggers but that was too much trouble. Instead, I ran out to the woods where she and her brothers and sisters were filling their pails and their bellies, from the look of their purple-stained faces, "The most wonderful news, Mattie," I said, gasping out the words. "Mrs. Powell is going to pay for me to go on to seventh grade."

Mattie set down her pail, came over and hugged me. I grabbed her hands and we jumped up and down laughing.

Then her face got serious. "I'm so happy for you, but some of the girls might feel bad they're not going on," she said.

It was a splash of cold water. Trust Mattie to always think of the feelings of others. I wished I was more like her.

"Do you feel bad?" I asked.

She waved her hand at her passel of brothers and sisters. "Mama needs my money, and I like having a little to spend on pretty things now and then. Anyway, I'm no scholar, you know that. Studying is pure pleasure to you. I had to work at it."

I gave her a quick hug. "I'll be as careful of their feelings as I can," I said.

The next day at the mill, my ankles covered in red chigger bites, I thought about what Mattie said and acted calm when I shared my news. The other girls seemed happy for me. They crowded around, hugged me and congratulated me. Everyone except Ruthann. She listened with a strange, almost hungry expression.

"It's like a dream come true for me," I told the girls.

"Bully for you," Ruthann said. "You're not the only one with dreams you know. But do we get to do them, oh no."

I looked at her, unsure what to do. Finally, I said, "Maybe your turn will come."

"Yeah, right," she said. Neither of us spoke a word the rest of the morning.

At lunchtime, watching her sit under a tree looking at the sky with a frown on her face, I wondered what her dreams were. But I didn't ask.

That night, my own dreams turned to nightmares. Sometime in the middle of the night, I heard Ma start coughing worse than ever. Every cough felt like a hammer blow to my own chest because I knew it must hurt her. She got up and padded out to the front porch. I lay still listening and after a few minutes, I knew what I had to do. I slipped out from under the covers and went to join her. The night was sultry, the air heavy. A sliver of a moon was visible over the tree tops, a gleam in the dark sky. In the distance a dog barked and an owl hooted. Normally, I'd enjoy all that.

Ma sat on the steps, leaning over with her arms wrapped around her. She was breathing in long gasps like she couldn't get enough air.

"Delia," she said. "You startled me. Go back to bed, child."

"I can't. Ma, you gotta get out of the mill. The cotton dust is ruining your lungs. It's only going to get worse if you keep on."

"How am I going to stop work? What would we live on? We're barely making it as it is." Her voice was as bitter as I'd heard it, discouraged in a way that wasn't like her.

I looked at the moon and tried not to cry. My first try at speaking didn't work. My throat just closed up on me. I cleared it, swallowed and tried again. "I can quit school and work full time in the mill. If we tighten our belts we can make it."

She gave a laugh that wasn't a laugh. "If we tighten them much more, there'll be nothing left of us. Oh Delia, don't listen to me. It's just nighttime blues. Things will look better in the morning."

"No they won't," I said. "I'm going to tell Mrs. Powell tomorrow to forget about seventh grade." It would have sounded better if my voice hadn't broken on the last words.

She grabbed my chin and turned me to look straight at her. "Now you listen to me, Delia Mae Hammett. You are not quitting school. Get that thought out of your head. The Lord done give you talent and a chance for something more, and it would be poor repayment to throw it back in His face. Promise me you won't quit on account of me."

"But Ma…"

"Promise me. I mean it." She started to cough. "Promise me right now," she ground out. There were tears in her eyes that I couldn't stand to see.

"I promise," I said.

"All right then. Go on to bed. And try not to worry. The Lord will provide some way or other."

"Yes, Ma'am," I said. I went back to bed, but I couldn't sleep for worrying about Ma. It seemed to me the Lord had been a bit backward about providing for us. I'd promised Ma I wouldn't drop out of school. That made me glad and frantic at the same time. All night I tried to think of ways to make money and came up dry. Maybe my brother and sisters would have some ideas. We had to do something or we'd lose Ma, too.

At lunchtime the next day, instead of going home for lunch, Ezra, Jewel, Naomi and I sat outside the mill conferring. They'd been as worried as I was so they were glad to talk about it. We needed a plan Ma would agree to.

"I could quit school," Ezra volunteered. "I only have one more term to go." He was hot to quit anyway, but Ma wouldn't stand for that either. Still, he could put in a few hours doffing after school and that would help.

Naomi and Jewel were already working full time, and there was only one shift at the mill.

"I could try again and say I decided school was too much work," I said.

Jewel shook her head. "As if she'd believe that. We all know you're crazy for more learning. Anyway, it would make her sad."

"But she'd be alive!"

"You're assuming she'd quit work. Maybe she wouldn't."

We went back inside the mill with no more plan than when we started.

Chapter Four

March 1957, Whistleton, Virginia

I was resting in my room when Mrs. Atwood came to my door. She tapped lightly on the door frame and I sat up.

"This came for you this morning after you left," she said, handing me a letter.

She stood there waiting, but when I showed no inclination to open the letter, she left.

I held the envelope a few seconds, looking at my son's bold, decisive handwriting. He rarely wrote, and I wanted to savor the moment. When his first wife, Bettina, left him a few years ago, he'd married a much younger woman. Wife No. 2, Shirley, was expecting any day now. He'd be a father again at the age of 61. And I'd be a grandmother again. I didn't see as much as I liked of my other two grandchildren, who lived in California. Probably I wouldn't see much of this one either. Nonetheless, visions of pudgy baby legs waving in the air, gurgles, little hands reaching out in exploration and wide innocent eyes filled my head. And when the wet diapers materialized, I could hand him back to his parents.

But when I read the letter, the message was quite different.

"I'm concerned about you," he wrote. "I know you want to return to your old house, but I question whether you'll be able to. Even if you can, it's too big for one person. I know it has a lot of happy memories, but you're not young anymore. I worry that it is too much for you. I could fly East, find a real estate agent and put the house on the market. Then, if somehow you can live on your own again, I can find you a smaller place, one you can manage."

I flung the letter on the bed, wishing it were heavier so it would make a satisfying smack when it landed instead of a faint rustle. I wasn't sure who

I was angry at. His concern was genuine. He had hinted at this before. But seeing it in writing made the prospect all too real. I'd lived in my house for more than 40 years and knew every creak and every crotchet of it as well as I knew my own creaky, crotchety body. It was an old-fashioned, two-story white house with a wide porch, very like, now that I thought about it, Mrs. Powell's house back in Felthame. True, it was a big house for one person, but that didn't mean I should sell it. I wanted to go back there, not to some tiny, strange apartment with no room for my beloved grand piano. There had to be another way.

I picked up the letter, tucked it back in the envelope and headed for the front door. My room felt confining, the way I imagined a smaller place, even if easier to care for, might feel.

When I reached the front door, drizzle greeted me. It was chilly on the porch and I went back to my room for a sweater, passing a poster advertising a raffle to benefit the local animal shelter. A benefit. I looked away with a feeling of sadness.

Henry was reading in his usual chair in the main room. "Damp day," he said.

"Indeed," I said, hoping he wouldn't join me. I needed to calm down and think, to quit acting like a stubborn old woman who didn't want to change. I passed Alice, who was hurrying toward Henry carrying a plate of cookies, so I was safe for a while.

I settled down in a rocker on the porch and read the letter again as if something might have changed. Things were always changing. The earlier letter from Ruthann had stirred things up. Memories of the Benefit and so much else were rising from the deep well of the past. I sat for a while listening to the sound of rain hitting leaves. A mist began to rise from the grass.

I looked up as Henry came to join me anyway.

"You OK?" he asked. "You looked upset."

"I'm fine. Just wishing for a time machine," I said.

"Oh, what would you do with it?"

"Change the past."

"It's tempting at times," he said. "But we wouldn't be the same people and neither would anyone around us."

"That could be both good and bad," I said, even as I wondered what my life would have been if the Benefit had gone differently.

Henry spoke again. "Maybe something worse would happen than whatever we tried to change,"

"I really don't think that's possible," I said. "Look, I'm sorry, but I'm not good company right now. Thanks for trying to cheer me up. I appreciate it. I think I'll call it a day."

"OK. You know where to find me if you need someone to talk to." He brushed a cookie crumb from his shirt, courtesy of Alice, no doubt. The action helped to restore my equilibrium. Whatever the past, the present still offered moments of lightness and pleasant possibilities. I patted his arm affectionately and retreated to my room, where I dropped the envelope in my top dresser drawer, out of sight, but not easily put out of mind.

A week later, Kate sat at the piano in the practice room at the end of our usual session. She'd seemed unusually tense. I looked down at her hands, so unmarked and soft, then at my wrinkled hands with the blue-green veins standing out like cords, and thought about how young she was. And how difficult it could be for the young to share with the old.

She shifted nervously on the bench and cleared her throat.

"Something's on your mind," I said. "I'd be happy to listen."

"I heard from Grandma. She's demanding to know whether you're coming to see her."

"I don't know," I said. "Our relationship was, is... complicated. I doubt a visit would be good for either of us."

She flushed. "It would be good for Grandma," she said. "I don't understand what the problem is."

"No, you don't."

"I know you're giving me free lessons, and I appreciate it," Kate said. "I just wish you would think about Grandma, too. She's had a hard life and now she asks this one favor. It's not as if you have a lot of other things to do. Your leg seems to be getting better. I bet you could make the trip just fine. Here you have a chance to help her, and instead you're hanging on to whatever old grudge you've got. It isn't right."

She banged one hand down on the keys. The sound reverberated in the room and inside me. Up to now, I'd seen her only as sweet and quiet. A part of me was actually pleased to see her flare up, because I'd wondered if Ruthann had squelched any display of temper when Kate was growing up.

I felt my own flare of irritation at her tone, quickly tempered by the knowledge Kate didn't know the truth. If I spoke my mind now, I might say too much and destroy her image of her beloved grandmother, a woman who still no doubt persisted in calling the act that changed my life forever "the accident."

"Things aren't as simple as they might seem," I said.

Still upset, she tried another tack. "Grandma's kinfolk are pretty much all gone. She's... well, she's lonely. And time's running out."

I understood loneliness, but I didn't want Kate's pleading to lead me into something I'd regret. "I promise I'll give you an answer soon," I said.

We stood to go, both a little stiff with each other. "I didn't mean to yell at you," she said. "But Grandma's done so much for me, and I want to help her."

"Of course you do," I said. "But this can't be rushed."

On the way out, I noticed a flier on a bulletin board for a concert to benefit a sick student. I thought of my own Benefit gone awry. I couldn't seem to escape it. Was God trying to tell me something? If so, maybe I should listen.

At the car, as she fished her keys from her pocket, I looked at her hair shining in the sun. She was so young, so vulnerable. I must seem ancient to her. Mrs. Powell, my piano teacher, had seemed ancient to me. Looking back I realized Mrs. Powell was probably in her fifties. Interesting how your fifties became young once you passed them. And how youthful you still felt in some ways, even in your eighties.

I remembered clearly the very day that Mrs. Powell took me under her wing, or perhaps more accurately, made me her project.

Spring-Autumn 1890, Felthame, North Carolina

Ma was still working and I was going to school and pulling a half shift at the mill. Her cough was worse. I'd catch her rushing to the barely open window at work to grab some clean air whenever she got a break.

I was standing in the back yard looking at the stars blazing in a cloudless black sky when she came up behind me. It was a soft spring night. After all day inside at the mill, I wanted a few minutes of nature before I went to bed. A bullfrog sounded a bass note from his home down by the pond. Cicadas added a shrill treble accompaniment.

"Listen to all the sounds," I said. "There's music everywhere if you listen for it. Sometimes, I can even hear it in the whir and hum of the mill machinery."

"Can you now?" she said. "Imagine that."

We stood in silence. I picked out the distant murmur of the river. A dog barked somewhere with a deep, rough sound and another one answered with a high yip. An owl hooted low and deep. It was a strange kind of choir that made a person feel almost sad.

"It is kind of like music, ain't it," Ma said. I winced, then felt ashamed. Mrs. Powell said refined folks didn't say "ain't." But I heard it everywhere. More and more I felt split in two.

"You've been right quiet lately," Ma said. "Something eatin' at you?"

"Seventh grade is almost over and I don't know if Mrs. Powell is going to continue her experiment — that's what she calls it — or not."

"What do you want to happen?" she asked.

"I want to go on. The piano lessons are fine. I love that part. And I'm doing good in school. But it seems like I can't do anything else right. Mrs. Powell is always after me to stand up straight, talk a certain way, comb my hair, sit ladylike. She wants to know if I'm praying every night. Last week, she warned me about the dangers of playing cards, as if we even own any cards. I know she's only trying to help, but... Don't pay any attention to me."

Then I was sorry I said anything. Ma had enough on her mind. So what if I was tired. Everybody was tired.

Ma didn't say anything. But the next morning when the mill's first warning whistle went off at 5 o'clock, commanding us to prepare for work she told me to rest a bit longer.

"Your sisters can do your chores this morning," she said. Jewel, Naomi and I slept three to a bed. Their added warmth was great in winter when the fire died down. It wasn't so great in summer when my nightgown stuck to me and I thought if one more sweaty arm poked me I'd scream. They crawled out of bed, and I lay there enjoying being able to stretch out without hitting anyone. I could hear them bustling around gathering eggs and feeding the chickens for me. I appreciated that because I hated the way our mean old rooster, Sergeant, acted every time I entered the chicken yard. While I walked around scattering the feed, he stalked along beside me, bobbing his head and staring at me with first one wicked eye, then the other. Every now and then, he'd let out a long, drawn-out whirring sound, flutter his wings and charge me with his feathers fluffed out. When I yelled and waved my arms, he'd retreat as if he'd won a big victory.

Suddenly, it occurred to me that he was kind of like Ruthann. I smiled in the darkness. If I could picture her as being like that rooster, maybe I could quit reacting whenever she made her snide remarks. Of course, one day Sergeant really might attack with those razor-like claws and that sharp beak. He'd jumped on the back of Jim, a neighbor boy, one time. Jim ran around the yard yelling and flailing his arms with the rooster pecking away until Ezra charged out and pulled Sergeant off him. Jim had bloody scratches all down both arms. Best not to dwell on that.

I got up in a better mood and gave Ma a big hug before I left for the mill. "My, my," she said, and smiled.

Ruthann was already at work when I arrived. She glared at me. I looked at her and thought of our rooster and smothered a laugh. It kept bubbling up inside me. The more I tried to press the laughter down, the more it wanted to get out. I turned away, my face red, then peeked back at her, envisioning her as a rooster bridling up and retreating. A strangled sound escaped me.

"What is your problem?" she asked, taking a step toward me. It was too much. The laugh exploded out of me and I made a whirring sound like Sergeant, looked at her with first one eye, then the other and ran at her with my arms flapping wildly. She backed up, eyes wide and put up her hands to fend me off.

"Stop it, you're crazy," she said.

"No," I said, pulling up short with the laughter dying all through me. "You're the one who's crazy. I am sick of your remarks. I am sick of your jealousy and I am sick of you ragging me. Leave me alone. Got it?"

"Oh yeah?" She bristled up and moved back to her usual spot. "Well, I'm sick of how you think you're better than everyone. You with your books and your big words. I can't help it if I'm not some piano genius so I get to go to school. I bet if I tried I could learn to play as good as you. You're not so special." She threw up her hands. "Oh, to the devil with it. I'm wasting my breath."

"I don't think I'm any better than anyone else," I said. "I'm sorry you're not in school. But that doesn't mean you can pick on me all the time."

Our gazes locked. The machines were as noisy as ever but there was a weird silence while something flowed between us. We stared at each other like two strange dogs trying to establish dominance. I was determined not to drop my gaze first. My eyes watered as I tried not to blink or look away. Ruthann must have felt the same because I could see her struggling. She blinked first. Triumph surged through me. Ruthann narrowed her eyes and her mouth drew into a straight, tight line. She took a step toward me. I'll never know what would have happened next because just then my sister Jewel poked her head down the end of our row.

"Did you hear about the accident in the card room?" she called, her voice high and excited. "They say a man got killed."

Ruthann and I, lost in our own world, jumped.

"What happened?" I asked.

"The man got his shirt caught in a belt and it threw him up to the ceiling and he bashed his head against the beams. It was awful."

The card room was a dangerous place, full of machines, belts and overhead pulleys to convert the cotton batting into a loose rope, ready to be turned into yarn and, when it reached the spinning room, thread.

"They're probably carrying him out about now," she said.

She ran to the window, with Ruthann and me right behind. Below us, four men lugged a board with a sheet-draped figure sprawled on it. While we watched, a hand fell over the side of the board and hung there until a worker hurried over and tucked it back under. Red stained the sheet. For a sickening instant, I thought of Pa's death and turned away.

"I'm glad I work here where it's safer," Jewel said, oblivious to my reaction.

"Oh, I don't know. Accidents can happen anywhere," Ruthann said, staring at me.

Jewel ran back to her spindles. Ruthann and I worked away without speaking until the quitting whistle blew. I'd never been so glad to leave the mill.

After work, I went to Mrs. Powell's house for my weekly piano lesson. While it was going on, I pushed everything else out of my mind and felt happy the way only music could make me feel. Afterward, I got down on my hands and knees to scrub the kitchen floor. The lye soap made my hands red and raw, so I always waited to clean until after my lesson. She stayed in the other room. Pretty soon I heard Mr. Powell come in.

I edged over to the kitchen door and peered out through the crack. Ma said nothing good ever came of eavesdropping, but maybe they'd say something about more schooling for me. Mr. Powell stood their ramrod straight in his usual three-piece suit. He'd lost his left hand during the war against the North and had a metal hook in its place.

At first, their talk was about the man killed at the mill. He was really upset, talking about how he hated to lose a worker. Mrs. Powell talked about helping the man's family. Then she put her hand on his good arm, smiled up at him and said, "I've been meaning to talk to you about Delia." Her voice was high and girlish in a way I'd never heard before. I felt almost embarrassed listening.

"What about her?"

"You've been very generous. It would make me so happy if it you would pay for another term for her."

I almost dropped my scrub brush I was so excited.

"I don't think so," he said.

"But she's doing well. My father always said…"

He brushed her hand off and starting waving his hook around, jabbing the air until I was afraid he'd hit her with it. "Your father. Your father. I'm sick of hearing about your father. I know he was rich and I'm not. He owned a plantation and I'm just a mill superintendent. But the plantation is gone and so is he."

Mrs. Powell said in a timid voice. "I'm sorry. But I do have a plan for Delia."

He ran his fingers through his hair and took a deep breath. "I know your plan. But there's no guarantee it will work. Then, more education will only have made her unfit for her station in life."

"But it's just one girl. She's talented, and I feel it's my duty to nourish that talent."

"Lady Bountiful," he said, "like your mother."

Her eyes widened.

"Oh yes," he said. "I've heard of Lady Bountiful. I'm not a complete know-nothing."

Her lip quivered and she stepped closer, reaching for his good arm again. Her little girl voice was back. "Of course you're not. You're smart and wise and a good businessman. I don't know what I'd do without you."

"Well," he said, lowering his hook. "I know you have a tender heart. Just try to be more practical. It's money out of my pocket and one more person lost to the mill. She's working half a shift as it is, which could look like special treatment. And now…"

A wagon rumbled by and I lost his next few words. I leaned so far forward to hear that I fell against the door frame. His head shot up. "What's that?"

"Oh my, I forgot that Delia is working in the kitchen."

His face flushed, from anger or maybe embarrassment at me overhearing them quarrel.

He strode to the kitchen and I dropped to my knees, scrub brush in hand. He gave me a stern look and turned to his wife. "I'd best get back to work. We'll talk later."

I finished scrubbing the floor, with Mrs. Powell avoiding me, and went home scared.

That night while Ma and I washed the supper dishes in the tub outside, I told her what he'd said. Ma only had a few years of schooling, but she was smart and she had common sense.

"Sounds like he's afraid if you get too much book learning, you won't be happy no more working at the mill. And like he don't approve of paying for your schooling."

That made my stomach feel like it did back when Ruthann was waiting to waylay me on the way home from school.

Ma wiped her hands on her apron and looked me straight in the eye. "Maybe you won't get to go to eighth grade. But don't let nobody tell you you're not good enough as you are. You understand me? And don't be ashamed of working in the mill. Good people work there."

"Yes, ma'am," I said. "I know that."

All summer I wondered whether I'd be going on. Finally, with the start of school only three weeks away, I couldn't stand the suspense. We'd just finished our weekly lesson and I was sitting on the piano bench with Mrs. Powell standing over me. "What are you thinking about eighth grade for me in the fall?" I blurted, twisting to see her face.

"What do you think I should do?"

Everyone is supposed to be modest and let other people say good things about them instead of doing it themselves, but I couldn't with something this important. "Send me on," I said. "I've worked hard and been a good student and done everything you asked."

She smiled. "That's true. I should have said something sooner, but there were a few… difficulties to work out. We've decided to pay for your books and tuition for one more year. Then we'll reevaluate."

"Thank you," I said. "Oh, thank you." I wanted to jump up and hug her, but I was afraid it would seem too familiar, so I said, "Thank you" again with all the feeling I could put into it.

She seemed amused. "You're welcome. And I have a little surprise." She went in another room, came back and handed me a package wrapped in brown paper. "This is for you. Open it."

It was a store-bought red and brown plaid dress with a white collar.

"I love it," I said. Then I was so excited, I up and hugged her anyway. She stiffened, but she didn't pull away. And she smiled at me when I left, so I suppose it was all right if I didn't make it a habit.

When I showed the dress to Ma, she stroked the material, her fingers catching a little on the fabric.

"It's right pretty," she said. "It's good of her to provide for you. I'm happy for you." But she looked sad as she turned away.

As it turned out, going to eighth grade was a blessing to all of us, especially Ma. She was coughing worse than ever, but insisted on working because money was short. Ezra was working full time now, which helped. But something more was needed. The final piece fell into place when one of the women in town wanted someone to do sewing and ironing for her. I volunteered to pick it up after school and take it home to do at night, for a price. After the first time, someone else wanted me to do their work.

It would be nice to say I had a plan from the beginning. But I didn't. Ezra came up with the idea, maybe because as a boy he wouldn't have to carry it out. I could try to find regular customers in town — there weren't many prospects in the village — and pick up more sewing and ironing after school. Then we could all work on it evenings and I could take it back when I went the next day or so. I was dubious, because we were all at the ragged edge of fatigue as it was. But we agreed to try it, for Ma's sake.

Maybe God does provide, although he could be faster about it, because soon, all of us except Ezra were working away a few extra hours by lamplight. We told Ma it was temporary to get ahead a little. She wasn't wild about it, but had to admit the money would help. When it looked like the work would be steady, we went to the next step of our plan and talked to Ma about quitting.

We all sat around the kitchen table after Sunday service with the dishes cleared away while Jewel did the talking.

"Ma," she said, "we got a little extra now, and Ezra is helping out. It's time for you to quit work and stay home so you can get well."

Ma stared at us. "So that's what this is about. It's a sweet idea, and I thank you, but there's no way I'll let you younguns keep on at this pace. No sir. I do my part like everybody else."

"Ma," Naomi said, "Please. We want you to get well and you won't get better breathing in cotton dust every day."

Ma shook her head. "No," she said. "I know my duty."

"But Ma," I said, "you've been missing work now and then lately. You know this can't go on."

"It will be a cold day in… well, you know where, when I let my children work their fingers to the bone supporting me. Now, I'll hear no more about this."

She bent over coughing while we looked at each other, faces grim. Jewel had tears in her eyes and I felt the same way. Ma jumped up and left the room, while we sat there.

"Now what?" Ezra said. No one answered. Ma could be as stubborn as our old mule. That's where things stood when we went to bed. None of us slept well, so we heard Ma slip out of bed in the middle of the night, smothering a cough, to go out to the kitchen.

"We gotta put a stop to this," Jewel said, listening to Ma's deep coughs and labored breathing.

"You're right," I said. "We have to get through to her somehow."

Naomi went to wake up Ezra in the other room. The four of us headed out to the kitchen.

"What's this?" Ma said. "Don't try to talk me around. I gave my answer."

"We don't accept it," Jewel said. "It hurts us so bad to see you like this, like a knife twisting inside every night. We can't sleep for worrying."

"Pa's gone," Ezra said, speaking up unexpectedly. "And now we might lose you, and then what will we do?"

"I'm tough," Ma said.

Ezra, who never cries, being a boy and eleven years old, burst into tears.

"Here now," Ma said, reaching out to him.

He pulled away. "Don't you care that we might be orphans?" he yelled. "Don't you care about what it's doing to us inside?"

I started to cry myself. "You're being selfish," I said.

Ma looked like a thunderbolt hit her. Selfish was a word no one would ever use for Ma. But now I had.

She stared at me. "I hadn't thought of it that way," she said. "Go back to bed. I'll think on it, I promise."

A few days went by with everyone looking at each other and no one saying anything. Ma stayed out sick from work on Tuesday. On Wednesday night, she called us together.

"All right," she said, smothering a cough. "I guess it's time. I don't want to make you kids suffer and I don't ever want to be selfish. But as soon as my breathing gets better, I'll take over the extra sewing and ironing. That way Delia won't fall asleep over her books at night and you all won't be stumbling to bed."

Ezra jumped up and down. My sisters and I hugged her. "Thank you, Ma," Jewel said. "Thank you."

So that's how it fell out. Once Ma was away from all that dust, her lungs got somewhat better. She still wheezed and coughed, but not like she had. It looked like we weren't going to lose her anytime soon.

At times, we got a break from the work. When the river was low, the hum of the machinery slowed and that meant the water level in the mill race had dropped and we stopped work until the machines cranked up again.

One fall afternoon, after I'd started eighth grade, I heard the rhythm of the machines wind down. Mattie and I looked at each other with mutual anticipation. Ruthann didn't seem as happy, maybe because we wouldn't get paid for the break. I have to say Ruthann was a good worker. She talked to her machines like they were children, wheedling them, praising them, scolding them. And it did seem as if her machines broke down less often. But when the river was too low, no amount of talking would get them going again.

Pretty soon, the boss man came in and told us we could take a break. I grabbed my eighth-grade school book from the floor behind me. Mattie and I had been reading aloud a story about a man named Professor Wilson who fell off a sailing ship at night.

"Come on," I told her. "Let's sit on the grass outside and read some more."

It was a warm, cloudless day, so we sat in the shade under a huge oak tree. Ruthann situated herself on the opposite side of the trunk. She often sat in earshot when Mattie and I read. Once Mattie asked her if she wanted to join us, but she said "no," so now we ignored her.

We'd just gotten to the part where the ship was firing its guns but no one could hear the man in the water yell for help, when the overseer called for us to come back to work. I lingered, wanting to finish the next few sentences, so we ended up the last to go in.

Ruthann came around to our side of the tree and looked at me with alarm. "Ooh, watch out. There's a yellowjacket on you," she called.

"Where," I said, batting at my hair and running toward the mill with

Mattie not far behind. I jumped inside the door as if that could keep it from stinging me.

"I don't see anything," Mattie said. "It must have flown away."

"Come on, ladies, back to work," the overseer called.

In the excitement, I forgot about the book for an hour. When I remembered, I felt panicky. Books cost money.

"Cover for me while I go get it," I told Mattie.

"Let me go," Ruthann said. "I owe you for filling in for me when I burned my hand."

"No. I can do it," I said.

When I went outside, the book was gone. I searched all around, but I couldn't find it so I went back inside.

"Where's your book?" Mattie asked.

"I don't know," I said, feeling worried. "I guess somebody took it." Ruthann kept working away. I looked at her suspiciously. She'd been the last one to come in.

"Don't look at me," she said.

"I'm not."

It was an hour until quitting time, a mighty long hour while I thought about how Mrs. Powell would lecture me about the book. She was always telling me that money didn't grow on trees.

When we got off, Mattie and I searched around the tree again without finding the book. Ruthann passed us without a word, holding her arms tight around her waist. I stared at her. She's got my book under her apron, I thought. Impulsively, I ran at her and knocked her down.

"Delia, what are you doing?" Mattie screamed from behind me.

Ruthann fell hard with an explosive grunt and I landed on top of her.

"Give me my book," I yelled, drawing my fist back. "I know you have it."

"You're crazy," she said, staring up at me with wide eyes. "Get off me or you'll be sorry."

"Look," Mattie said. The book lay on the ground a few feet away.

"You had it all the time," I shouted at Ruthann. "It must have fallen out when you fell."

"I did not have it," she said. "Let me up, or else."

I rolled to one side and she stood up.

"Maybe we missed it when we searched," Mattie the peacemaker said. The way she gave everyone the benefit of the doubt was a quality I loved in her most of the time. Right now, it irritated me.

"We didn't miss it. She stole it."

"You're crazy," Ruthann said again. "I never had your stupid book.

What would I want with it?" And she ran off into the twilight.

When I got home, Ma was getting ready to cook cornbread in the fireplace.

"I'm going to tell the superintendent about Ruthann tomorrow," I said, while Ma put the batter in the iron skillet and set it on the coals. "He won't put up with a thief in the mill." Earlier in the year, a woman who stole something was let go that very day and left town in disgrace.

"Hand me that lid while I think on this," Ma said.

I gave her the lid and she put it on the skillet and piled coals on top.

"Did you see Ruthann with the book?" Ma asked.

"No. But I know she took it. How else could it be right nearby after I knocked her down?"

"You may be right. But you could be wrong. Either way, think a minute. What will be likely to happen if you tell Mr. Powell?" Ma asked.

"He'll probably fire her straight away. It serves her right."

"And if he fires her, what will Ruthann and Vernell do then?"

I hesitated. Ruthann's aunt might be mean, but her health was poor, and if Ruthann lost her job, they'd have to give up their house and move. It would be a mess, and not just for Ruthann.

"She should have thought of that before she took my book," I said.

"You think on it and we'll talk later."

That evening, when we were alone, or as alone as we could be in our house, I brought up Ruthann and the book again. "I'm studying on it right now," Ma said. A little later she said, "Delia, read to me from the Bible tonight. Matthew 5 would be nice."

I liked to read to Ma. It was the only time she wasn't doing two things at once. She'd sit down, give a little sigh and just listen, because she said God's word deserved your whole attention. Sometimes I wished she'd give me the same undivided attention, but she had a lot to do.

I read the chapter aloud and it was all about forgiveness and loving your enemy. When I finished, she said, "Thank you, sugar. Let's turn in. It's been a long day."

Lying in bed, I thought about the verses. Darn Ma anyway. Why couldn't she have left things simple?

In the morning, we went to church and sang "There's A Wideness in God's Mercy," which didn't make my decision any easier. But one of the Ten Commandments said thou shalt not steal, and Ruthann was a thief, pure and simple. And a bully. My life would be easier without her around.

On Monday, when I went to the mill, Ruthann sidled up to me. Under our feet, the floor quivered as the machines started their roar. She put her mouth close to my ear. "You better not get me in trouble. Or you'll find out what trouble is," she whispered. I could feel her hot breath against my skin.

I stood silently, scared. She put her hand on my shoulder. "Did you hear me?"

"I heard you. Get your hand off me."

I'd decided to do the Christian thing until she threatened me. I simmered all morning while she stole periodic glances at me. At lunchtime, I whispered to her, putting my mouth close to her ear the way she'd done to me. "I'm going to see Mr. Powell now, and we'll see who finds out about trouble."

Then darned if her mouth didn't turn down and her face go all pale like she was scared to death. I walked away and I stood in front of Mr. Powell's office for five minutes trying to decide what to do until he came out and asked what I wanted. Ma's words echoed in my mind. I thought about Vernell maybe having to drop out of school.

"I just... Never mind," I said.

"Are you sure?"

"Yes," I said.

When I got back to the spinning room, I walked up to Ruthann and spoke close to her ear. "I didn't tell," I said.

"That was smart," she said, and kept working. But her fingers were a little unsteady on the thread.

After that, Ruthann was quiet around me, almost as if she was a little afraid. It made me uncomfortable because I knew what it was like to be scared of someone. A tiny part of me was glad. I knew that part was a sin, so I tried to think about the fifth chapter of Matthew, like Ma would want me to. But I still was a little glad.

After a few months, things went back to normal with Ruthann making occasional remarks that stung a little, the kind of remarks where if you protest, the person says you're too sensitive or you took it wrong or you didn't have a sense of humor.

It would be nice to say everyone saw the same side of Ruthann that I did. But that wasn't true. She had her own friends. Some rough, but some nice, and all of them seemed to like her.

With Mattie, especially, she was different, gentler somehow. But then, everyone loved Mattie. Sometimes I felt jealous. Another emotion Ma would say wasn't worthy of me. I tried to subdue the feeling, and mostly I did. But one day when Mattie and Ruthann sat together at lunch and laughed over some private joke, it got to me. When Mattie and I walked home after work, I couldn't keep quiet any longer.

"I don't get what you see in Ruthann," I said. "You don't hear the little snide remarks she makes when no one else can hear."

"What does snide mean?" Mattie asked.

"It means smart alec, mean-spirited," I said, reminded of how our two paths were diverging. I wondered if Mattie, like Ruthann, thought I was getting above my raising.

"Oh. I don't see that side of her. She's always nice to me. And she can be funny. She really can. She has a sharp wit."

"Sharp enough to prick me plenty of times. Sharp can hurt."

She stopped walking and turned to me with a look of distress. "It's not that I don't believe you exactly. But that's not the Ruthann I know. What am I supposed to do? I feel like a piece of taffy at a pulling party."

"Nothing, I guess. But it's almost like she's trying to steal you away from me."

"Don't be silly," Mattie said. "You can't steal someone if she doesn't want to be stolen. And I don't."

We started walking again. Just as she turned away to head for her house, she said, "I wish you two could be friends."

"I'll try again, for your sake," I said.

I did try off and on. There were times when it seemed as if we could mend our fences. Back when Ruthann and I were in sixth grade together, I'd noticed Vernell. He was in a lower grade, being seven, and as bright as they come, always waving his hand to answer the teacher's questions. He was bad to bite his lips though, when he made a mistake. Maybe he'd outgrow that.

In church the Sunday after I told Mattie I'd try to be friends with Ruthann, I noticed that he was actually reading some of the words in the hymnbook. After the service was over, I walked over to where Ruthann and Vernell were standing and smiled down at him. "I saw you reading in church this morning," I said. "You're doing really good."

He smiled back. Ruthann, who'd put her arm around Vernell when I approached as if I was going to harm him, raised her eyebrows.

"Ruthann, he's smart as a whip," I said.

She smiled straight at me, a sight as unexpected as the sun coming up at midnight and just about as dazzling.

"He is smart," she said, ruffling his hair. "He really is."

She said good morning to me after that, which I counted a huge success. She'd tell me little things Vernell was doing, or really that she was doing with him, like using a stick to scratch his ABC's in the dirt. I always said something friendly back.

But things soured again. One day, during a break, I was leaning against a wall studying a textbook when Ruthann came up. She glanced at the book and asked, "So what important things are you learning these days?"

Her tone was a little sharp, but I decided to take the remark at face value. "Well, there's this place in Canada, near Alaska, where they've discovered gold. Lots of people are going there to seek their fortunes."

"Alaska is where it snows all the time, right?" She leaned against the wall beside me and looked at the book.

"Right. They have polar bears that have white fur to match the snow."

"Yeah? What do they eat, with all that ice and snow?"

Her whole face changed when she was interested in something. Her eyes became brighter and her mouth softer. It was like moonlight shining through a cloud.

"They eat fish, mostly. But the Eskimos hunt them sometimes for the fur and the meat."

"I'd love to see Eskimos and polar bears."

"Me too," I said. Neither of us had ever been outside Felthame.

"Can I see your book?" she asked. I handed it over. She leafed through the pages, studying the illustrations and chapter headings until I became uneasy. I reached over, took it back and tucked it in the pocket of my apron.

"Time to get back to work," I said. "We could look at one of my books together sometime, if you like. It's got more stuff in it about other places."

"Are you afraid I'd steal your book if you let me look at it alone?" she said, her face clouding up.

"No," I protested, even though that had been in the back of my mind. "I just wanted..."

"Never mind," she said. "Go back to your stupid lessons. I'm not interested."

Chapter Five

December 1892, Felthame, North Carolina

The weather had been cold for days. Hog killing weather at last. Securely wrapped against the cold, Ma, my sisters Jewel and Naomi, Ezra and I headed for the hog pens with a feeling of excitement. Everyone would come and help, and then the meat would be divided up. We didn't own a hog, but we'd contributed table scraps all year to feed them, so we were entitled to a share. It would be a day of work and visiting and at the end of the day, we'd feast on fresh ham and biscuits, along with cracklins from the fried fat and skin.

Neighbors joined us, until we were a stream of hungry folks heading for the pens. I spotted Jediah, Naomi's boyfriend, ahead of us.

"Here come the prettiest girls in town," he said. "Alike as four peas in a pod." Which was true. We were all small-boned with dark brown hair and brown eyes, except for Ma and me with our blue eyes. And if we weren't the prettiest, we could hold our heads up. Ezra, though, had begun to get some growth and had lost the hated title of shortest boy in his class.

"Oh, go on with you," Ma said, but she smiled at Jediah and pink spread across her cheeks. Naomi put her hand to her mouth to cover the gap in her teeth, which she'd gotten self-conscious about since she started stepping out with Jediah.

I wished I had a steady boyfriend. Oh, a few boys had taken notice. But the things I was interested in, like music and books, didn't interest them. And it was boring to talk about hunting and fishing all the time. Secretly, I dreamed that someone from the big city of Charlotte or even someplace like New York, would come to town. He'd take one look at me and... What happened next, I wasn't sure. But he'd want to talk about more than just hunting and fishing.

I noticed Mattie sitting off to one side. "Go on over," Ma said. "We can get the fire started and the water heated. I'll call you when it's time to scald the hog and scrape the hairs off."

Naomi split off to walk with Jediah. Ma and Jewel headed for the women filling up the big iron pots with water. Ezra wandered toward the hog pens.

I saw Ruthann go over to Mattie. I hesitated, then decided it was a day for everyone to be neighborly and walked over to join them. Mattie smiled and patted the ground for me to sit down. Ruthann nodded coolly.

Off to one side, at the hog pens, rifle shots rang out. Squeals filled the air as the hogs fell, kicking in their death throes. I looked away. Every year, at this point, I was reminded for a split second of how a wild hog killed Pa. I wondered if Ma felt the same, but we'd never discussed it.

The men began slitting the hogs' throats and hanging them up so the blood would run out. Fires already blazed over some of the pots and steam from the water curled upward in the frosty air.

Children ran around everywhere. Four were playing nearby. Vernell, ten now, chased Peter, a neighbor boy. They flashed past us, laughing. Nearby, Crystal, the same age as Vernell and Peter, twirled in a circle, her blonde hair shining in the sun. She spun faster and faster until she fell to the ground giggling. Lydia was playing jump rope, breathlessly chanting "Miss Mary Mack, Mack, Mack, all dressed in black, black, black." She was special to me ever since she confessed she wanted to learn to play the piano. Our occasional lessons were pure pleasure, although she was the bounciest thing. She bounced down the church aisle to the piano, then she bounced on the piano bench, making it creak. I'd settle her down, but she'd get excited at some new success and be off and bouncing again.

"How is Vernell doing in school?" I asked Ruthann. Vernell was always a safe subject.

"Great, as usual," she said, plucking a withered piece of grass and shredding it. "He really likes Mrs. Allenby."

Mattie spoke up. "Did you know she's going to retire in a few years?"

I looked at the children playing in the sunlight and the thought leapt up inside me: I want to be a teacher. Up to then, work and school had consumed me, with no looking ahead. I was fifteen, and in two short years, I'd be through with eleventh grade and ready to go out into the world.

"When Mrs. Allenby retires, they'll need a new teacher," I said. "I think I'll apply to teach in the mill school."

Ruthann looked up. "You? Then you might teach Vernell."

"Yes, me. It would be a privilege," I said, looking out where he and Peter were chasing each other.

"Yes, it would be," she said.

Mattie laughed and jumped up. "Come on, y'all. They must be about ready for us to help scrape the hairs off." Ruthann and I smiled at each other. Only Mattie could find pleasure in that.

Later, when the biscuits were made, the ham sliced and we all sat around by the flickering light of outdoor fires eating, things changed. Someone began playing a banjo, making me think of Dad again. I felt suddenly furious that something like a vicious hog could take him away from us and he'd never hear banjo music again. Trying to distract myself, I looked around. Peter and Vernell had laid sticks on the ground a ways apart and were taking turns seeing who could jump the farthest, moving the sticks after each jump. Crystal lay on the grass near her parents, apparently worn out. Lydia stood a few feet away from us, her feet tapping in time to the music. When she noticed me looking at her, she ran over. "Can we have another piano lesson soon? Can we? Can we?" she asked.

"Sure, sugar," I said. "Maybe…"

Just then I heard a shout and turned to see Peter, legs flailing, jumping one of the smaller bonfires. He landed on the other side, barely clearing the flames, rolled once and leapt to his feet, throwing his arms in the air. A few of the men clapped.

"Triple dog dare," he yelled to Vernell, who stood on the other side. Vernell took a running start.

"Stop," Ruthann yelled, racing toward him, while Mattie let out a high piercing scream that seemed to go on and on. I followed Ruthann. Vernell's stocky form was silhouetted against the sky for a split second as he jumped, the orange flames grabbing at his feet. Then he was over, landing on the edge of the coals and clutching his ankle.

Ruthann grabbed for him. "Are you all right?" she demanded. "Let me see."

She touched his ankle and he winced, then he grinned at her, eyes shining. "He said I couldn't do it. But I did."

"That was stupid. I know you always gotta prove yourself, but Lord, you could of really hurt yourself."

Before Vernell could reply, she grabbed Peter by the shoulders, shaking him. "What were you thinking? My brother could have been burned bad." She kept shaking him until I grabbed her arm.

"Stop," I said. "He's only ten. They weren't thinking."

She whirled and we stood there staring at each other, until Vernell broke the paralysis by pushing himself to his feet. He put his weight experimentally on his right ankle, then took a cautious step. "I'm fine," he said. "I'm strong."

"Right. Headstrong," she said, but a smile tugged at her mouth. She reached over, grabbed a tree limb lying near the fire and handed it to him. "Here. Use this to walk with."

A chastened Peter was watching. Vernell glanced at him, then at Ruthann, seeming as if he wanted to refuse the help in front of his friend, but Ruthann stood there adamant and finally, he took it.

It was only then that we noticed Mattie was still standing frozen where we'd left her, face white and trembling all over.

"Oh Lord," Ruthann said. We rushed over to her.

I reached her first. "It's all over," I said. "Nobody was hurt." But her expression didn't change. It was almost as if she didn't hear me.

"Mattie," I said.

"Leave her be," Ruthann said, putting her arm around Mattie.

"Mattie," I said again.

Mattie ignored me, turned and laid her head on Ruthann's shoulder like some kind of wilting flower.

"Where's your folks, sweetie?" Ruthann asked. "I'll take you to them."

"Not yet," Mattie said, her voice all trembly. "Not quite yet."

So we sat there on the ground a few minutes, until we all traipsed over to Mattie's folks.

After we delivered her, Ruthann and I walked away, both of us silent, with Vernell trailing behind.

"What was that all about?" I asked when we were out of earshot.

"Don't you know anything?" Ruthann said.

"Apparently not. So why don't you tell me."

"Ask Mattie. If she didn't tell you, I'm not going to."

"All right, I will," I said.

I was silent after that, wondering what could account for the terror on Mattie's face, and why she'd told Ruthann but not me.

Ruthann took Vernell's hand and strode away while I walked slowly back home alone, full of questions.

The next day, at lunch break at the mill, I asked Mattie to go aside with me. We sat on an old log in the pale wintry sunlight and ate our sandwiches.

"About yesterday," I said. "Are you all right? You seemed mighty upset."

"I don't want to talk about it."

"OK," I said. "I didn't mean to pry."

I looked at an ant crawling along the log, carrying a sandwich crumb too big for him, and tried not to feel hurt.

We sat without talking for a few minutes. Just when things were getting awkward, Mattie spoke up. "Look, I can't talk about it and go right back to work. How about after quitting time?"

"Fine," I said. "Whatever you want."

It was dark and cold when we got off so we wrapped ourselves in blankets and sat on the grass in the back yard where we could have some privacy. A full moon shone down, lending a pale, unreal light and making the tree branches look like black fingers reaching up around us.

"It's like this," Mattie said. "When I was nine, before you and Ruthann came to Felthame, my mama set me to watching my baby brother, Gabriel." She stopped and I waited.

"We were in the kitchen. It was right after Christmas and the fireplace was blazing. And…"

She stopped again.

"You don't have to tell me if you don't want to," I said.

"No. It's just… Anyway, let me get it all out. I was eating an orange I got for Christmas and Gabriel was playing with a sock ball on the floor. My brother Billy Joe — he was ten then — grabbed my orange and ran out of the room. I ran after him to grab it back. We got to fighting over that stupid orange and the next thing I knew the baby was shrieking. I ran back into the kitchen and he'd crawled into the fireplace and he was all burnt. His hair was on fire. I pulled him out and batted at it. And his little arms were…"

She started sobbing, rocking back and forth, and pulled the blanket over her head like it could keep out the grief.

"Oh, Mattie," I said. I put my arms around her and she leaned up against me the way she'd leaned up against Ruthann the other day.

"Don't ever fight," she gasped between sobs. "Don't ever fight, Delia."

"Hush, hush," I said. "I won't. It's all right."

"It was my fault," she said. "Mama said it was my fault, and she's right. It was all my fault."

"No," I said. "It wasn't your fault. You were only nine."

"It was," she said, defeated like, and lay back on the ground, her sobs trailing off.

In a bit she sat up. "I know I should have told you," she said, "since I told Ruthann, but…"

"But what?" I said.

"It's complicated. Don't be mad," Mattie said.

"I'm not mad," I said, even though I'd thought some uncharitable thoughts the night before about how we were supposed to be best friends. But that was before I knew her story.

A cloud covered the moon. She looked up, her face blurred in the darkness.

"It's like this," she said. "You've got so much going for you. Oh, none of us have much in the way of things. But you've got your piano playing.

You're talented and you have a family that loves you. You've gotten to go on in school. Ruthann doesn't have any of that. But she's as smart as you. Now me, I'm not that smart. I'm happy to stay here. But Ruthann wants...." She waved her hand as if the rest of the sentence was self explanatory.

"Anyway, she needs me in a way you... you just don't."

"I do need you," I said. "You're important to me."

"And you're important to me. But you and me, we've got one kind of friendship, and me and Ruthann, we have another. Can you understand that?"

"I suppose so," I said, feeling petty for caring. "But it does seem like she always wants what I have."

Mattie put her hand on my arm. "I'm thinking you already have what she wants."

I smiled at her and put my hand over hers. "Don't fret," I said. "It's not worth fighting over."

"Nothing is," she said.

After that I looked at Ruthann and everyone else a little differently, wondering if they had a secret, too. If they did, would I ever know?

Chapter Six

April 1957, Whistleton, Virginia

Back then, full of self-righteousness, I was jealous of Ruthann, believing she cottoned up to Mattie and took my textbook to spite me. Now, staring out the window of Kate's car on the way back to Pleasant Oak after her lesson, I decided Mattie had it right and Ruthann's motives were quite different.

"Does your grandmother like to read?" I asked Kate.

"Oh yes. Mostly mysteries. She runs through them so fast she's read most of the ones in the library. Although she's slowed down recently. Her eyesight isn't as good."

"I'm sorry to hear that," I said. "Reading is a pleasure."

"Did she read much when you were girls?" Kate asked.

"There weren't many books around," I said. "Our school only had ten books that weren't textbooks. We didn't have a library. But she was smart and enjoyed school, for as long as she went."

"Grandma always regretted she didn't get to go on, but she tries to keep up with things as best she can."

"You look a lot like her when she was young," I said. "I have a photo of the girls in the spinning room years ago and she's in it."

"Oh, I'd love to see it," she said.

"I'd show it to you, but most of my photo albums are back at my house."

Longing struck me for the familiar sights and feel of my own home. "It's not far from here," I said. "Maybe we could go by and look if you have time."

"Right now?" She glanced at her wristwatch. "Um, sure. Just tell me how to get there."

"If it's inconvenient, we can skip it. But I have a concert grand, and if you've never played one, it's a different experience from a practice piano. The feel of the pedal, the touch, the tone, everything is different."

Mentioning the grand piano felt like bribery, but I wasn't ready to return to the rest home.

As we cruised down neighborhood streets, I wondered whether Kate was interested in me or in persuading me to see her grandmother. She was getting free piano lessons, but every week she had to drive out to what must be a depressing place for a young person. Already I looked forward to her visits. How strange it seemed to be wishing for the company of the granddaughter of my old nemesis.

"Nice house," Kate said as we pulled into my driveway.

"Thanks," I said. "We bought it years ago." And a good thing. I couldn't have afforded it now, on Social Security and a small pension. The neighborhood was gentrifying as young professionals moved in, and property taxes rose. Samuel would say it was a smart business move to sell it and move to a smaller, more affordable place. Not yet. Not yet.

The boy I'd hired had given the lawn its first mowing of the spring and the scent of fresh grass greeted us as we stepped out of the car. I'd donated my houseplants to a neighbor since there was no one to water them. Well, they could be replaced when I returned. I refused to imagine a For Sale sign in the front yard.

I fished the key from my purse and we entered through the side door to the garage, where my white Corvette roadster sat. Kate's eyebrows rose when she saw it, almost as high as my son's when I bought it. I loved the reaction. People expected me to drive something sedate, maybe a gray Studebaker. I had to wear "sensible" shoes because of what Ruthann had done years ago. But I didn't have to drive a sensible car. Yes, it was an extravagance, but when the wind blew past my face and hair as I drove, I counted it money well spent.

"Wow. Nice car," Kate said.

"Thanks. I like it."

Inside the house, everything was as I'd left it, neat and simple. I don't like fussy things. It had a stale feel from being closed up. I opened the front door wide to let in fresh air.

"Why don't you play the piano while I find my photo albums," I said, leading the way to the big living room. I'd removed most of the furniture, so that the concert grand dominated the space. The light of the afternoon sun spilling through the blinds highlighted a thin layer of dust on its usually gleaming surface. I'd scrimped to buy that piano, and it had been worth every penny. It was something else I couldn't imagine selling.

I walked quickly through the first-floor rooms, enjoying seeing my familiar things. The stairs were still too much for me to be able to check conditions on the top floor. While Kate played, I rummaged through five photo albums and assorted loose photos I'd periodically vowed to organize better. Finally I found what I was looking for and returned to the living room.

Kate was absorbed in playing "Some Enchanted Evening," her face soft and dreamy. She had her hair up in a ponytail and it swung softly as she played. I stood in the doorway, unwilling to interrupt her. As I watched her, I could understand that Mrs. Powell, in some ways, had seen me as the daughter she never had.

When the last notes died, Kate looked up and smiled apologetically. "It's not classical, but I like it," she said.

"I do, too. What other popular tunes do you enjoy?"

She ducked her head. "Oh, Elvis Presley's stuff."

I'd listened to a little of his music here and there. Hard to avoid it. While I didn't much care for all his hip waggling, his music had a certain raw energy to recommend it.

"Don't be cruel to a heart that's true," I crooned, all I knew of that tune.

Her head jerked up and she stared at me incredulously.

"We need all kinds of music," I said with a laugh. It was such fun to confound young people.

"I found the photos," I said. "Come take a look."

We sat at the kitchen table and I showed her the three photos I had, reproductions of those taken in 1894 when a researcher came around to document child labor in the mills, not that his report changed much in Felthame. Gossip around the mill was that Mr. Powell was opposed to the visit, fearing it might stir up trouble, but Mrs. Powell persuaded him to let the man come.

"Here's your grandmother," I said. "She's the girl in front." Three of us were lined up about a yard apart in the spinning room. We wore serious expressions. Ruthann's eyes were heavy lidded, as if she needed sleep.

"She looks sad," Kate said.

"Yes, I guess she does," I said. "Here's a group shot."

Six of us girls, of varying ages from about twelve to eighteen, were cutting up for the camera. Our hair, flecked with lint, was pinned back in the buns everyone wore. Mattie's arm was around my shoulder, and she and I were grinning, probably at something she'd said. Ruthann, in the center, stared straight at the camera with a sober, alert look.

"I like this one better," Kate said. "Is that you?" she asked, pointing to another photo.

"It is." I stood alone, lit by the huge windows, with rows and rows of spindles and yarn in front of me. There was a certain forlorn quality to it.

"Here's what Grandma looks like now," Kate said, pulling a snapshot from her wallet. "It was taken last year."

Ruthann was seated in an armchair, unsmiling. Light glinted off her glasses. Her short hair was white, of course, and her face wrinkled. She'd lost weight, judging by her cheeks, but not a lot. I didn't see any signs of ill health. I wondered what was wrong with her.

It gave me a strange feeling to see her photo and realize we both were old and the events that changed my life had happened more than a half century ago. Somehow, I still pictured her as younger.

I didn't wish her ill, but I didn't want to see her again either.

I handed the photo back to Kate, stowed the albums and cast a longing look at the piano, but Kate was eager to leave and I'd delayed her already.

"I'm leaving next Wednesday on spring break," she said. "I need your answer by then."

I was restless when I got back to the convalescent home, unable to settle down. As I'd often done, I took my troubles outdoors, working my way down the ramp to a huge elm. I stared up at the branches, enjoying the spring green and patches of blue sky against the brown limbs. It reminded me of the way I used to lie under a tree as a girl, look up at the sky and dream. I looked around. Should I do this? Getting down wouldn't be too difficult. But getting up would be a problem without a helping hand. Still, the tree called to me. I answered.

I lay down, spread out flat on my back, cane beside me. The earth was cool, solid and comforting. I stared up at the sky, arms flung wide, recapturing for a few precious moments those childhood feelings. Unfortunately, the ground was hard and bumpy, things that never bothered me as a kid. The longer I lay there, the more the cold penetrated. In a few minutes, with the aid of the sturdy trunk of my friend the tree, I levered to my feet, triumphant. Mrs. Atwood stood on the porch staring at me. When she saw me look her way, she shook her head, whirled and went inside.

After dinner, as I was leaving the dining room, she approached me with a guarded expression. "You were gone a long time today," she said. "Did you have a nice outing?"

"Yes, I did."

"Good."

If she wanted to be friendly, I'd give it a go. "How was your day?" I said.

She looked startled, as if no one ever asked. "Uh. Busy. People don't realize how much responsibility running this place entails. You have to be constantly on the lookout, watch things like a hawk. This isn't an easy job."

"I'm sure it isn't."

"I noticed you aren't pretending to play the piano any more. Frankly, I was worried about that."

"Worry no more. I assure you I am oh so totally in touch with reality."

"What in the world were you doing lying on the ground under the tree?" she asked.

"Enjoying looking up at the sky. Didn't you ever do that when you were a girl?"

She shook her head. "Lord, no," she said.

"Too bad."

We moved aside to let an elderly woman in a walker get past us.

"Your young friend must be good for you," Mrs. Atwood said. "Will you be seeing her regularly?"

"I might. Why are you so interested in my comings and goings?"

She straightened up taller, if that was possible. "I've seen this before. Residents think they can do more than they can. They overextend and have setbacks, then their families blame me."

"I promise my son won't blame you," I said. "He knows I'm hard-headed."

"I'm sure he does," she said.

I walked off, trying not to limp. I was tired and my leg hurt, but I didn't want her to know. I was grateful to reach eighty with my senses intact, but it was infuriating not to be able to do what I wanted without pain. I clearly hadn't mastered growing old gracefully.

I thought of Ruthann and wondered what was wrong with her and how she was managing. And I thought about how sad she looked in that one photo when we were both seventeen. It was taken just a month before I left the mill to start teaching school.

September 1894 — June 1895, Felthame, North Carolina

I pulled the bell rope at the mill school, excitement lending extra vigor to my first official task as a new teacher. It rang out over the village. The sound was still dying as I walked to the window to peer out. My forty six students were variously hurrying or strolling toward the school. Peter and Vernell were, predictably, roughhousing with each other. Lydia was clutching the only book she owned, "A Child's Garden of Verses." She took it everywhere as if it might disappear if she let it out of her sight. Crystal skipped along, lunch pail swinging. The four of them had had a special place in my affection since that day at the hog killing when I'd realized I wanted to be a teacher. As I watched, girls and boys began forming separate lines. Lydia spotted me and waved. I waved back, embarrassed to be caught so obviously eager, then went to my desk to await their entrance.

I stifled a yawn. I'd slept little the night before, rehearsing my lessons plans over and over. I'd been up with the dawn to finish decorating the classroom with cutouts of letters and numbers and signs encouraging the children to do their best.

Now, Mr. and Mrs. Powell sat in caneback chairs at the front of the room, chairs brought in especially for the occasion. Mr. Powell planned a welcome speech.

My new teaching certificate lay on the desk in front of me. I glanced at it as if to reassure myself that I had indeed graduated from eleventh grade, passed my exams and been authorized by the state of North Carolina to teach for the next year.

Mrs. Powell noticed my gaze. "You earned it. You'll be a wonderful teacher," she said.

"I'll do my best."

Mr. Powell nodded at his wife. "You were right, my dear. You had a good plan after all." We heard high, excited voices outside and we all smiled. "Ah, here come the children," he said.

They marched in in a ragged line, the boys bowing to me and the girls curtseying. I'd done the same thing when I was a student. Now that I was on the other side, I began to feel like a real teacher. Quickly, I sorted them by sex and age, from the wide-eyed five-year-olds there so their parents could work in the mill on up to the twelve-year-olds almost ready to leave school.

When everyone was seated, we began. I'd wondered what Bible verse would be good for our morning reading. Ma had suggested something from Proverbs, so I read the part of the first chapter about increasing knowledge, while the Powells nodded approvingly. When I closed the Bible, Mr. Powell stood up, straightened his waistcoat and began his speech.

"Good morning, young scholars," he said. "You are embarking on a new school year and I know it will be a profitable one. I admonish you to work hard and learn all you can." He droned on in that vein, talking about honesty, truthfulness, respect for authority until even the older students were squirming in their seats. Occasionally, they stirred to alertness when he jabbed the air with his hook to make a point. Finally, Mrs. Powell put her handkerchief to her mouth and cleared her throat softly. He glanced at her and wound down.

"We're counting on you," he told me as I ushered them out. "The mill needs good workers, workers who can read and write and know how to do an honest day's work."

I stood up straighter, understanding perfectly. The mill paid part of my salary. Accordingly, it specified in my contract that I would uphold mill work "as an honorable vocation." I thought of Ma saying that mill folks were good people. It was honorable work. But it wasn't for everyone, and I wouldn't pretend it was. I opened my mouth to reply just as Mrs. Powell caught my gaze and shook her head infinitesimally.

"Thank you for coming. I'll do my best," I said.

The morning sped by while I tried to find out who knew what, divided them into study groups so the older ones could help the younger ones, and began reviewing their reading and math skills.

I was impressed with Ruthann's brother, Vernell, now a husky, blond twelve-year-old. He'd remembered more than most and seemed determined to be the best student in his grade, sticking his hand up for every question, even though I called on everyone evenly.

During reading time, when a fourth grader mispronounced a word, Turner, one of the older boys, snickered loudly. Vernell shot him a look of disgust. Turner stared back at him as if to say, "Mind your own business." The two glared at each other, and Turner half rose from his seat. Vernell tensed and stood up as if to confront him.

I had to take charge fast. "Sit down, Vernell," I said. He nodded and subsided. Tradition would say I should smack Turner's hand with a ruler, but I wanted a different schoolroom. If my idea didn't work, I could always resort to the ruler.

"Turner," I said, "at recess, you will stay in and write one hundred times on your slate, I will be kind to others."

He groaned. I'd already noted that his penmanship was lacking.

"All that won't fit on my slate," he said.

"Then you'll have to erase it and write it over and over, won't you?"

We engaged in a brief staring duel, then he dropped his eyes and made a face that I pretended not to see. And at recess, he complied, scowling the whole while. I breathed a sigh of relief. One battle won.

At lunchtime, Mattie came by. We'd never talked about Gabriel's death again, but little by little we'd shared a few more things. I even told her about the day Pa died, which I'd never shared with anyone. It felt like being undressed in public, but it made us closer.

My students were racing around on the grounds, using up some of their prodigious energy. Mattie and I dragged the caneback chairs outside and ate our sandwiches while I kept an eye on my charges.

"So, how did it go?" she asked.

"Fine, I think. It's a challenge keeping everyone busy."

She handed me a bundle wrapped in plaid cloth. "This is for you, from all the girls in the spinning room," she said.

I unwrapped the cloth to find an illustrated book of maps of various countries. I leafed through it, admiring the pretty colors and the detail.

"We took up a collection to buy it," Mattie said. "I hope you like it."

"I love it. I can use it to teach geography. I'll come by when school is out and tell everyone how much I appreciate it."

She put her hand over mine. "We're proud of you."

Mr. Powell had been right in one way. I wouldn't say more education had made me unfit for my station in life, but it had made a difference. As I learned more, my vocabulary expanded, my grammar changed. Associating with the town students during high school, students whose parents in some cases were professionals, I saw more possibilities in life. I still laughed and joked with my friends at the mill and defended them fiercely from outside criticism, but things weren't quite the same. An invisible line had been crossed and I feared there was no going back.

Ruthann had begun calling me Miss HAM when she saw me, which she said stood for Miss High and Mighty, and she hinted to people that I thought I was too good for them now. That wasn't true. The growing gulf made me sad, and a little lonely, but I didn't know what to do about it. This gift showed they still cared about me.

"What's new at the mill?" I asked, sure Mattie, everyone's friend, would know.

"You'll never guess. Bobby Lee Winton is courting Ruthann."

Bobby Lee was another mill worker, a muscular, blond man a year older than Ruthann. He'd dropped out of school to become a doffer, changing bobbins at the mill. He was good-looking, but a little rough. Last year, he'd beaten up a man who insulted him, but word was Bobby Lee had calmed down. That's the way it was in the village. Everybody knew everybody else's business unless you were really careful. And sometimes even then.

"Really? How's that going?" I asked.

"Hard to tell. Next thing you know, you'll have a boy running after you."

"Like that store clerk is running after you?" I asked with a laugh.

She was keeping occasional company with a nice-looking clerk, who was a bit of a dandy. Mattie spent her leftover pay on clothes, so they were well-matched. I think she enjoyed the picture they made together.

She waved one hand dismissively. "Oh, he's fun, but nothing serious. He knows I like my freedom," she said. "You need to find someone to have fun with, too."

A few young men had made overtures, but no one had captured my fancy. I told myself that teaching and helping at home didn't leave much time for socializing. But really, I still dreamed of something more than a quiet life in the village. How or with whom, I wasn't sure.

"He'd have to run fast to catch me," I said. "I'm pretty busy."

In the field beside the school, Seth and David, two of the younger children, were playing leapfrog. Seth missed and kicked David in the nose. David lurched toward me crying, blood streaming down his face.

"I have to deal with this," I told Mattie as I pulled out my handkerchief and tried to stanch the amazing quantity of blood coming from David's nose.

"And I have to get back to work," Mattie said. "I don't envy you this job. I'd rather work in the mill than try to teach this crew. It would plumb wear me out."

By the end of the day I felt the same. Teaching was harder than I'd thought. Still, I found time to talk to Vernell before he left.

"I appreciate your help," I said, "but keeping peace is my problem."

"I just wanted to help," he said. "My sister sai…" he dropped his head.

"Your sister what?"

"Never mind."

"All right," I said. I could imagine she'd painted a less than flattering picture of me. "See you tomorrow. You did well today."

"Thanks," he said, then added almost in a whisper, "You're a good teacher."

The school year galloped along. Gradually, I got to know my pupils' capabilities. Vernell, Peter, Lydia and Crystal, all in sixth grade, were fulfilling the promise I'd seen in them. When I saw Ruthann on the street one day she unbent enough to ask me how Vernell was doing.

"Fine," I said. "He's a pleasure to teach."

"Good." She paused, looking down, then at me. "He likes having you for a teacher. He says you make it interesting."

I blinked at the idea of Ruthann complimenting me. "Thank you. I'm glad he feels that way," I said.

The subject of Vernell didn't come up again but when Ruthann and I saw each other in passing after that, she returned my nod of greeting with another nod or a faint smile.

At Christmas time, my sister Naomi married Jediah at last and moved out. Now Ma needed a share of my salary more than ever with one less worker in the family. Ezra was still at home, and so was Jewel, but a young man was sparking her.

And that store clerk was still after Mattie. She gave him little encouragement, which seemed to make him more determined. As for me, I went on occasional group dates with Mattie, but no one held my interest.

In May, Mattie came to my house after work one evening while I was planning lessons. A lightning bug darted in through the open door as she entered and flitted around the room, glowing off and on in the dim light.

"Did you hear?" she asked. "Ruthann and Bobby Lee got hitched today."

"Wow. Really?"

"Yep. The preacher married them on their lunch break and they went right back to work in the mill. Kind of sad, the way it happened so fast, because Ruthann used to talk about how she wanted a fancy wedding. This one sure wasn't fancy."

Mattie looked around to see if we were alone. Ma and Jewel were in the bedroom, and Ezra was out back in the privy. She lowered her voice. "Word is she's in a family way, and they had to rush to get the vows said."

"At least Bobby Lee was willing to do the right thing," I said. "Where will they live?"

"With her aunt for now, Lord help them. I gotta run. I thought you'd be interested."

After she left, I looked for the lightning bug, but it had found someplace to hide. I returned to my lesson planning, McGuffey's Second Reader open on my lap. The story was about a pony. Yet unexpectedly, as I looked at the spelling words, it struck me that some of them described Ruthann. Young. Pretty. Bright.

Yes, they applied to her. I shut the book with a bang as I thought about how smart she had been in school and how she and I had vied to be best in the class. Now she was up at five in the morning and on her feet all day watching for breaks in yarn in a noisy mill. Much as I disliked her, I knew she was not only capable of much more but yearned for it. If not for Mrs. Powell's help, I might be in her shoes. Now Ruthann was married and pregnant. I felt a twinge of pity. She would have hated that if she'd known. I opened the book again with a renewed determination to wait for the right man to come along. If there even was a right one.

The school year was almost over. I stood in front of my class and tapped lightly on the desk to get their attention. "Sixth graders," I said, "while the other children are working on their reading and arithmetic, I have a writing assignment for you."

Expressions of dismay, boredom or smiles greeted the news.

"Take out your copy books and write one page on the theme: If I could be anything I wanted, I would be…. And tell my why you chose that. You have ten minutes. Then it will be time for arithmetic."

I'd debated whether to give this assignment, because most of them had little chance of moving beyond the mill. Would it raise expectations that could never be met? But, I decided, my job was not just to educate them, but to help them imagine.

"Remember, neat penmanship. And use only one page." Paper was precious. Soon the scratching of soapstone pencils was added to the drone of younger children reading to each other and the sound of chalk on slates as fifth graders copied sums.

I lugged the copybooks home that night and read them on the porch in the fading light of a gold and pink sunset. Some of the students, the ones to whom writing was torture, had groaned when I assigned the topic. And when I read through the essays, I felt like groaning at times myself. For some, spelling and grammar were still terra incognita, as they said on old maps. Creative terra incognita with misspellings I'd never thought of. Their dreams were varied, ranging from becoming mill superintendent to being a good wife and mother.

I saved my four star pupils for last as a reward.

Peter wrote, "I want to build bridges and big buildings. It would be interesting to plan and to see things come out the way you saw them in your head." That urge was already showing itself in the wood and rope swinging bridge he and Vernell had built over a nearby ravine. How often did similar talents spring up all over Felthame only to wither for lack of opportunity?

Crystal, who loved movement, dancing, twirling, dreamed more modestly of being a secretary. Why? So she could buy "pretty clothes and enough books to fill my bedroom."

Lydia, my favorite, wanted "to play the piano, because it makes me happy. You can't make money at it so I would teach school during the day and play the piano at night. If I saved for a few years, I could buy a big piano like Mrs. Powell's."

The last essay belonged to Vernell, who tried to be best at everything and hated to lose. If he missed a word in the weekly spelldown, he'd be unhappy all afternoon. "I want to be a doctor," he said. "If there'd been a doctor when my mother was sick, maybe she would still be alive. And doctors make enough money to buy a house of their own."

I sat back, flashing back for a moment to Pa lying in bed breathing his last. What if a doctor had been a few miles down the road and we'd taken him there right off? No use plowing that furrow, though. I understood how Vernell felt. He'd been only seven when his mother passed and his father skedaddled. And what with living with his uncharitable aunt, a home of his own would be high on his list. I stacked the copybooks up with a feeling of sadness, wishing I could make all their dreams come true.

At the end of the year, all four children wanted to go on to seventh grade. Their families were willing, even though they'd lose the children's mill wages, but they had no money for tuition or books. I vowed to do what I could to help them. Finally I hit on an idea and went to call on Mrs. Powell.

"Come in, come in, my dear," she said, smiling and sweeping her hand toward the hall in a grand gesture. "Sit down and tell me how you are. I hear good things about the school."

"Thank you," I said, seating myself on a fragile-looking chair in the parlor. "I have four promising sixth graders who I'd love to see go on in school, but the families don't have the money."

"A shame," she said, her tone neutral.

I hurried on. "You were my patroness," I said, using her favorite word for herself. "I can never thank you enough for the difference you made in my life. I know you care about young people, so I wondered if you'd be willing to give a piano recital and invite some of the more well-to-do people here and in town to come. It would be a scholarship benefit."

Her eyebrows rose. "Me? Why, I don't know. I'm competent, but no virtuoso. And I've never done anything like that."

"Oh no, you're wonderful," I said.

She laughed. "Your experience of pianists is rather limited, but I'm glad you think so." She cocked her head to one side, considering. "It might be fun. And it's for a worthy cause. I'll have to ask Mr. Powell, of course. Come back tomorrow after school and we can talk more."

I left with a good feeling. All the next day, I enjoyed watching my four eager students and thinking about what a great surprise I had for them and their parents. We might even raise enough money to buy a few more books.

After school was out, I hurried to Mrs. Powell's house. She greeted me at the door, her smile of welcome missing. We stood in the hall this time.

"I'm sorry," she said, not meeting my eye, "but Mr. Powell thinks it isn't suitable for me to do a concert. It's a nice idea, but I can't. He wouldn't like it."

From the lecture Mr. Powell had given me at the beginning of the school year about upholding mill work as honorable, I suspected he disapproved of anything that might deprive him of workers. More education could certainly do that.

"Oh," I said, "but…"

"I'm sorry," she repeated.

I raced to come up with an argument that might change things. "Maybe if we gave some of the money to the church."

"Ah, my dear, I wish that would get his approval. But he was quite adamant. He'd have a conniption if I went against his wishes." She held her palms up as if she was helpless in the face of his demands.

"Maybe I could talk to Mr. Powell and explain things."

"I wouldn't advise that. The subject is closed. Remember what it says in Ephesians: 'Wives, submit yourselves unto your husbands as unto the Lord.'"

"I know, but surely…" She put her hand on the doorknob and I sputtered to a stop. When someone quoted the Good Book, it was useless to argue.

"All right. Thank you for considering it."

I walked into the sunlight, brimming with frustration. I'd dreamed that these four pupils would be my small contribution to showing that children who didn't want to work in the mill could hope for more. The hum of the mill three streets down seemed to mock me. Mill life was as unchanging as Mr. Powell.

Mattie stopped by the house that night after work. "It's so disappointing," I said. "It makes me want to scream every time I look at the kids. I know people would come to a benefit concert."

We sat in silence, and an idea began to form. "I wonder if I…"

Mattie clapped her hands the way she did when something excited her, which was often. "I know what you're thinking," she said. "You want to give the concert yourself. You should. You definitely should. You play as good as Mrs. Powell." She gave a delighted grin, making her plump cheeks look even more like ripe peaches. Her quick enthusiasm was one of the things I loved about her.

"Mrs. Powell did say she'd taught me all she could," I said.

"There. You see," Mattie said.

It was tempting. I'd been playing in church on Sundays so I was used to performing in public. A concert couldn't be that different. And I'd do anything to give my students the same chance I'd had. It would be like passing on what Mrs. Powell did for me.

"I just might do it."

"Maybe you could get Ruthann to sing," she said.

"What? Ruthann? I don't think so."

Mattie always wanted to bring people together, but this was too much.

"Hear me out," she said, pressing on. "She wants to help Vernell. And she has a lovely voice. You said so yourself. I know she'd do it. More people might come if it wasn't just the piano. It would be more interesting."

"Not in a million years. Anyway, is she showing yet? If she looks pregnant, it wouldn't be proper."

"She's not showing. At least think about it. You're not the only one who wants to help kids, you know."

"Not Ruthann," I said.

"Have you thought this concert idea through?" Ma asked me. "If Mr. Powell doesn't want his wife to do it, why do you think he'd want you to do it?"

We were sitting in the kitchen shucking peas by lamplight.

"He's not my husband. What I do won't embarrass him."

"Maybe not. But he can make it mighty uncomfortable for you. You'd be bitin' the hand that feeds you. And he has been mighty good to you, to all the mill people."

It was true. He donated firewood and food to needy families, was generous to the church. And, while Mrs. Powell was my supporter, it was Mr. Powell who had paid for my education. I knew he might object, but I didn't let myself think about it because then I might back out and let down my students. And feel like a coward to boot.

"We're not doing it in the village, so maybe he won't care that much," I said, ignoring the fluttering in my stomach as I dropped the last of the peas in the pan with unnecessary force. "I've already talked to Miss Holcombe, and we can have it there." She was my former teacher at the secondary school in town. "The school got a piano last year. We'll put up posters and make lots of money. It will be fine."

"It's a good thing you're wantin' to do, but I worry," Ma said. She stood up, pressing her hand to the small of her back, which ached more often these days. "Well, do what you think is right."

I hated it when she said that. It meant I was supposed to take the high road. To me, that meant giving the concert, and doing all I could to make it a success. And, drat it, I supposed that meant asking Ruthann to help.

But Mattie stole a march on me. At lunchtime the next day, Ruthann came by the school. "Mattie said you wanted to see me," she said. "Something about Vernell. He's behaving, isn't he?"

"He is," I said, silently cussing Mattie for putting me on the spot. Or maybe she was just trying to make it easier for me to ask Ruthann.

"I have an idea for a way we might raise money for Vernell and some of the others to go on to seventh grade," I said.

"I'm listening. Be quick. I don't have much time left on my lunch break."

As I outlined my plan, her expression grew thoughtful. "And this will help Vernell?"

"It should, if my plan works. And Peter, Lydia and Crystal, too."

"All right," she said. "I'm in."

Thus it was that a few days later Mattie and I sat on the front pew in the empty church waiting for Ruthann so we could practice for the concert, which was only a week away.

"I hope this works," I said.

She smiled reassuringly. "Relax. It's going to work out great. You'll see."

"I'll do my part," I said. "Did you tell her that Mr. Powell didn't want Mrs. Powell to do it and that's why we're doing it instead?"

"I told her and she didn't say anything except that she'd be here."

When Ruthann came in, she greeted Mattie and nodded to me. I nodded back.

"You know this could get you in trouble with Mr. Powell, right?" I asked, thinking about my conversation with Ma.

Ruthann put her hands on her hips. "I'm not afraid of anyone. Let's get going."

"Fine then. I've been thinking about the program. At first, I was going to make it all church music, but since it's at a school, I thought we could make it a mix."

Mrs. Powell had taught me a sprinkling of popular music, along with the classical and sacred. "I was thinking of 'Old Folks at Home' and 'I've Been Working on the Railroad,' and 'My Grandmother's Old Rocking Chair.' What do you think?"

"I don't know too many popular songs," Ruthann said. "I could sing 'Home, Sweet Home,' and 'Amazing Grace' and 'Sweet Hour of Prayer.' Would that be too strange with the other stuff?"

"I've never done this before," I said, "so anything sounds good to me."

"Not very reassuring," she said.

"We'll divide the program in half," I said, "with the popular stuff at the beginning, and then the hymns. We could end with 'Amazing Grace.' People always like that and it suits your voice."

"Let's practice then," Ruthann said. "I don't have a lot of time."

We did and it went well. She even smiled in my general direction when we were done.

So the night of the concert, I wasn't worried about her, just everything else. I'd decided on a freewill offering because selling tickets was too complicated. Miss Holcombe was going to give a little speech about helping the students. Miss Holcombe was old, maybe fifty, and lived alone. She wore her hair pulled back so tight you would think her forehead would hurt, and she always wore black like she was in mourning. We'd made up romantic stories in school about lost loves, but no one knew the facts. Strict but fair, she would jerk even big boys around by the ear if they misbehaved. Once, when one complained, she said, "You'll thank me later." I'd never been jerked around, but I certainly felt thankful to her now.

If her speech, combined with Ruthann's "Amazing Grace," didn't move folks, their hearts were made of granite.

Mattie stayed home at the last minute, which didn't help my nerves any. She said she had to baby-sit her five younger brothers and sisters. So Ruthann and

I walked over together early so we could get used to the room and run through the songs.

"Are you nervous?" I asked.

"I don't get nervous."

"Really? I do. I hope I remember the songs and that a lot of people show up."

"You'll do fine," she said, which was the nicest thing she'd said to me since the day she told me Vernell thought I was a good teacher.

At seven o'clock, people started filing in and sitting on the benches, not as many as I'd hoped, but maybe they'd give generously. They were dressed nicer than Ruthann and I were, even though we'd both worn our Sunday clothes, and I felt a little embarrassed. But Ma always said pretty is as pretty does.

Miss Holcombe stood up and the murmurs and rustlings died down.

"We're gathered here tonight for a good cause, the education of our young people. I know you'll enjoy hearing these two talented young ladies perform. I'll speak more later, but now, without further ado, I present Delia Hammett and Ruthann Winton."

Polite applause filled the room while Ruthann and I bowed to the crowd. Ruthann might claim she wasn't nervous, but the hand that rested on top of the piano was trembling.

So we played and sang, and I only muffed a few notes. Halfway through, Miss Holcombe talked some about helping young people fulfill their dreams and how more and more we needed an educated work force in a changing world, then she passed a wicker basket up and down the rows.

When we moved to the hymns, Ruthann's voice was shaky on the first song, but on "Amazing Grace" at the end, she let it all out. She had a powerful voice with a throaty quality that spoke to you somehow. A few of the ladies dabbed at their eyes with handkerchiefs. I felt the flash of warmth that some music gave me, as if I'd bathed in sunlight.

Everyone was quiet for what seemed like a minute after the last notes, and Ruthann's face froze. I wasn't sure what to think either. Then the clapping began, and I relaxed. Ruthann and I bowed while people clapped. I could get used to this, I thought. The applause was like a spring freshet, sending the blood racing through my body.

Miss Holcombe reminded people that if they hadn't given, there was still time and that the donation basket would be by the door as they left.

"Give generously," she said.

When the last of the audience had left in a swirl of congratulations, Miss Holcombe brought up the offering basket and sat it on top of the piano. We stood beside her and watched while she counted.

"It's enough for three children," she announced.

"That's all?" I said. "Not all four?"

"Not the way I calculate it. I'm sorry. But that's very good," Miss Holcombe said. "Without you, there'd be nothing. You both should be proud."

I was proud. But I hated having to tell one student he couldn't go on.

Walking home with Ruthann, clouds covered the setting sun, creating shafts of light in the sky.

"It looks like rain," I said. "I love to listen to the rain."

Ruthann looked at me and smiled. "Yeah? Me, too."

"I like it best when I'm lying in bed at night hearing it hit the roof," I said. "It's like a different kind of music."

"I like rain all the time," she said. "Before my folks died, when we were on the farm, we'd have rain parties. That was fun."

"What's a rain party?"

She hesitated. "It's when you see it's going to rain hard and you can't work outside, so everyone gets a biscuit with butter and honey, and you all sit on the porch and listen to the rain. It pours off the roof like a... like a veil in front of you. You just sit and watch. That's all. My mother always called it a rain party." She gave an embarrassed laugh. "It's hard to explain. Forget it."

"No. It sounds great," I said, glimpsing a totally different Ruthann.

We walked in silence after that. By the time we reached the village, raindrops began to patter against the trees by the side of the road and hit our skin.

"Well, see you later, Ruthann," I said. "Thanks for your help. You were great." I felt the warmest I'd ever felt toward her. Maybe it would be a new beginning for us.

"It was for a good cause," she said. "But we only raised enough money for three students. Which three get to go on?"

"I don't know. I guess I'll talk to the parents."

She grabbed my arm and turned me to face her. Raindrops from her swinging hair splashed in my face. "What do you mean you don't know? I didn't risk my job so Vernell could drop out after sixth grade," she snapped. "You owe me."

"I'll do the right thing," I said.

"What does that mean?"

Rain began pelting down, soaking through our dresses, dripping off our hair. The scared feeling that Ruthann gave me when we were girls swept over me. I'd thought I was over it.

"Just what I said. I'll do the right thing," I said, forcing myself to look her straight in the eye, a move that might have been more impressive if raindrops weren't running down both our faces so it looked as if we were crying.

"As long as you're clear that Vernell goes on," she said.

"We're getting soaked," I said, feeling welcome irritation rise in me and push out the scared feeling. "For heaven's sakes, let's just go on home. I told you I'd do the right thing."

As soon as I figured out what that was.

Chapter Seven

I lay awake long into the night, wrestling with what to do about Vernell. Did he deserve special consideration because Ruthann helped raise the money? Or was that unfair to the other students who didn't have a relative with the talent to help them? Ruthann would be furious if I didn't choose Vernell. But that wasn't a good enough reason to favor him. If I gave in to my uneasiness about her reaction, it would be the same as if I was a scared kid again and she was still bullying me, a thought I despised.

It was natural for Ruthann to favor Vernell. And she had helped make the concert a success. But she didn't see the children day after day the way I did. I loved all four. I could picture them so clearly.

Crystal's mother must have known when she named her that she'd be delicate because at twelve, she looked like a picture I'd seen of a ballerina. Her limbs were long and slender. The flaxen hair of childhood still shone brightly. Crystal loved words, was a crack speller. She'd written in her essay that she wanted to be a secretary. But I could easily imagine her as a teacher.

Then there was Lydia. This was her best chance at schooling, what with eight children in the family. In a town where we all got by, they had less than anyone. Her musical talent deserved to be nurtured.

To look at Peter, he seemed nondescript, like every other brown-haired, average mill kid. But he loved to build things. Maybe he'd be an engineer or an architect someday. I knew no engineers or architects, but I liked to think anything was possible for my students.

Then there was Vernell, who was deserving too. How could I deprive any of them of a chance at more? What was fair to them?

I veered here and there like a rabbit fleeing the hounds, until I finally made a decision. Right was right, and fear shouldn't enter into it. Now all I had to do, much as I hated it, was discuss it with Ruthann.

We met after church the next day, lingering in the pews. Maybe being in God's house would hold her temper in check.

"I've decided we should draw straws to see who gets to go on to seventh grade," I said.

"Good idea," she said. "That sounds fair."

"I mean that everyone would draw straws."

She scowled. "Vernell, too? I don't think so."

I launched into all my reasons for the drawing, but she wasn't buying it. Her expression grew darker by the second. So much for the tempering influence of God's house.

She jumped up, ready to do I knew not what.

"Think, Ruthann," I said. "These parents are your friends and neighbors. You have to work with them at the mill every day. You see them in church, on the street. They have to feel it's fair to their kids."

She stood still, fists clenched by her sides, staring at me. "I can see that," she said slowly. "They're good people and their kids deserve a chance. I just can't see leaving Vernell out. That's not fair either."

"There's three chances out of four he'll win," I said.

"Oh sure. And we've been so lucky in life up to now, right?"

My heartbeat pounded in my ears, but I'd made my decision. "I think it's the right thing to do," I said. "Maybe I'm wrong. But I can't shut the other kids out of their chance. You can be there for the drawing or not. Your choice."

She looked at me speculatively. "I'll go along with drawing straws if I get to hold them."

Stung, I snapped, "You don't trust me?"

"I'm just saying, I'll hold the straws. Take it or leave it."

"I'll take it," I said.

The next morning shortly after daybreak, a doffer from the mill knocked on our front door.

"Mr. Powell wants to see you right away," he said, then scampered off without waiting for a reply. Fifteen minutes later, I stood in front of Mr. Powell's desk in the mill like a naughty pupil.

The room was hot and he'd removed his suit coat. I wished I had something I could take off because I was sweating, and not just from the heat.

"I hear you had a little musical event Saturday night," he said. "You and this spinning room girl Ruthann."

"It was all my idea," I said quickly.

He waved his hook dismissively. "I'll deal with her later."

"The concert was a big success," I said. "We raised enough to send three students on to seventh grade."

"Three this year. And how many next year? Your contract explicitly says you will uphold mill work as honorable. But here are three children probably lost to the mill. And the mill is the future of this town. Where would people be without it?"

"But look how it benefited you to have me teaching school."

"Yes. Look at how my wife's little experiment benefited me and the mill."

I'd been avoiding his gaze. Now I raised my head and looked him in the eye. "I am not an experiment. I'm a teacher. I respect mill work. My own family works here. I worked here. But these children deserve a chance to go as far as they can. Maybe they'll choose mill work, maybe they won't. But I won't discourage them from learning more."

He rubbed his wrist where leather attached his metal hook to the stump of his arm, studying me a moment while my heart pounded. Then he shook his head and sighed.

"You're young yet. You'll learn," he said. "You're not thinking of the mill's need for workers and the overall future of the village. I have to."

He paused, then leaned across the desk toward me. "It's done now. But the mill pays your salary, and you have a one-year contract coming up for renewal. This bears serious consideration. Do we understand each other?"

Shaken, I said, "We do."

Ruthann and I both wanted to do the drawing as soon as possible, so Tuesday, during lunch break from the mill, Vernell's aunt and the parents of Crystal, Lydia and Peter came to the school. Everyone stood in a circle at the front of the room as if we were getting ready to play a children's game. I handed Ruthann the straws. She turned around and adjusted them, then turned back to us.

"We'll draw alphabetically by the child's first name," I said.

Ruthann looked at me with alarm. "No," she said. "Vernell draws first."

The father of Crystal, who would go first under my plan, spoke up. "I go along with alphabetically," he said. "It's as fair as any other way." He jerked a straw from Ruthann's fist and held it up. "Long," he announced triumphantly. Lydia's mother drew a long straw before Ruthann could react. Now everyone's eyes were on her fist as Peter's father, Pete Senior, stepped forward. You'd have thought King Arthur was getting ready to draw Excalibur from the stone.

Ruthann's brows drew together. "Wait," she said. "This isn't right." She drew her fist back, the two straws still in it.

"Is there a problem?" Pete Senior said. "Because if there is…"

"No problem," I said, eager to get this over with.

Ruthann glared at me, but there was something else in her eyes, something almost pleading.

"Good," Pete Senior said, and plucked out a straw. "Long," he said, holding it aloft. Ruthann opened her fist and the short straw fluttered to the floor. She stared at it in disbelief, then lifted her gaze to stare at me, face white and stricken. She raised her hand and for a second, I thought she would strike me. Instead, she whirled and stalked toward the door.

I was tempted to let her go, but the anguish I'd seen in her face tugged at me. I had to let her know how sorry I was that Vernell lost out.

"Excuse me," I said to the others and hurried after her.

"I'm so sorry," I told her.

"How could you?" she whispered, which was scarier than if she'd yelled. Her fists were clenched by her side like they'd been after church the other day, and her whole body was stiff as if she were restraining herself from hitting me by force of will.

"How could you?" she repeated. "You *knew* the only reason I did that concert was for Vernell."

"But you agreed to the drawing," I said. "You knew there was a risk."

"But I thought we had a deal. I had it all set so Vernell would draw first and get a long straw. Then you threw in that alphabetical thing without telling me."

"We didn't have a deal," I said. "You misunderstood. I thought you agreed to hold the straws because you didn't trust me and wanted to be sure the drawing was fair, not that you wanted to fix the results."

"So you say now." Her gaze raked me up and down. "I thought maybe I was wrong about you, Miss High and Mighty. I see I'm not. I won't forget this."

"I'm sorry," I said again.

"Not as sorry as you will be."

She made a low sound in her throat, spat on my foot and strode off while I stood staring after her, the fear I'd made a terrible mistake rising in me.

I walked back, stomach roiling and spit still on my shoe, to face Vernell's aunt. "I'm so sorry," I repeated, feeling like a parrot. "I can tutor Vernell after work if he wants. He'll get some schooling that way. And maybe something will change."

Her mouth tightened and she glared at me. "Ruthann said he'd go on, that it was all set," she said. "What went wrong?"

"That's the way the draw went," I said. "You saw for yourself."

"I did. I reckon there weren't any mischief in how it was done." She said the words, but she didn't look like she believed them. "Well, it's too late now. But I hate to tell him. He was so sure things were set. He's been talking about it ever since the concert."

"I'm so sorry," I repeated. What a useless phrase.

She shook her head and left without another word. The other parents, who'd been watching silently, crowded around me now, smiling and happy. But my pleasure in their happiness was dimmed.

The next day, Mattie told me that Mr. Powell called Ruthann into his office, but nobody knew what was said. She looked like thunder when she came back to the spinning room and she didn't work for two days — so I guess that was wages lost — but at least he didn't fire her. And Mattie said that Vernell had applied to be a doffer at the mill and they'd taken him on right away.

I stood near the entrance waiting for him when he left work. "Walk with me," I said.

He looked as if he would refuse. "Why should I?"

"Please," I said. "I need to talk to you."

He shrugged. "All right."

The setting sun cast long shadows ahead of us on the dirt street.

"I wanted you to know I'm willing to help you keep learning," I said. "You're smart, and if you work hard, you might be able to go to school later without being too far behind."

"I surely want to learn, but it won't be the same," he said.

"No, but it's all I have to offer."

He looked at me for what seemed a long time while I waited, hoping he'd say yes and I'd have a chance to redeem myself. The last rays of the sun cast a golden light on his fair skin and blond hair.

"I don't hold with what you decided, although I reckon Crystal, Lydia and Peter are happy," he said. He scuffed at the red dirt with the toe of his work shoe. "It don't hardly seem fair. But tutoring is better than nothing." He raised his head, mouth grim. "I'll do it," he said. "When can we start?"

"Tomorrow," I said. He nodded and walked away.

After that, we studied during the brief snatches when he wasn't changing bobbins. Soon the long work hours and the lure of horsing around with the other boys overshadowed the idea of lessons. He seemed conflicted, pulled by his friends to be one of them, pulled by me and whatever was inside him to aim for more. We switched our lessons to Saturday afternoons, when he was off. But now I was competing with warm summer days, fishing, swimming in the river, playing ball with friends, powerful draws for a twelve-year-old boy. At night, I lay awake trying to think of fresh ways to make the lessons interesting. At least, I thought, this will make me a better teacher in the fall.

Ruthann ignored me, if you can call pointedly looking away when she saw me ignoring me. Her threat that I'd be sorry lurked in the back of my mind, cropping up at odd times when I spotted her.

A month went by, then Mr. Powell sent word for me to come to his office at the mill. I stood in front of his desk in a duplicate of the scene after the concert. This time, though, my heart wasn't pounding with apprehension. The concert was history, and nothing bad had happened. A new school term was beginning soon. And Mr. Powell had acknowledged that I was doing a good job as a teacher, even if I had deprived him of three potential workers. I doubted I'd get a raise in pay, and maybe I'd have to listen to a lecture, but we could move on from there.

I smiled as I greeted him. "How are you today, Mr. Powell?" I asked.

"Well enough, Miss Hammett." I stood there a moment, waiting for him to invite me to sit down. Instead, he tugged at his collar as if it was uncomfortable.

"Let me come straight to the point," he said. "That's always best in these matters. We've decided not to renew your contract in the fall."

"What? But I've done a good job."

"I don't question your teaching ability. Just your attitude, which doesn't fit with what we are looking for in a teacher."

"If you mean the concert…"

"Ah yes, the concert. I made my position quite clear before that you were to uphold mill work, but you chose to go your own way."

"My job is to encourage the children to go as far as they can go," I said.

"My job is to be sure the mill has enough workers, contented workers." He waved his hook in the air. "Well, no need to rehash the past. I'm sorry things didn't work out."

"But…" I stared at him, trying to take in a scene so at odds with what I'd imagined.

He took a deep breath. "No arguing, please. Let's keep this as pleasant as possible."

Pleasant? How could it be pleasant to be fired?

When I opened my mouth to protest, he waved his hook in the air again with a slashing motion. "The decision is final. We've already retained another teacher. Good day, and the best of luck to you. I wish you well."

After I left his office, I leaned against the wall in the hallway, breathing hard. For a second, I sought for a way out. Maybe Mrs. Powell would go to bat for me. But then, she hadn't had the gumption to support me about the concert. Much as she might like me, she'd never go against her husband.

I left the mill in a daze. I'd been naive to think I could buck Mr. Powell and get away with it. At least, I told myself, three children had benefited. I'd done something good and he couldn't take that away from me. I started home, head down, feeling like a whipped puppy.

As I walked along, I started to get angry. This was so unfair. I was a good teacher, one eager to try new ideas, one who cared about the children. But mixed with the anger was a hollow feeling of uncertainty. What would I do now? It would have to be a job in town, where there were more opportunities. My mind scurried through the immediate possibilities, ranging from laundress to seamstress, not that I sewed a fine seam, to clerk in a ladies' clothing store and back again. Yes, I could probably find work. But I wanted to teach.

That night, Ma looked so tired, what with constant chores, that I put off telling her until after supper. She sat on a stool in the kitchen, removing her shoes and stockings. It had been a hot day and even with the windows open, the house held the heat. I ran my hand across my sweaty face and swatted at a fly that tried to land on me.

Ma let out a long sigh and rubbed the soles of her feet. "Fetch the wash basin, would you, please?" she said. "Then bring in a bucket of water. My feet are hurting something fierce tonight from standing all day. Maybe a little foot washing will help." She laughed. "It was good enough for Jesus."

I sat the enamel wash basin by her feet and picked up the bucket of water, steeling myself to tell her.

"Mr. Powell didn't renew my contract," I said. "Because of the concert. He said I didn't have the right attitude."

"Oh my. I'm sorry you was let go." She came over to me, walking slowly. She patted my shoulder and I realized that I was an inch or so taller than her now.

"Your attitude is fine," she said. "Don't let anyone tell you different. You done what you thought was right, which is what we all ought to do. You're smart. Things will work out."

She went over and sat down again. I loved her so in that moment it filled me clean up to the brim.

"I've been trying all day to think what to do next," I said. "We need my salary."

"If you're desperate, maybe if you apologized, Mr. Powell would take you back at the mill until you find something."

"I doubt that. Even if he would, I don't want to. I can't apologize. I just can't." I poured water into the wash basin, splashing a little on the floor in my agitation at the idea of apologizing to Mr. Powell.

"Can't say as I blame you," she said. "We all got our pride."

I knelt to sop up the drops of water. "I've been thinking," I said. "This isn't the only school in the world. I bet I could find a teaching job in another town, get a room in a boarding house and send money back."

"I bet you could. I'd miss you something awful. But there's not much here for you."

She stuck her pale feet in the wash basin, wriggled her toes and gave a sigh of relief. The lamplight flickered on her tired face. I yearned for the wider world, but I felt a stab of loss at the thought of leaving her, my family and friends, the only world I'd known. The farthest away I'd been from the mill village was the town three miles away.

"What do you want to do most in the whole world?" Ma asked.

"Something to do with music," I said, surprised by the way the words burst out of me. The second I said it, it felt right. "When I play the piano, I feel so... alive. I can't explain it."

"I don't know anybody who makes a living with music," she said.

"Neither do I. But I have to find a way to make some money. If I could do it with music. That would be... well, it would be wonderful."

"I hope you can. It's been a long day," she said. "Things will be clearer tomorrow."

The next morning Arthur Benning came to town.

Chapter Eight

April 1957, Whistleton, Virginia

Resting in my bedroom at Pleasant Oaks, lost in memory, I could see more clearly my mixed motives for insisting on the drawing and how little my teen-age self understood all the ramifications. I'd lost touch with the three students whose parents drew the long straws, winning them more education. I hoped their lives were better because of my decision. But if Vernell had gone on to seventh grade, my whole life would have been different. And so would his.

I'd been resting long enough. I sat up slowly to give the blood time to get to my head, a precaution I'd learned after my fall, and went out to the main room. It was midafternoon, a slow time when lots of residents rested or napped.

Henry sat in an armchair, staring straight ahead, a book resting in his lap. I heard the sound of shoes on tile behind me and saw Alice the Loquacious heading his way. He grabbed his book and stood up with a panicked look, then saw me. I stifled a laugh at his expression.

"Care for an afternoon stroll?" I asked as I outflanked her.

"Please. Now would be a good time."

We headed for the door as rapidly as possible.

"Wait," Alice called. "I have a question."

We kept going. Once we'd manipulated the handicapped ramp, we ducked around the building and stood there, laughing.

"Makes me feel young again," he said. "Like the time old Mr. Adams almost caught me stealing his persimmons."

The ground was uneven and not ideal for me, but it was clear Henry didn't want to go back inside and chance being cornered by Alice.

"What now?" I asked.

Pleasant Oaks had an acre or two of land around it. He pointed toward a maple tree about fifty feet away, just showing the tiny reddish leaves of spring.

"It's a sunny day. We could sit over there until the hunt dies down."

I worked my way carefully over and settled down on the mixture of fallen leaves and scraggly grass underneath the tree. We sat quietly and a bird started to sing. The call was pleasant and complex but unfamiliar.

"Listen. Isn't that cheerful?" I said, keeping my voice low.

He cocked his head. "It's an indigo bunting," he whispered. Then he pointed. "Look there it is, on the lowest limb of that tree."

His pointing startled the bird and it flew away in a flash of brilliant blue.

"I'm impressed you recognized the call," I said.

"Comes of being a Boy Scout, among other things. I used to roam the woods every chance I got. Being cut off from nature is one of the toughest parts of being here."

"I know," I said. "It's the simple things, the loss of control over your choices. You can't go in your own kitchen and fix what you want. You have to choose from the two items on the menu that night. If you don't happen to like either, too bad. You can go hungry."

"Yes, but I'd rather be here than live with my daughter and have her take care of me. She says I'm too proud to let her help, but that's not it."

"I know," I said. "Oh well, being here is only temporary."

He looked at my cane dubiously. "Yeah?"

"Yeah."

"I might be here a while," he said. "Things aren't going too well."

"I'm sorry to hear that."

"That's life. When I was younger, I thought if you tried hard enough, you could change anything. Not true."

"Not true," I echoed. "Except maybe your attitude."

"Enough whining," he said, although I wouldn't have classified our conversation as whining. More like acknowledging reality. "I've vowed I won't be one of those old people who can only talk about their ailments. Although, I must say there are more ailments to talk about now, and since they're happening to me, they've become a lot more interesting. Tell me about yourself. I heard you were a piano teacher."

"That's right. For many years."

"I wish I could play a musical instrument. The closest I come is listening to records, especially cowboy songs. Do you sing, too?"

"Some," I said. "The voice changes with age."

"I can't sing worth a lick. In the shower maybe."

"Everyone can sing," I said. "They just need to stop caring about how they sound."

"Not everyone." He let loose with a few words from "Sweet Betsy from Pike" in a droning voice that made me wince. He was right. He couldn't sing worth a lick.

"See?" he said with a laugh.

I laughed, too. "Music is about enjoyment," I said. "If you enjoy singing, don't let anyone stop you."

"Bird songs. That's the kind of music I know," he said.

The wind rustled in the trees, blowing strands of his sparse, silver hair across his forehead and giving him an almost boyish look. My interest stirred along with the breeze.

"What did you do before you retired?" I asked.

"Forest ranger with the National Park Service. Listen, I bet the coast is clear. If you want to know more about me, come to my room and look at some of my photos. They say a picture is worth a thousand words. I'm a pretty good nature photographer. I might have a closeup photo of an indigo bunting."

"I thought it was etchings that men wanted women to see."

He grinned. "I work with what I have."

Here we were flirting. How pleasant it was to feel that old male-female interplay, that awareness of the opposite sex that probably only departed at death. My son would have been embarrassed at my thoughts. And Mrs. Atwood, I felt sure, frowned on what I'd once heard her refer to as "hanky panky." Too bad. I liked it, and I had no doubt Henry did, too.

"Lead on," I said.

He helped me up, a process that would have made a good slow-motion scene in a movie. We went back inside and marched — or more accurately, maneuvered — down the hall without sighting either Alice or Mrs. Atwood.

His room was cluttered with Outdoor Life and Field and Stream magazines along with field guides to birds, butterflies, moths, trees and stars and a well-thumbed stack of Louis L'Amour westerns.

"You're welcome to borrow any of my books," he said. "That L'Amour is a good storyteller."

"Thanks. I'm more of a science fiction fan. Isaac Asimov. Robert Heinlein. That kind of thing."

He pulled a tan photo album from a bottom drawer. "My daughter put this together for me," he said.

He guided me through lovely nature photos of trees in all seasons, brooks covered with leaves, snowy mountains, winter branches silhouetted against the sky.

"Did you take these?"

"Most of them. Now, not this one."

The black and white photo showed a man in a National Park Service uniform atop a horse.

"That's me and old Bucky at Yosemite in the 1920s," he said. "Bucky for buckskin. I still miss that horse. I remember when feet or horses were the only ways to get around."

"Me, too," I said, thinking of my long walks to high school. "How things have changed."

Toward the back were various photos of his daughter and son, smiling over a birthday cake, sunbathing at the beach, riding bicycles. Then there were the obligatory photos of the grandchildren: A grandson reached for a ripe tomato. A granddaughter sat pensively in the crook of a tree, oblivious to the camera. A lovely young girl in a flowered dress carried a red balloon across a field.

"These are wonderful," I said.

The last two photos in the book were of him with a woman. In one, they were young and smiling, posed in front of a fake backdrop of clouds. It was an old sepia print, badly faded. In the second photo, their rounded faces were wrinkled with age, their hair silver. His hand rested on her shoulder, and her hand covered his.

"My late wife, Jeanette," he said. "She died three years ago. We were married for more than fifty years." His gaze lingered on her face. "I miss her still. But she wouldn't want me to grieve forever. She always said that life goes on, with or without us."

"Relentlessly," I said. My husband had been gone a year and I missed him, too. But he'd been gone in another sense for several years before that. I still felt sad when I thought about the day, deep in his dementia, when he looked at me puzzled and asked if I'd ever learned to play an instrument. Our joyful musical sessions together had become dust on the wind of fading memory. Yes, I'd almost gotten used to being alone, to thinking of myself as single before the fact of his death.

"Had you lived alone before?" I asked.

"Not really. But, of course, I spent a lot of time alone in the woods. But you've got birds and squirrels and such around you."

"I thought I knew about being alone, because of my husband's illness," I said. "But after he died, I realized that here I was at age seventy nine, and this was the first time in my whole life I'd lived truly alone. Always before, I had family around."

"It's a challenge," he said.

It had been, but I'd also discovered surprises about myself and what I liked and disliked when there was no one else to consider.

"I've kept busy since she died," Henry said, staring at the photo of his wife. "I walk. I read. I study nature. My daughter and grandchildren come to visit. I'm grateful. But still… there's no substitute for daily companionship." He looked at me. "You know what I mean?"

"I do. Indeed I do." Some gaps not even music could fill.

He closed the album firmly. "I don't know why I ran on like that," he said. "Pay no attention to me."

"I understand," I said. "You're not asking for pity. It's just the way things are."

He met my eyes for a long second, then looked away. "What about you, Delia? Do you have any photos here? Unless you're too tired or maybe tired of listening to me. I've just enjoyed this so much…"

"I only have one album, but I'd be happy to show it to you," I said.

We walked down the hall to my room. I closed the door for privacy, feeling a little odd, even excited, at being alone with a man in a bedroom again. We had barely settled on the edge of my bed, there being no other place to look at the photos together, when someone knocked briskly on the door.

"Come in," I called.

Mrs. Atwood opened the door and peeked in. "Just saying hello," she said, looking at where we sat, elbows touching, with the album on our knees, which were also touching.

"Hello there," I said. Oh the temptation to fall backward on the bed and scandalize her.

"Is everything all right?" she asked.

"Couldn't be better," Henry said.

"Well, uh…" She frowned, then opened her mouth as if about to speak again. And I gave in to temptation.

"Oops," I said, leaning hard against Henry. Over we went on our sides on the bed in a tangle of limbs while Mrs. Atwood stared at us, then whirled and disappeared down the hall.

After she was gone, we lay there a moment, hugged each other and erupted in laughter like two kids who'd outsmarted the hall monitor at school. The laughter faded and there was a long moment while we held each other. Then, as if by mutual consent, we sat up and returned to the photo album, in pleasant accord. It was the best moment since I'd come to Pleasant Oaks.

Knowing that we're always more fascinated with our own family photos than other people are, I quickly worked my way through mine. In the middle of the book, I came to a faded photo of Felthame mill workers lined up on the brick steps. I remembered the year well: 1903. Unexpected tears stung my eyes.

"What's wrong?" Henry asked.

"Old memories. I'm sorry. I'm a little tired. Let's finish up later."

"All right," he said. "I'd like that. And I'm sorry for whatever made you sad."

"Just getting overemotional in my old age." How could I ever explain? Fortunately, with a concerned glance, Henry accepted my statement.

After he left, I thought about my reaction to the photo and I realized that as much as Ruthann might need to see me, I needed to see her, too. I'm going to do it, I thought. I'm going to Felthame. Before I could change my mind, I went to the phone and called Kate. I could hear someone yell down the dorm hall for her. My heart pounded annoyingly while I waited. Maybe this was a mistake.

But when I heard her fresh, young voice, with a certain timbre to it that reminded me of Ruthann, I strengthened my resolve. I was through running from the past.

"I'll go back with you," I said, my voice tense. "Tell your grandmother I'll be there."

"Great. Thanks a bunch," she said. "I know she'll appreciate that."

When I hung up, I felt drained but calm. I could stay with my sister Naomi and her husband, Jediah. It would be good to get away, to test how ready I was to be on my own again. As to the actual meeting with Ruthann, time enough to worry about that when it happened.

Later that day, Mrs. Atwood showed up at my door again.

"I wanted to remind you that it is inappropriate for unmarried men and women to be in each other's bedrooms," she said. "We have a sitting room that you're more than welcome to use."

"Yes, ma'am," I said, my tone the opposite of Southern politeness.

She shook her head. "You really don't like it here, do you?"

"Do you?"

"I do my best, even when some people don't appreciate it," she said. "If you can't fit in, perhaps you should find another home, one more suited to your... personality."

I could just see myself phoning my son to explain I'd been kicked out for having a man in my bedroom and general insubordination. But something in me resisted all these attempts to control me. Perhaps, it smacked too much of Mr. Powell and the way he disapproved of my benefit concert. Or how Ruthann made me afraid as a girl.

Mrs. Atwood tapped her foot, waiting for some response.

"I'm not trying to make your life more difficult," I said. "But we weren't hurting anyone. I don't think we need so many rules around here. We're not children."

"Then don't act like children," she said, and stalked off.

I watched her go and resolved to invite Henry back to my room soon to see the rest of my photos.

Naomi was delighted when I called.

"It's about time you came to see us," she said. "What's it been? Four years?"

"About that."

It would be good, no matter what Ruthann wanted, to see Naomi. And I'd love to see my best friend, Mattie, again. She had spent her life at the mill and chosen never to marry. Yes, there were a lot of positive things about this visit.

"You'll be staying with us, of course," Naomi said.

"Of course."

I'd have to sleep on their convertible couch for a few days, but she'd be insulted if I stayed in a motel. Family didn't do that.

"Ruthann's granddaughter, Kate, is giving me a ride," I said.

"Kate?" Her voice rose with surprise.

"It's a long story. How is Ruthann these days?"

"Fine as far as I know. I don't have anything to do with her and she doesn't have anything to do with me. Live and let live."

"A good philosophy." And one I wasn't following.

I hung up with a warm feeling. Naomi was eighty four now and, while bothered by arthritis and failing eyesight, still mentally sharp. Her marriage to Jediah had lasted. She'd found mill work satisfying and worked her way up to the weaving room before she retired with a small pension. Her six children lived within fifty miles, along with a smattering of grandchildren and great-grandchildren. All in all, a good life.

When Mrs. Atwood heard of my plans, she called me into her office. It was a model of neatness. Papers were carefully stacked, with a small brass clock facing her. Stapler, pencil sharpener and a gold pen in a holder were lined up precisely. All the necessary administrative accouterments. But no family photos or personal touches. I wondered briefly about her home life. Did she have a husband? Children? If so, I imagined they marched to whatever tune she chose. Or maybe she fussed over them endlessly, monitoring their comings and goings.

On the wall behind her was a big photo of a maple tree in autumn. Patches of snow lay on the ground under the tree; red and gold leaves glowed against the white. It was similar to the nature photos that lined the halls at the nursing home.

"That's a lovely picture," I said, while she seated herself behind her gray metal desk. "All the photos here are. It's a nice touch, especially when so many residents can't get out in nature anymore."

"Thank you," she said. "My brother took those. It was his idea to hang them in the halls."

"He's very talented," I said.

"Yes." She paused. "He was. He died not long ago."

"I'm sorry."

She motioned me to a chair opposite her and looked at me over her steepled fingers. "So, I hear you're planning a lengthy trip."

The nursing home was as bad as the mill village for lack of privacy.

"That's right."

"Does that seem wise?"

"Perhaps not. But it's something I have to do," I said, beginning to feel irritated, as usual, when she questioned me.

"I can't be responsible if you get worse because of this," she said. "I've been watching you. You're not as healed as you like to think you are."

"I'm not asking you to be responsible."

"Have you talked to your doctor?" she persisted.

"I appreciate your concern, but I'm eighty years old and I believe I can make my own decisions, wisely or unwisely," I said.

She frowned. "My brother was just like you. He had this chronic cough. I begged him to see a doctor, but no, he put it off until…" She broke off. "Never mind that. I'm just saying don't be foolish."

"No more than usual," I said.

As I left, she muttered, "No fool like an old fool." Maybe she thought my hearing was bad, like so many other residents, or maybe she wanted me to hear her remark. In response, I warmed even more to the idea of the trip.

Still, consulting my long-time doctor was sensible. The problem with seeking advice is that you can be told things you don't want to hear. He shook his head at my plan. "This isn't prudent," he said. "It could make your hip worse."

"But," I countered, "it might not, right?"

He shook his head again. "Ah, Delia, you are a determined woman," he said, discarding I suspected "stubborn" or, as Ma would have said, "mule-headed." "Yes, that's true. Your hip might not get worse."

He'd left me a loophole and I jumped through it with alacrity. This might be my last trip home. Life had taught me nothing is certain. A convalescent home only reinforced that lesson. I had tried not to let my physical limitations rule my life and I didn't plan to start now. He did caution me not to walk long distances. That I could promise.

When Kate and I were ready to leave, Henry came out on the porch and gave me a warm hug, then waved as the car pulled away. I waved back, a little bemused at the fondness I felt for him already. His short, rotund body wasn't the type that usually appealed to me. I leaned more toward tall and dark, with handsome as a bonus. I glanced back to wave one last time and saw that Alice had come out on the porch to stand close beside him.

I faced forward and gave a little laugh. Kate glanced at me. "Something funny?"

"Just life," I said.

The miles rolled by. Here and there, in the distance I spotted ramshackle, abandoned barns covered with vines, a familiar sight from childhood. The sight made me wonder what ever happened to our farm. As we moved closer to North Carolina, the pitch of the roofs of houses changed from the sharper angle of the North to a more gentle angle, better suited to the sunny South where less snow accumulated. The hum of the car motor made me sleepy. I often felt sleepy in the afternoon, a stereotype about old people that annoyed me, but that seemed to be true more and more these days. I drifted off. When I woke up, we were nearing Greensboro. My hip ached when I moved and I gave a yelp of dismay.

"Are you OK?" Kate asked.

"Just stiff. Can we stop and move around a bit?"

"Sure thing."

We pulled in at a roadside park and I walked back and forth, loosening up, while Kate searched the grass on her hands and knees.

"What are you looking for?" I asked.

"Four-leaf clovers. Grandma collects them. She presses them in a book."

"How many has she got so far?" Automatically I looked down to see if I could spot any clover, but things tended to blur a little at that distance, despite my glasses.

"About eighty. One for each year of her life, she says."

"That's a lot of luck," I said. "Maybe some of it will rub off on me."

She continued scanning the grass. From time to time she glanced at me, as if to reassure herself I was all right. I must seem decrepit. If only she knew how young I still felt inside. Henry had reminded me of that.

"Do you have a boyfriend?" I asked, lowering myself to the grass beside her.

"Um, yes. His name is Alec."

"Tell me about him." I searched the grass while we talked.

"We knew each other in high school. He works in a furniture store in Felthame. As soon as he gets enough money saved, he's going to college."

"Is it serious?"

Her face colored slightly. "I don't know. We like each other a lot, but being separated has been harder than I thought." She plucked a clover, examined it and tossed it aside. Not lucky, apparently. "Everything will be fine when we see each other again," she said. "It will all work out."

I smiled without comment. No one can tell the young that things might not work out. Certainly, no one could tell me when I was her age.

Chapter Nine

June 1895, Felthame, North Carolina

I sat on the grass and plucked daisies from the field behind our house. The sky was clear, the sun warm and soothing on my shoulders as I slit the stems, weaving them together. It was a mindless activity, one that let me escape from worries about Mr. Powell firing me from my teaching job and my pressing need for money.

I often went to the river when I needed to think. Something about the music of the flowing water soothed me. Ever since I'd read a poem by Robert Louis Stevenson about how the river flowed "out past the mill, away down the valley, away down the hill" on its way to the sea, I'd thought of the river as a connection to something larger than the village. It led to places I longed to visit, adventures I yearned to have.

A shadow fell on my hands and I looked up into the smiling face of the best-looking man I'd ever seen, what Mattie would call "easy on the eyes." He was tall, seeming even taller from my low vantage point, with dark, wavy hair, deep-set eyes and even features. He looked to be about thirty, but a youthful, well-preserved thirty.

"What are you doing?" he asked.

"Making a daisy chain for my hair," I said, embarrassed to be caught at the mature age of eighteen in such a juvenile activity.

"Don't stop," he said. "Mind if I watch?"

"No." Any other answer would have been rude.

"I'm Arthur Benning," he said, as he sat down beside me. His accent was strange, clipped, and the vowel sounds different from what I was used to.

He reached for a daisy and plucked the stem high up near the flower.

"You need a long stem to make it work," I said.

He plucked another stem close to the ground and handed it to me. "Is this better?"

"Perfect," I said, flustered by the warmth of his fingers.

"And you are...?" he asked

"Delia Hammett."

"Ah. Miss Hammett."

"What does 'Ah. Miss Hammett' mean?"

"Just that I've heard your name. You're the giver of the infamous concert."

I stopped weaving and stared at him, chin lifted, "The same, and proud of it." Maybe he wasn't as handsome as I'd thought.

"No need to fire up," he said. "I approve, although I realize my position is not universally held."

"Oh." I didn't know what to say, so I concentrated on finishing the daisy chain, conscious of his eyes upon me. As I started to get up, he leaped to his feet and offered me his hand, helping me stand. We stood facing for a few long seconds.

"Allow me," he said. He took the daisy chain and placed it on my hair, his face closer to mine than was proper. My heart beat faster at his nearness.

"There," he said. "A crown for a charming, pastoral princess."

If I was a princess — and I'd never been called one before — did that make him Prince Charming and this a modern fairy tale?

I gave a little curtsey. "Thank you, kind sir."

He bowed and we smiled at each other.

"I'm new to your fair hamlet," he said, which was obvious, since everyone knew everyone in Felthame, and a stranger stuck out. Plus no one from the village would ever call it a hamlet. "I'm here to sell some new equipment to the mill," he said. "Would you mind showing me around?"

The request was ridiculous because the village wasn't big enough for people to get lost. After you saw the mill, the company store, a few other businesses, the school, the church, there wasn't much left. But all at once I realized this was his way of saying he wanted to spend time with me.

"Of course," I said. "I'd be happy to. Where are you from, if I may ask?"

"Pennsylvania," he said, which explained his strange way of talking. He was the first Yankee I'd met, an interesting, exotic find. I asked him questions about life in Pennsylvania, forgetting my manners, but he didn't mind, judging by his smiles. It turned out they had dark brown dirt there instead of our red clay. They ate a plant called rhubarb in pies, but he'd never tasted grits or chitterlings until he came South.

"Have you ever seen the ocean?" I asked, thinking of how our river ran to the sea. "It's supposed to be beautiful."

"It is. The ocean is extremely beautiful." The way he caressed the word "ocean" sounded like the way I felt about music.

"Tell me about it," I said. "Sometimes, I try to imagine being there."

The corner of his mouth quirked up. "Let's see. The water is dull green, or sometimes blue and sparkling when the sun hits it. The waves roll in in a series of long lines. They build and build until they hit the shallows. Then they collapse in a long curl of white, racing in parallel to the shore."

He waved his hand in the air, then let it fall like collapsing waves.

"It makes a dull roar," he said. "The foam hisses up on the beach and washes back to sea. By then another wave is thundering in. All the time, seagulls are squawking overhead. And sometimes sandpipers skitter along making tracks in the wet sand."

"It sounds like a kind of music," I said. "A symphony of the sea."

His stride faltered as he stopped and looked at me as if he hadn't really seen me before.

"I never thought of it that way," he said. "But yes, it is. Lord Byron wrote a poem about it." His voice took on a deep timbre. "There is society where none intrudes by the deep sea and music in its roar."

I clapped my hands together before I thought that it might make me look childish. "I love the idea of the music of the deep," I said. I could imagine the sounds eternally repeating, powerful, rhythmic. Automatically, I began thinking about what notes you would use to create that feeling on the piano.

He smiled down at me. "You're delightful," he said.

I smiled back and my cheeks felt hot. "Oh well," I said. "Not really. You know so much more than I do. Thanks for telling me about the ocean."

By the end of the walk, I concluded that he was a gentleman and nice, despite what most folks said about Northerners. I wondered how Mr. Powell, who'd lost his hand to a Yankee soldier in the war, liked working with him. But I couldn't ask Mr. Powell, and it seemed rude to mention it to Arthur. He couldn't help where he was born. I suppose that in business they both did what they had to, like everybody else.

It took perhaps fifteen minutes to show Arthur the wonders of our fair hamlet. I stretched it out by showing him the field of cotton in full blossom outside the village, in case that was new to Yankees. They were fifteen delightful minutes. I'd never met a man who was so witty and could make me laugh so, one who obviously found me attractive. After our stroll, he asked if he could call on me in the future.

"Yes, I suppose," I said. Inside I was saying, oh yes, yes, yes.

"May I have the pleasure of walking you home?"

"No, thank you," I said. "I have some things I need to do."

I didn't really, but suddenly I was afraid that because I was a teacher, he thought I was closer to his social level than I was. His manner, his clothing all spoke of someone well-to-do. When he saw our house and realized our differences, his interest would ebb. But how pleasant it had been today.

The next morning I walked to town and visited Miss Holcombe, the teacher who'd made the concert possible. When she invited me in, I looked around curiously. An oil painting on the wall showed a stern-looking, middle-aged man with red hair and blue eyes. I longed to know who he was. There was a model of a sailing ship on the table beside him in the painting. Maybe he was a captain who was tragically lost at sea, sending her into perpetual mourning. Or maybe not.

"What can I do for you, Delia?" Miss Holcombe asked.

"I was wondering if I could use the school piano to give music lessons this summer," I said.

She tilted her head consideringly and smoothed her black dress.

"Hmm. That's an interesting idea. I'd have to check with the school board, but it might be possible. So few people have pianos yet that I don't know how many students you'd have."

"They could practice their singing," I said. "Everybody likes to sing."

She reached her hand out as if she was going to touch my shoulder, then drew it back.

"I heard about you losing your job," she said. "I'm sorry. I wish we had an opening here, but we don't. If I hear of anything anywhere I'll let you know. Don't give up on teaching. We need good teachers."

"Thank you. I won't." The implied compliment warmed me. I am a good teacher, I thought, reassured. Surely something would turn up for me.

She approached the local school board, and they approved my plan, but only until school started. I had two months to find pupils, earn a little cash and come up with a more permanent plan.

Arthur was coming to visit our house for the first time. What would he think of our home, so much plainer than what he was used to? Ma said life wasn't made up of possessions but of treasures we should be laying up in Heaven. Likely she was right, but a few more treasures on earth wouldn't have been amiss about now to my way of thinking. I imagined Arthur's world as filled with glittering people and possessions. My mental picture was fuzzy, but it involved things I didn't have, like satin dresses that rustled when I walked, dresses someone else would wash for me, flowered china dishes that matched and weren't chipped, an indoor toilet and a bathtub with clawed feet.

Now I looked around the front room, trying to see it the way Arthur might. I'd scrubbed the plank floor with lye soap that left a sharp, clean scent. A braided rag rug Naomi had made covered part of the floor. Our wooden chairs and table were plain but sturdy, mostly made by Pa. He'd better not turn his nose up at those. The Bible lay open on a table as usual. I'd chosen morning for the visit before the house heated up. And I'd baked fresh biscuits in case he wanted a bite to eat.

Ma came to stand beside me, smothering the faint cough that still cropped up from time to time from when she worked in the mill.

"Do you think everything looks all right?" I asked.

"It looks fine, honey. Them flowers is a nice touch." She pointed to some Indian pinks I'd picked from the meadow at daybreak. They sat in a glass jar on the table where they lent a fiery spot of color. "Goodness gracious," she said. "He's just a man like any other. If he don't like us the way we are, it's best you find out right away."

That's exactly what I wanted to find out. And he'd better not look down on Ma, I thought fiercely, or he'd soon be fishing in another pond. At the same time, I wanted to make a good impression. Ma must have felt the same, despite what she said, because she'd put on her best calico dress, the one she wore to church on Sunday.

"Tell me about him again," she said.

"He's a widower. His wife and son died last year of the black diphtheria."

"I'm real sorry to hear that."

"But his parents are alive and he has two married sisters. He and his father are in business together, Benning and Son. They sell textile mill machinery."

"Plenty of opportunity for that around here." She smoothed her hair, sat down in a chair and picked up some knitting.

It was going to be just the three of us. Naomi was home with Jediah, and Jewel had gone to the store to buy groceries. Ezra was off with his buddies fishing for catfish. That made things simpler, since we only had five chairs and if everyone was here, someone would have had to stand. Plus it might have been overwhelming for a first visit.

When the knock came, I waited a few seconds before answering so he wouldn't think I was too eager.

"Good morning," he said, removing his hat with a smile. Ma put down her knitting, stepped forward and he bowed and greeted her.

"Welcome to our home," she said. "Please come in and sit down."

He took a chair, settling into it without comment while I wondered what he was thinking. When Ma went into the kitchen to fetch some tea and biscuits, he looked around. "Lovely flowers," he said. After that, he chatted with Ma about the prospect of rain and how low the river was. They moved on to discussing the best time to plant cabbage while he sipped on his tea and exclaimed that my biscuits were nice and light. I'd dabbed them with honey that Ezra had gathered from a hive in an empty tree. So we talked about that. He told a funny story about running from bees as a boy. It was different from our private conversations, which were more about books and his travels. I couldn't decide if it was good or bad he was talking about things Ma knew about. Was he being condescending or polite?

After he left, Ma turned to me. "He seems nice enough," she said. "And he has good manners. Not snooty. But be careful. Hear me?"

"I hear you, Ma," I said. That was praise enough, coming from her. Yea, I thought, the visit was a success.

After that, Arthur continued to seek my company. We walked sedately in public. In the meadow behind our house, we sat in the grass in full view while he read to me from various books, corrected my grammar, widened my horizons about how people outside Felthame lived. When no one was looking, I let him steal a few exciting kisses. On Sundays he drove me to the Methodist church in town, where I encountered new hymns and an organ, instrument of the gods. Or, I suppose, of God.

It was a strange summer with more leisure than I'd ever had, despite my household chores. Arthur was gone from time to time on business and when he returned, each time I felt as if I loved him more.

While my social life had looked up, my finances were worse than ever. By the end of July, I'd garnered only three piano students. I enjoyed teaching them, but I needed more money. Miss Holcombe gave me the names of a few schools in other towns and I sent applications, listing her as a reference. When the first rejections came back, I wondered if they'd talked to Mr. Powell, who I doubted would give me a recommendation. Undeterred, I wrote to schools farther afield and waited with increasing uneasiness. So far Mr. Powell hadn't evoked the rental clause that said we needed one mill worker per room. I'd never heard of a family being evicted for that reason. I didn't want us to be the first.

One evening after I'd spent part of a Saturday with Arthur, Ma asked me to sit on the porch with her for a private talk. It was dusk and we waved our paper fans vigorously to deter hungry mosquitoes.

"This Mr. Benning," she said, "he seems nice enough, like I said. But where do you see this goin'?"

I'd begun to dream of marriage, but I didn't want to say so. When I'd mentioned the idea to Mattie, she shook her head and said she doubted it. I didn't want to believe her.

"I don't know, Ma," I said, swatting at a mosquito. "Can't I just enjoy it?"

"Honey, I don't want you to get hurt." She sighed. "I wish your Pa were alive. He'd talk to him straight, if need be."

Alarmed, I said, "Please don't say anything to Mr. Benning. It would be too embarrassing."

"Delia, you're young and tiny and pretty and innocent. I can see he'd like that. I reckon you're like some strange woodland flower to him, but men like him marry their own kind. If not marriage, they're after one thing."

"He's not like that," I said.

"He'd be the first man since God created Adam. What do you think he wants then?"

"He likes me. He knows so much, and he's always teaching me things. I think he's wonderful."

"Huh. I imagine you're feeding his male pride, puffing him up like an old rooster. And when the bloom is off the rose, what then? When he goes back home, you're gonna be hurt."

"But Ma, he says he's going to settle here. Well, not in the village, but in town. He's tired of all that cold and snow up North. Since he deals in textile machinery, there's lots of work for him in the South. He says changes are coming to the mills, and he wants to be in on them."

She fanned more vigorously. "So he'll be staying around. I see. Well then, I'm sorry to talk so plain, but don't let him get in your britches."

"Ma," I protested. My cheeks felt hot.

"I'm just saying."

The next time I saw Arthur, her words stayed with me. It was true he seemed to enjoy telling me things, answering my questions, suggesting how I should behave. At times, I almost resented it. Was something wrong with me the way I was? But it made him feel good, and he was only trying to help me improve. Besides, hadn't I told my pupils that if they wanted to learn, they had to be willing to listen?

As to the other comment Ma made, about what men are after, that part was true. The more we hugged and kissed, the more he wanted to go farther. It was hard to remember how to behave when my insides felt quivery and my pulse pounded in my temples, but when I'd start to weaken, I'd remember Ma's words. The more I said no, the more he pressed for yes, and the more difficult it became to hold fast. Finally I told him that I felt like a chicken being eyed by a hungry fox.

"You drive me crazy," he said, his voice husky. "You have ever since that day I saw you sitting in a field of daisies like some kind of bucolic painting."

Then he laughed. "I guess I have been overeager. I'll try to behave myself."

Which lasted maybe two days.

About then, I got a letter inviting me for an interview for a teaching job in a tobacco town up Durham way. Miss Holcombe drove me up in her buggy. The town was a little larger than Felthame, with a two-room public school, more books and fewer students per teacher. Miss Holcombe was there to vouch for me. After the school authorities talked to her in private, they made me an offer on the spot. I accepted calmly. Inside, I felt relief, excitement, regret at leaving Felthame and Arthur.

The next morning I told Arthur about the job. It was a hot August day and we sat in the shade on the river bank far enough above the mill race that we could talk without shouting. Out on the water, a red-tailed hawk swooped down on broad wings, then soared upward.

"You're moving away? I hadn't counted on that," he said, frowning. He plucked a blade of grass and began methodically shredding it.

"I have to make a living," I said. "And teaching is what I know. There's nothing for me here."

"I suppose not," he said, his voice flat. He tossed the blade of grass into the air where the breeze caught it for a second, before it drifted to the ground. I felt a pang of disappointment at his reaction because secretly I'd hoped Ma was wrong, that the thought of losing me would spur him to propose, that men like him did marry outside their social circle.

"I thought you'd be happy for me," I said.

"I am. It's just... unexpected." He stared at me so long I became uncomfortable, then he said, "I'm sorry, but I have to go." He stood and held out his hand to help me up.

"Just like that?"

"I'm sorry. Duty calls," he said.

Duty — or something — certainly did call because days went by with no word from him. Bewildered and hurt, I talked it over with Mattie late one night, drinking lemonade at her house by the dim light of a lantern that I hoped would hide any tears that arose.

"I don't understand what went wrong," I said.

"He's a damn Yankee," Mattie said. "What else can you expect from him? He's a scoundrel, pure and simple, and not worth losing an ounce of sleep over."

"Too late," I said, with a weak grin.

She patted my shoulder. "You'll see. Someone will come along who will treat you the way you deserve. Just be patient."

But I didn't want someone else. I wanted Arthur. After that, I held my head up and pretended it didn't hurt, except when I was alone when I had to admit it hurt like the devil. Gradually, hurt changed to anger. I didn't deserve to be treated this way. If I ever saw Arthur again, I'd give him down the country, for sure. Or maybe I'd ignore him, sweeping grandly by with a cool "Good morning, Mr. Benning."

I knew I was a hot topic of conversation, because everyone talked about everyone, but people made no comment to my face. In fact, I was treated with extra consideration, which was touching and humiliating.

Well, most people made no comment to my face. One afternoon, I passed Ruthann on the street. She had Violet, her baby girl, slung on one hip and a sack of groceries in her free hand. The baby looked at me with the bold, inquisitive stare that babies have and I smiled involuntarily.

I was ready to pass on when Ruthann stopped and spoke to me. "Nice day for a walk." Her tone was dry. She paused and looked me up and down, "But I see you're all alone. Too bad."

"I'm doing fine," I said, wishing some stinging comment would come to me. Unfortunately, I only seemed to think of comments too late to use them. She knew she'd scored a hit. She smiled while I swept on, hurting, but head held high.

Later, I realized that Ruthann had done me a favor. I *was* alone and I needed to accept it and move on, to focus on myself and my future, not mope over Arthur, who probably wasn't wasting one second moping over me. New adventures awaited me. Soon I'd be leaving Felthame and seeing new places and new people. That was something to be excited about, even though I'd miss my family and friends and, for a while at least, Arthur. I had to remind myself frequently because what might have been and what was yet to be wrestled for domination in my heart.

As the time to leave approached, I sought out Vernell. I caught him on his lunch break. Overhead, huge white clouds pregnant with rain, the kind that turned into thunderheads in the afternoon, scudded by, driven by a stiff wind. We walked across the street and sat on the wooden steps of the company store. Mr. Powell came out of the mill and hurried toward his house, consulting his gold pocket watch as he walked. When he saw the two of us, he nodded stiffly.

"Good luck in your new job," he said.

Good manners were called for. "Thank you," I said.

He'd never tried to stop Vernell from taking lessons from me, and I'd been careful not to give the lessons on mill property. Now he wouldn't need to worry about it.

I looked at the three-story mill across from us, the highest building in town, and wondered if this was Vernell's future.

"This is our last lesson before I leave," I told Vernell. "I have a present for you." I handed him a McGuffey's reader I'd bought with the last of my savings.

"Thank you," he said. "I appreciate it." The wind lifted his blond hair like a ragged halo.

"I hope you'll keep studying," I said.

"I will. I surely will." He clutched the McGuffey reader to him. Maybe he would.

We could hear the constant hum of the mill in the momentary silence that fell.

"But the mill isn't so bad," he said. "One of the men is showing me how to fix the machinery. I'm catching on real fast. One of these days I'll be a supervisor."

I thought with a pang of his dream of being a doctor. "I bet you will," I said. "You're smart."

He bit his lip and looked away for a second. Then he shook his head, the way we'd been taught to do when we got a compliment so we wouldn't seem uppity. "Yeah, well. Thanks."

"They're going to let me work in the card room, starting next week," he confided. The card room was where they transformed cotton fibers into a loose rope. "They put me in there because I'm strong," he said proudly. He flexed his arm, then grinned. He was only thirteen, but he was big for his age and husky.

"I'm sure you are," I said, forcing a smile and thinking how much I'd miss him. "I hope things work out for you. Please keep studying."

I watched him walk away, sorry it had to end this way. Now he'd no longer have the breaks that doffers got and he'd be even tireder at the end of a long work day. There wouldn't be much energy left for learning on his own.

I felt as if I'd failed him, but later Ma said sometimes you just had to do what you had to do and that his future was in his hands. She said she'd try to encourage him.

That night, Vernell brought a blackberry pie and a jar of pickles over to the house.

"Ruthann said to give this to you for the book," he said, pink rising in his face.

"Thank you," I said. "That wasn't necessary." I didn't know if it was a peace offering or a way to avoid being beholden to me for helping him. Ruthann was proud that way.

"She said it *was* necessary."

Not a peace offering then. I was sorry about that.

A few days before I was to leave town, Arthur showed up on my doorstep while everyone was at work.

"I thought I'd catch you alone. I need to talk to you," he said.

"I have nothing to say to you," I said, glad I was showing some starch in my backbone.

"Please. I know I've behaved badly. Give me a chance to explain."

I hesitated, looking at his earnest face. "All right. Come in." So much for starch.

We stood awkwardly in the tiny front room.

"I had to have time to think," he said. "And I have. Will you marry me?"

"Will I *what*?"

"Marry me. Do me the honor of becoming my wife?"

I stared at him. A surge of joy raced through me, strong as one of those ocean waves Arthur had described. It was really happening. Arthur wanted to marry me. I swayed on my feet, as if the waves were real. He put his hand on my arm.

"Are you all right?"

His touch brought me back to reality as another wave of emotion broke over me, one of anger at the humiliation and anguish he'd put me through.

"Let me get this straight," I snapped. "You disappear for two weeks with no explanation. Then you come sashaying back in and propose."

His hand dropped and he took a step backward. "I know," he said. "But you have to understand."

"That would take some doing."

"We're from two different worlds. My family expected me to marry elsewhere. They even had someone picked out. She…" His voice faltered. "I… well… You're right. I treated you badly. I apologize. But I have my head on straight now. I want to be with you forever. Please say yes." He dropped to one knee like a character in a book, took my hand and looked up at me imploringly.

I looked down at him. Could I trust him? I couldn't bear to go through this again. But as I looked at his earnest face, I made my decision. Everyone made mistakes. The good Lord knew I'd made some. Here was the man I loved, repentant and eager at my feet.

"Yes," I said. "Yes."

He grabbed me and whirled me around, hitting the table and knocking the Bible akilter, then put me down, leaving me dizzy with more than the motion.

"Let's keep it a secret for now," he said. "I need to inform my family first. They'll love you, but it will be a shock to them. Just give me a little time to prepare them."

"All right," I said doubtfully. "But I don't see what harm it would do to tell Ma."

"It's only for a week or two. Then I swear we'll tell anyone you want." He leaned over and kissed me gently. "Trust me on this."

"All right," I said again, unwilling to let my resurrected dream die.

"You're such a sweetheart," he said. He traced his finger down the curve of my jaw, making me shiver with pleasure. "I'm lucky to have you."

But keeping a secret from Ma wasn't easy. That night, when she heard me singing softly while I peeled potatoes, she said, "You seem mighty happy. Are you glad to be leaving us?"

"Oh no," I said, "It's not that. I mean, I'm looking forward to teaching, but of course I'll miss all of you."

"I hear tell Mr. Benning came to visit today," she said.

"Yes," I said. Heat rose in my cheeks and I bent my head over the pan to conceal it.

"Something's going on," she said. "Out with it."

"It's a secret."

"Is it an honorable secret or one that needs the light of day shed on it?"

"The first one."

"Hmm," she said. "Let me help you with those taters." When we finished peeling them, she asked, "Would you read to me from the Bible tonight?"

"Yes, Ma."

She selected Proverbs 31: 10-31, about how the virtuous woman worked from dawn to dusk doing chores. That passage always tired me out, what with planting vineyards and clothing the whole household in scarlet. I think it made Ma feel good about her own hard work, especially the verse where "she layeth her hand to the spindle." But the part I'm sure was aimed at me was about how a virtuous woman's price is far above rubies.

Arthur and I leaned out into the main street of town, trying to see past the mob of laughing, chattering adults and children. Two days ago, Arthur had spotted the poster advertising a traveling circus and invited me to watch the parade through town with him. In the distance, I could hear the brass band playing "Stars and Stripes Forever." I loved the liveliness of the Sousa marches. Back when I was teaching, I'd save a little money out to buy sheet music, even if it meant doing without something else.

I especially liked this tune. It made a person feel happy just to hear it. The band strode into view, all shiny in gold braid with brass instruments reflecting sunlight. In front of the band, a man in a blue jacket with red piping pulled a bass drum on wheels, beating it in tune to the music. The sound vibrated in my chest and I turned to Arthur with delight.

"Thank you for bringing me," I said. "This is great."

"My pleasure, princess."

Behind the band came horses with tassels on their harnesses pulling red and yellow painted wagons with cages of animals I'd only read about or seen in drawings. A lion with a bedraggled mane and solemn yellow eyes stared morosely through the bars, then dropped his head on its paws. What must it be like to be confined to a tiny space when you were used to roaming the jungle? The circus seemed less glamorous for a moment. But then the band struck up another Sousa tune that set my foot to tapping.

People cheered when a huge gray elephant with a scarlet blanket tromped by with a woman on its back clad in fewer clothes than were proper in public. She waved at the crowd. Arthur winked at her. She winked back. He smiled like he'd gotten a present. I poked him in the side, and he whispered, "Sorry. Just looking."

The elephant was followed by a camel and a dog dressed up with a frilled skirt who pranced on his hind legs periodically. Then came jugglers and acrobats dressed in gaudy colors. They smiled with lips closed, as if a big, tooth-baring smile was too much effort. They looked tired, as if they could use more sleep.

"I wonder what it would be like to travel from town to town like that?" I said. "Would it get boring after a while?"

"Probably. Work usually does. But we do what we're born to do, like it or not. Look there."

He pointed at the final person in the parade, a clown with a monkey with a tin cup. The monkey ran into the crowd, then back to the clown with coins jingling. I didn't think I'd like being a clown.

"If you could do anything in the world, what would it be?" I asked Arthur.

He paused, as if weighing his words. "Live in a house by the ocean, I suppose, with a big porch where I could sit and watch the ocean. It's quiet there, not like the mill. I mean, there's noise, but it's still quiet somehow.

"Every morning I'd walk the beach and see what the waves had cast up in the night. You can find all kind of treasures, especially after a storm. Then I'd go back and read to my heart's content. And be waited on hand and foot by a beautiful woman." He laughed self-consciously. "Sounds silly, doesn't it, for a grown man to talk that way?"

"Not at all. But you can skip the beautiful woman part, unless it's me."

His hand tightened on mine as we headed back for our horse and buggy. "It's just a fantasy," he said. "There's no money in picking up seashells. I sell mill machinery with my father and that's that."

"I'd live in a nice house and wear pretty clothes and raise lots of children," I volunteered.

"Sons," he said. "Lots of sons to carry on the Benning name. The line stops with me right now."

"Sons," I agreed, although how one could deliberately bear a boy was beyond me. "And I'd play the piano and teach music to children. And if they couldn't pay, I'd teach them anyhow."

"But you won't be working," he said. "No wife of mine is going to work."

"I suppose not."

I'd miss teaching something fierce but I had Arthur to tend to. And someday children — girls as well as boys.

"Would you like to see my house?" he asked, handing me into the buggy and taking the reins. He'd bought it soon after he arrived, but I'd never been there.

"I'd love to." The horse clopped down an unpaved residential street lined with young trees. I hadn't been to this area before even though Felthame was just down the road.

"It's a new neighborhood called Bellewood," he said. "It's going to be *the* place to live. All the best folks will be here. The town plans to pave the streets and they're going to put in electricity soon. Word is the streetcar might come out this far before much longer." I could imagine how it would look someday with mammoth oaks shading the houses and electric lights shining from the windows in the evening, casting a glow on the sidewalk.

A woman on the street looked our way curiously as we passed. Arthur tipped his hat and smiled at her. She nodded in return with a big smile.

He called the horses to a halt in front of a two-story gray frame house with a pillared front porch. The yard was almost bare, with new grass poking up here and there.

"Do you like it?" he asked.

"It's very nice," I said. I studied the yard critically. A rose bush would be a nice touch.

He hitched the horse's reins to a tree branch and helped me out. "Let's go inside," he said. He turned a big brass key in the lock, then pushed the door open on a broad hallway. Sunlight streaming through white lace curtains made a complex pattern on the wooden floor. I could easily imagine living here with him.

On the wall in the hallway, a photograph in an ornate gilt frame showed an unsmiling woman with ringlets and a long, horsy face but nice eyes standing beside an equally serious portly man with a dark, bushy mustache. His resemblance to Arthur was clear, although some fifty extra pounds blurred the man's even features. This might be Arthur thirty years from now.

Arthur saw my gaze. "My father and mother."

"I can't wait to meet your family."

"No rush," he said.

"What is your mother like?" I asked.

"Oh, you know, doting on her only son like all mothers."

I thought of Ezra who'd never been doted on a day in his life and was reminded again of the differences in our background.

"What about your father?"

His voice tensed. "Not much to tell. All business all the time."

"Do you and your father not get along?"

"Well enough, I suppose. We're different," he said. "Come on. Let me show you the rest of the house."

We wandered into the dining room, which held a long wooden table atop a flowered rug, six caneback chairs and a sideboard heavily carved with images of fruits and nuts. A separate room for dining. It seemed extravagant. A folding door separated it from the parlor.

"The house and furnishings aren't that fancy, but it's a start," Arthur said.

"I love it already."

The rest of the house was marvelous, especially the little room with the indoor toilet. No sink or clawfoot bathtub that I'd dreamed of, but no more visits to a smelly outhouse, freezing in winter and stifling and wasp- and spider-ridden in summer.

Best of all was the kitchen. Arthur led me to the door and paused. "You'll like this," he said.

"A cast-iron stove," I said, staring at all its black, scroll-worked beauty. "And with a container to heat water." I threw my arms around him. "Oh Arthur. You're wonderful."

He gave a delighted laugh. "So are you." He gave me a quick kiss, then pressed his mouth harder against mine. I pulled away, conscious of him as a man as never before. He loosened his arms reluctantly and I looked at the stove again. No more cooking over an open fireplace. It couldn't be that hard to learn to cook on a stove. Lots of town people did it. Suddenly, everything crashed in on me. My life would be so different as Arthur's wife. I'd move in different circles, be expected to entertain, to call on people, probably dress differently, serve unfamiliar foods. Despite Mrs. Powell's tutelage, there was so much I didn't know about how women in Arthur's world behaved. Momentary panic welled up in me and my hands shook.

"What's wrong?" he asked, stepping closer.

"Nothing. It's a lot to take in." I was terrified, but I'd just have to learn quickly. I was smart, wasn't I? I could do it. I had to.

"And now," he said, "let me quickly show you the bedchamber."

"A closet," I exclaimed as I stood in the doorway peeking in. There'd be someplace to hang my clothes beside nails on the walls.

He laughed. "There's one in every bedroom."

My gaze wandered to the massive four-poster bed with its white coverlet, then away. On the dresser, I spotted some seashells and moved toward them. I'd never seen real seashells. Nervously, I picked up a hinged shell with white fluted sides. The shell was thin and felt fragile. "It looks like angel wings," I said. He came and stood behind me. I could feel his breath warm on my neck.

"That's what I call it," he said. "I found it on the beach one morning at high tide. It's a wonder the hinge didn't break."

Delighted, I picked up a small, flat white shell with a delicate swirling pattern. "What's this one?"

He nuzzled the nape of my neck, sending a shiver through me. "I don't know the scientific names. Someday, when I get a chance, I'll study them. It looks like a baby's ear to me."

"So it does." I put it down and reached for another. His hand closed over mine before I could pick it up. He turned me around and carried my hand to his lips.

"Delia," he said, "forget the shells for now."

He pulled me closer and kissed me. My lips parted involuntarily and my hands went around his neck. He steered me toward the bed and half dazed, I let him. Suddenly, I stopped short.

"We're engaged," he said, keeping a firm grip on my hand. "Why wait?"

He stroked my arm as if I were a nervous horse that had to be gentled, then his hand moved upward toward my bosom. A thrill ran through me. At the last second, I jerked away, remembering Ma's warning. Even more strongly, an image of Ruthann flashed through my mind. Ruthann, who'd gotten with child out of wedlock and been the subject of gossip. I'd had enough of gossip. And I wasn't going to be like Ruthann.

"We've waited this long," I said. "I plan to wait until after the preacher pronounces us husband and wife."

He let his hand drop and frowned.

"Is this a ploy to get me in bed?" I demanded. "We haven't told anyone in town yet that we're getting married. And I bet your family doesn't know either."

"Not yet, but I'll tell them soon. I've been busy." He reached for my hand again, but I pulled back.

"Let me know when you do," I said. "And when it's no secret in the village, too. Then we can talk about bedchambers."

"I see that you don't trust me," he said, his voice tight. "If you feel that way, perhaps I'd better take you home."

"Perhaps you'd better," I said in a voice cold as iron in January.

We rode without speaking back to my house. Ma was in the backyard washing clothes but I couldn't face her right now. I hurried to the river before she could question me and flung myself on the ground, sobbing. Disappointed anger filled me. How dare he proposition me like that, engagement or not? I might be a mill girl, but I deserved to be treated with respect. Yes, I'd been tempted, but that only made me mad at myself. I hated to tell Ma. She wouldn't say she told me so, but, always practical, she'd say there were other fish in the sea. I didn't want other fish. I still wanted Arthur. I stared sightlessly at the water until a semblance of peace returned.

Arthur found me there. He stood over me, face flushed. "You win," he blurted before I could say anything. "Tell your family."

"I wasn't trying to win," I said.

He ran his hand down his face. "I know. I'm sorry I behaved badly. I just got a little… ahead of myself in the way men can do. You don't know what it's like to be a man alone in a bedroom with a lovely woman. "

I shook my head. "Obviously not." Lingering caution held me back. "I don't want to go through this again. Are you absolutely sure this is what you want?"

"I'm sure." His voice was firm. He sat beside me on the grass, keeping his distance.

I'd heard the phrase "being of two minds." Part of me thought this was too rushed. Another part looked at him, handsome, apologetic, desperate to have me share his life. I thought of the fascinating conversations we'd had, so unlike any I'd had with village boys, and of the way he'd opened up a wider world, and I pushed the doubting part down. I knew I could be a good wife. And he wouldn't have come back if he didn't want to wed. It must be hard for him to go against his family's expectations.

"Do you love me?" I asked, my voice trembling more than I liked.

He started to put his arm around me, then stopped. "I'm crazy about you," he said. "And I'll prove it. Let's get married right away."

"Right away? Won't your folks want to be here for the wedding?"

"It's a long, tiring trip. And I want you to be married here surrounded by your friends and family. We'll invite my family when we're settled and present them with a fait accompli. I promise you. How does that sound?"

"What's a fait accompli?"

"When something's done that can't be undone."

"Oh." I'd been nervous about meeting Arthur's family and about all the things I had to learn about his kind of life. As a bride, not a fiancée, my status would be settled, my welcome more assured. I'd be a fait accompli. That was what I wanted, wasn't it?

"That sounds acceptable," I said. "As long as it's not a secret. I want to tell my family today and I want you to mail a letter before the sun sets telling your family we're getting married."

"That's fine. Tell your mother. Tell the whole world."

He did mean it. Happiness filled me again. The past week, I felt like I was on one of those merry-go-rounds I'd heard about. Up and down, round and round. Maybe finally I'd be able to get off.

Arthur left with a promise to come back and talk with Ma after I'd talked to her. "It will be better coming from you first," he said. That suited me fine. I'd get her honest reaction, like it or not.

When I returned to the house, she was still in the back yard scrubbing clothes in the washtub. She held up one of Ezra's shirts and pointed to a black spot on the collar. "I declare, I don't know how your brother gets his clothes so dirty."

"Ma," I said. "Can you stop for a minute? I have something to tell you."

She dropped Ezra's shirt in the tub, wiped her hands on her apron and turned to face me.

"Arthur and I are getting married. Isn't it wonderful?" I said, hugging her.

"Really?" Her arms were at her sides and her expression uncertain.

"Really. Truly. Aren't you glad for me?"

At that, she put arms around me, then pulled back. "If that don't beat all," she said.

I let her go and did a little dance. "Yes. It beats all. And we're getting married right away."

Her face clouded over. "Right away. Delia…," she began. I knew what she was thinking.

"It's all right, Ma," I said. I laughed. "My price is still above rubies."

"Then I'm happy for you, darling. I'm happy. We got some planning to do." She paused. "But first I gotta finish scrubbing these clothes."

I ran off to tell Mattie, who decided Arthur wasn't a scoundrel after all.

The next few days seemed to race by. There were a few people I especially wanted at my wedding. Mrs. Robinette was one. She was in a family way again and doing poorly, so she declined, but wished me well. Mrs. Powell was the surprise. I went to her house to tell her. We sat in the parlor where she served me tea and beaten biscuits just like I was a fine lady.

"Arthur Benning and I are getting married," I said. She reared back in her chair so fast she spilled her tea.

"You're marrying that Yankee?" she said.

I stared at the dark stain spreading across the rug.

"Yes," I said. "I don't understand. You know I've been seeing Mr. Benning."

"But I didn't think it would come to marriage. Oh my dear, you haven't seen Yankees in action like I have. Yankees burned my father's house, after promising they'd spare it if we gave them our silver and money.

They destroyed our cotton, stole our livestock and left us with nothing but destruction and debt." She shook her head vigorously, as agitated as if it had happened yesterday. "In my experience, and that of a lot of folks around here, they're rude and loud and you can't trust them. And now you're planning on marrying one, and a man who treated you badly from what I hear."

I ignored that remark because it was true, but now everything was fine and it was best to forgive and forget.

"Then why does Mr. Powell do business with a Yankee?" I asked.

"One does what one must for the good of the mill," she said. "We have to live. And Mr. Powell says Mr. Benning is a good businessman."

I sat the teacup on the side table and she dabbed at the spot on her dress. "Well, it's your life. But you're dear to me and I hate to see you marry a Yankee."

"I'm sure some Yankees are like that, but Arthur's different," I protested. "I wanted to invite you to the wedding because of all you've done for me."

"I appreciate that. But no, thank you," she said.

I stood up stiffly, feeling as if she was attacking me as well as Arthur. I'd heard other older people talk like Mrs. Powell. The war of Northern aggression was long over and we'd lost. It had been terrible, but it was time to move forward.

"I'll be going then," I said.

She walked with me to the door. "I'm sorry I got so upset just now. Good luck, my dear. You'll likely need it."

You're wrong, I thought. Fleetingly, I wondered if other people felt the way she did. So what if they did. Ma said it was what was in your heart that counted, not what other people thought. And love for Arthur was in my heart.

It was my wedding night, and I was excited and scared. It was one thing to know about farm animals, and another to be undressing in your new home with your husband lying on the bed waiting for you. I knew generally what would happen, but I also didn't really *know*. Ma had been embarrassed to talk about it. All she said was, "It might hurt some, honey, but it will soon be over. It gets considerably better. Don't worry." Which made me worry more.

To cover my nervousness, I began to talk to Arthur as I took off my stockings. "The wedding went well, didn't it? It was so nice of Mattie to make a rose wreath for my hair. The flowers smelled so pretty, too."

I carefully laid my dress on a chair and looked at it a moment. Mrs. Powell, perhaps by way of apology for her comments about Arthur, had given me a bolt of cream-colored organdy to make a wedding dress. Most folks got married in their Sunday best or even their everyday clothes. I'd thrown my arms around her in gratitude and she'd patted me awkwardly on the back. Then, Miss Holcombe donated some white lace for trim. With Ma's help, I'd sewed up the prettiest dress ever. Ma said I looked beautiful in it, and I felt beautiful too.

I smoothed a fold in the dress, with my back to Arthur, who lay on the bed watching my every move. I was intensely aware of him and the fact I was standing there in my flimsy cotton shift. "This was the fanciest wedding I can remember in the village, what with being in church, instead of at home," I said, "and both of us all dressed up. You were so handsome in your black frock coat. When we stood in front of Rev. Robinette, while everybody sang 'Christian Hearts, In Love United,' I was so happy, I thought I'd burst."

Arthur chuckled. "I'm glad." His deep male voice brought home to me how different my life had become. It was the first time I'd been alone in a bedroom at night with a man. Nothing could be more different from sharing a bed with my two sisters.

I picked up my white linen nightgown that I'd embroidered with pink roses and prepared to remove my shift and slip on the gown. Faint moonlight shone through the window, illuminating my body. I felt shy and exposed. I'd looked at my breasts the day before while the family was at work, trying to imagine how they would look to Arthur. Would he find me beautiful? What if he didn't?

"Forget the nightgown. Come here," Arthur said in a husky voice that sent a shiver through me.

I walked slowly toward the bed, resisting the temptation to cover myself with my hands. I had nothing to be ashamed of. I was a wife now, and all this was as it should be. A strange tingling filled me. He pulled me down beside him in the bed. As he took me in his arms, he felt me trembling.

"Don't be afraid," he said.

"I'm not exactly afraid. Just, well, nervous. Excited. I don't know."

He kissed me gently. "We'll take our time," he said, following that statement with a considerably more eager kiss.

We did take our time. More and more wonderful feelings rose in me as he caressed my body. Despite the quick pain Ma had talked about, I found sensations I didn't know existed, sensations that left me unsettled and craving more when we finished. Maybe, like Ma said, that came later.

When our lovemaking was finished, and we lay on our backs, with Arthur's arm flung across my stomach, he spoke suddenly. "If we're lucky, you got with child tonight," he said.

I'd thought about having his children, but still I was startled. "I want children, of course," I said. "But I was hoping we'd have a little time to ourselves before babies started arriving." Not that I knew how to keep from getting pregnant, despite the rumors of old grannies with secret herb knowledge.

"I understand that. But I'm hoping for a son, and as soon as possible."

"It could be a daughter," I said.

"A nice, healthy son to carry on the family name and business. Arthur Benning III. My father will be so pleased. Nothing could endear you to him more."

I felt a flash of dismay. I'd yet to meet his family, but I hoped they'd value me as more than a vessel for their grandson. "I can't control what God sends," I said. "Wouldn't a daughter be nice, too?"

"Yes. A daughter would be lovely. But later."

I said nothing more. Arguing would be like what Ma called plowing the river, nothing to show for your efforts. Secretly, I still hoped for a little time to adjust to this new life, so different from what I'd known, before I became a mother.

I lay in bed exhausted. Only ten months after our marriage and already I had twin sons. I'd never known such pain, but at least I had something to show for it. My hair lay limp in sweaty strands on the pillow and the smell of fresh blood filled the room. The midwife finished cleaning me up while Ma put a baby on each side of me.

"Are they all right?" I asked.

"Perfect," she said. "Ten fingers, ten toes. Perfect." I knew their lungs were perfect from the way they wailed when the midwife spanked them.

"Shall I call your husband in now?" the midwife asked.

I nodded. "He'll be over the moon," I croaked. My throat was sore from screaming, but that would fade.

Arthur had been standing outside the door. Now, he rushed into the bedroom, fell to his knees and kissed my hand. Then, he pulled a pearl necklace from his pocket, lifted my exhausted head and fastened it around my neck. "I knew it would be a boy," he said. "But twins! This is twice as good."

He'd had a boy's name picked out for months: Arthur Benning III, to be known as Trey, but no girl's name. I'd selected one, just in case: Matilda, the name of my mother's mother.

"Let's call the other twin Samuel after my father," I said. He looked at me tenderly, still on his knees.

"Of course," he said. "Samuel it is."

Even while I lay there, one dark-haired son nestled on each side of me, part of me wondered, how he would have reacted if I'd borne a daughter.

As Arthur predicted, his parents were over the moon. The coolness they'd shown since our marriage melted into appreciation, first of the mother of their precious grandsons, then for me as a person.

Life settled into a pattern of trying to balance the needs of Arthur and the boys while fulfilling my duties as a housewife. My dreams of long walk and talks with Arthur were just that, naive dreams. He proved an attentive father, if stricter than my pa had been. My occasional worry over what Ruthann's threat meant faded in the face of my busy life. In fact, I didn't see her again, except at a distance, for more than three years.

Then, on New Year's Day of 1899, Ma sent me word about Vernell.

I shivered in the chill air at the graveside and thrust my hands deeper into my coat pockets. The clods of dirt striking Vernell's pine coffin felt like blows. The earthquake of grief and guilt I'd felt when I heard of his death in an accident in the card room had subsided, but aftershocks still shook me without warning. I hoped seeing him laid to rest would help me begin letting go of all that had happened.

"He is safe with the Lord," the pastor intoned. "His earthly toils are over and even now he is sitting at the feet of Jesus."

"Praise be," a few people murmured. From my place at the edge of the mourners in the church cemetery, I felt no comfort. I shivered again, and Arthur put his arm around my waist. Almost everyone in Felthame was there, dressed in black on a gray, cloudy day that seemed appropriate for laying to rest a sixteen-year-old boy.

Ruthann stood close to the open grave, holding the hand of her daughter, Violet, with her husband, Bobby Lee, beside her. Her expression was grim. She and Bobby Lee had pierced me with venomous looks when I arrived, then ignored me.

As the service ended and people began to disperse, Ruthann turned Violet over to Bobby Lee and charged toward me. People parted to let her past and watched curiously as she drew near where Arthur and I stood. Her quick steps and stony face told me this would be unpleasant. Ma and my sisters started to move my way to support me. I shook my head to stop them. Arthur took one look at Ruthann's expression and tugged on my arm. "Let's go," he said. He knew Ruthann and I didn't get along, although not the extent of it.

"No. I have to face this," I said. "It's my problem. You go on ahead. I'll join you in a minute."

He looked at Ruthann barreling toward us and let go of my arm. "If you're sure." He stood a few seconds more until I motioned again for him to leave.

He walked a ways off, out of earshot, and stood looking toward us, a frown on his face.

Ruthann stopped in front of me, hands on her hips. "Did anyone tell you how Vernell died?" she demanded.

"He slipped and caught his leg in a machine," I said, taking a step backward as she thrust her face toward mine.

"But did they tell you how he lay on the card-room floor moaning and screaming with the blood spurting out of his leg, right there in the midst of all the tobacco spit, and them trying to stop the bleeding, but they couldn't. And the floor turning all slick and red and his voice getting fainter and fainter until he..." Her voice broke.

I shook my head, trying to block out the vivid image. I wanted to remember Vernell laughing while he chased Peter at the hog killing. Or waving his hand eagerly in class, making little bouncing motions in his seat in his excitement to be called on. That was the Vernell I wanted to remember, not a boy I'd failed dying in agony on the card room floor.

"Oh, Ruthann," I said, reaching out toward her.

She retreated a step. "Don't touch me," she said, snapping each word out like the crack of a whip. "It's your fault. If not for you, he'd have been in school instead of working in the mill. You killed him as sure as if you'd taken a gun and shot him."

The accusation struck straight at the uncertainty I'd felt since the night of the benefit concert. Any protest I might have made died on my lips. "I'm so sorry," I said. "I truly am."

She leaned toward me. "You will be," she said, her voice low and dead calm. She spun on her heel and walked away, leaving me shaken.

On the way home in the buggy, I kept returning to the image she'd painted of Vernell bleeding on the floor. Guilt overwhelmed me, irrational or not. I tried to talk to Arthur about it. "Maybe it is my fault."

"Don't be foolish," he said, clucking the horse to a faster pace as if to escape the conversation. "You did what you thought was right. Put it out of your mind."

The next day, he bought me a piano.

I lost myself in playing it, taking care of the children, spending my limited free time with Arthur. Whenever I saw a stocky, tow-headed boy on the street, I thought of Vernell.

A month after Vernell's funeral, on a sunny, unexpectedly mild afternoon in early February, I took the twins over to Ma's house to see her, and to get a break from mothering. Bad weather had kept us indoors for several days. I yearned to be outside and away from the restless, energy-filled twins.

"Would you watch Samuel and Trey for me while I get a little air?" I asked Ma.

"Of course," she said. "Take your time. We'll be fine."

I strolled across a field to the edge of the river and stared at the water rushing by. The noise drowned out the footsteps behind me so I jumped when Ruthann spoke. I spun around to face her.

"I saw you come this way," she said. "I want to talk to you."

Wariness sprang up in me, but her expression was neutral, the best I could hope for.

Southern politeness won the day. "How are you doing?" I asked.

She shrugged. "Busy. You know how it is with a youngun to take care of."

"Or two of them, in my case."

"Yes. A double handful for you." Her voice was still even.

"Do you ever think about Vernell?" she asked, her tone changing.

"Almost every day," I said.

"So do I. So do I."

Her expression darkened. She gestured to the gray, sullen river. "That water sure looks cold, don't it?"

"It does indeed."

She moved closer to the bank, almost teetering on the edge. She lurched as if she was about to lose her balance. "Delia," she called. "Help!"

I reached out a hand to grab her. Instantly, she leaned back toward safety and jerked my hand forward. My hat flew off and, propelled by the force of her grip, I tumbled into the river.

I gasped, stunned by the coldness of the water, and inhaled dirty river water. My sodden long skirt clung to my legs, dragging me down. Coughing and choking, I swam downstream, angling toward the steep bank, searching for a place where I could climb out.

"Help," I shouted, my voice almost lost in the roar of the river. I lost sight of Ruthann as the current tugged greedily at me. The cold was a living thing, stealing life from me. Frantically I struggled with numb hands to undo my skirt and petticoat to free my legs. With a final tug, I wrenched them loose. Now I could kick more easily but whatever warmth the garments had offered was gone. It became harder and harder to move my arms, kick my legs. I was going to die.

No, I thought, I refuse to give up. The twins need me. With a final desperate rush of energy, I fought my way toward a boulder at the edge of the river. When I reached it, the force of the water thrust me against a cleft in the huge rock. I felt my leg catch. Pain surged through me as the river tried to pull me downstream while my leg remained stubbornly caught. I screamed in agony and struggled to keep my head above the rushing water.

"Ruthann," I yelled, staring upstream. "Help!"

She stood frozen upstream, a distant figure with her hand to her mouth. Now she raced along the edge toward me. "Hang on. I'm coming," she yelled. My hip was a mass of pain, but the sensation was blanketed by the chill creeping through me. I retched and coughed up river water. Suddenly, Ruthann was there, knee deep in the shallows, reaching out. She grabbed my numb hands and tried to pull me across the boulder. I screamed again.

"Stop," I moaned. "My leg is trapped."

She crawled up on the boulder and jerked on my leg. The bone made a horrid grating noise, and I screamed. For a moment, I thought I might vomit with the strength of the pain.

"You're still stuck," she said. "I'm sorry to hurt you, but I have to try again. You can't stay in the water. You'll freeze to death."

"Wait a second," I whispered, bracing myself against fresh pain. "All right. Go ahead."

She moved to a different angle and jerked again. Even as I let out another scream, my leg pulled free. Ruthann grabbed my shoulders and dragged me up on the rough rock, above the level of the water, where I lay shivering in my wet shirtwaist and underdrawers. Nausea overcame me and this time I did vomit, turning my head to one side.

"Don't move. I'll get help," she said, her face ashen. She flung off her coat with its sodden hem and laid it over me, then ran full tilt toward the village.

I drifted in and out of consciousness, jolted to wakefulness by the agony of my leg and the shivers wracking my body, then pushed back into blackness. What was taking so long? Had Ruthann abandoned me? The cold and pain could finish what the river started. Panicked, I struggled to stay awake. Maybe I should try to crawl to the village. I looked down to see my foot turned outward at an unnatural angle. Could I even crawl? We do what we must, I thought. And I am *not* going to let Ruthann win. I moved my leg experimentally and yelped as pain flared through me. I gritted my teeth and braced myself, ready to try again rather than die here on the rock like a dead branch flung up by the river.

Just then I heard Ruthann call out, "Hurry," followed by other voices and the sound of running feet. She had brought help after all. Relief flooded me. Arthur hurried forward and bent over me, his face full of concern.

"Oh my God. Are you all right?" he demanded.

"She…" I lifted a hand to point at Ruthann and tell what she had done, but it fell weakly to my side. Arthur's face blurred before my eyes. "She…"

"Don't talk," he ordered. "Explanations can wait."

But Ruthann rushed to explain. "She got too close to the edge and fell in," she said in a voice tight and high with tension. "I reached out and grabbed her hand. I tried to hold on." Her traitor voice cracked. "But her hand slipped away. I should have tried harder."

My eyes snapped open and I stared at her. She dropped her gaze. Tears ran down her cheeks. "I should have tried harder," she repeated. A mill worker with lint in his hair patted her shoulder. "You done all you could," he said. Behind him, a man in overalls muttered, "She's a real, live heroine." People in the growing crowd gathered near the rock began to whisper her name.

"No," I croaked. I wanted to tell them what happened, but unconsciousness overtook me. Even as I slipped away and felt Arthur directing the other men to be gentle, I struggled to say something. Only a scream came out as they lifted my legs.

After that, things were broken up in my memory like slivers of glass. Voices, Pain. Lying in my bed at home shivering. Concerned faces of my family.

I was jerked back to consciousness by a bearded doctor standing over me, examining me. I looked down to see a swollen, lacerated leg I could hardly recognize as belonging to me. All sense of embarrassment at having my leg exposed fled at the sight.

"We're going to put you under," the doctor said "and try to fix this leg.'

"Fix this leg?" Did he mean amputation? If I could have sat up, I would have. "What are you going to do?" I demanded.

"Your thigh bone is fractured. We've got to pull the broken bones into position and put splints on your leg. You'll have to wear them for at least two months. If you're awake while we do it, the pain of setting the bones will be too much to bear, so I'll give you some anesthetic."

I looked at Ma, who had her fist pressed to her lips. Arthur stood beside her, his face white.

"Mr. Benning," the doctor said, "once she's under, I'll need your help. You pull when I tell you. The muscle is strong and will resist, but we must put the ends of the bone in place, and even then it may not heal properly."

He looked at Ma's small frame doubtfully. "Your daughter will be excitable even while unconscious. We'll need someone to hold her shoulders to keep her still."

Ma nodded. "My son, Ezra, is in the other room with his sisters. I'll call him in."

Arthur reached down and took my hand. "Is there no other way?"

The doctor shook his head.

As soon as Ezra was in position, the doctor turned to me. "Are you ready?"

I nodded, suppressing a groan of pain. He placed a cloth over my face, poured something on it and told me to breath deeply. I looked up into his serious brown eyes. A sweet smell filled my nostrils, then nothing.

When I returned to muzzy consciousness, the doctor was wrapping two cotton-padded boards around my leg, one on each side. Arthur and Ezra looked pale and shaken. Ma was gripping my hand tightly.

"She should rest now. No visitors or excitement," the doctor said when he finished, snapping his black bag shut decisively. "I'll be back to check on her later."

I lay there alone, replaying events and trying to ignore the agony in my thigh. One thing was strong in my memory: That moment when Ruthann deliberately jerked me forward, her face grim. She knew and I knew what she'd done.

My overwhelmed body slipped into an exhausted sleep. When I woke up, Ma was standing over me. I looked down at my immobilized leg. My first thought was that I might not walk again.

"How bad is it?" I asked.

"The doc says time will tell," she said. "We'll know more later. How do you feel, sugar?"

"Words can't describe it." Nothing could describe the whole series of events.

"The doctor left some laudanum," she said. "I'll fetch it. He said you could eat something light when you woke up."

"Where are the twins?" I asked.

"Arthur hired a colored woman to look after them so I can tend to you. Don't you fret. They're fine."

They would have to manage without me. I felt weak as winter sunlight.

"Where is Arthur?" I asked. "I need to tell him something."

"At the mill," Ma said. "He said he had some business to tend to. He'll be back shortly."

"He's gone?" A hollow feeling filled me. Anger flickered in me, adding to my anger at my injury and the way I'd gotten it.

"What about Ruthann?" I demanded, my voice still rough from screaming.

"Ruthann? At home, I guess. I can't thank her enough. You were wrong about her, honey. I owe her everything for saving you."

"She didn't save me," I burst out. "She pushed me in. Deliberately."

Ma's mouth fell open. "Pushed you in? Pushed you in," she repeated, then gathered herself. "What… what happened?"

"After I left the twins with you, I went to the river and was standing there thinking. Ruthann came over. We talked and she teetered on the edge.

I reached to help her keep her balance. And then — Ma, I swear on Pa's memory, which you know I wouldn't do if it wasn't God's own truth — she jerked my hand and deliberately pulled me in."

"Oh no," Ma said, sinking down in a chair by the bed. She sat without speaking for a moment, then she shook her head and her face turned red. "Hellfire," she ground out, the first curse I'd ever heard from her, a sound so shocking I stared in disbelief. The word reeked of a deep fury.

"Hellfire is what she deserves," Ma said. "I've a mind to go over there right now and have it out with her. Or go straight to the police and let them handle it."

She stopped, trying to master herself, but her face was red and her voice no calmer when she spoke again. "You could have died. Instead, she's telling everyone how it was a dreadful accident and she's glad she was there to save you. Sweet Jesus, what a hypocrite. Lord knows, there's lots I'd like to do to her for what she done. Don't nobody lay a hand on a child of mine and get away with it."

Ma stared upward as if seeking divine guidance. "I guess the Lord does know what I'd like to do. The Bible says we're supposed to forgive those who despitefully use us, and I try to be a God-fearing woman. But it's easier said than done when it's your own flesh and blood that's been hurt. Oh my. This is tough." She rocked back and forth, wrapping her arms around herself.

For a few minutes she didn't speak while I lay motionless afraid to move for fear of making the pain in my hip worse. Then she stood up and kissed me. "You don't need me running on like this. Act in haste, repent at leisure, they say. I gotta be smart about this. Take this laudanum and we'll talk more later."

I sank back into dazed sleep. When I awoke, Ma was there by my bedside, dozing in the caneback chair, her head nodding forward. I made a croaking sound, and her head snapped up.

"Feeling any better?" she asked.

"A little. Oh Ma, what are we going to do?"

"Eat, then we'll talk. I made you some chicken soup with black-eyed peas to keep your strength up. And there's cornbread with honey if you want it."

"Just soup for now." I couldn't face more than that with my raw throat.

In a few minutes, she came bustling in with steaming soup in our best brown earthenware bowl. She sat beside me, holding the bowl, and pulled her chair closer.

"The doctor said we shouldn't prop you up. Let me help you with this."

Feeling like a baby, I let her feed me half the soup, then waved my hand to show I was full.

She took the bowl, then sat back down beside me. "Honey, why do you think she did what she done?"

"She blames me for Vernell's death," I said.

Ma nodded. "That's what I figured. But that don't make it right. And don't you go blaming yourself."

Too late, I thought.

"I've been pondering how to handle this," she went on. "I'd truly like to tell everyone about Ruthann, but the more I ponder, the more I wonder how it would all turn out. I believe you. But there's no witnesses to dispute her side of things. And yet, it's powerful hard to think she might get away with hurting you. It's a tough row to hoe, no doubt about it." She gave my hand a little squeeze. "I gotta pray about this."

"I have to study on what to do myself," I said. "But I'm not as good as Christian as you are, Ma. I'll tell you that right now."

Just then, Arthur came into the room. He knelt by my side and kissed me gently. It felt good to have him here at last. Now I'd get the support I yearned for.

"How are you doing, sweetheart?" he asked, his voice low and tender.

"Fair." The laudanum was wearing off; pain was lurking, waiting to seize me again. Beyond the pain, one thing was foremost in my mind. "I need to tell you about Ruthann," I said.

"I know. Ruthann told me what she did."

My eyes opened wide. "She told you?"

"About how she saved you. Everyone's talking about it. Mr. Powell gave her tomorrow off, and there's talk of a little party to honor her."

"A party?" My voice rose to a shout. "A party?"

"What's wrong?" he asked.

When I told him what happened, there was a silence. Then he sat back on his heels and stared at me. "Good Lord, Delia. That's terrible. Incredible." He paused, and cleared this throat. "I hate to say this, dear, but it's a huge thing to accuse her of something like that if there's any doubt."

"I know what I remember," I said grimly.

"All right. All right. Don't upset yourself." The uncertainty in his voice stung me.

Ruthann's performance while I lay on the rock must have been convincing.

"Of course I'm upset," I said. "You look like you don't believe me. No wonder. Ruthann's had hours to spread her lies."

"It's not that I don't believe you. But the idea that she would try to kill you, that's hard to swallow. You were pretty out of it when we found you. Maybe you're not remembering it right...." He let the sentence drift off. I stared at him, tears springing to my eyes. He wasn't going to support me. My own husband.

Suddenly I felt differently about Arthur. The armor was tarnished, and it made me feel empty.

"Think what you want. I need to rest," I said. "Go on back to the mill and do whatever you have to do."

"Don't be angry. You're what's most important now. I can stay here if you need me."

"Ma can take care of me." He might say I was important, but he hadn't been acting that way.

He bent down to give me a gentle hug and laid a kiss on my cheek.

"Oh, Arthur," I said, tears spilling from my eyes.

"I love you," he said. "Everything will be fine. Just get some rest."

After he left, I stared into space thinking about our marriage. I'd assumed that it would offer the same support that my family had offered growing up. Times might be tough, but Arthur and I would face them together. But Arthur, who shied from unpleasantness, wasn't proving to be the strong, supporting arm I'd pictured. Maybe he never would be. I might have to be the strong one, and I felt anything but strong right now. Or maybe my expectations had been naïve all along, a young girl's dream of a shining knight. Worries flooded my mind. What if this were permanent? I feared that Arthur wouldn't react well if I was crippled for life. And what of the twins? Would I be able to run and play with them? I pushed my concerns away, mindful of Ma's admonition not to borrow trouble.

My thoughts circled back to a more immediate problem. What was I going to do about Ruthann? Whether she had come to the river with the idea in mind or it had been an impulse, she could have killed me. She did pull me out and run for help. So somewhere inside, she might regret her impulsive action. But last-minute repentance didn't change things. True, I couldn't prove anything, but I could make people suspicious of her. Down deep, a spark of guilt struggled to ignite, guilt that I'd indirectly taken her beloved brother from her, and she had a right to be angry at me. I shifted position slightly; the pain that shot through me doused the guilt as effectively as water on a fire.

I woke up the next morning determined to expose her. I was lying in bed planning what I'd say when there came a knock on the door. Our preacher, the Reverend Robinette, had come to visit. Perhaps, I thought, I should talk to him about what had happened. The Lord had called him to the ministry when he was seventeen but hadn't seen fit to give him a fulsome voice or the urge to short prayers or sermons. But he was kind-hearted and not given to gossip. It might be good to talk to someone outside the family, someone who wouldn't be so full of hurt and anger over what had happened to someone they loved. My own anger raged in me like a wild animal, yearning to be set loose.

Ma led him into the bedroom. The Reverend was stocky, with wispy red hair, freckles, and blue eyes with pale lashes. When he preached, his florid complexion turned even redder. He hurried toward me and clasped one of my hands. "I'm so sorry to hear about what happened," he said.

"Thank you." I looked at Ma. "Could the preacher and I talk in private?"

She nodded and left the room.

"Thank God you were spared," he said as he settled into the chair by the bedside.

"Thank God," I echoed. "I need to talk to you about all this. But first I need you to promise that you won't tell anyone."

"Of course not. You have my word." He leaned forward attentively.

"My accident wasn't an accident," I said. "Ruthann deliberately pushed me in the river. Then, she had a change of heart, ran downstream and helped me to shore."

He sat back in his chair. His freckles stood out against the sudden paleness of his skin. "Ruthann? Pushed you, my heavens. That's... that's hard to believe."

"Believe it. I wouldn't lie about something this serious."

"But why would she do that?"

"Her brother, Vernell," I said. "She blames me for his death a few years ago. Anyway, I'm too upset to think straight. I want to tell everyone, make her suffer the way she's made me suffer." I waved my hand, unable to voice all that I felt.

"Let's pray on this," he said. He closed his eyes. I was in no mood for a long-winded prayer so before he could open his mouth, I cut in with a prayer of my own. "God, help me to sort this out and do the right thing. In Jesus's name. Amen."

"Amen," he said feebly. He cleared his throat. "I can understand your anger. Anyone would be angry." At least he wasn't doubting me. "But Jesus said we should forgive those who trespass against us."

"I know that. But I need to talk, all right?"

Thankfully, he only nodded.

"On the one hand, if I speak out, there are no witnesses. It's my word against hers. And some people know we're not friendly. So they might not believe me." Like my own husband. "People will likely take sides. It could divide the village into factions, cause bad blood."

He nodded again. "It very well could."

"If they believe me, Ruthann could be tried and sent to prison. Then her husband and daughter would suffer for something that wasn't their fault."

Frustration filled me. Everything seemed to be stacking up against speaking out. But, devil take it, it wasn't fair.

"Somebody shouldn't be able to hurt someone and get away with it. It isn't right. We have laws against attempted murder," I said.

I gestured down my body where my bandaged leg lay out from under the cover because it hurt too much to have anything extra weighing it down. The pain, blurred now with medicine, was a wolf lurking just outside the campfire waiting to dart in and seize me.

"Look at me," I said. "I don't know if I'll ever walk again."

"I understand. Things that aren't right happen all the time. It wasn't right for our Lord to be crucified. But on the cross he forgave his persecutors."

"I'm not Jesus," I blurted out.

He shook his head as if he agreed, then he sighed. "I know it's not easy," he said. "With this so fresh, you're likely in no mood to hear this. But maybe later it will help. Just remember that Jesus counseled us to forgive seventy times seven, and to love our neighbor."

"But I don't," I said.

His voice took on a touch of sternness. "That's our sinful nature speaking. Pray to overcome it." He laid his hand over mine. I wanted to push it off. His tone softened. "Some neighbors are easier to love than others. It can take time. Be patient with yourself."

I doubted I'd get anything more from talking to the Reverend, although it had helped to lay out the consequences. "Thank you for coming," I said. "I appreciate it."

"I'll keep you in my prayers," he said. "God will guide you."

After he left, I thought about Vernell. He wouldn't want his friends and neighbors to be at odds with each other. He wouldn't approve of what Ruthann had done either. And I thought about how my decision on his schooling had led to this moment. It wasn't that I deserved what had happened, just that the more I thought about it, the more I reluctantly suspected Ma was right, that nothing good would come of speaking out. If I did speak out, Ma and my family would have to live daily with the consequences, which wasn't fair to them.

It took a few days, but finally I made the hardest decision of my life: To leave things be. I suspect it wasn't so much God guiding me, as the preacher suggested, as the fact I had no way to prove what had happened. If I had to endure neighbors calling her a heroine, so be it. It would have to be enough that my family knew — and, of course, Ruthann. But I certainly wasn't ready to forgive her.

As for Arthur, he was sympathetic, but he said nothing more about Ruthann, willing to let my accusation fade away like morning mist on the river. I'd started to notice that he often took the easy way. Marrying me when his family had other plans for him must have taken a lot of courage on his part. I clung to that thought. He did love me as much as I loved him. We would surmount this bump in the road and go forward.

A few weeks later, the doctor gave me the bad news. My leg was so badly damaged, he doubted I'd ever walk normally again. I'd be able to manage, but running, if it proved possible, would be an awkward affair at best. Dancing was out of the question. No, I wanted to scream. No. I don't deserve this. It can't be happening. But it was. And all my wishing wouldn't change it.

Chapter Ten

April 1957, en route to Felthame, North Carolina

I sat in the grass by the roadside with Kate and rubbed my bad hip, remembering that long-ago day, the day that left me with a permanent limp, and pain that flared up whenever I overdid.

"Are you OK?" Kate asked. "You had such a sad expression."

I stared at her a second, reorienting myself to the present. She looked so much like the grandmother she loved that it evoked old emotions in me, emotions that weren't fair to her.

"I'm all right," I said. "Just remembering."

Kate stood up, hands empty, then reached down to help me up from the grass. "No four-leaf clovers?" I asked.

"No. Maybe next time. We'd better get on the road."

The miles ticked away while I thought about Vernell and about death. Gloomy thoughts perhaps, but the nursing home, where two residents had died since I'd arrived, made reminders of mortality impossible to escape. I didn't dwell on it as a rule. Death was a visitor who might show up unannounced any day, but I didn't plan to sit around waiting.

Kate knew about death too. Her mother, Amanda, had died of brown lung, in 1949. I cast a sidelong glance at Kate, who'd been left motherless at ten. Much too young. But then Amanda was only forty two when she died, too young, also. The mill took its toll.

My thoughts began to weigh on me. Time to think of pleasant things. I turned in my seat to face Kate. "How are you finding it to be so far from home? Sometimes it can be daunting at first. I was certainly homesick when I moved North."

She spread one hand, palm up. "Pretty much it's great, but it took getting used to. My schooling was behind the level of the classes here, but I'm studying hard and catching up. Some of the people talk faster and I can't always understand them. But then again, they think I talk funny so I guess it evens out. It's strange, though. I miss the simplest things."

"I know," I said. "When I went North, my sister Naomi packed me a basket filled with pound cake, hominy grits and persimmon jelly. She said there was no telling what kind of food Yankees ate. I was glad to have it. It was a literal taste of home."

"I spent a weekend last month with a girl from Pennsylvania," she said, "and they had rhubarb and some other stuff I never heard of. But she had never sucked the nectar out of a honeysuckle flower."

"Poor thing," I said.

She smiled and looked directly at me for a second, reminding me again of her grandmother, yet the resemblance didn't jolt me this time.

"I was in upstate New York," I said. "For me, the biggest surprise was seeing only white faces on the street. That was a first."

"That's hard to imagine," she said.

"When was the last time you went home?" I asked.

"At Christmas."

"How was that for you?"

"Good. But it's harder than I thought to keep up friendships. We're interested in different things now, have different experiences. I don't want that to happen with Alec and me."

She stared straight ahead. "Grandma warned me when I left not to get above my raising. It's not that. It's more like I'm on a boat that's drifting away."

"I know," I said. "But you'll always be connected to them. And if being poor teaches you anything, it's that poverty has nothing to do with what kind of person you are."

"What about your father?" I asked. "How does he feel about you going so far from home?"

"He doesn't much hold with college for a woman, but he allowed as how he wouldn't hold me back. Anyway, Grandma's dead set on me graduating and nobody goes against her when she decides something."

"I can imagine. She's..." I searched for the right word. In deference to Kate's love for Ruthann, I settled on one less potent than I might have used. "She's strong minded."

Kate's laughter had a bit of an edge. "Yes, she is. I like hearing you talk. Your accent reminds me of home. You know what the weather is like at home and how the dirt is red and about kudzu and you knew my mother when she was a girl. It's... a connection."

"I feel the same way," I said. In that moment, my heart yearned toward her, Ruthann's granddaughter.

Felthame, when we finally arrived, seemed much the same as on my last visit. The town and I had both grown older, a little more rundown in places, but recognizable.

The three-story brick mill with its huge, arched windows still dominated the village. The town had crept out to meet the village, so the sense of isolation was gone. The mill houses looked subtly different. The mill had finally sold them to the workers and now the homes were no longer identical peas in the same pod. Tan, pale green or blue siding replaced the white wood. People had added on modern kitchens and bathrooms.

It was late afternoon and on a playground girls were jumping rope and playing hopscotch while boys played baseball or shot marbles. The school was new, the children's clothing different, but the games, the sounds could have come straight out of my days as a teacher here.

A few years ago, the town had paved the streets and put in sidewalks. Here and there a TV antenna sprouted from a roof. Felthame was catching up to the modern world.

"There used to be chicken coops out back of these houses, and cows, too," I told Kate. "Many's the cold morning I got up before work to draw water from the well, feed our hens, collect eggs for breakfast. Everyone did it."

"Grandma, too, I suppose. She doesn't talk much about those days."

"Her aunt didn't have a cow, just chickens. We all drew our water outside, and carried it indoors because we had no indoor plumbing, just pumps and outhouses."

Kate made a face.

"When everyone is in the same situation, it doesn't seem strange," I said. "You don't know you're poor. It's just the way life is." Although Ruthann had been poorer than most.

"I like the way things are now better," she said.

"So do I." I shifted uncomfortably in the seat, my hip reminding me I'd been still too long and would walk more stiff-legged than usual when I first got out of the car.

"Can you take me directly to my sister's house? I'd like to rest before I meet your grandmother," I said.

"Sure thing."

"Going to see your boyfriend?" I asked.

She blushed. "First Grandma, then Alec. Can I tell her when you'll stop by?"

"Tomorrow afternoon, around two o'clock. If that doesn't suit her, we can find another time."

"I'll tell her," she said. "She'll be glad to see you."

I wasn't so sure, even though she'd invited me. "Turn left here for my sister's house," I said.

Naomi had bought one of the newer mill houses and as Kate drove down aptly named Cotton Street, I saw Naomi and Jediah sitting in rockers on their front porch. When we pulled up, Naomi stood up with a big smile. Jediah waved from his chair, while she shuffled down the walk to greet me, a cane in her hand. We hugged awkwardly, with our canes getting in the way, then she laughed.

"What a pair we make," she said, shaking her head. "At least we're still alive and kicking — sort of. Come on in and rest your bones."

She looked me over critically. She'd put on twenty or so pounds, but I still weighed the same as when I graduated from high school, although things had shifted south over the years.

"Gracious. We've got to fatten you up," she said. "I've got some pinto beans, turnip greens and ham on the stove and cornbread fresh from the oven. And I made a peach cobbler. Canned peaches. But I think you'll like it."

"Sounds terrific," I said. And it did. Southern home-cooked food again.

"Kate, you're welcome to eat with us," she said.

"Thank you kindly, but I'm sure Grandma has something waiting for me."

I thanked her and she drove away.

"I have a surprise for you," Naomi said as we entered the house. A smiling Mattie, plumper than ever, stepped out from behind the door and we hugged amid mutual squeals of delight. For a few moments, I felt like a girl again. It was a perfect start to my long-delayed homecoming.

At the same time, it was a shock to see her sagging chin — well, her sagging everything. There is nothing like reuniting with old friends to drive home the fact you've gotten old, too. But the sweet smile was unchanged, even if time had thinned the lips and added lines to her mouth.

After Naomi fed us in her usual extravagant manner, Mattie drove me to her place so we could catch up. Her neat house was tiny, more like a cottage, and full of statues of angels. Big ones, little ones, porcelain, wood, glass — covering end tables, perched on the mantle, peering at you as you walked down the short hallway.

Mattie waved her hand helplessly at the packed curio cabinet in the living room. "It started with just a few," she said. "I didn't plan on collecting angels. But people would see them, and they'd give me more. It makes an easy gift if you don't know what else to buy." She laughed. "At least, I can say I have angels watching over me. I'm surrounded by them."

"That's quite appropriate," I said.

She smiled prettily, reminding me of the girl she used to be. "Oh well. You would think so."

"What are you up to these days?" I asked as we sat down. She took the rocker with a crocheted green and white afghan on the back.

"Church work, a little gardening, visiting with my nieces and nephews and grandnieces and grandnephews. It's funny. I never wanted children, and now kids are in and out of the house all the time, and I love it. Especially the part where I can send them home when I get tired. It's a good life."

"I'm so glad." I brought up the question most on my mind. "What do you hear from Ruthann?"

"Ruthann? Why, not a lot recently, come to think of it. She keeps to herself these days. I need to get by and see her. Why do you ask?"

"She wrote and asked me to come see her. I think she wants to make peace."

"Make peace? Do you still resent the way she teased you as a girl?" I remembered with a jolt that she didn't know the role Ruthann had played in maiming me. Telling her now would only upset her to no good end.

"That was long ago," she said. "It's best to let bygones be bygones."

Best, but not easy.

I'd arranged to meet Ruthann the next afternoon, but her house was only two blocks from ours and I spotted her on the sidewalk earlier that day. I stepped back into the shadow of Naomi's house, not ready to face her yet. Her tall, slender figure looked thin to the point of emaciation. She crept along, head down, with her right hand pressed to her abdomen. Every few steps she paused as if she was at the end of her strength. The wind lifted her gray wispy hair, revealing a flash of pink scalp. Looking at her, I was reminded of one of the last times we'd talked seriously. It had been a time when life and death were all mixed up together.

Summer 1906, Felthame, North Carolina

It was a Saturday morning almost ten years into our marriage. Our sons had turned nine. Samuel, the active twin, squirmed in his chair at the breakfast table, eager to be outside in the glorious summer day, but knowing he dare not leave until his father dismissed him. Trey, the quiet one, looked longingly out the kitchen window as well. Arthur read his paper, oblivious to the yearnings of his offspring, while I turned from the stove to put a fresh plate of biscuits on the table. A bored Samuel chose that moment to torment his brother. Whether it was a poke in the ribs, a kick under the table or some other mischief, I don't know.

"Ow," Trey yelped and glared at his brother.

Samuel returned a guileless stare. "What?"

Arthur peered over the top of The Daily Observer. "Samuel," he said.

Samuel had the good sense not to claim that Trey started it. "I'm sorry, sir," he said. Trey looked down at his plate with a faint smile.

Arthur nodded and returned to his paper while the boys sat fidgeting. Arthur would keep them there an extra ten minutes as a lesson. He was strict with the boys, but he loved them. I wasn't so sure if he loved me anymore. More and more, it seemed he basked in the public attention of various admiring young women who reminded me of myself at eighteen, while our conversations seemed to be mostly about the boys and the household. I told myself it wasn't his fault women found him attractive. After all, I'd found him attractive enough to marry. But I didn't like it. I also didn't like the way he seemed even more impatient with my limp lately. Not that he said anything, but I sensed it in the way he sighed when he had to slow down on our walks. I'd tried to talk to him about it, but he turned silent or left the house for a walk "to clear his head" if I persisted. Well, things were what they were, and I told myself to enjoy what we had, not what we didn't have. Still, his attitude hurt.

After breakfast, Arthur announced, "I have an appointment with my lawyer about problems with the contract for some mill machinery. Don't wait lunch for me."

"Can we play catch later?" Samuel asked.

"Probably. It depends on how long I'm gone."

Samuel looked disappointed.

"I'll see what I can do," Arthur said.

Samuel smiled. "Maybe we can practice batting, too?"

"Sure thing," Arthur said.

"Don't be too long," I said. "It's shaping up to be a beautiful day. Maybe we could have a picnic this afternoon, after you play baseball. Would you like that, boys?"

"With chocolate cake?" Samuel asked.

"Or white cake," Trey chimed in.

"We'll see," I said. "One or the other."

"Or both?" Samuel said.

Arthur laughed. "Don't pester your mother. She has enough to do keeping up with you scamps."

He turned and kissed me on the cheek. "I can't say for sure when I'll be back."

I sent him off with a hug and a smile, but as I watched him hurry down the walk, I wondered if this was to be our future: Him preoccupied with business and me busy with housework. Our main connection, the children. Maybe passion always faded with time.

I passed the portrait of his parents in the hall and stopped to look at his father. Meeting his father had been the key to understanding Arthur better. I hated how that stern, practical old man had shaped Arthur's life to one of obedient duty to the family business. Or to be fair, how Arthur had let him shape his life. Would our marriage have been happier if Arthur hadn't struggled to fulfill his father's expectations, if he had followed his own dreams? Did he even know what they were? He loved poetry, books, the ocean, exploring nature, all the things his father despised as unmanly. Maybe if his father had been different, Arthur wouldn't crave the attention of women so. But then, what ifs were useless. I'd tried to understand him, but sometimes I doubted you could ever understand another person. Sometimes I felt like Arthur and I were like people looking down a well. We peered into the depths and glimpsed water, thinking we saw bottom, but it was only a distorted reflection of ourselves.

I thought about taking the boys and visiting Mattie for the morning. She might help me sort out whether I was imagining things with his latest admirer, Nora Lemond, an unmarried member of our church who made her living as a seamstress. Where I was black-haired, petite and blue-eyed, she was my opposite, with womanly curves, flowing blonde hair and green eyes. She was perhaps twenty, while I would soon be thirty. There had been incidents between her and Arthur recently that troubled me: Glances held a little too long, a dropped handkerchief he gallantly picked up with a bow, a smothered laugh, a blush.

No, I decided, I wouldn't talk things over with Mattie. She was still happily single and I wasn't sure she'd understand married life. Truthfully, I was embarrassed at how things seemed to be turning out. Even Ruthann, who'd given birth to another daughter, Amanda, seemed more content than I was.

I turned to washing the dishes and tidying up the kitchen while I sent the boys out back to play. A watermelon would be a nice addition to our picnic, I thought. I'd heard the farm wagons rumbling by bringing fresh produce to market. Yes, another ripe watermelon, a favorite of Arthur's — would be refreshing on a hot summer day. I finished sweeping and dusting, then called to the twins, who were playing on the two rope swings — one for each of them — tied to the limbs of the huge oak in the yard.

"I have to go to the store for some watermelon for our picnic," I said. "You can come with me."

They jumped off the swings in a hurry. A visit to the store meant penny candy. Jelly beans were the current favorite. We headed off, with one boy skipping along on each side of me. On our way, we passed the office of our lawyer, Franklin Snyder. I glanced over, noting that the door was closed and no lights were on.

I was puzzled. When we got to the store, I mentioned it to the clerk, a skinny, gregarious man who collected tidbits of gossip the way a farmer's wife collects eggs. "Oh, Mr. Snyder left town Friday. I heard tell he won't be back until Sunday," he said. "Did you need him?"

I smiled, hiding my apprehension. "No. I just wondered."

How could Arthur have an appointment with the lawyer this morning? Had he lied? Oblivious to the turmoil inside me, Trey and Samuel stood in front of the glass jars with the jelly beans and began discussing whether green or red beans tasted better.

Once we returned home, laden with watermelon and different-colored beans for each boy, I sent them back outside to play and paced back and forth in the parlor. I thought about my growing suspicions over the past few months, about Arthur's disinterest in me. Was he with Nora, or was I a jealous wife who was adding things up wrong? I had no proof of anything. I'd say nothing for now.

Arthur came home two hours after lunch, giving me plenty of time to make and remake my decision. He put his hat on the hat tree by the door and sauntered down the hall, whistling. At the sound, my pent-up emotions spilled out of me like water rushing down the millrace.

"Where have you been?" I demanded.

"I told you before I left this morning. At my lawyer's office. It took longer than I thought." He frowned at my tone.

"You're lying," I said. "Mr. Snyder is out of town and I know it." My voice rose with every sentence. "If you weren't at the lawyer's, where were you?"

Arthur's face whitened, then he drew himself up. "I had business to attend to. I don't have to answer to you for my whereabouts. I'm the master of this house."

"You may be the master of the house, but I have a right to ask questions. I bet you were with adoring little Nora. I've seen the way she looks at you."

"Nora? You're imagining things. Get a hold of yourself, woman."

He paused, then shook his head as if clearing it. "I... Delia, I need to think," he said. "I'll be back shortly, when we've both cooled down. We can talk then."

"What? You're leaving?" I stepped forward as if to physically restrain him. Here he was running away again.

"Calm yourself," he said, brushing past me. "I said I have to think."

With that, he turned and hurried out the front door. I stared after him, my body shaking. In a few minutes, I heard his horse's hooves clattering on the street as he rode away. I picked up a book off a side table and, in an uncharacteristic act, threw it at the door. It didn't help. All it did was dent the cover. I bent to pick it up, then turned to find Samuel staring at me with wide eyes.

"It's all right," I said. "Your father and I are a little upset, but it has nothing to do with you. Come on. You can help me pick some tomatoes for dinner."

Hours later, when dinnertime arrived with no word, I began to worry. Arthur's anger was usually not flame, but frost: Cool while it lasted, but quick to melt. For the first time I wondered if there had been financial reverses that he didn't want to tell me about. He'd said there were problems with a contract for mill machinery, unless he lied about that. Maybe he couldn't face me with the truth. His work was his life, and he was proud of his ability to provide for us. If money was the problem, we'd get through it together. I'd been poor. I could be again. If it was something else… I shook my head impatiently. It was worrisome enough that he hadn't come back, without my imagining things.

The boys had been as boisterous as ever soon after Arthur left, but by bedtime, they were uncharacteristically silent. There had been no picnic that day, no playing catch with their dad.

I fed them both cookies at bedtime, something I didn't usually do. As they munched away, spilling crumbs on the floor, Trey studied my face. I'd tried to be upbeat, but my worry must have leaked out in my expression. "Is Father mad at us?" he asked.

"Of course not." I reached over and ruffled his hair.

"When is he coming home?"

"He had… business to attend to. He'll be home soon," I said. I thought of other times he'd come home later than expected, times I'd worried for nothing. But not this late. "Finish your cookie and I'll read you a story."

"I want a story, too," Samuel said.

"I'll read you both a story at the same time. All right?"

After some discussion, we decided on another chapter from "The Wonderful Wizard of Oz." One boy sat on each side of me, following along. I think they were as glad to snuggle up as I was to feel their sturdy bodies.

The further adventures of Dorothy and company soothed the boys, but not me. I left them still awake but with hopes they'd sleep soon, and went to the living room, not sure what to do now. Maybe I could get Mrs. Purcell, our neighbor, to stay with the twins on some pretext so I could stroll by

Nora's house to see if Arthur's horse was there. I paced back and forth, went to the front door, where I stood with my hand on the knob for long seconds before I turned on my heel and retreated to the kitchen. Skulking by her house would be humiliating. Surely I had more pride than that.

That was at seven o'clock. At eight with darkness coming on, my pride seemed less important. What if something had happened to him? He'd been upset, distracted when he left. If he was at Nora's house, at least I'd know he was safe. I tucked the boys in and hurried over to Mrs. Purcell's. She had just pulled an apple pie out of the oven and the cinnamon smell filled the house.

"Have a piece," she urged, untying her apron and reaching for a knife.

"It looks wonderful, but I have to get back. The boys are alone. I need to run an errand and I wondered if you could watch the boys for fifteen minutes," I said. "Arthur is out on business so I can't ask him."

"Do you think the boys would like a nice piece of pie?" she asked.

"I'm sure they would, but I just got them settled for the night."

"Too bad. It's best when it's still hot. And there's more than enough for my husband and me." She gestured hopefully toward the pie.

"Maybe they're still awake," I said, forcing a smile. "If they are, a little sliver wouldn't hurt."

She looked at me more closely. "Is everything all right?"

"Everything's fine. Come over when you're ready. And thank you."

She showed up in a few minutes with three slices of pie that could never be described as "little slivers."

When I left, the boys were sitting in their nightshirts gobbling pie and telling her about Munchkins.

"Take your time," Mrs. Purcell said, between bites of pie. "We're all fine here."

Nora's house, two streets over from ours, was dark and the door to the shed where she kept her horses was closed. I contemplated sneaking through the back yard and opening the shed door to see if Arthur's horse was inside. Or would he tie it farther away? Something in me rebelled at the idea of checking the shed. A marriage should be built on trust and I wasn't acting trusting. Or was trust sometimes another way to say foolish? Regardless, it felt demeaning to check further. With stomach-clenching visions of the two of them together inside her house, I returned home.

I sent Mrs. Purcell home, sat in the living room and tried to read "The Wheel of Life," a novel Arthur had bought me a few weeks ago. But I was in no mood for a book that included a woman vainly trying to interest a straying husband. Unfaithfulness was an old story, but it seemed painfully new when I feared it was happening to me.

Restless, I got up, and went to my piano. The boys, stuffed with pie, were finally asleep, so I ran my fingers noiselessly over the keys so as not to wake them, hearing the notes in my head.

Just as the grandfather clock in the hall chimed nine times, someone knocked loudly on the front door. I jerked in my chair, tenser than I'd realized. Arthur wouldn't knock. We didn't lock our door at night. No one did. For a moment, I tried to believe that Mrs. Purcell had left her shawl or one of the flowered plates. But I knew she hadn't. I stood, but my legs had turned to glass. If I moved, they might shatter. Stop it, I thought. Whatever awaits, it won't go away if you ignore it. Resolutely, I walked carefully to the door and flung it open.

A grim young man stood on the porch, his hat in his hand. He looked like he wished he were home in bed, anywhere but pinned in the yellow light spilling out from the hall. A bolt of fresh fear shot through me at his expression.

"Yes?" I said. "Can I help you?"

"Mrs. Benning, I'm sorry to tell you this, but there's been an accident," he said, his voice low. He met my gaze for a split second, then stared down at his suddenly fascinating hat, turning it over and over. I followed his gaze a moment, staring stupidly at a spot of dirt on the brim. Then reality pierced me, and I raised my eyes to his face.

"It's my husband," I said. "How serious is it?"

"He's…well, ma'am, I don't know exactly how to say this. I'm afraid he's dead."

The blood seemed to leave my head; dark spots filled my vision. I grasped the doorknob and with an effort stayed on my feet.

"What? What happened?" I whispered. I didn't invite the messenger in, as if keeping him outside would keep his news at bay.

He shifted from foot to foot, then dared another glance at me. "It looks like his horse threw him. They found your husband in the meadow behind your mother's house."

"Oh," I said. "It's where we met. Our favorite spot." Had Arthur gone there to think about us, remind himself of the happiness of our early days, or perhaps to decide how to tell me bad news? It hardly mattered now.

"Someone saw his bay mare running free in the village and a few of us started searching," the man went on. "Then Ruthann Winton said as how when you all visited your mother, sometimes you and him liked to visit the meadow so she said we might should search there. We looked, and there he was on the ground. His head… Well, never mind about that. Anyway, we put him in a wagon and carried him to town, but it was too late. I'm powerful sorry."

"Where is he?" I said. "I want to see him."

He looked at me with concern. "He's at Doc Chapman's office. I just come from there."

Then the doctor likely would still be there.

"Let me fetch my neighbor, and I'll be right there," I said, seized with the idea I had to see Arthur now. Maybe he was unconscious, and the young man was mistaken. The desire to do something, to put off the moment when I had to absorb the news drove me forward.

The messenger waited while I rushed next door. When Mrs. Purcell answered my frantic knock, she was ready for bed. She'd donned her night wrapper and her long gray hair was undone and straggled to her waist. But she came at once.

As the messenger and I set forth, the night sky was clear and moonless and the stars blazed forth. A lovely night under other circumstances. Most houses were dark, their occupants asleep, their lives unchanged. How could that be? Once, I stumbled on the rough cobblestones in the dim light. My guide grabbed my arm and I held on to him like a lifeline.

At the doctor's office, I hurried past him to where Arthur lay on his back on a wooden examining table. Blood matted his hair and bruises disfigured his face. I'd heard someone say that her dead loved one looked like she was asleep. Arthur didn't look that way. Something essential was missing. I couldn't deny the truth any longer. Still, I took his hand, wanting to touch him. Dr. Chapman watched uncertainly while I leaned over and kissed Arthur's slack, unresponsive lips. I put my hand up to his bruised cheek, as if I could heal what was wrong with a touch. I stood there silent, stroking his cheek over and over, dimly aware that a door had closed prematurely, a door that could never be opened on this earth. There'd be no second chances at understanding each other, at mending our marriage, at anything.

I knew I should turn away, that I couldn't stand there forever touching him, but I felt frozen. Finally, the doctor came over and took my arm, startling me to awareness. "Mrs. Benning," he said gently, "come and sit down. You're swaying on your feet."

"I am?" At his words, a wave of dizziness overtook me.

"Can I get you something?" he asked.

"No. Nothing." I swallowed hard, put a hand on the table to steady myself, and schooled my voice to calmness. "If someone will bring Arthur home in the morning, my mother and I will lay him out," I said. "Please tell them not to come until after nine o'clock. I need time to tell our sons."

My voice was even now because I looked out from a little cave in my mind where nothing could touch me. This might not even be happening. Perhaps I was dreaming. Dreams could seem like reality.

"All right," the doctor said. His forehead was wrinkled with concern and his eyes were kind. "Do you need a sleeping powder? Is there anything I can do for you at all?"

"No," I said from my cave. "But thank you."

Most of the night I lay awake. Twice, I turned toward Arthur's side of the bed and stretched out my hand to nothingness. The darkness seemed to close in. Needing to see the room to give me a sense of reality, I lit the lamp. It was hot and the window was open to let in a breeze. But nothing stirred. Moths beat their wings against the screen, trying to get in. Otherwise the room was silent, too silent. No familiar sounds of Arthur's even breathing, no rustle of the sheets or creaking of the bed as he turned over in his sleep.

The emotions I had pushed down surged against the dam I'd built, demanding to be let out. I closed the windows for privacy, despite the heat. Burying my face in my pillow so the boys wouldn't hear me, I sobbed until nothing was left.

Spent, exhausted, I wiped my face, got up, fixed some tea and sat in the rocking chair trying to gain control. When Pa died, I cried and cried. At first, I cried in front of Ma until I saw how hard that was for her. After that, I slipped away to a clearing in the woods, my secret place, where I tied two sticks together to form a cross and knelt and prayed and cried alone. But at the end of all my crying, Pa was still dead and we still had to go on.

I had no secret place now, but I did have two sons who needed me. Ma had held together when Pa died, mostly for our sake I now realized. I had to do the same. Fighting the onslaught of fresh tears, I rocked and rocked as I tried to figure out how to tell the boys about Arthur. But really, there was no way to lessen the impact. With that decision, I returned to my empty bed and fell into a restless sleep in which a giant bay horse threw Arthur again and again and again while I watched helplessly, unable to move, unable to scream.

Chapter Eleven

Our usual Sunday morning ritual called for Arthur to drink his coffee and read the newspaper undisturbed in his study while the boys ate breakfast in the kitchen. Later, we went to church together as a family. The morning after Arthur died, there was no thought of church. Instead, I stood in my bedroom irresolute, trying to decide what to wear, as if it were the most important decision I had to make. It was better than thinking about the rest of the day. I couldn't bear to wear black, not yet. It was too final a statement. Finally, unable to focus, I picked out a blue organdy dress with sprigs of daisies on it, dressed mechanically, then woke the boys and got them dressed. The week before I'd bought them identical navy blue playsuits with white, striped collars. Arthur liked the way they looked in them. "My little sailormen," he called them. Now I pulled the suits out and handed one to each boy. "Let's wear these today," I said. They raced to get dressed and were set to clatter downstairs for breakfast until I stopped them.

I patted the edge of Trey's bed. "Come sit here," I said. "One on each side of me." When they were settled, they turned wide eyes toward me, curious about this break in the routine. I put an arm around each boy.

"I have some sad news," I said. The quiet safety of my mental cave deserted me at that moment and I had to stop. I swallowed hard and discovered you really could get a lump in your throat that kept you from speaking.

I tried again, in a voice borrowed from somewhere else since it didn't sound like my own. "Last night, your father's horse threw him. He was hurt. By the time they found him, it was too late. He was dead." I'd thought about using softer words, words like "gone to be with the angels," "resting in the arms of Jesus," "with his heavenly Father," phrases people used to comfort themselves and obscure the reality that their loved one was never coming back. But those phrases would only confuse the boys at their age. They knew what "dead" meant. You couldn't live around animals and not know. Simplest was best. At least I hoped so.

They stared at me, unable to take it in. "Dead?" Samuel said. "He can't be. He's going to play catch with me."

"I'm sorry. I'm afraid he really is dead," I said.

He burst into tears. Trey, the stoic one, struggled unsuccessfully not to cry. I hugged them, and they hugged me back so tightly I felt my breath constrict in my chest. Tears trickled down my cheeks despite my earlier resolve to be calm. We sat there unmoving until I realized I should still see that they got a good breakfast. All the decisions would be mine now. It was a lonely feeling.

At the sight of Arthur's empty chair, Samuel began to cry again. Trey swallowed hard, but said nothing, while I busied myself in serving the boys grits and ham in silence. I toyed with my food, trying to order my thoughts for the tasks that lay ahead. Finally, I scraped it into the garbage uneaten. Naomi would say now was when folks most needed to eat to keep up their strength. Perhaps she was right, but I wasn't hungry.

That night, after Arthur lay in the parlor, washed and decked out in his best black suit, I put the boys to sleep and fled to the quietness of the bedroom. My gaze shifted to our dresser. The seashells Arthur had shown me when we were courting were still there. He had never gotten back to the ocean in the time we were married. There was always more work to be done for Benning and Son. I picked up his angel-wing shell, walked into the parlor and slipped it into his coat pocket. "I can't go with you on your new journey," I whispered. "But here's a piece of the ocean to take with you."

In the next two days, I put on a black mourning dress, contacted Arthur's shocked family, accepted condolences, talked with the boys as they struggled to accept the new reality, ordered a casket from the furniture store. His family and I decided on a small service in Felthame with a graveside service to follow in the family cemetery in his hometown in Pennsylvania.

The Felthame service was on a sweltering day with the coffin closed. Mourners jammed the parlor. Even Mrs. Powell came, despite her dislike of Yankees, murmuring expressions of sympathy. Although all the windows were open, sweat dripped off the seated mourners, and added to the overpowering mixture of perfume, flowers and sweat that filled the air. The world, through my veil, was appropriately misty and gray. Samuel and Trey sat on each side of me on borrowed chairs, clutching my hands, and listened stoically while our minister praised Arthur and declared he was not dead, but "asleep in Jesus."

Trey tugged my hand and whispered in my ear. "Does that mean Father might wake up?"

"No," I said. "He won't wake up."

I'd selected the funeral hymns myself: "There's a Land That Is Fairer than

Day," with its sweet promise that we would all meet again "on that beautiful shore." And "Shall We Gather at the River," which I'd loved since childhood. The music comforted me even while it threatened to break the dam on the emotions I was holding back until I was alone. Joy might be public, but grief, I was learning, was private, no matter how many condolences people offered. They moved on with their regular routines, as they should, and the boys and I were left to deal with the blank spot in our lives. I knew that we would. People did. But things would never be the same.

When the service was over, Nora came up and put her black, gloved hand in mine. The scent of lavender water drifted toward me.

"He was a wonderful man," she said in a soft voice. "We'll all miss him." Her eyes sparkled with what could have been unshed tears. I stared at her uncertainly. Had there been anything between Arthur and her beyond his usual flirting?

"Yes, we will all miss him," I said, glad the veil hid my narrowed eyes and my desire to shake the truth out of her. As I turned abruptly away, I noticed Ruthann by the front door. She must have stayed in the back during the service, hidden behind the crowd. I wondered what had motivated her to come, given our history.

Jewel, who was standing beside me, spotted her at the same time. Usually slow to fire up, this moved her to some emotion besides acceptance of what life sent. "What's she doing here?" she demanded. "She's got her nerve."

My nerves were frayed with the events of the last few days and my encounter with Nora. But I owed Ruthann for finding Arthur, and I paid my debts. I turned to Ma. "I need to say something to Ruthann," I said.

"Oh, honey, are you sure?"

"I'm sure."

Jewel scowled. Ma said nothing more. She'd pretty much stopped offering advice once I became a mother. She said if I didn't have good sense now, I never would. Not a totally comforting thought.

Ma put her hand on Jewel's arm. "This is none of our affair. Let's go in the kitchen and help get the food ready. Come on, boys. You can help, too. There'll probably be extra cookies around."

I walked quickly over to where Ruthann hovered, her 11-year-old daughter, Violet, beside her and her baby girl, Amanda, cradled in her arms. Ruthann lifted her chin and stood her ground, but she clutched Amanda more tightly. Bobby Lee put his arm around her and looked stolidly at me.

"Ruthann, I understand you told the searchers where to look for Arthur," I said. "Thank you for that."

Her cheeks flushed. "Anyone would have done it. I just came to say that

I'm sorry for your loss. I'm… sorry for everything."

I knew what she meant. Perhaps she thought this was the only place where I'd listen to her without attacking or turning away. Or maybe she was genuinely sorry for maiming me. But stretched thin with grief and worry, I was in no mood to hear her long-overdue apology. Anger flared in me, swift as summer heat lightning. I opened my mouth to respond, then glanced around.

Nearby mourners watched us spellbound, waiting for me to greet Ruthann the heroine, who not only had saved me from the river years ago, but now had found my fallen husband. If I spoke a single word to her, filled as I was with grief and loss, I'd turn Arthur's funeral into a sideshow in front of my children. This wasn't the time to air our differences. Maybe that time would come someday, but not now. Instead, Ruthann and I stared at each other in a silence filled with unspoken words.

Finally, she cleared her throat. "All right then. I said my piece, done what I came for." She turned and walked away, back straight. I took a deep breath, and returned to the business of learning to be a widow.

April 1957, Felthame, North Carolina

I stood in the shadows of Naomi's home and looked after Ruthann's bent, retreating form. She looked frail and not at all well.

The next morning, as I approached her house, I could see what Kate meant when she told me that the bulbs she and Ruthann had planted were a sea of gold in spring. Daffodils lined the walk and gathered in clumps under the tree. They were withered now, only traces of yellow remaining, but I could imagine how riotous they looked a few weeks ago.

Ruthann's house was one of the older ones, but well-kept up. A tin tub of pansies with cheerful purple and yellow faces sat beside the wooden steps. In one shady area of the yard, grass refused to grow. Someone had wielded a broom and swept it clean of sticks, leaving neat patterns in the dirt.

I scanned the sky, delaying our meeting a few seconds longer. The low-hanging clouds held the promise of April showers. I hoped it wouldn't rain, since I'd left my umbrella at home, not wanting to wrestle with both an umbrella and a cane.

I walked up on the front porch, raised my hand and knocked briskly on the door. Sleep had been hard to come by the night before, making me tired, and my hip ached, an unneeded reminder of the past that Ruthann and I shared. But I felt strong inside, ready to enter the lion's den and be Daniel to Ruthann's lion if necessary.

She opened the door and motioned me in. Her flowered housedress hung on her, further evidence of her weight loss. I'd wondered what I'd feel at this meeting. Trepidation, yes. Curiosity. Some old anger. All of that was present. The one emotion I hadn't expected was a vague pity when I compared the Ruthann in front of me with the Ruthann of memory, the one who strode tall and defiant through life.

"Thanks for coming," she said. "I know it wasn't easy."

The beige walls of her tiny living room were adorned with a sampler saying Bless This House, various family photos, and a painting showing a bearded Jesus calming the storm.

She motioned me to a seat and I leaned my cane against the arm of the easy chair. She looked at the cane, then away. "I made some sweet tea and pound cake," she said. "Let me fix you some."

Before I could respond, she'd hurried into the other room. Almost immediately she returned with the tea and the cake neatly sliced on white plates. Even under these circumstances it seemed we had to observe the traditions of Southern hospitality. We sipped in tension-filled silence as I waited for her to explain what she wanted. I took a bite of the pound cake, which I'd have found delicious under other circumstances.

Ruthann toyed with her slice, then set the fork down with a clatter and cleared her throat.

"This is harder than I thought," she said. "First off, let me say, I done wrong that day by the river when... when things happened. I didn't mean to hurt you. Vernell's death was fresh on my mind and eating away at me. Suddenly, with you standing there, something come over me. I'm sorry. I tried to tell you I was sorry at Arthur's funeral way back when, but you were in no mood to hear it."

"You could have written me a letter, tried again at a better time," I said, my voice chilly. "I wonder if you're only apologizing because you want something from me now."

To her credit, she didn't shrink from my words. Her chin lifted. "I deserve that. Yes, I do want something. But I mean it when I say I'm sorry. It's festered inside me all these years. I can't go back and do things over. None of us can. We just have to go on the best we can. For a long time, I tried to convince myself it really was an accident, that you slipped out of my grasp and into the river. I wanted to be a heroine and have people think I was special. But I'm through fooling myself. I was wrong. And I am truly sorry."

I looked at the direct gaze of those brown eyes and decided to believe her.

"I appreciate your apology." I couldn't quite say I accepted it. But I did appreciate it. It eased something hard inside me.

"I don't have much time left," she said. "And I don't want to die with things left unsaid. I'm hoping..."

The front door opened and Kate burst in laughing, with a lanky, young redhead in tow, who I assumed was her boyfriend.

"Oops. Sorry to interrupt. We'll only be a second," she said. "I have to get something in my room. Hi. This is Alec."

Alec acknowledged me with a soft "Pleased to meet you, ma'am."

Kate rushed to the back of the house while Alec waited uncomfortably near the door. "How are y'all?" he said.

"Fair to middlin'," Ruthann said.

"Looks like it's fixin' to rain," he said. His freckles stood out against his fair skin.

"Yes, it does," I replied.

He nodded, then looked hopefully down the hall for Kate, obviously not sure how to make small talk with two elderly women.

Thunder rumbled in the distance. "Oh good, it is going to rain," Ruthann said. "We need it."

"I remember how you like rain," I said. "You used to have something you called rain parties, right?"

"Yes. But that was a long time ago. People would think I was in my second childhood if I did that today."

"Half of them think eighty-year-olds are in their second childhood anyway," I said. "Sometimes they treat us like children at the nursing home."

"Not just at the nursing home," she said with a strained laugh.

There was an unsettling, surreal quality to our conversation. While I knew we were speaking in generalities until Kate left, it felt strange to be talking almost normally with the same woman who'd tormented me as a girl and left me crippled for life. For her part, Vernell's death stood between us.

Kate hurried down the hall. "Bye, Grandma. See you later." She planted a kiss on Ruthann's cheek and flung open the door. I could hear the patter of rain outside as Kate and Alec dashed off.

"He's a nice boy," Ruthann said, "but I hope she don't get too serious too soon. Well, young people will do what they want, wise or not."

"How true," I said, thinking of the mistakes we'd both made.

She turned to face me. "Kate tells me you've been giving her piano lessons. Thank you. She's taken a shine to you. She's a good girl and after I'm gone, I hope you and she... well, I'm jumping all over the place. Here's the thing."

Ruthann leaned closer and lowered her voice, even though we were alone.

"The doctor says I got the Big C," she said.

"Oh, Ruthann, I'm so sorry."

Cancer. The word struck terror into everyone. Some people survived, but a lot didn't.

"Does Kate know?"

"Nobody knows except my doctor, and now you. And I don't intend to spread the word. You know how some folks are around here. They act as if they can catch it if they get too close or think God must be punishing you for something."

"I don't think God works that way," I said. I wanted to ask more questions about her health, but wasn't sure how or whether I'd be invading her privacy. And I was at a loss as to why she'd invited me here or confided in me.

"It's…" She dropped her eyes. "It's in my woman parts, and the doctor says nothing can be done. I'll be gone by Thanksgiving at the latest. I can feel the pain gnawing away like a rabid fox inside me. The doctor gives me pills, but they're starting not to work. And they make me feel hazy, like I'm seeing things through a widow's veil. I hate that." She closed her eyes as if to gather strength. Then she took a deep breath and went on.

"The end is near and I got more to say to you. It may sound strange, but I always admired you at the same time I was jealous of you. You had a family that loved you and my folks were dead, my aunt a holy terror, always taking a switch to me. You got to go on to school and I didn't. Folks made a fuss over your piano playing. Then it seemed as if at least Vernell would get his dream, even if I didn't get mine. But…"

She stopped short. "I vowed no excuses, and I won't make any. You know, all these years I've felt bound to you somehow because of the things that happened when we were younger. It's like we're close, even though we're not friends."

I had to admit that I, too, had felt connected to Ruthann in a strange way, a twisted dark thread running through the pattern of my life.

"Promise you won't tell Kate anything about this," she said.

"Don't worry. That news is yours to tell. She won't hear it from me."

"All right then." She winced and rubbed her abdomen. "I got something else mighty important to talk with you about, mighty important. But I get wore out so easy these days, plus it's kind of upsetting and it will take a while to tell. Best to leave it be for now. Can you come back tomorrow when I'm fresher?"

"Of course," I said, even while I wondered what was coming next.

I walked home thinking about Ruthann. She'd been such a presence in my life, even when we were apart. Somehow, I'd never thought she'd be gone even though I knew that death stalked us all. Perhaps for her, death would be a friend. I wondered if I would feel that way as time went on. When I was younger, the idea would never have occurred to me. Death was a villain then, robbing me and the boys of a future together. I thought of the difficult days after Arthur died. I hadn't thought about them for a long time, but being back in Felthame and seeing Ruthann brought it all back.

Chapter Twelve

August 1906, Felthame, North Carolina

It had been two months since Arthur's funeral. Visitors who'd showered us with food and condolences had returned to their lives. I'd seen a lawyer, gotten the boys back into a regular routine and mostly stopped crying when no one was around. Mattie said to give things time, but I felt adrift, a leaf borne on a stream with no destination. I missed the strangest things: The sound of Arthur's deep male voice, counterpoint to my lighter one; his body weighing down the bed so that I slid toward the middle and fetched up against his warmth in the night; the smell of his cigar, which I'd have said I hated until it was gone.

Arthur had left us a little money, but I needed to earn more. His parents had offered to take us in, but that was a last-ditch option. There had to be more than living off the bounty of your dead husband's aging relatives. I barely knew them. When we'd visited their home, I'd been welcomed as the mother of their grandsons, but I couldn't imagine living every day with Arthur's controlling father. He'd teach the boys what he'd taught Arthur, that business was the most important thing in life, that being male was superior to being female. I didn't agree with either opinion. The sexes were different, each with their own proper roles. But that didn't make one inferior or superior to the other. No, Arthur's parents weren't an option. It was time to move forward, if only a little.

I decided to start by giving away Arthur's clothes. One cloudy morning while the boys were in school, Ma and I looked through his chifforobe together. I pulled out a tweed suit. A faint aroma of Arthur's bay rum tonic clung to it. Quickly, I put it back.

"Is something wrong with the suit?" Ma asked. "I might could mend it."

"No. It's just that everything reminds me of things we did together. He liked to wear this on Sunday when we went for buggy rides after we were first married." The smell of bay rum seemed to linger in my nostrils.

"I know, honey. Your pa didn't have clothes nowhere near as fine as these, but I hated getting rid of them. It was like letting go of him." She touched the material. "Arthur surely liked fine clothes."

"He did," I said. "How he looked was important to him. They're top quality and I need to pass them on to someone who can use them. It's just hard."

Resolutely, I reached in, took the suit out again and draped it across our bed, smoothing the fabric and laying it straight. Next, I pulled out his striped bathing suit. "This reminds me of going swimming in summer with the boys. He said he'd take us to the ocean before school started this year so I could finally see it."

I'd hoped a visit to the ocean would rekindle something in Arthur that I'd loved when we met, that he'd feel again the enthusiasm that talk of the sea gave him and remember there was more to life than work. I'd pictured us strolling hand in hand, the surf wetting our bare feet, gulls flying overhead. I put the bathing suit aside with a sigh. The trip had never happened. The ocean was still there. The boys and I could see it. But it wouldn't be with Arthur.

I grabbed a hat. "This black derby. I can picture him doffing it to women we passed on the street. He gave an especially deep bow to the elderly ladies. They always smiled at him."

My voice caught on the last words. Ma pulled out a white waistcoat. "There's a button missing on this one," she said, handing it to me.

I fished in the shallow pocket to see if Arthur had tucked the button in there. If so, I could sew it back on, a final act of caring. Paper crinkled under my fingers. I laid the waistcoat on the bed and unfolded a small, white square with a heart in black ink drawn in the center. Below the heart in graceful handwriting were the words "I Love You" and the letter N.

I felt an inner jolt. Of course. N for Nora. The note smelled faintly of lavender, just as she did. Nauseated, I crumpled it and closed my eyes as if I could shut out knowledge of what this meant. When I opened them, Ma was staring at me with concern.

"Are you all right?" she asked. "I know it's hard. We can do this later if you want."

I'd felt guilty at times about Arthur's death. Intellectually, I knew I wasn't to blame. But if I hadn't spoken angrily to him, he wouldn't have dashed off and he'd still be alive. Now, a flash of anger rose up and overwhelmed the guilt. I'd had suspicions about him and Nora. But when Arthur died, I'd decided to let my suspicions die also. It was unfair to suspect him when he couldn't defend himself. Now I felt a renewed sense of loss as my view of our marriage rearranged itself to accommodate this new evidence.

I stuffed the note deep in my pocket. "I'm all right," I said. "Let's sort through the rest of this and get it over with."

Without comment, she helped me whip through his wardrobe. I saved his catcher's mitt for Samuel, and his pocket watch for Trey, who was given more to reading than sports.

That night, when the children were asleep and I was alone at last, I sat at the kitchen table. Nora's note in my pocket loomed large out of all proportion to its actual size. I reached in, uncrumpled it and stared at it fixedly as if it somehow could reveal its secrets if I only looked long enough. I turned it over, but the back was blank. What was the truth here? Was this Nora's fascination with an older, worldly man who flirted with her? I could understand that. Or was it a sign that Arthur had betrayed our marriage vows? He was dead now. In one way, knowing wouldn't matter, but in another way, it meant everything to know he'd been true to me, that our marriage, strained as it may have been, wasn't a lie. I'd accepted his need for female approval. But betrayal, that was different.

The note held no answers. I crumpled it again and stuck it into the unlit stove. Taking a candle, I reached in and set the note aflame. I thought about confronting Nora. But to what end? It would change nothing. I'd try to remember the good times, not dwell on things that could only bring me pain. Watching the note crumble to ashes, I resolved to start over in a place with fewer memories and more possibilities. I'd pursue the love that had always been true to me: music.

"I don't see why you have to run off to Yankeeland. It seems to me like you could stay in North Carolina," Naomi said plaintively, folding my best dresses into a neat pile.

I'd sold the house at last and had only a few days to move out. Naomi was helping me sort through what possessions to take to my new life studying in New York state. From her mournful tone, you would have thought I was going to the moon. But being married to Arthur had helped me understand that Yankees were not the enemy from a war over long ago. I imagined they were like the folks in Felthame, worried about their families and their jobs, most of them good people, a few of them bad. I hoped that was right, because by selling the house and getting rid of my furniture I was gambling with not just my future but the twins' future, too.

"North Carolina is a great state," I said, determined to be upbeat. "But this move is what I want. Merrimont College takes women and it offers the courses I need. I want to become the best musician and the best teacher I can. It's harder to do that here."

Despite my brave words, I still woke up at night at times wondering what I was doing. Then I thought about my father eking out a hardscrabble living on the farm, my mother, brother, sisters working in the mill and barely getting by and resolved anew to do whatever it took to build a different future for me and my sons.

"Bloom where you're planted is my motto," Naomi said. "Give me Jediah and a good day's work at the mill with my friends and I'm happy. Well, I see you've made your mind up. I hope it works out."

She held up a dented frying pan. "What do you want to do with this? It's still got some wear in it."

"Give it away. I won't have room for much for a while."

Ma had been more supportive. "I know this isn't the way you thought your life would go," she'd said. "But life goes as it will. Our job is to make the best of it." She'd looked at me speculatively. "If you're scared, there's no shame in that. I was scared when your Pa died and I had to move to town and fend for myself with four younguns to support. I managed. You can, too."

Jewel wandered in from the parlor. She hadn't questioned the move the way Naomi had, but then Jewel went along with whatever was happening, neither happy nor sad, a cloud drifting where the wind blew. Every now and then I thought that might be a better way to be. Or a less painful one. She'd even married that way, dating the first boy who showed an interest and wedding him at eighteen because he was "steady."

"What do you like about him," I'd asked once, thinking how different that was from the passion I'd felt for Arthur.

"No surprises." It sounded boring, but it suited her.

"Did you see any furniture you want?" I asked her now.

"Oh I don't know. Maybe that flowered settee."

"It's yours."

Most of my household goods were jammed into the front parlor. I'd already given Naomi my white dishes with the yellow roses. She said she'd think of me whenever she used them. Ma was getting the kitchen stove. They were pieces of me left behind, a promise I'd return. A sign in front of the house invited people to stop by and make an offer for what furniture was left. It had been a hard decision to sell my furniture. But every bit of money would help me in New York.

I laid sheet music in one of the trunks we were taking on the train. Naomi looked at it, then at me. "What are you going to do with your piano?" she asked.

"I'm going to sell it," I said in a strangled voice. "A buyer is coming tomorrow."

I could cope with leaving my furniture, but the piano — that was tough. "I'll buy another one someday," I said.

"What a shame, with you loving it so," Naomi said. She put her arm around me. "Don't go. We'll all help you manage here. Now isn't the time to hare off on your own with two children."

"Now is exactly the time," I said, fighting tears as I tucked a wool blanket into the trunk. It would be cold in Weysauk, New York. "I won't be alone. I've found another widow with a child and we'll share expenses and child rearing."

"You don't even know this woman," she protested.

"True," I said. "But the college gave me Barbara's name and we've exchanged letters. She's a secretary with a young daughter. We don't have to love each other, just get along." How hard could that be?

I hurried on, seeking to reassure her and maybe myself. "Barbara has a four-room apartment. We'll share the rent and that will help with expenses. It's within walking distance of the college. Anyway, I'll be so busy, what with watching the boys and taking classes and working part-time as a..." I hesitated, since I didn't have a job lined up — "at something that I won't have time to be lonely." I paused. "Naomi, can't you understand? I'll be pursuing my dream."

"But the people there won't love you the way we do."

A knock at the door saved me from responding. Mattie stuck her head in. "Hello the house. Anybody home?"

"Come on in," I said. Mattie, at least, would cheer me on, whatever her doubts.

She swept into the room and gave me a hug.

"I have something for you," I said. "Come with me." Almost every time Mattie visited, she played the carved walnut music box in my bedroom. I picked up the box from the dresser and held it out to her. "To remember me by."

Her eyes lit up. "Oh no. I couldn't take that."

I paid no attention. Her refusal was part of the Southern ritual of accepting a gift. The recipient had to say no at least once, before politely getting to yes.

"I insist," I said. "It will mean a lot to me for you to have it."

I placed the box in her hands.

"All right. If you insist."

"I insist."

She gave a little laugh, wound the key and lifted the lid. Tinkly music filled the room. I smiled, looking at her face. I would enjoy thinking of Mattie playing the music box. It would make me feel connected to her when I was in a strange place.

Her eyes fell on the wicker rocking chair in the corner. "Um, do you have any plans for that?" she asked.

"Do you want it?"

She hesitated. "Oh, I don't know."

"Please, take it." I'd rocked the twins in that chair many a night, nursing them or singing them to sleep. The rocker was hard to give up, connected as it was to my sons, the enduring bright spots from my marriage. But it helped that Mattie would be the one to have it. Maybe she'd rock children of her own in it and tell them about her friend Delia.

"Actually, I wasn't thinking of me," Mattie said. "It's just…" She fell silent and seemed torn.

"Out with it."

"It's just that Ruthann and I were talking the other day. She has that new baby. It's got the colic, and she drags in to work all worn out from not sleeping. I bet rocking would soothe it, and they'd both be able to get some sleep."

"Ruthann?" I said.

"Never mind," Mattie said. She looked at me sadly. "It was just a thought. Really, forget it. Let's talk about something else."

Mattie loved us both, and I loved Mattie. I couldn't bear for her to think badly of me. Plus, I was leaving for a new life. I could start by being generous about my beloved rocker. "I'm giving it to you. If you want Ruthann to have it for her baby, that's all right with me," I said.

Mattie smiled, and I felt glad I'd done the right thing.

After she left, promising to return for the rocking chair, I sent Naomi and Jewel home to their families. Naomi gave me a hug as she got ready to leave. "Remember," she said, "we're always here if things don't work out."

When everyone had gone, I busied myself with more sorting of household goods. How had we accumulated so much? A knock on the door interrupted me. When I opened the door, Nora stood on the front steps. I swept my gaze over her, trying to look calmer than I felt. She wore a dark green dress that set off her eyes, a dress looser and more subdued than she usually wore. Her blonde hair was tucked back into a bun. It was as if she had deliberately tried to look plain for this visit. I had seen her only in passing at church since the funeral. Several times, she'd looked my way, her expression bleak and I'd averted my gaze, my loss still fresh. Once or twice, she'd approached as if she wanted to speak to me, but I turned away to chat with friends and she retreated. Whatever she was thinking, I didn't want to know. Now here she stood. Her signature scent of lavender wafted toward me, reminding me of her aromatic love note to Arthur.

"Yes," I said curtly.

"I apologize for intruding, but I need to talk to you before you leave town," she said.

A woman pushing a baby carriage walked by on the sidewalk, looking our way with a friendly smile. I smiled back with an effort.

"Come in, Nora," I said. This wasn't a confrontation I wanted to have on a doorstep.

She stepped inside and Southern courtesy deserted me. I closed the door but left her standing.

"What's on your mind?"

"I'll come right to the point since I know I'm not welcome. I can tell from the way you act at church when you see me, that you, well, suspect something."

"Why wouldn't I, what with your flirting?" I demanded. "It was excruciatingly painful to me. Then there was your little love note that I found when I was sorting Arthur's clothes."

Her face was white and her hand trembled as she lifted it to her mouth. For a second, I realized how young she was, how susceptible to Arthur's charms, just as I had been. She, too, had lost someone she cared about. I faltered for a second in my anger. Then, I thought of my fatherless boys and it surged again, flaring up like brushfire before the wind.

"I'm sorry," she said. "Just let me explain. I came here because our preacher said letting someone believe a lie was the same as a lie, that we need to make things right with those we've harmed if we want God to forgive us. He says confession is good for the soul."

"Whose soul?" I interrupted, suspecting I knew where this was going.

She stopped startled, as if the question had never occurred to her.

"Uh, mine. I have to get right with God. After church, I told the preacher that I did someone wrong, but I didn't say who or what I did. He prayed with me and the Lord convicted me of my sin. It's been heavy on my mind ever since. I can't sleep for thinking about what to do. So finally, here I am to apologize."

"I can't sleep either. My husband is dead," I said. Nausea rose in me as I thought about Arthur coupling with this woman. "But I don't feel the need to dump my sins on someone else's doorstep. You've delivered your message. You'd best go now."

"No, wait," she said. "You don't understand. It was only one time, I swear it on the Holy Bible. I wanted you to know that on the day Arthur died, he told me he was going to break it off with me. He said he loved you and he was sorry he ever got involved with me. I got so upset that he left and said we'd talk later, that he couldn't deal with it right then. I upset him so much he went riding off and got killed. I'm the reason he's dead."

She burst into tears.

"Nora," I said. "Please. Calm down." She sobbed hysterically until finally, against everything I was feeling, I put my arms around her. I held her and patted her back while she sniffled on my shoulder, wetting my dress.

"We're not responsible for how other people act. Don't blame yourself," I said, remembering how I'd had similar thoughts. "Honestly, though, I cannot deal with this right now. You've unburdened yourself like you wanted. Now, I'd like you to leave."

"I need to wash my face," she said. "I can't go out looking like this. What will people think?"

She was right. Speculative gossip flourished like kudzu in the mill town, spreading everywhere and growing in the telling.

"In here," I said, leading her to the kitchen sink and handing her a towel. When she bent over the sink to wet it, I fantasized for a second about pushing her head under the running water. She finished dabbing her face, unscathed, and I showed her to the door. She looked at me, hand on the knob.

"I'm sorry I hurt you," she said. "I know it was a sin. But Arthur was so…"

I cut her off with an upraised hand. "Please don't say any more. Just leave."

She scurried down the walk and I locked the door behind her. I didn't want anyone to come near me.

I walked to the back yard and sat on the steps, staring unseeing at the rosebush I'd planted and the bees buzzing around it in the sultry summer air. I didn't cry. I'd done enough of that recently. Crying made you feel better for a while, but problems still had to be faced. My anger had cooled or gone underground. Mostly I felt an overwhelming sense of tiredness. I searched my mind for a song that would lift my spirits. None came to mind. My thoughts were still fixed on Nora's visit. What in the world was she thinking? That she would confess and I'd say it was fine? Believers who felt convicted by the Lord did all kinds of things to atone, some healing, some that would have been better left undone. I wasn't sure which category this was in. Right now, I felt like I'd have preferred ignorance.

But as I calmed down, I decided it was better to know the truth. Yes, Arthur had been unfaithful. Lord, that hurt. I'd have a lot of grieving and healing to do over that fact. But he'd also told Nora it was over, that he loved me. I liked to think he would have stuck to his resolve, even though the admiration of young women was as alluring to him as wild honey to a bear. I was glad I'd never know what would have happened if he'd lived.

The sun was slanting lower in the sky, casting shadows where I sat. It was time to start the cornbread for supper. The boys had gone fishing with friends, but they'd promised to be home before dark. They'd want me to cook up their catch. Daily life was going relentlessly on despite straying husbands and death. I stood up, wiped dust from my dress and went inside. Nora, I decided, had done me a favor. I didn't need to wonder any longer. I could put the uncertainty behind me as I went forward to my new life in upstate New York.

April 1957, Felthame, North Carolina

It was good to be back in Felthame and walk the familiar streets. One morning shortly after Kate and I arrived, I spotted her outside the village grocery story looking happy and rested. The dark circles I'd noted earlier were gone from her eyes.

"Are you getting caught up on your sleep?" I asked.

"Getting there. It's hard to get enough sleep. At least for me."

"I know. I felt the same way when I went North to study," I said.

She looked at me for a long moment, perhaps trying to wrap her head around the idea of me as a young woman literally burning the midnight oil.

"I can imagine," she said, rallying.

I couldn't resist adding to her image. "Of course, I was a widow with two young sons to care for at the time along with going to school and working evenings in the mill."

"Sounds rough," she said.

"Four years worth of rough," I said, then wished I hadn't. It sounded like an appeal for sympathy. Those years had been a blur. On one hand, there was the joy in learning more about music, the pleasure in seeing my sons grow. On the other hand was the utter exhaustion that brought moments of despair when I wondered whether I should quit. Letters from home had been my lifeline, even though they'd mostly been news about the weather and which villager was "doing poorly." Ma always signed her name carefully at the end of each of my sisters' letters and drew a heart. I hated that I'd lost some of those letters over the years.

"It was all worth it though," I said. "You'll say the same thing when you get your diploma."

"You had to work in a mill up there, too?"

"I did. It was the only job I could find that would fit my schedule. I worked in the weaving room, which was…" I broke off as she looked over my shoulder and her face broke into a big smile.

I turned and saw, as I expected, her young man, Alec, coming down the street toward her. There'd be no more interest in the half-century-old reminiscences of an elderly lady.

"Oh, before I forget," Kate said, "Grandma has a piano. She plays a little, not like you, of course. But I bet she'd be happy to let you play it while you're here."

"What?" I said. "She has a piano?"

"Yes. Gotta run. It was nice seeing you."

She walked toward Alec, leaving me to absorb the news about the piano. Ruthann's house was small and I would have noticed a piano in the living room. I always noticed pianos. It must be in a back room. I stood there stock still for a few seconds, unable to tell what I felt about Ruthann playing the piano. If I were still a girl, I suspect I would have felt a little dismayed. Piano playing had made me feel special at a time when I wanted, perhaps even needed, to feel special. Now, with the passage of time and experience, I felt pleased that Ruthann had a piano. Music was for everyone. Although I did wonder if her attitude toward me had had some role in her decision.

Maybe somewhere during our visit there'd be a lighter moment when we could talk about pianos. Or maybe that would seem as if I was trying to outshine her yet again. No, best to let her bring it up if she wished. Everything between Ruthann and me was so complicated, but then there were so many reasons why, reasons that went far beyond "the accident."

I was curious about the piano, but even more curious about the mysterious secret Ruthann wanted to share, a secret so big she was too exhausted to talk about it until she had rested. Well, she wasn't shy. She'd let me know when she was ready to talk.

I headed on toward the corner store and the tea I'd been seeking before I met Kate. As I walked, memories of those first years after I got my diploma were fresh in my mind.

May 1910, Weysauk, New York

I looked around the tiny apartment one last time. I'd boxed up my things and the boys, ready for the move to my first post-college job — teaching at a high school in Polkington, New York. Last to be packed would be my most precious possession: My college diploma. Four years of my life were in that piece of paper. Years of studying, working, watching my sons grow, dealing with a variety of roommates and child-care arrangements, dating sporadically but finding no one who touched my heart.

Now I felt as if I'd climbed an incredibly hard mountain to be greeted by a wonderful sunrise at the top. I couldn't stop staring at my diploma.

When I'd gotten my high school diploma, I'd been ecstatic. This was even better. I picked up the diploma and sniffed it, imagining that the black ink still smelled fresh. I half-danced awkwardly around the bedroom, holding it up in front of me. I laughed out loud with pleasure. I'd done it. I'd done it.

"What the heck are you doing, Mom?" Trey asked from the doorway. I set the diploma on the bed and smiled at him. "Celebrating graduation," I said. "Celebrate with me." I grabbed him and tried to whirl him around. Already he was taller than I was so it was more of a stumble than a whirl.

"Polkington, New York, here we come," I said and laughed again.

He smiled in return, even though neither of my boys was happy about leaving friends and starting at a new school. In Samuel's case, now that he was a teenager, I suspected there was a young lady involved. It was startling to think of them in that light. But then they were only three years younger than I was when I married Arthur. How naïve and inexperienced that seemed now. Arthur had seemed old to me — or at least mature — but here I was in my early thirties, the same age as he'd been when we met, and I didn't feel old at all. I felt ready to tackle anything.

"You act as if Polkington is paradise," Trey said.

"No. It's just a small town, but it's on a river, and I've missed the river. And it has hills, just like North Carolina. We'll have enough money and I'll be able to spend more time with you."

He groaned slightly. Having your mother spend more time with you wasn't a priority when you were his age.

"I'll get enough sleep — very important to me — and, Trey, I'll be able to buy a piano. A piano I can play for as long as I want."

"I know, Mom. I'm glad for you. It's just... you know, a change."

"We've had a lot of changes," I said, "but things will settle down at last."

"If you say so," he said, shaking his head. "But I bet you're wrong."

January 1912, Polkington, New York

School was out for the afternoon. I stood in my classroom alone waiting for Duncan O'Toole, wondering if this was wise.

A week earlier I'd asked a fellow teacher, Rupert, for help in finding a musician to talk to my class about brass instruments. That's when he'd introduced me to his friend, Duncan, who played the cornet. We'd met at the club where he played. I still carried the image of him wailing away to the lively "Hurricane Rag" in the smoke-filled air, his cornet glinting as it hit the light. The image made me uneasy because he reminded me of Arthur. Not so much in his looks. He was tall like Arthur, but his features were more rugged. Arthur's hair was straight, while Duncan's was curly and a little long, so that he kept brushing it out of his eyes.

It was more his manner, the way he focused totally on me when he was with me, flirting in a charming way. Then, after he left my table, I watched him flirt with three separate women on his way back to the stage.

"He's a ladies' man," Rupert had warned me when he saw the way my gaze followed him. "Oh, he's smart and funny, a good friend. He loves kids and music, and I know you do, too. But watch out. He's a bachelor, a guy who flits from flower to flower, and likes it that way. Charm is his middle name."

"Don't worry," I'd said. "I've been vaccinated against charming men."

So why did I keep remembering how he looked, the way he raised one eyebrow and grinned easily?

I looked around my classroom, trying to see it as Duncan would. I straightened the ink stand and blotter on my desk, nudged my history textbook over so it lined up with the other books. I'd just cleaned the blackboard. The smell of chalk dust lingered in the air. My gaze went to the table at the front of the room. I was teaching the children about Eskimos. I'd told them the story of Agoonack, a girl who lived in the frozen north. On the table was a tableau, with a white cheesecloth to represent snow and a misshapen white igloo the children had made from plaster of Paris. A doll to represent Agoonack leaned against it. The coat the class had made for her looked more like a bizarre furry mouse than a parka.

As I looked at the display, I thought of that long-ago time when Ruthann and I were children and she'd been excited to talk with me about what I was learning about Eskimos. It had been a rare moment of rapport.

Footsteps sounded in the hall. I stood up, smoothed my hair and looked expectantly at the open door. The principal led Duncan in and introduced him. "Your guest is here," he said.

Duncan nodded to me, his face serious until the principal left.

"Nice classroom," Duncan said, looking around. He spotted the snow scene. "What's this?"

So I told him about Agoonack.

"Boy, I wish you'd been my teacher," he said. "All that drilling and memorization. I hated it. But this looks like fun."

"Oh we drill and memorize, too. But the pupils need a break from all that."

Suddenly he leaned forward and brushed at my cheek with his fingers. Startled, I stepped back and put my hand to the spot.

"Chalk dust," he said with a smile.

"Oh," I said, flustered. "Thank you. Won't you have a seat and we can get started?"

He looked at the rows of wooden desks, sized for elementary students, then at my desk, the only other spot in the room where one might sit. Oh dear, I thought. I should have brought in a chair.

"Yes, Teacher," he said. He took a seat at a desk in the front row. His knees stuck out awkwardly and he hunched over it like Ichabod Crane. He grinned broadly. "I'm ready to be taught."

"Please, Mr. O'Toole," I said, "wouldn't you be more comfortable at my desk?"

"This is fine. Please call me Duncan."

I seated myself at my desk, feeling more secure in the familiar position.

"All right. Duncan, tell me about your background."

He laughed. "I better give you the brief version. I was Rupert's college roommate until I got kicked out at the end of my sophomore year. My fault. I wanted to play music and party more than I wanted to study. Since then, I've played at dance halls, weddings, balls, charity affairs, dances held by fraternal lodges, anywhere they needed someone. Is that enough? Oh yes, I love children and I'm excited to talk to your class."

He grinned at my serious expression. "Why don't you tell me a little about yourself, Mrs. Benning?" he said. "It seems only fair."

"Me? There's not much to tell. I'm a teacher and I play the piano. Now about the class."

"Right. The class," he said. "Tell me about your students. How old are they? What do you hope to accomplish?"

Good questions and ones that put me at ease as they shifted the emphasis to our joint venture. "They range in age from eight to eleven," I began. "They've been exposed to the piano and the violin. I want them to learn about brass instruments, to see that there are all kinds of ways to make music."

"Great. I thought I'd play for the kids, show them how the cornet works, let them try to make a sound with it," he said, moving his fingers as if depressing the keys on a cornet. "Maybe talk about ragtime since that's so popular."

"That sounds swell," I said. "Most of all I want the children to learn to enjoy music, to see that it's not just for a few people. Anyone can make music part of their lives, even if it's just singing around the house or listening to someone play an instrument."

"Your eyes shine when you talk about music," he said.

So do yours, I thought.

We drifted into talk about songs we liked until I realized with a start I'd better get home to fix the boys' supper.

"I'm looking forward to meeting your class," Duncan said as I showed him to the schoolhouse door. He grinned, leaned forward and kissed my hand, eyes raised to look at me. "And, I'm looking forward to seeing you again," he said, standing up.

As I jerked my hand back, I could feel the spot where his warm lips had pressed. His grin widened.

"I'll see you in class then," I said.

After he left, I went back to my classroom for my purse and stood for a moment staring at the desk where he'd sat, still feeling his lips on my hand, remembering his engaging grin. The mica in the streams at home wasn't gold, I reminded myself, no matter how much it sparkled in the sun.

I still felt the sparkle of his personality the following Monday when he spoke to the class, drawing them in. Students crowded around him, eliciting squawks and squeals from the cornet. One small boy actually produced some clear notes. He whispered something to Duncan, and Duncan patted his shoulder and whispered back. I let the session run over into our arithmetic class, but finally I had to call a halt. When Duncan let loose with his final ragtime solo, the kids listened entranced, feet tapping in time to the music. Mine were tapping, too. At the end, I thanked him profusely and thought I'd seen the last of him.

Three days later, I found a large brown envelope in my mailbox. I turned it over curiously. The bold handwriting wasn't familiar and neither was the return address, 5208 Brookdale Road. When I tore it open, I was greeted by the bright red cover of the sheet music to "Hurricane Rag," the catchy tune Duncan had played at the dance hall when we met for the first time, a tune that had set my foot to tapping under the table.

A note was stuck inside the music. "Please accept this as a minor gift from one musician to another. I thought you might enjoy playing this song. You seemed to like it the other night. Perhaps I can hear you play it sometime. Best wishes, Duncan O'Toole," it read.

I looked at the sheet music in dismay and admiration. It seemed like a prelude to more interaction, but what a thoughtful one. I dashed off a thank-you note and sent it on its way. I played the piece on and off that day. Every time, I thought of Duncan.

The next afternoon, wandering through the music store, I spied the sheet music for a collection of syncopated piano pieces, "Nothing But Rags," and leafed through it. It was thirty two pages of rags and marches by everyone from Scott Joplin to W.C. Powell. I wondered if they would work with a cornet. Duncan might have to transpose the key, but perhaps that wouldn't be a problem. He'd like this, I thought. I bought it and mailed it to him, thinking it made us even. It wasn't good to be indebted to a charming man.

Four nights later, the phone rang. It was Duncan. "Thanks so much for the ragtime book," he said. "I love it."

"I'm enjoying the music you sent me, too."

"Good." He paused and I was ready to end the conversation.

Then he blurted out, "I have an idea that might interest you. It's a way to introduce more children to music."

Bull's-eye. Children and music were dear to my heart. "That sounds... interesting," I said. "Tell me more."

"It's too complicated to do over the phone. How about if we discuss it over some ice cream at Goode's soda fountain?"

"It's January," I protested. "Ice cream in January in New York?"

He laughed. "Ice cream is always in season."

I laughed too. "You're right. When did you have in mind?"

We arranged to meet and I hung up, intrigued and uncertain. This man was clever. He knew how to draw me in. Clever men could be trouble.

Mr. Whitman, the clerk behind the soda fountain counter, stared at us over the top of his glasses, then shifted his gaze to the store window and the snow pelting down outside. "You want ice cream sodas?"

"That's right," Duncan said with a grin.

Mr. Whitman was a fussy, middle-aged man with a mania for neatness. When he wasn't stroking his mustache, he was busy polishing soda glasses or invisible specks on the big mirror behind the long marble counter, wiping off the stools, sweeping the clean floor..

"Ice cream? In this weather?" Mr. Whitman said. "Let me see what we've got, if anything."

He rummaged around and came back. "Vanilla. That's it." He glanced out at the snow and shook his head.

"Vanilla sounds fine," Duncan and I said at the same time, then laughed.

Mr. Whitman added the soda water and we watched it fizz up. A burly man sitting on one of the counter stools eating his sensible hot soup, looked at our sodas and shook his head. I suppressed a laugh at his expression. This visit was worth it just for the reactions.

Duncan plunked twenty cents on the counter, which Mr. Whitman promptly picked up. As we moved to one of the round, marble-topped tables, he was wiping the spot where the money landed.

I took a sip of my drink. "What do you think?" Duncan asked.

"You were right. It does taste good in winter — if you're where it's warm."

I could see our reflections in the big mirror behind the counter and I tucked in a stray curl. "So, what's your idea?"

"One of the boys in your class asked me about learning to play the cornet. So I thought you and I could do a concert for the families to drum up interest." He laughed. "Drum up. Wrong instrument. Eventually the school might even get a small brass band going. I'd be willing to help."

"It's a nice idea. But most of the children don't have instruments," I said.

"Then, let's make the performance a communitywide benefit to buy some for the students."

An image of Ruthann and Vernell sprang into my mind. "I don't know about a benefit," I said sharply.

I glimpsed my grim expression in the mirror. "Let's just say I'm leery of benefits. They don't always work and someone gets left out."

"OK then," he said, his expression quizzical. "Think of it as a concert, something simple where we happen to pass the hat to buy instruments for the school. No specific students involved."

"Maybe."

A pretty young woman, cheeks flushed with cold, hurried into the parlor. Tousled blonde curls peeped from beneath her bonnet as she shook her head to dislodge snowflakes. Duncan looked at her appreciatively, then quickly away when he saw me watching him.

"Sorry," he said. "I didn't mean to be rude. It's just that I..." He lifted his hands in the air and let them fall as if he were helpless. "I love women. I love their perfume, the sound of their voices, the way they look, the way they move, the way they look at life. To me, every woman has something to admire about her. You have plenty. For example, I like your black hair. When you stood in the schoolhouse door the other day, I noticed how it gleamed in the sun. But it's not just that. The first time I saw you I thought, she looks like a little doll."

It was an unfortunate phrase, the same one Arthur had used when we met because I was tiny. I frowned and Duncan rushed on.

"Then, when I talked with you, I found out you had a mind of your own. And you were full of enthusiasm for one of my passions, music. When I visited the classroom and saw the Eskimo tableau, I could see you were a good teacher, too, that you cared about your pupils."

"Thank you," I said, my hand straying toward my hair. His words felt good. I could see why women were drawn to him.

"Perhaps we should get back to business," I said.

He smiled. "By all means. Back to business. I thought you could play a few songs. I could play some. For the finale, we could do a piano-cornet duet." He put his left hand on the table as if playing a piano and used his right hand to pretend to blow a horn, then grinned. "See what fun it would be."

"I'll think about it. But don't count on it." Already though, two thoughts were running through my mind. It seemed low risk, like no one would be hurt. And the musician in me was stirring. I'd never done a duet with a cornet player. It would involve transposition, always interesting. Yes, it might be fun. And I'd learn something new about music.

"You know," Duncan said, studying me, "when I saw you tapping your toes to the music and the expression on your face when you looked at the pianist in the dance hall that night I thought, now there's someone who loves music as much as I do."

"I do love music. I've loved it my whole life."

His hand halfway reached for mine. He stopped and let it lie on the table between us. I lowered my gaze, tempted for one second to inch my hand toward his. Instead, I took another sip of my soda.

"Where did you learn to play the cornet?" I asked.

"Down in New Orleans."

"That's a long way from New York."

"So is North Carolina. Sometimes, life takes strange turns," he said.

"Yes. It does."

"My dad was a farmer in this area," he went on. "He wanted me to farm like my two brothers. He loved the land. But I hated farming. He decided if I wasn't going to be a farmer, I should go to college and become a doctor. He could see some use for that. Looking back, I suppose I was a mystery to him and he was a mystery to me."

He made an inarticulate sound deep in his throat and took a quick pull on his straw. "Anyway, things went south between us so I dropped out of college and went South literally, to New Orleans, where I found the music that... it may sound strange, although maybe not to you... that spoke to something inside me."

We looked at each other in perfect agreement.

"So," he said, breaking his gaze, "I started hanging around with musicians. All that freedom was intoxicating, in more ways than one. I went a little wild. But I learned a lot about what I wanted and what I didn't want. So even the mistakes were worthwhile. Sometimes I wonder what it would be like to have taken a different path, to have a wife, kids, stability. The idea gets more attractive as you get older. Anyway, I didn't take that path. I went to New Orleans instead. It was there I first heard the cornet. That was the day I knew I'd found the instrument for me."

"I felt the same way when I first heard the piano," I said, flung back for a moment to that little Felthame church.

Our gazes locked again. The attraction I felt scared me. Don't fall for this man, I told myself. You have enough going on in your life without getting involved with some musician who plays in nightclubs and has a reputation as a ladies' man. He admits he was wild in his younger days, drank too much. You can't be sure he's over all that. Your sons need a responsible adult male in their lives. And you need someone stable, not this man so like Arthur in his charm and flirtatiousness.

This time, I looked away first.

A strange expression crossed his face, like someone who just realized something surprising. He shook his head as if to clear it.

"I learned to play the cornet," he said, "and the next thing you know, I was making a living… of sorts as a musician. Then my father died and my mother took sick. So I came back here to be close to her. What's next for me? Who knows?"

He shrugged self-consciously. "Probably more than you want to know. I do like to talk. What about you?"

So I told him my mill-girl-to-teacher story, leaving out Ruthann because it was nothing I wanted to share.

My growing attraction to Duncan worried me for other reasons. There had been other interested men who'd backed off. Some when they realized I didn't like to be told what to do; others when they saw I limped and had two children. I didn't want to get hurt again.

But he handled the news I had twin sons with aplomb. "I hope I get to meet them," he said. "Kids usually like me, and I like them."

I hesitated, then pressed on. Best to get this over with. "I'm sure you've noticed I have a permanent limp. It's the result of an accident when I was young," I said, stuffing a trunkload of trauma into a single sentence. "I can get around well enough, but I can't dance."

"I'm sorry," he said. "But there are lots of ways to enjoy music."

I was surprised at his acceptance. I suppose I expected him to react like the other charming man in my life, Arthur, who'd been put off by my lameness. My injury was the point when things changed between us. He wanted a perfect wife and I was no longer perfect.

I'd made excuses for Arthur, but maybe his reaction had hurt me more deeply than I wanted to admit. Suddenly, I realized I had in some ways accepted his view of me. I was lame so I was no longer perfect. Maybe I'd been too hard on some of the men who expressed interest in me, assumed rejection when none was there.

I drew in a deep breath at the thought.

"Is something wrong?" Duncan asked.

"No," I said slowly. "Nothing is wrong. Nothing at all."

I tucked away this new thought and moved on to talk about other things.

Before he left, he reached into the bag he'd brought and handed me some sheet music. "While you're deciding, look at this. I thought we might play it together," he said. "Do you know it?"

The cover showed a riverboat on a lake with the full moon reflected in a pool of orange. "'I Want to Be in Dixie' by Irving Berlin and Ted Snyder," I said. It was a clever choice, given my origins. I studied the lyrics about never forgetting or forsaking the sunny land of cotton. The words brought a sudden longing for my family back home and the warmer winters of the South.

"I don't know it. And I haven't agreed to your plan," I said.

"No harm in playing a new piece of music," he said with a grin.

The minute we stood up to leave, Mr. Whitman scurried over to collect our glasses and wipe off the table. Duncan and I looked at each other and smiled. I hadn't had this much fun in a while.

Outside the snow had stopped. Duncan offered to walk me home, but I felt unsettled by my conflicting emotions. "It's still broad daylight. I'll be fine," I said. He smiled and tipped his hat. When I looked back half a block later, he was standing on the sidewalk watching me. Flustered, I turned and crunched through the snow at a deliberate pace, not looking back again.

At home, I put the sheet music on the piano and played through it. It was in the key of B flat and I wondered what key a cornet was in.

I thought, too, about what it would mean to my students to be able to have instruments to play. I owed it to them to give the benefit a chance. In the end, I agreed to his plan, and we arranged to practice.

It was our first practice session, one I'd been looking forward to. Duncan arrived promptly, bringing a small box of chocolates. "Rupert told me you like these," he said. Another thoughtful gift. I could feel myself softening toward him as I thanked him and led him to the parlor where my upright piano sat.

"The twins are at baseball practice," I said. "They'll be back in a bit. I've told them you'd be here."

He nodded and I sat down at the piano while he took his cornet from its case. Our practice went well, with a lot of laughter over our mistakes. The cornet was, in fact, pitched in B flat so he could play a major scale on the horn while I played the B flat major on the piano. No transposition required for our duet.

"Fate," he said. "It must be a sign."

"A sign we better get to work on fine tuning our performance."

He laughed appreciatively at my feeble play on words. I wasn't much given to making jokes, but Duncan brought out my light-hearted side.

Halfway through, the boys came bursting in. Not boys anymore since they were seventeen. It seemed as if they should still be wearing knickers and knee socks.

As Duncan shook hands with each twin, I looked at the three of them together. With short people on my side of the family and tall people on Arthur's side, the twins had settled in at five foot ten. They had their father's brown eyes, but the dark hair came from both sides of the family. Lately, they'd taken to parting their hair in the center and slicking it down with macassar so the house smelled faintly of coconut oil and some unidentifiable fragrance. Duncan, about six feet tall, with his dark hair and brown eyes looked like he could be their older brother or uncle. If you looked more closely, there were clear differences: the twins' full lips and their long lashes that were attracting the attention of girls, Duncan's thinner lips and his nose, slightly crooked and with a small scar. I wondered what the story was on that. It felt right somehow to see them together.

"So how was baseball practice?" Duncan asked.

"Fine," Samuel said stiffly. His glove was in his hand.

"Nice glove," Duncan said. "They don't make that style anymore."

"It's my dad's. He was great at baseball."

"It looks like the glove's in great shape."

"Thanks."

It should be. Samuel oiled it regularly to keep it from cracking. For both my sons, their dead father had taken on a larger-than-life quality that no other man could match.

"What big league team do you like?" Duncan asked.

"The New York Giants. I have great hopes for them," Trey said.

"I like the Giants, too," Duncan said.

Samuel's brows drew together a little, as if he wondered whether Duncan really liked the Giants or was saying that. Or maybe I was reading too much into it.

"I especially like their pitcher, Christy Mathewson," Duncan said.

Trey nodded. "Me too."

I smiled inwardly, then wondered why I cared what the boys thought of Duncan. This was, after all, a practice session, not a date.

Samuel shifted from foot to foot. It was time to end the conversation on a positive note.

"We need to practice more," I said. "Y'all run along now."

In parting, Samuel, with unnecessary but sweet protectiveness, made a point of informing me that he and Trey would be in the kitchen "if you need us."

"Nice young men," Duncan said when they were out of earshot.

"They are, aren't they?" Arthur would have been proud of them.

When we finished practicing, we each showed off a little. I played him part of Mozart's C Major Piano Concerto, No. 25, and he applauded.

"My turn," he said. He lifted his horn and pronounced solemnly, "Madam, I give you 'Southern Cross,' by the renowned cornet player Herbert Clarke as performed by the somewhat renowned player Duncan O'Toole."

When he finished, I clapped loudly. He bowed. "Thank you, madam. Every musician loves an appreciative audience."

Indeed. I loved sharing our varied music.

After Duncan left, I strolled out to the kitchen. The twins were seated at the table drinking hot chocolate and eating sugar cookies I'd made earlier. I poured a cup of chocolate from the pan on the stove and sat down beside them. Silence reigned.

"So, what did you think of him?" I asked.

Samuel shrugged. "He seems nice enough." He thought a moment. "I liked his playing."

"Yeah," Trey said, then added, with the Southern accent he hadn't quite lost despite his years in the North, "You laughed a lot, Mom. Y'all seemed to be enjoying yourselves."

"I suppose we were," I said.

He contemplated his cup for a few seconds. "Good," he said.

That was the end of that discussion. I was sure they were wondering what role Duncan had in my life. So was I.

Duncan and I practiced a few more times, talking long after the music ended. The night before the concert, he lingered on the doorstep as we said goodbye, staring down into my eyes, then leaning down tentatively toward my lips. I stretched up to meet him. We kissed again and again until that old familiar quiver I hadn't felt in years rose in me.

I broke off the contact at last.

"I'd like to keep seeing you when this is over," he said.

"I'd like that," I whispered, caught in his spell. He left with a final hug while I stood transfixed, leaning weak-kneed against the door. I hadn't felt so energized, so happy, so aware of myself as a woman since well before Arthur died.

This can't last, I thought. For all I knew there were other women in his life. I wouldn't stand for that. Either Duncan or I would break it off eventually or he'd push for bedplay. Appealing as the idea was, I wasn't prepared to go there without commitment. Rupert had warned me Duncan flitted from flower to flower. So I doubted he'd want marriage. That suited me. The years of independence, of making decisions without consulting a husband, had changed me. I knew the joys of marriage. I also knew its strictures. A husband would expect to make final decisions about our lives. He'd expect me to quit work. No, I had no interest in submitting to a husband's will.

Still, I was tired of being alone. Duncan temporarily could fill that void that children never can. Thus reassured, I retreated to my bedroom and slept soundly.

Yet the next day at school, I pulled Rupert aside during recess.

"Your friend Duncan was great with my class. Thanks for introducing us. We're doing a concert together now to raise some money for instruments."

"So I heard," he said.

"I'm enjoying practicing with him."

He looked at my face. "Uh, oh," he said. "Duncan strikes again."

"No," I said. "It's not like that."

"I hope not. Last I heard, he was seeing a singer at the Safari Club." He paused. "Do you want me to try to find out if he still is?"

"Good heavens, no," I said, face burning. "It's nothing to me who he sees."

"If you say so."

As I walked back to my classroom, I was surprised at the depth of hurt I felt. Clearly, I'd been fooling myself about my feelings for Duncan.

Then came the night of the benefit concert. It was a rousing success, with two calls for encores. We'd only prepared one piece so I asked Duncan to handle the second encore, figuring he had more practice at performing than I did. When the final applause died down, the principal took the stage.

"We've raised enough to buy five instruments to be kept at the school for future use," he announced. "We owe special thanks to Mrs. Benning and Mr. O'Toole for their performances."

The crowd applauded again enthusiastically. Elation filled me. We'd helped the school and no one had suffered.

People prepared to leave and the principal went down to mingle with the parents, Duncan and I stood backstage in the wings behind the red velvet stage curtain, listening to the people praising our performance as they filed out. We looked at each other with big smiles. "It went well, didn't it?" I said, waving my hands in the air with a happiness I couldn't contain.

"It did. We were great together," he said. He looked around, spotted no one nearby, then hugged me. Flush with enthusiasm and adrenaline, high on applause and music, I hugged him back. The feel of his masculine body warm against mine gave me an unexpected jolt of electricity.

Suddenly, he wrapped the edge of the red curtain around us with one hand, shielding us from view and creating a dark, soft cocoon of intimacy. "What...?" I asked.

"Marry me, Delia," he said. "I love you. I've been thinking about this ever since that day at the ice cream parlor when I suspected I'd found the woman I'd been searching for all these years. Please say yes."

I stood stunned, searching his face for I knew not what. His features were dim and told me nothing. The silence stretched between us. In it, I could hear his breath move in and out. There must have been other sounds, footsteps on the stage, murmurs of the audience leaving, but all I was aware of was the feel of his body, the sound of his breath.

"I'm sorry," he began, his voice miserable.

"Yes," I whispered. The word leapt out of me, puncturing the silence. My heart soared even as I put my hand to my mouth, astonished at my certainty. Some deep, hidden part of me had answered. What, the more rational part wondered, had I just done?

Duncan removed my hand and clasped it, letting the curtain fall away so that we stood together on the bare boards inches apart. He must have been thinking of the long silence before I spoke, because his next words were flat. "I shouldn't have surprised you. If you need more time, I can wait." His expression was carefully neutral. But nothing could hide the hope in his eyes.

"No," I said. "I mean, yes."

He gripped my hand tightly as if to prevent me from bolting like a startled filly.

"I'm not sure what that means," he said.

A sudden sureness settled over me. "It means, no, I won't change my mind. Yes, I'll marry you."

Just like that I made the craziest, most spontaneous decision I'd made since I ran at Ruthann like a demented rooster in the spinning room.

"You won't be sorry," he said and kissed me fiercely, just as the principal walked into the wings, frowning as he took in this public show of affection.

"Mrs. Benning has just agreed to marry me," Duncan said. The words made my acceptance more real.

His frown vanished. "Oh? Well, then." He reached out to shake Duncan's hand. "Congratulations. You're a lucky man."

"I know," Duncan said. "The luckiest."

I felt lucky, too. The feeling lasted through putting on our coats and heading out into the winter night. As Duncan walked me home under a sky filled with brilliant stars, the giddiness evaporated. We walked in silence, my head whirling with questions.

"Duncan," I said. "This is crazy. We barely know each other. And I thought you were seeing someone else."

"Not since the ice cream parlor," he said. "Never again."

"There are so many things we haven't discussed. Where will we live? Do you want children? I would have liked to have had a daughter as well as sons. But that didn't happen. Now the boys are about ready to leave home, and I've reached the point where I don't want to start over with a newborn."

I stopped short. "Oh dear. I just realized. I'd have to quit work. They'll never let a married woman teach. I suppose I could give private lessons, but maybe you don't want your wife to work. And I love teaching."

He reached out a hand and laid it on my lips.

"Delia, stop," he said. "I'm happy just to be a stepfather to your boys. As for your continuing to work, that's no problem." He gave a rueful laugh. "Besides, my income is uneven. Whatever you earn will help. I know this is no bargain for you in some ways. But I promise you we'll have fun together. That has to be worth something."

I subsided into silence, still uncertain. What of my reservations about controlling husbands? Duncan hadn't shown any signs of trying to tell me what to do. But then, courting behavior was no guarantee of how a man — or woman — would behave once they'd captured the other person's heart.

He kissed me at the door, a long, lingering kiss. "I love you so much," he whispered. "I'll do all I can to make you happy."

"I love you, too," I said.

That night in my bedroom, I considered what I wanted in a husband. Stable, faithful, good provider, good father to the boys. I believed Duncan would be a good father. The other points on the list were more uncertain. He hadn't been too stable in the past. He wasn't a great provider. And he clearly loved the attention of women.

But he had other qualities I hoped for in a mate: Loves music. Makes me laugh, makes my heart pound when I'm near him. They were important, too. Once Ma had told me that when she first saw Pa, she knew he was the one. I understood that better now.

I thought about Arthur and how he'd been a good father and an excellent provider. He'd made my heart pound with passion, taken me into a world I'd longed to join. That courtship had happened quickly, like this one. I'd been sure then, too, and it turned out badly.

This was different. I'd been mad for Arthur, but he was never in love with me the way Duncan was. Together, we could work out any problems. Six months later Duncan and I were married in a simple ceremony with the twins in attendance. And so, I launched into an uncertain future, hoping that this time I'd made the right choice.

Chapter Thirteen

December 1912, Felthame, North Carolina

Duncan lay in bed beside me in the chilly darkness, whispering because my mother was asleep in the next room and the twins were sprawled on blankets on the floor in the front room. The fire had died down to coals and neither of us wanted to replenish it. Besides, this situation had its merits. I huddled closer to him under the patchwork quilt Ma had made from patterned flour sacks.

We were at the stage, six months into our marriage, where there were lots of new things to learn and share, where the other person appeared fascinating territory to explore and the habits that might become irritants — or worse — hadn't emerged. So far the worst revelation about Duncan had been that he snored when he was tired. What flaws he'd found in me, I could wait to be told.

"We'd best get some sleep," I said. "Our rooster will crow at dawn whether we've had enough sleep or not."

The rascally Sergeant had gone to his heavenly or, more likely, hellish reward and been replaced by Corporal, a rooster lower in rank but no kindlier in disposition.

I lay still, feeling his warmth. The quilt and the darkness created a cocoon of intimacy, of safety. "I have something to share with you," I said. "It's about how I got my limp." I'd put off telling him, mindful of how it had hurt when Arthur hadn't believed me.

"I wondered," he said. "But I figured you'd tell me when you were ready."

"It all began with a benefit concert that went wrong."

"Ah." His grip tightened as if to hold me as close as possible. And so I shared the story of that terrible day at the river for the first time ever with someone who wasn't kin.

"That's terrible," he said when I finished. "What you've gone through. It's horrible."

Tears came to my eyes. My family had said it. Yet coming from him, it had an added impact, an extra validation of my experience.

"We may see Ruthann on the street while we're here," I said. "I just nod and pass on."

"I don't know as I could do that," he said in a hard, low voice. "I see red just thinking about someone hurting you. But I'll try."

"I've struggled with this," I said. "But it's gotten easier with time and distance." Or perhaps the hurt just found a deeper place to hide.

Suddenly, he kissed me in the middle of my back, a kiss I could feel through my flannel nightgown. I turned and kissed him, on the cheek first, then on the lips. He kissed me back less sedately, rising up on one arm. The quilt slipped down and I started to reach for it.

"Let it be," he said, his voice thickening "I have an idea for how to keep warm."

"Oh, I see. I like your idea. But the boys and Ma might hear us," I protested.

He stopped my mouth with a kiss, then another. His hand slid toward my breast and the passion he always ignited in me began to overcome my reservations.

"We'll have to be really quiet," I said.

He bounced experimentally on the feather mattress, which gave out a soft bumping noise. I smothered a laugh as his motion threw me against him.

"A minor challenge, but possible," he declared.

We kept very warm.

Afterward, I lay awake taking in the smoky smell of burning firewood that permeated the house in winter. How many nights had I lain here as a child? But never like this. If I looked, I could find the marks for my height on the wall and the spot near the floor where for some unremembered reason I'd scribbled the word "think" in pencil. Ma had scolded me and I'd scrubbed, but it was still there. "Think" That was good advice, but right now the farthest thing from my mind was thinking. I wanted only to feel Duncan beside me and enjoy being home.

Soon he started to snore. I poked him and he stopped, at least temporarily. A coonhound bayed somewhere; an owl hooted in the distance. Despite myself, being home waked other, less palatable memories. What would happen, I wondered, when Duncan met Ruthann for the first time?

The next day, Mattie, still single and enjoying it, had some pointed questions as she and I sat in her front room wrapping Christmas presents. Duncan and I had brought harmonicas, a few wooden toys and clothes for my nieces and nephews with us, plus gifts for the adults. Ma had laid in oranges and candy. It would be a good Christmas.

"So," Mattie said, while she wrapped a jaw harp, "you said y'all are moving to Virginia this summer so you can teach college there. Does the school know you're married?"

"Yes," I said. "It took me a while to find a school who'd take a married woman. The dean went out on a limb for me. I'm an experiment." Just like years ago with Mrs. Powell, the mill superintendent's wife, I thought.

"He won't be sorry," she said. "How does Duncan feel about his wife working?"

"He knows how much I want to teach music so he's behind me."

"A point in his favor," Mattie said. She reached for more white tissue paper and wrapped it around a harmonica. "If I could find a man like that, one who didn't think God gave him the right to tell his wife what to do, I might take the plunge." She cocked her head to one side. "Or I might not."

I laughed. She didn't lack for male admirers. How would she feel when she was older and alone in a village where precious few women stayed single or childless by choice? Happy, I hoped. Better that than a bad marriage.

"And what will Duncan do while you're teaching?" she asked.

"Make music. They have dance halls and charity balls in Virginia, too," I said, picking up a piece of red ribbon.

"Hmm. Seems like you'll be the main breadwinner. How do you feel about that?"

Only Mattie or my family could get away with questions as personal as these. Love gives you certain privileges.

"I'm fine with it."

"But is he?"

"Naturally, he wishes he could shower me with luxury, but that's not the way it is."

I laid down the ribbon and turned to face her. I wanted my dearest friend to understand. She was only echoing the doubts of my family. Ma, as much as she'd liked Duncan, had been uncertain about how he would provide for his new family.

"I doubt we'll ever be rich in money. But, Mattie, he makes me laugh. We have music in common. He loves the boys and they're learning to love him. Those things are what are important to me."

Some doubt still must have been in Mattie's mind. "That's all well and good. But I've seen the way he flirts. It's kind of cute, but I don't want you to get hurt," she said. "You know what I mean."

"Yes, he does like to charm women. But he says that he appreciates women in the same way he appreciates a fine piece of music. You can listen, but you don't have to play it yourself. Mattie, everything will be fine. I've never been happier."

"Good," she said, giving a final, vigorous twist to a red bow. "It better stay that way or heaven knows what I'd have to do to him."

"It would be nothing to what I'd do," I said.

Sunday morning the whole family went to church together. A Christmas tree stood in front, decorated with strings of red holly berries and white paper snowflakes the children had made. The smell of fragrant cedar branches and burning candles filled the air. I looked over to see Ruthann and her family slip into a pew across from us. I felt wary around Ruthann, in the way you are wary of dogs if you've been bitten by one, an atavistic, unthinking reaction. I wished I didn't react that way because it seemed that it still gave her power over me.

Duncan, his mouth stern, nonetheless took my lead and we nodded politely to Ruthann and her husband. It was after all church and almost Christmas. Her daughter Amanda was six now, dressed in a red velvet dress with her blonde hair curled prettily.

The surprise was Violet. I hadn't seen her in a few years. Neither had the twins. My memories of her were of a silent, shy child, tall for her age, with even features and huge brown eyes, who usually looked away when she talked to you. Now she had blossomed into a pretty young woman. A white blouse with a high, lace-trimmed collar was tucked into the waist of her gray skirt. Her long curly hair was braided demurely atop her head, but tendrils had escaped and shone faintly auburn in the light streaming through the church windows.

My sons noticed her, of course. Samuel nudged Trey and inclined his head toward Violet. Trey glanced at her, give a tiny nod to his brother, then looked at her again. Violet flicked her eyes his way, and immediately gazed straight ahead with a faint smile.

Ruthann seemed oblivious to the interaction, but I wasn't. I nudged Trey. "Stop staring," I whispered.

Trey and Samuel both kept stealing glances, but how often can you reprimand practically grown young men in church without attracting attention? Instead, I lost myself in the familiar carols of childhood until the spirit of Christmas swept over me. Ruthann's lovely soprano soared out on the hymns, and my alto and Duncan's tenor blended with hers in the best harmony we could achieve from a pew away. On the last verse of "Joy to the World" I looked Ruthann's way. Her eyes shone as if she felt the same way

I did, transported to a higher, better place. And so we sang "wonders of His love," looking at each other so we could hear our voices blend, harmonizing perfectly. It reminded me of that moment after the ill-fated concert when we were girls. I was struck with the possibility that, in a different world, Ruthann and I could have been friends, enjoying music together.

The song ended and Ruthann shook her head as if casting off a spell. The preacher motioned us to our seats and started a prayer that went on and on, gathering speed like a departing train. He prayed for the sick, the well, the old, the young, the church, the town, the nation, the world, the hungry, orphans, widows, missionaries, those who had lost their way, drunkards. I peeked from lowered lids to see Ruthann tapping her fingers restlessly on her lap. Beside her, Violet sat quietly with eyes closed. The twins used this opportunity to gaze at Violet. I shook my head at them, and closed my eyes again. Duncan stirred restlessly. He wasn't used to services that went on and on. Finally, mercifully, the pastor had run out of either energy or groups to pray for, and we could move on to our final song, "Silent Night." It restored the Christmas glow, which lingered inside me as we walked down the aisle after the service.

"Nice prayer, very comprehensive," Samuel told the preacher as we shook hands at the church door. The pastor smiled while Trey, Duncan and I smothered grins.

In the church yard, we lingered to exchange Christmas wishes with neighbors.

"Let's go wish Violet and her family a Merry Christmas," Trey said. He and Samuel walked over toward Violet, who stood quietly with her parents. I trailed them reluctantly while Duncan took my arm and stared at Ruthann as if ready to defend me against dragons. But it wasn't necessary.

When Ruthann noticed their approach, she turned to Violet. "Let's go. We have food in the oven," she said, and hustled everyone away while I called to the twins that we didn't want to keep Aunt Naomi waiting.

Trey stared after Violet, his interest plain. He'd been depressed and moody since his most recent love had dumped him three months ago. So I was glad he was showing interest in the opposite sex again. But why did it have to be Ruthann's daughter?

After our big Sunday dinner, Trey and Samuel stood on the porch whispering to each other. Then they stepped inside and Samuel let out an exaggerated groan, holding his stomach. "That was delicious," he said. "But I ate too much. I need to walk off some of that good food. I'll just take a stroll around the neighborhood."

"Me, too," Trey chimed in.

I was pretty sure their stroll would take them by Ruthann's house in hopes Violet was there and they could invite themselves in. In their ignorance of the tangled history between Ruthann and me, they would be in for a surprise.

"If you want to work off your dinner, your grandmother could use some more firewood cut, boys," I said. "Why don't you stay here and help her?"

Samuel and Trey looked at each other. "Mom," Trey protested.

Samuel shrugged. "You go on, brother. I'll take a stroll later."

Trey went into the bedroom and emerged with his hair freshly slicked down. I watched uneasily as he walked briskly down the street in the direction of Ruthann's house.

An hour later, he was back. Curiosity and a little anxiety consumed me.

"Did you have a good walk?" I asked.

"Nice enough," he said.

"Meet anyone?"

"Not really," he said. "I'll see if Samuel needs a hand with the firewood."

He went out to the back yard, where Samuel was finishing up. I looked out the kitchen window to see them talking animatedly, but too low for me to hear. Shortly, Samuel went off for his walk. He returned with no better luck, apparently.

That night, I dreamed that Samuel and Trey were in a fight over a patch of violets while a tall, thin woman joined me in throwing wads of cotton at them. Many of my dreams were incomprehensible. I took this one as an omen that it would be best to turn the twins' fledgling attraction elsewhere. There were always bright, pretty, young women on campus. I could host a music gathering and introduce some of them to the boys. And soon Trey would be off to the University of North Carolina in Raleigh to study for the law and Samuel would be enrolled at William and Mary in Williamsburg to study history. There'd be plenty of young women to interest them there. I lay awake planning and hoping not to get further entangled with Ruthann.

The day after Christmas dawned cold and clear with a cloudless blue sky. Duncan headed out into the country to talk with an old-time musician he'd found, while the twins and I went to the company store to buy groceries, a farewell gift for Ma. As we left the store, three blasts from the mill whistle shattered the calm. Across the street, plumes of gray smoke rose from the roof of the mill. A crackling sound split the air as a third-story window shattered and smoke poured out, followed by a lick of orange flame.

"Oh my God. The mill's on fire. Come on," I yelled. Naomi, Jewel, Ezra, everyone we loved was inside. The twins plopped the groceries on the sidewalk and we hustled across the street, with my leg making me lag behind.

People raced toward the building. The fire engine, horses running at full tilt, came barreling down the street. Mill workers streamed out the front door, some coughing and retching. As I watched, a man broke a window on the second floor and leaned out, yelling for help.

"Can't they get out through the front door?" Samuel asked.

"If flames don't block it," I said. "If they do, they could try the back door on the third floor. It has a fire escape that goes down to the second floor. People would have to jump from there. But the management usually keeps the back door locked so no one can sneak out for a smoke."

Fear filled me. With the openings for the belts running from floor to floor, the fire would spread rapidly upward and downward. The mill kept buckets of water at the ends of each row of machinery for the occasional small fires that erupted. They wouldn't be enough to douse a fire like this.

The pump of the ancient fire engine gushed water, but with little results. The flames grew with a roaring, crackling sound as the cotton and ancient wood ignited.

Around us, spectators screamed and cried. The town's two police officers motioned to the old-timers who played checkers on the porch of the store, and they shuffled over to help the officers keep people from rushing into the building in search of their loved ones.

I led the boys around back to the fire escape, hoping the exit door wasn't locked. Already the heat of the fire warmed my face. It didn't do to think about what it was like inside the building.

"Your aunts and uncle will come this way if they can," I said. "Years ago Ma told us to head for the fire escape if there was a fire in the spinning room. It's the closest path to safety."

Trey nodded, and we stared at the exit door. Loud thumps came from inside, then with a crash the door yielded to battering and fell outward. Workers stampeded over it down the fire escape and dropped heavily the last eight feet to the ground.

"Come on," Samuel yelled to his brother. He and Trey rushed forward to help lead people farther away from the fire.

A cacophony of sound filled the air as the fire roared and crackled. Now and then, a loud pop or boom rose above the rest. The workers' feet clattered on the steps. The thud of their landing when they jumped and the scattered screams and groans added to the uproar.

The wind caught the rising smoke, thrusting it downward to wrap the stairs in a shifting gray curtain. I peered through the haze. "Do you see your aunts or uncle?" I asked Samuel, who'd come to stand by me for a minute, breathing heavily.

"No," he said.

"I'd have thought they'd be out by now," I said. I pushed down a wave of panic.

Samuel patted my hand. "Don't worry. I'll go find them." He sprinted past me and jumped to grab the bottom rung of the stairs. "Help me up," he told a startled worker.

"You crazy?" the guy yelled, but then hoisted him to the landing before jumping to safety. Samuel raced up the steps, dodging workers coming down while I screamed after him, "Samuel, come back."

Trey had been standing stunned by my side. "I should help him," he said. I grabbed his hand firmly. "Don't you dare go in there. One of you in danger is more than enough."

Worry for Samuel filled me. I told myself that he had an idea of the mill's layout. He'd visited his aunts and uncle often enough in childhood. But finding his way amid smoke and flame would be a different matter.

"I've got to help somehow," Trey said, shaking loose and rushing forward to where workers were jumping to the ground. A young woman stood frozen at the bottom of the landing. "Jump," Trey called. "Jump."

She stared at him. Behind her a worker yelled, "Jump or I'll push you."

Bending her knees and thrusting her arms in front of her, she launched herself with a wild scream. Trey stepped forward to break her fall and they tumbled over backward on the ground. They lay stunned a moment, then he helped her to stand. As the young woman turned toward where we stood, I could see it was Violet. But where were Ruthann and her husband, Bobby Lee? Trey helped Violet to her feet, put his arm around her and led her farther away to make room for the stream of people still pushing, shoving and coughing their way down the fire escape.

But I had no energy to spare for those who were safe. My son, my sisters and brother were still inside. My world had dwindled to one wooden door at the top of the mill that held either joy or tragedy.

"Did you spot my folks?" I asked Violet.

"No. I'm sorry. It's a madhouse in there." She looked at my stricken face. "But there were places the fire hadn't reached. They might be all right."

She coughed violently.

"Don't try to talk," Trey said, patting her shoulder. "Just rest."

I yearned to go look for my family. But with my bad leg I'd be no help. I felt full up with frustration. We stared at the fire stairs as the stream of workers dwindled. "There," I shouted as relief crested over me. "There's Samuel and Ezra."

I limped over to the edge of the stairs, despite the smoke and heat, and waited impatiently while Samuel jumped, then Ezra, falling to the ground. They sat for a long second, then Samuel helped Ezra scramble away.

Once we were a safe distance, I hugged Samuel and Ezra as if I'd never hugged them before, then hugged them again to reassure myself they were really safe.

"What about Naomi and Jewel?" I demanded.

Ezra's face was red from the heat and his eyes watered. "I lost track," he rasped. "The smoke was so thick. I had to detour to get to the exit. About that time, I saw Samuel and we got out together." He stopped to cough. "Some of the others went the other way. They was going to slide down the rope they use to haul up cotton. If it didn't burn through, they probably got out the front." He closed her eyes. "I pray so."

Trey gripped his brother's arms and stared into his eyes without speaking, then nodded his head in approval. Samuel wiped his face, smearing it with soot, and looked at Trey.

"Don't ever do something like that again," I admonished Samuel, my fear turned to anger at his impulsiveness. I could have lost him.

He gave a slightly hysterical laugh. "No, Mom," he said. "I promise I won't do that again."

We straggled out front to search for the rest of the family. People wandered here and there chaotically. Some sat on the steps across the street watching, while others stood and stared unmoving. A few women wiped away tears, but most people looked on with grim, stoic faces. A line of empty buckets showed where an effort at forming a water bucket brigade had been abandoned as useless. From time to time someone rushed forward to embrace an emerging worker. But where were Jewel and Naomi? I watched with rising anxiety until suddenly I spotted them. "Look," I shouted. "There they are."

"Oh, thank God," I said. Trey and Samuel hurried forward, with me bringing up the rear. I reached out to hug Jewel. She wrapped her arms around me, then yelped and held up blistered hands with torn strips of skin.

"Are you all right?" I asked.

"I've been better," she said. I turned to Naomi, who had a bad burn on her ankle and one on her cheek. She reached up to touch it, then jerked her fingers away.

"It will heal," I said, knowing how she prided herself on her fair, even complexion. "You're alive. That's all that matters."

A ragged cheer rang out behind us and we looked toward the entrance to the mill where Ruthann had just limped out, followed by Mattie, Bobby Lee, and several other workers. Soot streaked Ruthann's face, giving her a fierce appearance. Her dress was ripped and her white petticoat blackened. Beside her, Bobby Lee carried a teenage girl, whose head lolled back. He laid her gently on the ground. Ruthann knelt beside her and patted her cheek, urging her to wake up. Beside them, Mattie sank to her knees, then fell over on her back, her long brown hair streaming out around her. She lay without moving. Let her be resting, I thought. Don't let anything serious be wrong with her.

"I'll be right back," I said and hurried over to Mattie. I dropped to my knees, heart pounding. She looked at me, then grabbed my arm. "Delia, is anyone dead?" she asked, her voice frantic. "Is everyone safe?" I thought of how her baby brother had died in a fire and how she had blamed herself. Today must have been a nightmare for her.

I hugged her close. "Yes," I said, even though I couldn't be sure. "Everyone is safe."

"Thank God," she said, and burst into tears.

In a few minutes, we all straggled or were helped across the street while the fire roared on.

"That's food for our children's bellies going up in smoke there," Naomi said.

Jewel nodded. "I thank God we're alive. But what are we gonna do with no work?" she asked. "We barely make it now. What are we gonna do?"

In silence, we watched as the town's livelihood burned to the ground.

When I took my eyes away from the glare and roar of the flames, I spotted Trey in his undershirt. He'd stripped off his outer shirt, despite the cold, and was wrapping it around Violet's ankle. When he finished, she put her hand over his and they stared at each other with obvious tenderness. I watched uneasily.

"Did you hear about Ruthann?" the man beside me said, making me jump.

"What? No, what about her?"

"She's a real-live heroine. The gals near her in the mill were panicking and she slapped one of them to bring her to her senses." He laughed. "Don't that just sound like Ruthann? Anyway, she told them to shut up and follow her. Her and Bobby Lee had everybody crouch down low and they led them to the rope and got them out pretty as you please. It was a hell of a thing. Beg your pardon, Ma'am. I mean, a heck of a thing."

"A heck of a thing, indeed," I said, unable to quite grasp the concept of Ruthann being labeled a heroine again.

"Hey, Molly," the man yelled, and Molly Caudle, a heavy-set store clerk with a head of gray, thinning hair, bustled over.

"Did you hear about how Ruthann saved a bunch of folks," she called out as she came nearer.

"I heard," I said.

Once on the playground, I'd seen a child stand in the middle of a seesaw, carefully balanced between the two ends. I felt the same now. On one end was my memory of the time Ruthann claimed she had saved me from the river and had false praise heaped on her while I kept silent with the truth locked inside me. On the other end of the seesaw was my sense of fairness. I'd seen her lead folks out of the burning mill. She *was* a true heroine this time and deserved credit. I stood balanced in the middle of my two emotions, then came down on the side of truth and fairness.

"Good for her," I said slowly. And I meant it.

After the fire burned itself out, tales of Ruthann's and other workers' heroism and close escapes were told and retold, chewed on like pork rind as people tried to make sense of the tragedy. When the injuries were counted, the village had been lucky. A fourteen-year-old girl broke her spine in a leap from the third floor and died within hours. But the other workers, despite broken legs or arms, sprained ankles or bad burns, would recover. Now the problem became, how would the town survive?

The village was resilient though. A few days later, while the smell of smoke still hung in the air, the charred timbers had already been hauled away. I joined Ma and some other women in setting up planks on sawhorses to lay out a community meal.

To one side of us, men and boys sorted through a jumble of bricks, passing along those that could be saved to a chain of boys to stack for reuse.

"Folks are really pitchin' in, aren't they?" I commented to Ma as we lugged over containers of hot coffee.

"I always said mill folks were like a family," she said. "Them that has helps them that don't." She lowered her voice. "The money you been giving me helps a lot. I hate to take it, but..." Her voice trailed off.

"You did for me when I was little. Now it's my turn," I said.

"I suppose. At any rate, I appreciate it," she said, and busied herself pouring sugar into a bowl. "They're going to rebuild the mill," she said. "With a decent fire escape this time. Some folks have talked about heading to other towns to find work, but most people are going to hang on. The superintendent talked the mill owners into canceling our rent payments for six months, so that helps. And the store is giving credit. Of course, when there's work again, they'll have to pay them back. Time enough to worry about that when it happens."

I spotted Violet heading our way with a pan of cornbread and was glad Trey and Samuel had left.

"Is Violet seeing anyone?" I asked Ma.

She looked at me, eyebrows raised. "Not that I know of. Why do you ask?"

"Just curious. Here, let me help you with the stew. We're gonna have some hungry workers here any minute."

April 1957, Felthame, North Carolina

A scrawny Negro boy knocked on Naomi's door after lunch and when I answered it, he thrust a note into my hand and ran off.

I unfolded the note to see Ruthann's wavery handwriting. "Come by this afternoon at 2 o'clock and we can talk," it said. I looked at the clock. It was 1:30, time enough to freshen up and mosey over.

But when I got there, Ruthann wasn't home. Kate, her eyes swollen as if she'd been crying, answered the door.

"Your grandmother asked me to stop by," I said.

"Oh, right. She had a doctor's appointment, but she thought she'd be back by now. Her rheumatism was acting up and she was going to get something for it. Probably the doctor is running late. He always seems to have an office full."

"I'll just wait, if that's all right," I said.

"Of course. Can I get you anything to drink or eat?"

"No, thanks," I said. "Kate, I don't mean to pry but you look as if you've been crying. Is everything all right?" I wondered for a moment if she knew about Ruthann's cancer.

She shrugged and reddened with embarrassment. "It's just... Alec and I had a fight."

"Do you want to talk about it?"

"Not really." I waited and in a few seconds, she burst out, "Why are men so stubborn?"

I stifled a laugh. She sounded as if she had vast experience in the matter of men.

"What's Alec being stubborn about?"

"He wants me to transfer to a college in North Carolina next year so we can see each other more often. And he won't listen to reason."

"How do you feel about transferring?"

"I'm not doing it," she said. "I can't because of my scholarship, and even if I could, I...he...we... oh, never mind." On that incoherent note she stopped talking. I waited until it was obvious we were through for now. I felt sorry for her, but there was nothing I could do.

"You said your grandmother has a piano?" I said, looking around.

"In the bedroom. Where she can play with the door shut and not bother my dad."

"Has she had it a while?"

Kate went to the front window and pulled aside the white lace curtain.

"About ten years," she said, peering at the street outside. "Grandma saved up for it. A college in Charlotte had a sale on used pianos so she made Dad take her to Charlotte in his truck and bought one, just like that. Sure surprised us. We always thought she didn't like hearing the piano."

"Did she say why she changed her mind?"

"Just that it was time to try something new. She got an instruction book and taught herself to play a little. And when I started taking lessons, I helped her some. Sometimes in the evenings, when it was just me here, she would play hymns."

I pondered the image of Ruthann at the age of 70 buying a piano and decided I liked it, whatever her motives.

"Oh, here's Grandma coming up the sidewalk now." Kate dropped the curtain and patted her eyes. "Do I look all right? She gets upset if I get upset."

The redness and swelling had faded some as we talked. "You look fine," I said.

"Good. I'll slip out as soon as you're settled. Just don't say anything to her about Alec."

"I won't," I said. I sat forward in my chair and waited to see what Ruthann had to tell me.

August 1916, Felthame, North Carolina

The laundry flapped in the morning sun. I reached in the basket for clothespins and another pillowcase. I'd come home for a week to visit Ma, who was complaining of back pain more and more. She was in her sixties now, still living alone, but her health was declining. Was it time for her to move in with one of her children? For us to hire someone to help her so she could stay at home? Persuading her to do anything that curtailed her independence wouldn't be easy.

Despite the decisions ahead, I felt almost like a girl again. I was alone on a beautiful, still-cool day in the place where I'd grown up. Tonight, I'd eat buttered corn, candied sweet potatoes and fried chicken around the table with family and I'd sleep on sheets saturated with the smell of fresh air and sunshine.

Duncan and Samuel had stayed in Virginia. Ma was inside making iced tea, and Trey had gone to the hardware store to get materials to fix the broken board on her front steps. The mill kept up its houses, but sometimes they took a while to make repairs. I wanted everything to be shipshape before we went back to Virginia.

A mockingbird burst into song on a nearby cherry tree. The sun kissed my arms, and I was like to burst with pleasure.

"Listen to the mockingbird; listen to the mockingbird, still singing where the weeping willows wave," I sang softly.

The bird cocked its head as if listening. Suddenly, it darted away and Ruthann jerked aside one of the sheets on the line and stepped through the gap, startling me.

"Do you know what your son has done?" she demanded, hands on her hips.

"Good morning to you, too," I said.

"Bad morning. Do you know what your son has done?"

"No. But I have a feeling you're about to tell me."

"He's been romancing Violet, that's what. She thinks she's in love with him. They want to marry when he graduates next spring."

I dropped the pillowcase in the basket. "Whoa. Slow down," I said. "Violet and Trey have been seeing each other?"

"For six months now. You didn't know?" A gust of wind blew a sheet against her face and she batted at it irritably.

"Good Lord, no. He never mentioned it."

"It seems he come down from UNC a while back to visit his grandma and he and Violet ran into each other again. Next thing you know, she's sneaking off to see him every chance she gets. And vice versa. I won't have it."

"The idea doesn't delight me either," I said.

Her tack shifted faster than a weather vane in a thunderstorm. "So you don't think Violet is good enough for your son?"

"That's not it. Their experiences have been very different, but from what little I've seen, she seems to be a lovely girl. I was thinking more that neither of us would enjoy being in-laws."

"You've got that right. What are you going to do about it?"

"I'll talk to Trey when he gets back, see how serious it is. But they're both nigh grown. I'm not sure how much we can, or should, do about it."

"We need to scotch this," she said. "If you won't, I will." She left as quickly as she'd come.

While I waited for Trey to return, I thought about what she'd said. Trey knew that Ruthann and I were cool to each other, but that was all. Should I share our tangled history? How would it affect the way he felt about Violet? About Ruthann? I was letting my experiences with Ruthann color my reaction, but I couldn't seem to help it.

When unsuspecting Trey came back, whistling, I dove in. "Sit down," I said, patting the top front step.

He looked at my serious face, put down the board and nails he was carrying, and plopped down onto the step.

"Uh oh. You've got that expression. Am I in trouble?"

"No. But we do need to talk. Ruthann Winton says you and Violet have been seeing each other for months. That you want to marry her. Is that true?"

His face reddened. "Yes, ma'am. I was going to tell you soon. I know you don't much cotton to her mother, but Violet's wonderful."

"You still have a year of college left," I said, my voice sharper than I intended. "This is not the time to get serious about a girl."

"We wouldn't get married right away. I know I need to finish school and get a job. But we could get engaged now."

I looked at his eager young face, swallowed hard and decided the past would stay between Ruthann and me. I barely knew Violet. There might be a lot of reasons she wouldn't be a good match, but her mother shouldn't be one of them. But oh, I didn't relish being thrown together with Ruthann at family gatherings if marriage came to pass.

"Getting engaged is a big step," I said. "A commitment to be honored. Don't do anything drastic. First, we'd like to get to know this girl, and you need to talk to your father."

His face set in the stubborn look he'd sometimes gotten as a child. "I won't change my mind," he said.

Chapter Fourteen

September 1916, Whistleton, Virginia

The train had just steamed into the station. Violet stood by herself, satchel on the ground beside her, searching the platform for sight of us. Tall and slim, she looked ethereal in a long lavender dress with a matching lavender ribbon in her dark, curly hair. I hadn't been sure she'd accept my invitation to visit us. Or that Ruthann would let her. But here she was, come for a long weekend.

I could tell the minute she spotted Trey. Her huge brown eyes lit up and her lips curved into a sweet smile. I turned my head quickly to catch a huge grin on his face.

Oh my, I thought. This is serious. He hurried toward her while Duncan and I lagged behind, unable to keep up with Trey's long legs. When he reached her, he gave her a peck on the cheek, remembering we were in public, and picked up her satchel.

"Did you have a good trip?" I asked, ignoring the faint flutter her resemblance to Ruthann gave me.

"Yes, ma'am," she said softly, casting her eyes downward. That's the way I'd remembered her, quiet and shy.

After she was settled and we'd eaten dinner, she offered to help clean up in the kitchen. Here was my chance to get to know the woman who had captured Trey's heart.

"So, Trey tells me you work in the mill office as a stenographer," I said as I started washing dishes. "How do you like the work?"

"Fine."

"What do you like about it?" I handed her a flowered plate to wipe dry.

"The pay is good and it's kind of interesting."

"What else?"

"It's not as noisy as what I was doing. I like quiet."

"So do I," I said. I cast about for more to talk about.

"What did you do before?" I asked.

She held out her hand for another plate and wiped it dry with serious concentration. "I started out in the spinning room, like Trey said you did."

"Oh. How did you make the switch? That doesn't happen that often."

"I took a correspondence course and learned how to type and take shorthand, so they gave me the job in the office." I could hear the pride in her voice.

"Good for you," I said. She gave me a smile that held echoes of Ruthann's rare, radiant smiles.

Unsettled, I paused to scrub the frying pan that had held the ham. "Is that the kind of work you want to do in the future?"

She hesitated and her cheeks turned pink. "Not really. When Trey and I marry, I plan to stay home and be a wife and mother. That's what I'd like best."

"I loved staying home with my boys when they were small. Those early years never come again." I said.

Silence fell. "What do you enjoy doing when you're not working?" I asked.

"Mostly read."

"I love to read, too," I said. "Maybe we enjoy some of the same books. What do you like?"

"Uh, romantic kind of books." She looked at me anxiously as if I might judge her as flighty.

"Romantic books can be enjoyable."

"I also like Willa Cather," she confided. "And I like 'Pollyanna,' because she's always so positive."

She was twisting the dishcloth in her hand and I took pity on her. We had the whole weekend to get acquainted. Anyway, I wasn't marrying her. Trey apparently was.

"Let's leave the rest of these for now, and join the men," I said.

That evening while Violet was taking a bath, I stood on the back porch with Trey watching the sun set over the hill behind our house.

"What does Violet's mother think about her visiting us?" I asked.

"Um. I don't know." The nervousness in his tone caught my attention.

"She does know Violet is here, doesn't she?"

"Actually, no. When the idea for a visit came up, her mom was really upset. She said Violet was too young to go off alone on the train. But Violet's plenty old enough. So I urged Violet to come anyway. She told her mother she was visiting a girlfriend overnight in the next town. I know it was wrong."

"Yes. It was. She lied to her mother," I said. "That doesn't bode well for how independent she is. Or for your relationship with Mrs. Winton."

He looked at the ground. "I know. But I wanted you to meet her so bad. And she wanted to meet you. Once we're married, her mom will accept the situation."

Boy, did I doubt that. At the same time, I thought of how eager I'd been to marry Arthur and be a "fait accompli" before I met his intimidating parents. I could understand her concern. But the subterfuge was troubling.

"It's done now," I said. "But if her mother finds out she lied, it will hurt that relationship and yours, too. Lies destroy trust."

"I know," he said again. " But Violet sets too much store by her mother's opinion. She's got to break away sometime. After all, I'm going to be her husband. She should be turning to me."

The sun had slipped behind the hill and a huge bank of clouds above it were turning pink and gold, a sight I usually gloried in.

"Let's leave the lying aside. How did you and Ruthann get along when you saw her?" I asked, my eyes on the sunset but my mind on the implications of my son's relationship.

"She was polite, but standoffish." He paused. "It was like she was sizing me up. She asked a lot of questions. How often I came home, stuff like that. She wanted to know if you and I were close. That seemed strange."

Not so strange, I thought. Judging from my encounter with Ruthann at the clothesline that day, her concerns about the relationship ran even deeper than mine.

"How does Violet's father feel about all this?"

"He seems to like me well enough. He's pretty quiet so it's hard to tell."

Trey had had enough of talking about Violet's parents. She was the center of his universe. "How do you like Violet?" he asked. "Don't hold this against her."

"I won't. She seems very sweet." If unwilling to buck her mother.

The bottoms of the clouds were turning gray and gloomy as the gold faded.

"I know she's quiet, Mom, but that suits me. She likes being outdoors and reading. And she likes to write little poems about nature and stuff."

"Oh? I'd like to hear one."

"Really?" He thought for a minute. "She wrote this after we watched a cardinal together. I memorized it." That sentence alone told me something about his interest in Violet. He wasn't given to memorizing anything he didn't have to.

He cleared his throat tentatively, then intoned in a deep voice that reminded me of his father, Arthur, when he used to declaim poetry to me:

"How I'd like a bird to be
If I could fly beyond the sea
To other people, other lands
Far away on golden sands
To see strange sights
And lovely nights.
But more I'd like to fly quite far
To other worlds or to a star."

"Very nice," I said, moved and a little surprised. "I felt the same way when I was a girl, longing for something beyond where I was." I patted his hand. "I like Violet from what little I know so far. I just hope she learns to be more independent."

By now, the sky had turned totally gray. "Let's go inside," I said.

There was more to Violet than I'd thought. But my misgivings were as strong as ever.

December 1916, Whistleton, Virginia

Trey slumped in his chair at the kitchen table. This was his first morning home from college for the Christmas holidays and he'd been angry and depressed since the moment he'd arrived. Duncan was sleeping in after a late-night performance at a local club.

"How's Violet?" I asked.

"Don't ask me," Trey said, staring morosely at the tea I'd fixed him. "I don't know and I wish I didn't care."

"Oh dear. That sounds bad. What happened, son?"

"I don't want to talk about it."

We sat in silence, each with tea we were neglecting, while I waited.

"I don't understand it," he burst out. "Violet and I were getting along fine. But last week when I went down to visit her, wham, she told me she's not going to see me any more, that nothing will change her mind. I asked her if she loved me and she said 'yes.' Then she started crying and said love wasn't everything. That it wasn't working out. She said she was sorry, but we weren't right for each other. I haven't seen or heard from her since."

"What a shock that must have been. I'm so sorry," I said. I reached across the table to take his hand. "I know this hurts terribly."

"You've got that right," he said. He stood up. "I'm going for a walk. I need to think."

"All right. I'm here if you want to talk," I said.

Trey did a lot of walking and staring into space during his time at home. As I watched his anguished bewilderment, I wondered if Ruthann's spoon was stirring this pot. I had no proof, but it seemed likely. Hadn't Ruthann done enough? Did she have to meddle in my son's life, too?

Two days before Trey was to return to college, I talked the situation over with Duncan. We sat on the bank of the frozen pond near our house, strapping on our ice skates. I'd discovered that basic ice skating, with its gliding motion, was possible for me, even with my bad hip. I'd never be graceful at it, but I reveled in the sense of motion and freedom it gave me, risky though it might be.

"You should tell him about Ruthann's opposition," Duncan said, helping me to my feet. "He's been so miserable. He's acting as if this is because there's something wrong with him. If he knew the background, it would help him understand that maybe Ruthann forced Violet to make this break."

We glided out on the ice, which complained around us with low creaks and moans. Our skates made skritching sounds over the uneven surface and the wind whistled past our ears as we moved in unison side by side, with Duncan holding my hand to help me along.

"I know how determined Ruthann can be," I said. "But unless she held a gun to Violet's head, she didn't force her to do anything."

"Did Violet strike you as someone likely to stand up to her mother?"

I shook my head as we rounded one end of the pond in a giant circle, Duncan stroking and me gliding on two feet. "No. But if I tell Trey, he'll be prejudiced against Ruthann for hurting me. Violet will wonder why. He'll tell Violet, and she'll want to defend her mother. It will be a mess. Better to let Trey and Violet sort out their relationship uncomplicated by all that."

"Two points," Duncan said. "Right now they don't have a relationship to sort out. And second, the truth is usually better than secrets."

"I agree," I said. "But I've seen how one well-intentioned act can unleash a chain of unintended events."

We skated in silence a few minutes, a cold wind whistling past our faces and turning them pink.

"Do what you think is best," Duncan said finally. "I trust your judgment."

That evening Trey and I sat before a blazing fire listening to the crackle of the logs. I looked at him as he stared into the fireplace. His face was set and his mouth tugged downward.

"If only I knew what I did wrong maybe I could change things," he said.

His pain and the way he blamed himself struck at my heart. The roots of this problem lay in the past, long before he was born. I had to say something.

"You know, Trey," I said, "this may not be all about you. Ruthann's mother has been opposed to the relationship from the start. She might be influencing Violet to break off."

"I know you two aren't friends, but I've never done anything to her. Why would she do that?"

"You'd have to ask her."

He studied my face, then stared into the flames again.

"Maybe I will," he said. "Maybe I will."

Two weeks later, Trey showed up, suitcases in hand

"What are you doing home?" I asked with alarm. "I thought school was still in session. Is something wrong?"

"Not now, Mom," he said. "I'll tell you tonight."

I started to press him, but he looked so weary, his eyes so bloodshot and tired, that I swallowed my questions and said only, "We'll talk later then."

My reward was a crushing hug like the kind he gave me when he was small, but had put aside as he grew to manhood.

At nightfall, I sat in front of the fireplace in an overstuffed armchair, mending one of Duncan's shirts. Trey sat across from me.

"Tell me what's going on," I said.

He stood abruptly and rubbed his hands in front of the fire.

"It's like this," he said, turning to face me. "I talked with Violet again, demanded to know what was going on. She said we lived in two such different worlds that it wouldn't work, that she wouldn't be comfortable in mine and I wouldn't fit into hers. Then I got upset and said her mother had put that idea in her head. She said her mom thought our backgrounds were quite different, but told her to do what she thought was best. I said you and Dad came from different worlds and that worked out fine."

"Violet might be afraid," I said. "I was terrified when I married your father and realized what a leap it was from the mill village to his world."

"Maybe. All I know is she wouldn't budge. I got upset and so did she. I said her mom was sabotaging our relationship because she didn't like you. She denied it. Finally, she said if I didn't believe her, I should ask her mother. So I got a ride down to Felthame and talked to her mom directly."

"How did that go?" I asked, my voice carefully neutral. Would Ruthann tell the truth?

"She said she didn't forbid Violet to see me, that she just pointed out some facts. And, Mom, she said that when you were girls, there was an accident at the river, that you fell in and injured your leg and that you blamed her. She said she blamed herself in a way, too, because she saw you were standing too close to the edge and she didn't pull you back in time. But that you couldn't let the past go."

"Oh," I said. "Did she now?"

There was some truth to Ruth's accusation about hanging on to the past. But I'd done my best to put that aside and give Violet and Trey a chance at happiness. Now she was lying again.

Anger flared in me, hot and high as the flames in front of me. I jabbed the needle into the shirt, pricking my finger and making me cry out. I dabbed at the drop of blood on my fingertip. "We have different versions of what happened. Quite different."

He looked at me alertly. "Different how?"

"She deliberately pulled me into the river, then repented and tried to save me. That's how different."

"Oh no, Mom. Really?"

Stung, I snapped, "Really. I wouldn't lie about something like that."

"Does Violet know about this?"

"No," I said. "I didn't see anything to be gained by telling her."

"She'd never believe it. And her position is pretty clear." He punched his fist into his palm with a loud smack that made me jump. "I feel furious at her mother for hurting you," he said. His voice was shaky on the next words. "But what difference does it make? It's all over between Violet and me. I can't force her to marry me."

A log burned through and rolled forward on the grate, unleashing a flurry of sparks. He pushed it farther back into the fireplace with unnecessary vigor, releasing another storm of sparks.

"I'm so sorry," I said. Sorry for many things. Sorry he was suffering, sorry that the troubled past Ruthann and I shared had hurt both our children. Perhaps I should have said nothing, but Violet would still have broken up with him. I looked at his stiff form and wished that everything, everything were different. But only in H.G. Wells' world were there time machines.

"It hurts like the devil to lose someone you love," I said. "I wish I could make things better, but I can't. Try to concentrate on finishing your education, son. Staying busy with school might help."

"I don't think it's possible to stay busy enough for this," he said. "I'm going for a walk. Don't wait up for me."

I didn't. But I spent a sleepless night worrying and wishing I could help.

The next morning, Trey joined Duncan and me at breakfast. "I need to talk to both of you," he said, standing beside the drawing-room table.

"All right. But first sit down," I said. "Have something to eat."

"I wasn't sure about this," Trey said, ignoring my request. "But I am now, after what Mom told me last night. I know you'll be disappointed, but my heart isn't in school. I'm tired of studying. My grades are suffering. I'm on the verge of getting kicked out. I've decided to join the Army. I need to get away, take my mind off Violet."

"Oh no," I said. "Please don't do that." Alarmed, I cast about for logical arguments. "Once you drop out, it will be harder to go back. Give yourself some time before you make a rash decision, one you'll regret."

"I agree with your mother," Duncan said. "It would be a mistake."

"It's my mistake to make," he said, "whether you like it or not. I've been thinking about it since Christmas, and this is what I need to do."

"You'll hate the Army," I said, thinking of my quiet, gentle son being shouted at and ordered around, even sent to war.

"You mean *you'd* hate the Army," he said. "My mind is made up. I'm sorry if you don't understand."

He walked out of the room, leaving Duncan and me staring after him.

"We can't let this happen," I said.

Duncan shook his head doubtfully. "We can try to talk him out of it. But young people have always had to make their own mistakes. I certainly did. And I'd hate to pressure him to do something his heart isn't in. I had enough of that with my dad when I wanted to drop out of college. Anyway, it may not be so bad. Before we know it, his tour of duty will be up and he'll be back, all grown up and ready to finish school."

"I'm afraid we'll get drawn into all this fighting in Europe," I said.

"Oh, I don't think so. Let's not borrow trouble."

"Just the same, I hate this," I said. "He's no soldier."

Trey went off to the Army. Time passed while we waited eagerly for his letters. It wasn't long before they hinted that he had made a mistake. The Army wasn't the solution to his wounded heart. I consoled him that his tour would soon be over. But then the country got drawn into the Great War after all, and his unit was among those chosen to go overseas. It was hard to see what was great about this war when your son was heading to the battlefield. As a child, I'd seen Civil War veterans limping around or missing an arm or leg. Now, those memories rose to haunt me.

Trey got to come home on a brief leave before he shipped out for Europe, then it was time to say goodbye again. Fog covered the train platform the morning he left, softening the outlines of the soldiers in their brown uniforms. Red Cross workers in long aprons were flashes of white in the mist. The scene seemed surreal. We all chatted with forced smiles about inconsequential things. None of the parents, wives, sweethearts wanted to send their loved ones off to war with tears, whatever they were feeling.

All too soon the conductor called all aboard. One after another, Samuel and Duncan clasped Trey around the shoulders, then stepped back for my goodbye. I hugged him close, his uniform coarse against my face, the feel of his cheek warm on my lips in the chilly air. "Don't you dare get wounded," I said.

"I won't, Mom."

He smiled down at me, my tall son. His spirits seemed to have lifted somewhat with the prospect of travel or battle or both. His eyes shone with excitement.

"And write often," I said. "Promise."

"I will, Mom. I have to go." With a last hug, I set him free, and he piled on the train with the other soldiers, all so young. They hung out the windows waving while we waved back, a sea of handkerchiefs fluttering farewell, until the train was lost to sight in the fog.

Every day after that we scanned the newspaper for war news as things deteriorated.

Then, on a snowy December morning in 1917, there came a soft knock on the door, so tentative I almost missed it. I had just finished fixing my hair, which I'd been thinking of getting cut short in the new style. I opened the door and a teenage boy in a uniform thrust a telegram at me. He left quickly while I stared at the impossible phrases: "deeply regret," "killed in action."

My shaking hands knew before I did. They refused to accept the news, opening involuntarily so that the telegram fluttered to the rug to lie there like a spent, pale yellow butterfly. I stared at it, then sank to my knees beside the telegram, rocking back and forth and moaning. I wrapped my arms tightly around myself to hold together, but the pain leaked out and filled the world.

Duncan found me in the hallway leaning against the wall.

"Delia, what's wrong?" he asked, bending down. Mutely, I handed him the telegram.

"No," he said, "No. It's a mistake."

"Do you think so?" I asked, hope flaring briefly.

He looked at the telegram again, his lips moving silently as he repeated Trey's name. He shook his head sadly. "No," he said, "I don't think it's a mistake." He put his arms around me and we hugged and cried and sat silently, staring into emptiness. Finally, we got wearily to our feet, locked in mutual, unbelieving sadness.

It reminded me of the hurricanes that passed through North Carolina from time to time, leaving devastation in their wake. The next few days were full of such wreckage as I called my family to tell them the news and listened to my mother sob, called Trey's grandparents and listened to his grandmother sob, called Samuel to tell him his twin was dead. He didn't sob either then or later, that I knew of. He retreated into a stony, stiff-lipped silence that spoke more loudly than tears.

Unlike a storm, which left brilliant blue skies in its wake, the devastation went on and on.

Five months later, on a sunny Saturday morning, I stood at the door to Trey's room, a door that had remained closed since the telegram arrived. Every time I walked past, it was a mute reminder of our loss. It was time to clean out as much as I could bear of his things. Duncan had offered to help, but I wanted to do it alone, where I could let my emotions have free rein without worrying about distressing Duncan anymore than he already was.

Taking a deep breath, I pushed the door open. Sunlight fell across the wooden floor, its gleam muted by the thin coating of dust. As fresh grief rolled over me, I staggered back feeling as if someone had struck me. Sorting through Arthur's clothes after his death, I'd thought that was the worse sorrow I'd ever experience. I was wrong.

Trey's blue and white striped cotton bedspread was neatly tucked in just as I'd left it months earlier. When he joined the Army, I'd straightened his room, washed, ironed and put away the piles of rumpled clothes he perpetually left on the floor, making everything ready for his eventual return. This current neatness seemed depressingly sterile. For a moment, I was tempted to flee and come back when I was ready. But I doubted I'd ever be any more ready.

I walked over to the wooden desk where his books were lined up with brass lion-head bookends at each end. Our brand-new public library could use some of the books to expand its fledgling collection. The textbooks might help a college student, a student like Trey had been. I made three trips out to the hall with my hands full of books, laid them on the floor, then went back.

His dad's old pocket watch sat on top of the dresser. He'd left it there when he joined the Army for fear he'd lose it. It hadn't been wound in months and it lay there mute, stopped at 10:15. I picked it up and closed my hand around it. It was cool and hard. For a few seconds, touching something Trey had touched, I felt connected to him. How often had I seen him wind the watch or take it from his pocket to glance at it? However careless he was with his other possessions, he'd treated the watch and his books with care. I would pass it on to Samuel, who would treasure it. With a trembling hand,

I laid the watch down and opened one of the desk drawers. It was full of seashells, all kinds, tiny and large, clam shells, a white fluted bivalve of the kind Arthur had called an angel's wing, a tiny whorled shell that looked like a baby's ear. My sight blurred as my eyes filled with tears.

When the boys got older, I'd told them how their father loved the ocean and shown them the seashells he'd collected. They knew a special one was buried with him. After that, Trey asked anyone who went to the seashore to bring him back a shell. I left them where they were. I couldn't bear to throw them away.

In the next drawer was a pile of letters with a Felthame postmark and Violet's return address. I stared at them, fighting anger. If she hadn't dropped him, he'd still be alive, and if Ruthann hadn't interfered, Trey and Violet might even now be planning a wedding.

I picked up the letters and sat on the bed, pulled one out of the envelope, then slid it back in. Reading them seemed like a violation of Trey's privacy, even though he'd never know. And I doubted it would ease my heart. Momentarily, I thought about returning them to Violet. Would that be kind or cruel? The fact Trey had kept them, showed he had cared about her feelings. Mailing them back might hurt her, remind her of what she'd lost. That decided me. I wouldn't return them. But keeping the letters would remind me of the tragic way things had turned out. No, I would burn them, let them go up in a flurry of ashes and smoke like all the dreams Duncan and I had had for our son.

Sobs shook me. I rocked back and forth on the bed, keening softly, until the wave of grief passed, then walked out of the room, leaving the door open, the way it would stay from now on.

I thought I had learned to live with the daily weight of my grief until I went back to Felthame for a visit that spring. Duncan and I went for a walk that took us past Ruthann's house. She stood in her front yard watering a patch of purple and yellow pansies. Her life was so normal and mine was so full of loss that at that moment I hated her. I marched up the walk toward her, determined to get her to admit that she broke up Trey's romance, that she started the events that led to his death. She put down the watering can and turned to face me, as wary as someone encountering a strange, hostile dog.

Rage and grief overtook me. "This is your fault," I said, grabbing both her arms tightly. "You killed Trey as surely as if you fired the rifle." Words poured out of some deep cistern inside me. "Do you know what it's like to lose a child, Ruthann?" I demanded. "I'm going to tell you. It's like you've been sentenced to a horrible prison. It's a strange place, full of tears, where everyone has lost a child. Other people can visit you and say how sorry they are for your loss. But, mercifully for them, they don't truly know what it's like to be there. They can leave. You can't. It's a life sentence, and there's no parole, ever."

Beside me, I dimly felt Duncan touch my arm as Ruthann made an abortive effort to get away.

"Leave me alone," she snarled.

"Oh no. You don't get off that easy," I said, tightening my grip. "You've seen a raccoon caught in a trap with the rusty teeth closed around his bloody leg? Losing a child is a little like that. You'd saw off your leg if it would end the pain and set you free. But it wouldn't help. Nothing can."

Ruthann stared at me. "I'm sorry about your son, but I didn't kill him," she said. "The Germans did that. You're not the only one who lost someone. What about my baby brother, what about Vernell? You want somebody to pay, but it isn't me. Now, for the last time, let me go."

Mention of Vernell hit me hard and I would have let her go if my bad hip, its muscles stretched tight and painful by my anger, hadn't reminded me of still another loss. "You pushed me in the river," I said.

She responded before I could go on. "You fell in. I fished you out. I saved your life."

I stood stunned at the depth of her denial. Duncan pulled gently on my arm. I ignored him and thrust my face closer to hers. I wanted her to understand the pain she'd caused.

"We can't even see our son again," I said. "We can't have the comfort of visiting his grave. They bury the soldiers where they fall. My son is somewhere in France. And I don't even know where."

My composure broke and I sobbed the last words, making them barely understandable.

Despair filled me and I fell silent. No description could do justice to the feral grief of losing a child. Despite her threat, Ruthann had made no effort to break free. I let go of her arm and she stared at me, mouth working. Surprised, I realized she had tears in her eyes. She blinked them away.

"I'm truly sorry for your loss. But this isn't my fault, no matter what you and Violet think," she said. Violet? For a split second, I was thrown out of my rage. So Violet blamed her mother for Trey's death. Before I could process the thought, Ruthann whirled around, strode up onto her porch with her usual erect walk and disappeared inside the house. I stood there so full of tangled emotions that I felt no one person could contain them all.

"Let's go," Duncan said in a soft, shaky voice.

Later, exhausted from the outpouring of emotion, I stood in the back yard as darkness fell. Duncan stood beside me, holding my hand. Around us, insects began to chirp their night song. "How are you doing?" he asked.

"All right, I suppose," I said. "I thought if I could get Ruthann to admit her part in this I'd feel better. And I do, a little, even it didn't turn out the way I thought. But Trey is still dead."

He didn't say anything for a minute. "I don't want this to poison our lives," he said.

"I don't either," I said. "It's just... hard."

I raised his hand to my lips and kissed it. I wasn't the only one who was hurting.

"I know it's hard," he said. "You're tired. Let's go inside."

"You go on. I'll be in shortly. I need to think."

After he left, I sat on the ground and stared up at the sky, trying to unravel the tangle of my thoughts. If Ruthann hadn't interfered, Trey might not have joined the Army and he'd still be alive. But honesty forced me to admit that she didn't make him join. Just as I didn't directly cause Vernell's death.

Duncan was right. Dwelling on past and present hurts led nowhere useful. I had to let things go. Above me the first star came into view, bright against the blackness. Ma called it the Wishing Star. There were so many things I could have wished for. Most of them things that couldn't be changed. Right now, the best wish might be for some peace when it came to Ruthann.

My lips moved in the rhyme familiar since childhood, then I stood up and went inside, still not as calm as I'd have liked.

When we returned to Virginia, Duncan and I buried ourselves — the perfect verb — in our music. Our shared loss made us more tender than ever with each other.

Samuel handled his grief in his own way, studying harder, trying to be the perfect son. He refused to talk about his brother, despite my efforts. Only once did he refer to his loss, when he told me he'd dreamed about Trey and that Trey said he was happy and not to worry about him.

Watching two geese glide across our pond one day, I realized that in many ways we were like them: Serene on the surface, but paddling madly underneath. The trick was to keep paddling so you could move forward. But on trips home, I avoided walking by Ruthann's house.

Chapter Fifteen

October 1918, Felthame, North Carolina

The town had turned the church into a hospital. People lay variously gasping, moaning, flailing, comatose in the pews covered with whatever sheets or blankets we could find. The air reeked of vomit, sweat and the pungent smell of the camphor balls or goose-grease poultices people had hung around their necks in an effort to repel the flu epidemic.

Duncan and I had fled to Felthame hoping to escape the Spanish flu. But death had followed us here.

I stood up from wiping the forehead of my sister Jewel and pressed my hand against my lower back, trying to ease the ache from standing and bending for hours. Across from me, Ruthann straightened from tending her daughter, Violet. Our eyes met for a long moment. Gauze masks obscured our mouths and nose, but I could read the terror in her eyes as well as she could read the weariness and fear in mine.

I raised my eyebrows questioningly and she nodded. Violet, then, was still alive. Maybe Violet would be one of the lucky ones. But she was twenty four and it seemed as if the Spanish Lady took those in the prime of life first.

Ruthann walked outside and I joined her. It was a gorgeous October day. Clouds scudded overhead in a blue sky. Sunlight poured down like a blessing. I pulled my mask down and took long, deep breaths of the fresh air. We stood without speaking because what was there to say? We were doing our best. But it wasn't enough. Who lived and who died was out of our hands.

Ma walked slowly up the street toward us. "How's Jewel?" she asked me.

"I think her fever is down," I said.

Her mouth quivered and tears sprang to her eyes, but all she said was,

"Good. Mighty good."

She looked at me critically. "Take a break, daughter," she said. "I got some rest and you're plumb wore out. I'll take over now. Naomi's coming along shortly to help. Duncan's at the house, and the two of you can rest together."

Duncan had been toiling at the mill, where the sick men were being tended. The mill was closed like almost every other business in town and now served as an infirmary, although the upper floor held bodies ready to be buried. Thank God the weather was cool.

Ma looked at Ruthann. "How's your youngun?" she asked.

"Holding on," Ruthann whispered, and slid slowly to the floor, face white, eyes closed.

Ma and I rushed over to her. I put my hand on her forehead, but it was cool, with none of the raging fever that often seemed to signal the onslaught of the flu.

"She's just tuckered out," Ma said. "She needs to sleep. Wearing herself out won't keep her daughter alive."

Just then Ruthann's eyes opened. "What happened?" she asked.

"You fainted," I said. "You're pushing yourself too hard."

She struggled to a sitting position. "Fainted? I don't faint."

"Apparently you do," I said. "You're exhausted. Let us help you home."

She stared at me. Accepting help was hard for her. Especially from me.

"That's all right. I can manage," she said.

Ma said, "I'll keep an eye on Violet for you. You get some rest."

"I'll have Duncan check on Bobby Lee," I said. Her husband was sick over at the mill infirmary. My sisters' husbands, Jediah and Mack, hadn't been stricken and were helping to tend the sick men there.

"Thank you," Ruthann whispered.

She levered to her feet, then staggered down the road to her house. Her other daughter, Amanda, was still well. Ruthann insisted Amanda stay inside in one room and that no one come near her. Maybe it would help. My son Samuel and his new bride had fled to a cabin in the mountains of Virginia, hoping the isolation would keep them safe. I prayed so. Surely this horrible epidemic would soon run its course.

Duncan was sprawled asleep on the bed when I got there. I crawled in beside him and pulled a coverlet over me. He stirred and wrapped his arm around me. I clasped his hand close to my waist, gave it a squeeze, glad for his love and strength, and plunged headlong into sleep.

I awoke an hour later, muzzy-headed, and realized that Duncan wasn't in bed. I found him in the kitchen sipping a glass of water. "Time to head out again," he said. He was helping at the men's infirmary in the mill just as I was helping in the church.

"How's it going?" I asked.

"This must be what hell is like," he said.

The days blurred into each other. One glorious morning, I checked on Jewel. Her fever was down. She stared at me out of bleary, confused eyes. "What day is this?" she asked.

"A wonderful day," I said, planting a kiss on her forehead. I could tell she would recover. Thank God, I thought. Although it was hard sometimes in the midst of so much death to see where God was in this.

Later that day, after a brief break, I returned to the church. Before I entered, I tore the camphor sack from around my neck and threw it in the street. It hadn't made a difference in protecting people. I was tired of being terrified. Inside, the same groans, rasping breathing and odors greeted me, making me gag until my nose got used to them.

Ruthann was there, bending over Violet. "How is she?" I asked. This epidemic had wiped away all previous enmities for the time being. I knew firsthand the fear you felt when your child was in danger. And I didn't wish that fear on anyone.

She gestured mutely. Violet's lips were the deep purple of cyanosis and blood trickled from her nose. While we watched, she gave one or two rattling breaths, then her chest stopped moving.

"No," Ruthann said. Then more fiercely, "No. No. No." She shook her fist at the sky, then lowered her arm. Her head drooped forward as if grief made it too heavy to keep upright. I reached out to steady her; for a long moment she leaned against me. Moved, I put both arms around her and hugged her. She hugged me back. Then she stiffened, withdrew, bent down and kissed Violet's cheek. She stood and slowly, so slowly, pulled the white sheet up to cover Violet's face.

"I have to go," she said in a strangled voice and hurried from the church like a wounded animal seeking a den to hide in. I watched her, knowing afresh the grief I'd felt when I got the news about Trey. In that moment, I felt her pain almost as deeply as my own.

In the days that followed, the death rate slowed. Bobby Lee recovered and joined Ruthann in seclusion in her house and I didn't see her again. Mattie, who'd fought her own battle with the flu and won, said that Ruthann wasn't seeing anyone. I thought about trying to talk to her since I knew the pain of losing a child. But when I knocked on the door, no one answered. Perhaps she wouldn't welcome my comfort anyway. Everyone had to grieve in her own way.

Duncan and I took the train back to Virginia, where the college had reopened, and resumed what passed for our normal life. After that, the months and years passed quickly as we learned to endure the Trey-sized hole in our lives and find pleasure again in daily happenings and in our remaining son, Samuel. As time went on, Duncan became more and more absent-minded. He was always losing things: his glasses, his sheet music, later his hearing aids, and finally, devastatingly, his mind.

April 1957 Felthame, North Carolina

I sat in Ruthann's living room waiting to hear what else was on her mind besides the dreadful news that she had terminal cancer. Kate was nowhere around. As before, we sipped on tea and pound cake and talked about the weather for a moment. She seemed more nervous than the day before.

She put down her saucer and looked straight at me. "No use beating around the bush. I got something really big to say. Hear me out before you say anything, all right?"

"All right." I sat up straighter in my chair, pound cake forgotten.

"Things are gonna get worse and worse for me. There'll be more suffering. I've lost weight. It's hard to eat. And I'm getting weaker. I don't want to die in pain, a burden to everyone. I don't want to be moaning and groaning and twisting, or doped up so much I don't know what's going on. I want to go out quicklike, since I got to die anyway. Spare everyone."

It was what we all hoped for. I thought of some of the nursing home residents, demented, incontinent, unable to get out of bed. Locked in their bodies. All-too-real evidence of what she was talking about confronted me every day at Pleasant Oaks.

"I can understand that," I said.

"So I've been thinking about not waiting for the end."

"Oh, Ruthann, do you mean suicide?"

She nodded.

Shaken, I protested, "But surely, Kate and her father would want to take care of you in your final days. She loves you."

"I don't *want* them to have to take care of me. I done for myself all my life. I don't intend to stop now. There's lots of other reasons." She began ticking them off on her fingers.

"He has to work in the mill. He can't be caring for me. Miss too much work and he'll be fired. I can't let that happen. Kate and him need his paycheck.

"Then there's the fact we don't have health insurance. I've managed to pay the bills so far, but if I linger, they'll mount up.

"Plus, Katie needs to finish her schooling. She can't be running home to tend to me.

"I don't want to die in some hospital room either, with tubes stuck in me like I was some kind of pin cushion."

"Tell your family and friends what's wrong," I urged. "You said you don't want things left unsaid. Don't deprive them of the chance to say goodbye, to repay you for helping raise Kate and everything you've done for them. Katie told me you saved your pay from the mill to help put her through school."

She shook her head. "My way is best. I got me a little life insurance I been paying on for years. It goes to Kate, so that will help. But as to the other about leaving things unsaid, if folks don't know how I feel by now, a few more months won't tell them any different."

I searched for a way to jolt her into a new way of thinking. "Are you sure you're not being selfish?" I asked.

"Don't talk to me about selfish," she said, her voice rising. "I done for everybody all my life, starting with my aunt on up to working in the mill all my life, caring for my husband and children. When does a body get to do something for themselves, I ask you? When?"

"I know you've worked hard."

She leaned forward and reached both hands out toward me as if she wanted to pull me toward understanding.

"It's a terrible thing to watch someone you love in pain and you can't do nothing about it," she said. "Believe me, I know. I want to spare them that. Now please, let me finish. This is a hard row to hoe as it is."

I took a sip of tea to salve my suddenly dry throat. "Go on," I said.

"See, this is where you come in. I can still get around some, but it's getting harder. I'm afraid any day now I'll be too weak to do what needs to be done. And I want Kate to have someone with her besides her daddy when I pass. He's a good man, but he's a hard man. I guess the way I used to be. He won't be able to help her grieve. But I think you care about her and would stand by her some. So it needs to be done soon, while you're still in town."

I sat back in my chair, feeling as if I'd been punched in the stomach.

"If I understand you correctly, you're asking me to help you commit suicide. Ruthann, I can't do it. Anyway, if your mind is set on killing yourself, you don't need me for that."

"I do need you. I tried to walk to the river by myself, but I couldn't make it that far. The ground was too rough and I tuckered out halfway there. I thought about rat poison, but that's too messy. Anyway, my life insurance won't pay if it looks like I killed myself."

"They put people in prison for this," I said. A sudden thought struck me, perhaps unworthy, but honest. "Is that what you want? Still trying to punish me for Vernell's death?"

"No," she said fiercely. "No."

"Why me, then? Surely you have friends here you can ask."

"I want someone who won't be faced with seeing my house every day, the church, the cemetery, and start feeling bad about their decision. You'll be far away, and you and I weren't close. I thought it might be easier for you."

"I doubt this kind of thing is ever easy," I said.

"I reckon not. But strange as it may seem, I trust you to understand and to do the right thing." Tears rose in her eyes, but she refused to acknowledge them. "Delia, we can do this so no one will ever know. I wouldn't ask you to do something that would get you put away."

"The answer is no," I said. "I'm truly, truly sorry for your situation and your pain. And I understand why you want a clean death. But I can't do it."

"Won't, you mean. Won't do it. You always wanted to be in control, be the one with the power to decide other people's lives, like you were with Vernell."

She picked up her tea glass, then set it down hard. "I'm sorry. I shouldn't have said that. But will you think about it?"

"There's nothing to think about," I said.

Overwhelmed by the turn the conversation had taken, I stood up so fast I felt lightheaded. I clung to the arm of the chair until it passed. "This is a lot to take in," I said. "I'd best be going."

She started to get up, then sank down in her chair as if exhausted. She swallowed hard and sat up straighter. "I won't beg," she said. "I never beg."

No, I'd never known her to beg.

I hurried to the door, let myself out and stood on the porch, staring at the scattered rain that had begun during our conversation. Ruthann must surely have an umbrella she'd lend me. But I didn't want to go back inside and ask her. I just wanted to get away. I limped home in the rain, reminding myself that a little water wouldn't kill me.

Her request wasn't that easy to dismiss. I'd told her there was nothing to think about. But I couldn't help thinking about it. What would I want someone to do for me in the same situation? My church and the law would say it was murder. Confronted with a hurting human being at the end of her life, one who I knew, things seemed more complicated.

Later that day, Kate stopped by Naomi's house. "Mrs. O'Toole, I need to talk to you," she said. "It's about Grandma."

We sat on the rockers on the porch where she rocked with a nervous energy that made the boards creak. It reminded me of sitting with Henry at the nursing home. I spared a fleeting thought for how he was doing, then focused on Kate.

"I'm worried about Grandma," she said. "She's gone downhill since I saw her at Christmas. She's thinner and weaker. She says she's fine. That it's just old age. But I'm scared. Did she mention anything to you?"

I hesitated, searching for words that wouldn't be an outright lie.

"She's getting old," I said finally. "We all are. The body starts to fail."

"I know but... I offered to go to the doctor with her, but she said no. And getting her to do something she doesn't want to do is impossible." She rocked harder. "I just know something is wrong."

"You may be right," I said, edging as close as I was comfortable with to the truth. "I can't say."

"Could you try to find out? Talk to her? Please."

"You don't need me in the middle. You two need to talk to each other," I said.

She looked at me, stricken. "I tried that. She just says I shouldn't worry."

I blew out my breath, then nodded. "All right. I'll see her again before we leave. But I can't promise anything."

"Thank you. Oh, thank you." Spontaneously, she jumped up, came over and hugged me. I put my arms around her in response, her young body warm and sweet against mine.

Then the moment was over. "Gotta go," she said. "I'll talk to you later."

The feel of her hug lingered. There was too little touching in my life. And I bestowed too few touches myself.

The next morning was Sunday, a day I'd been looking forward to until my conversation with Ruthann. It would be a treat to be back in my home church. The building was new, but I still knew a few people. I'd sit with Naomi and Jediah and some of her children, surrounded by family. We'd sing the old hymns I grew up with. The church had graduated to an organ, but a piano still sat up front, ready to be pressed into service for children's songs and the like.

We settled into a pew, and I looked around, smiling at people I recognized. During the part of the service where the pastor made the announcements and asked if anyone had something to share, Mattie stood up.

"We have an old friend back with us this morning," she said, gesturing toward me. "Delia O'Toole, whom some of our older members knew as Delia Hammett. She played the piano in this church many years ago and went on to teach music up in Virginia."

"Welcome," the pastor said. "Would you like to say a few words?"

I stood up. "Just that it's good to be here and I am grateful to this church and especially to the wife of one of the first pastors, Mrs. Robinette, for letting me play the church piano and getting me started on a lifelong love of music." Unexpectedly, my voice broke on the last words as a wave of gratitude crested over me.

People applauded and smiled.

"Perhaps you'd like to play us a hymn, for old-times' sake," the pastor said. I hesitated.

"Please," he said. "Don't be shy."

"All right." I stood and limped toward the piano.

"Does anyone have a favorite hymn to request?" the pastor asked.

"Shall We Gather At The River," Ruthann called out in a quavery voice.

"Ah, a fine old hymn and one everyone knows," the pastor said.

I shot her a look that could easily have slain her on the spot and spared her any future misery.

Obediently, I began playing, while the congregation sang, all through the four verses to the last with the words about our pilgrimage ceasing in heaven, where we would end our lives "with the melody of peace."

I banged the keys harder than necessary, resulting in anything but a peaceful melody, but I think the congregation took it for enthusiasm, not a riot of complicated, conflicting emotions.

"That was rousing," the pastor said, raising his eyebrows.

"I'd like to play one more," I said. "A favorite of mine."

He stole a look at his watch. "Of course. One more."

I swung into "It is Well With My Soul," emphasizing, "Whatever my lot, Thou hast taught me to say, it is well, it is well with my soul." When the last note faded, I glanced at Ruthann, sitting in her pew beside Kate and Luther, Kate's solemn father. Ruthann stared back, eyes bright and, it seemed to me, pleading. With a flourish, I finished the hymn and returned to my pew.

After the service, when hands had been shaken, greetings exchanged and Naomi and her family were ready to head home to prepare a Sunday dinner much bigger than anyone could eat, I lingered.

"I'd like to stroll through the cemetery by myself for a bit," I told Naomi. "I want to visit the family graves."

She nodded. "We'll eat in about an hour," she said. "Bring your appetite."

Naomi believed that it was fine to feed your soul, but it was just as important to feed your body. Once I'd quoted to her the verse about music having charms to soothe a savage breast. After raising her eyebrows at my use of the word "breast," she said tartly, "So do spoon bread and red-eye gravy."

I wandered among the tombstones, a mix of new and old, some shiny with still sharp markings, some stained with black or green spots of mold, the letters worn by time. Fresh and plastic flowers sprawled on some graves. Tiny American flags fluttered over the burial places of veterans. Confederate soldiers, a smattering of Union troops, soldiers from the world wars and now Korea all slept together in peace.

In the old part of the cemetery, I found Mrs. Powell's grave and said a silent thank you for all she'd done for me. I owed her, Mrs. Robinette, Miss Holcombe and many others a debt I could never repay, although I'd tried to show my gratitude by never turning away a needy piano student. There was always some household chore to be done in return for lessons. I probably had had the cleanest house in Virginia.

Somewhere near here were the graves of various members of Ruthann's family. The cemetery carried the whole history of the community and our intertwined lives.

Two rows behind Mrs. Powell's marker was my mother's grave, with Jewel's and Ezra's not far away. Ma had died of old age, Ezra died of a heart attack in 1950, and Jewel passed on in 1953 after she broke her hip in a fall and never recovered.

I wished I'd brought flowers, but I spotted a patch of violets growing by the wrought-iron fence that surrounded the graveyard, plucked a bunch, not without a groan as I bent over, and started to put them on my relatives' graves. At the last minute, I saved out two violets and walked a little farther to where Vernell lay buried. A weeping willow, symbol of eternal life, adorned his headstone. I leaned over and dropped the violets on his grave, a bright spot against the somber, gray stone.

"I'm sorry things turned out the way they did," I said softly. I wondered what kind of life he might have had if he'd drawn the long straw back then, or if I had made a different decision.

Ruthann's remark from the day before that I wanted to be in control, to wield power stuck in my head. Was that how she saw it? I'd put Vernell's name in with the other three students for a chance at more schooling and she hadn't been able to do anything about it. I'd certainly had the power then.

Questions churned in my head as I stood over his grave, the spring-red leaves of a huge oak whispering above me in the breeze. Was I still exercising power over her by refusing to consider her latest request? Did some small part of me see this as a way to get back at her for the years I'd been unable to walk normally, to run, to dance? Or was her request a way to continue to torment me, knowing I'd agonize over the decision? It didn't feel that way, though.

She'd be dead soon anyway. We both would. This graveyard was testimony to the way of all flesh. Did it matter that much if I helped her to die the way she wanted, spared her a few months of pain? Before I moved to the nursing home, I wouldn't have considered the idea. But after some of the suffering I'd seen there, helping a terminally ill person to ease into the next life didn't seem the same as hurrying someone along without their consent.

I remembered the day five years earlier that Duncan, his memory problems just beginning, looked at me with terror in his eyes and said, "Something is happening to my brain." For a while, I struggled along with two Duncans —

the old, laughing, music-loving one and the new, confused, cranky one who eventually didn't recognize me. Music reached him for a long time after other things did not. His body lingered, but gradually he left me in every other way. I cherished his physical shell at the same time I was worn out with caring for him. In the end, I couldn't do everything. I had to send him to a nursing home. But through it all I never wished him gone one second sooner. Still, I knew that if he'd been able, he'd have wanted to die before his dementia stole everything from him. From us.

My thoughts returned to Ruthann. I wasn't willing to go to prison, but what if no one *would* ever know? Except me and God, of course. A big "except."

There were no answers here. And I had no one to talk things over with without violating her confidence. I felt alone, just as I did at the nursing home. It was a way station, and except for my budding friendship with Henry, I hadn't formed a close relationship with anyone.

As I started back toward the street, looking idly at gravestones as I went, my stomach rumbled, reminding me I was hungry. The body always made its wishes known, even at times like this. With that thought, I left the province of the dead and headed for Naomi's house and the pleasures of a Southern Sunday dinner.

Over peach cobbler, I asked her, "Back when I was teaching here, Ruthann and I had a concert and we raised enough money for three students to go on to school in town. Do you remember?"

"I do indeed. That was a good thing you did."

Her comment soothed like balm.

I fished in memory for the students' names. There had been so many students over the years, but these held a special meaning. "There was Vernell, of course. Crystal Dickson, Lydia Moore and Peter…Wilson, wasn't it?"

She paused with her fork partway to her mouth. "That sounds right."

"I wonder whatever happened to them." I should have asked about this long ago. But I'd needed time and a little more wisdom to follow this thread of my life backward in time. Seeing Ruthann, had helped me be ready.

"It's been a long time. Let's see. Seems like Crystal was a good student and somebody in town helped with money for more schooling after you left. She stayed in the village after eleventh grade and got a bookkeeper job before she married and moved out West. I don't know about Peter. He won some kind of prize in a county spelling bee. That's all I recall. His folks left town after a few years and I lost track. But I remember how proud Lydia's mother was of her. She bragged on her all the time. Lydia became a teacher, worked her way through school, taught a little piano on the side. Then she moved to Charlotte to teach there. I'd say they did all right for themselves."

"That's good to hear," I said. "Very good to hear."

Chapter Sixteen

April 1957, Felthame, North Carolina

The next morning, I knew I had to see Ruthann again. Time was running out. We had only one more day before Kate and I had to head back to Virginia.

Standing in Naomi's kitchen after breakfast, savoring her homemade biscuits slathered with butter and dripping with homemade strawberry jam, I thought of Ruthann's childhood rain parties, when she and her family sat on the porch eating biscuits and honey while rain poured off the farmhouse roof.

"What's the weather forecast?" I asked Naomi.

"The paper says rain, probably just sprinkles."

Moved by an impulse I didn't quite understand, I asked, "Have you got any honey?"

"Honey? I reckon so."

She reached in the cupboard and pulled out a jar of clover honey.

"I'm going to visit Ruthann and I thought I'd take her some of your great biscuits with some honey," I said.

"You're seeing her again? I thought you and she were on the permanent outs."

"We were. But time softens things," I said, reaching for the honey jar and a knife.

"If you say so. She doesn't look none too good, does she?"

"No," I said. "She doesn't."

"What was that thing yesterday at church with the hymn request? I wondered if it had something to do with her pushing you in the river."

"Hard to say what's in Ruthann's mind. Does anyone but you and me know about that anymore?" I asked.

"No. we never told anyone. Unless you told Mattie."

"I never did," I said. I paused to wrap the biscuits in a red and white checkered napkin.

"Is something going on I should know about?" Naomi asked.

"No," I said. "Ruthann and I have a long history. It doesn't go away overnight. Now that we're both eighty, we're trying to make peace."

She looked at me. "The idea does you credit. But I'm not sure I could do it."

"I'm not sure I can either," I said, "but I want to try."

One thing about the South, you didn't have to make an appointment to visit someone. You could just stop by. So I took my biscuits and walked over to Ruthann's house under an overcast sky.

Kate's father was at work in the mill, but Kate was at home. After Kate greeted me, she discreetly disappeared into a back room, giving Ruthann and me some privacy.

"Here. I brought you something," I told Ruthann.

She pulled open the napkin and peeked inside. "Biscuits and honey."

"The forecast calls for rain," I said.

"Oh. I see." Her mouth quivered. "I don't know what to say."

"It was just an impulse," I said.

"Hmmm. A nice one. Thanks." She motioned me to a seat and silence fell. It was hard for us Southerners to come straight to the point. It seemed that, like a car engine on a cold morning, we had to warm up first. Especially with something as big as this.

"We could use the rain," she said.

"The grass does look a little parched." I wanted to get on with it, rude or not. "It's been a long time," I said. "A lot has happened. And now here we are."

"It's funny," she said. "I thought when you went North after Arthur died, we'd lose track of each other. But it seems like we know a lot of the turns in the road we've each made."

"We can thank Mattie for that," I said. "She's been a friend to both of us."

"We've had some tough times," Ruthann said. "That's for sure. We're both widow women now. You know that Bobby Lee died of a heart attack in 1948."

"Yes," I said. "I'm sorry." From what Mattie had said, he'd turned out to be a good husband despite his roughneck start.

"Twice widowed for me," I said. "I lost Duncan, my second husband, to dementia a year ago."

"Then you know what it's like to watch someone go into a decline and not be able to do anything about it," she said. "Have you thought more about what I said, about helping me leave this earth?"

"It's not that simple. Kate is worried. She asked me what was wrong with you. You're fooling yourself if you think you can pass your symptoms off as old age and loss of appetite."

"I don't know what else to do, feeling the way I do about hanging on," she said. "That's why I need you. I thought about asking Mattie, but she might feel like she couldn't keep it a secret. And I know firsthand that you can keep a secret."

I thought of the McGuffey's reader Ruthann had tried to steal. And of how she jerked me into the river. Yes, I could keep a secret.

"Lord, we don't let animals suffer the way we do people," she burst out. "Delia, don't you think I know I'm asking a heap of you? What would you want someone to do for you if you were in my shoes?"

"I'd want them to honor my wishes if they could do it safely, and if I was in my right mind," I said slowly.

"Do I seem in my right mind?" she demanded.

"Very much so," I said, unable to keep from smiling.

"All right, then."

My smile faded and I sat lost in thought, while she watched my face intently. Perhaps helping her *would* be a final grace note to a long, hard life. But did I really want to help her, or was I trying to even the score?

"I'm not committing to anything, do you understand?" I said. I waited until she nodded. "Hypothetically, then, how would you plan to kill yourself?"

She'd let out a breath of satisfaction. Was there a hint of something, triumph perhaps, in her eyes. I felt a momentary misgiving.

"I got one more thing to say before I tell you my plan," she said. "I meant to say it yesterday but I forgot. Seems like I'm always forgetting the things I want to remember and remembering the things I want to forget. Anyway, about Violet and Trey. I thought I was doing the right thing to turn her away from him at the time. I didn't think she'd be happy. And I wasn't keen on being around you more. I'm sorry. It's a lot easier to see your mistakes looking back than when you're in the midst of things."

"True," I said. "But more and more I realize I have to let some things go or I'll spoil what I have now. The past can't be changed."

"No matter how much we want to," she said. "Now, do I take it you've decided to help me with my plan?"

"I'm not sure what I think yet."

"Do you remember when we were young and the preacher baptized us in a side branch of the river?" she asked. "We wore those pretty white dresses and they floated up around us when we walked into the water so we had to hold them down for modesty's sake. Then the preacher dipped us over backward and we came up drenched, but smiling because we were born into new life?"

"Those were simpler times, but yes, I remember."

"Do you think it's like that when you die? You wake up smiling in a new, wonderful life? They say there's no suffering in heaven. And you're reunited with your loved ones."

"I don't know," I said. "I hope that's how it is."

"I do, too. Anyway, I thought the river would be best. People have drowned there before. The current is swift and the water's cold right now. It would be over soon. And it would look like an accident."

I wasn't so sure. There was bound to be an investigation that might point squarely to me. Then again, no one knew our tangled history. They might not suspect an 80-year-old, white-haired wisp of a woman who walked with a cane.

"Oh Ruthann," I said, not sure if it was an exclamation of dismay or despair or even a complicated affection.

Still she watched me, face serious and with the closest look to pleading that she could probably manage.

I thought of all the reasons she'd given. The wish to avoid pain or being doped up, wanting to spare Kate and Kate's father. Dying with dignity the way she wanted. They wouldn't be my reasons, but they were hers. I thought of Duncan's final days and made a decision.

"If you're sure this is what you want, I'll do this much for you. I'll walk with you to the river. If you change your mind at any time, we can turn back."

Ruthann broke into a smile. "Thank God," she said. "Oh, thank God."

I hoped God was somewhere in here, that he understood, forgave both of us if we needed it, looked with some level of compassion on two old, ailing women coming together at last in a way neither of us could have envisioned.

"When did you want to do it?" I said.

"You have to head back North soon. So, there's no time like the present. Today."

I sat back in my chair. I felt like I'd mounted a horse, only to see it take the bit in its mouth and run away with me. "Today? Before I change my mind?"

"Something like that."

"Or you change your mind?"

"I won't. I've thought on this for months. I want this. I really do. Be sure of that."

"Don't you need to prepare or something?" I asked.

"I've been prepared. Just waiting for you. My affairs are in order. So why put it off? Let me just get my sweater and tell Kate I'm leaving so she won't worry."

That seemed paradoxical in light of our plans. But she was right. Why delay? If we waited, I'd be gone and she'd be left with no one to help her while the pain grew worse and worse and she grew weaker. For a moment, I wavered. That might be best. Best for whom, though?

"Katie," Ruthann called, "Delia and I are going out for a while."

Kate's poked her head out. "Take an umbrella. And don't overdo."

"Oh, it won't rain yet." Ruthann picked up the cloth with the biscuits in it. "We're going to have a little spring picnic," she said, "like we did when I was a girl."

"Sounds like fun. See you later. Be careful."

Ruthann hesitated. "We will. I love you, Katie."

"I love you too, Grandma."

Stunned at the swiftness with which things were happening, I stood shakily to follow Ruthann.

She looked at my face. "Don't fail me," she said.

Outside, the sky had lightened and rain seemed less likely. We made our way toward the river, encountering no one. Most people were either working or in school. We took our time, time during which I reminded myself of what I would want someone to do for me under similar circumstances.

As we neared the river, we stopped to rest. By now, blue patches were showing through the clouds. "It looks like it won't rain after all," I said.

"Either way, it's a good day," she said, gasping for breath. She looked at the sky. "I'll miss this beautiful world. The trees and flowers and birds and all. But they say the next one is even better. I'm counting on it. There's one thing I need to know, though, before I go. Do you truly forgive me for what I done to you?"

"Yes," I said. "I truly do."

"And I forgive you for Vernell," she said. "It's taken me a long time to be able to say that and mean it. We both were young, and I reckon you did the best you knew how."

"Yes," I said, feeling that regret ease at last. "We both did the best we knew how."

I unwrapped the biscuits, handed one to Ruthann and took a bite. The faint smell of honey wafted upward on the chill air. "We'd better stand," I said. "I don't think either one of us could get the other up again if we sat down."

She nodded and bit into her biscuit. Honey oozed out the side. "Good, very good," she said. "But sticky as all get out. Only one cure for that." She lifted her hand to her mouth.

"I'm with you," I said. We licked our fingers like children, and our eyes met. It seemed to me as if something like love vibrated between us for a few seconds.

Ruthann sighed. "It's been a long journey," she said. "I'm so ready for the next bend in the road. It's a good thing you're doing. Truly."

Suddenly, it struck me that Arthur must have been thrown from his horse and killed not far from here. The river had woven itself in and out of my life, from the time I started work in the mill on up to now.

"Look after Kate," Ruthann said when we started toward the river again, with her leaning heavily on my arm for support. "You'll be close by."

"I'll do everything I can for her. I promise."

"Good. Some folks might not understand this. But by bringing me here, you've given me a gift. Don't worry yourself none about it later, you hear? And don't you go telling nobody, especially not Kate."

"I hear you," I said.

When we reached the high bank above the river, Ruthann hesitated.

"I know our voices ain't what they used to be," she said, "but could we sing a verse of 'Amazing Grace,' the one about how when we've been dead ten thousand years we'll still have time to sing God's praise?"

I had to wait to reply until the catch in my throat subsided. "Sure," I said. "You start us."

So there we stood, singing an old hymn in quavery voices that floated on the air with hints of their former strength and richness.

When the last note died away, Ruthann was silent except for the wheezing sound of her breath. She moved closer to the edge of the river and stood there. Her position brought back so sharply the day she pushed me in that I gasped. I remembered my terror, the frantic floundering, the shocking cold, the way I gulped water and the force of the current. This wouldn't be the peaceful end she imagined.

"Ruthann," I said, "Don't do this. Let's go back. I'll…" I reached down deep to the best part of me, past my son's death, past the years of my lameness, past even perhaps a sense of righting old wrongs that might have played some ignoble part in my being here. "If you want me to, I'll come back to town in a few weeks and stay with you until the end, take care of you." I said. "Kate can stay in school that way. Her dad can continue working. I promise."

She stared at me. "You'd do that?" She put one trembling hand on my shoulder. I reached up to touch her papery skin, cold as mine in the winter chill. A rush of compassion for her swept over me.

"Then, you're a true friend," she said, giving me a tremulous smile. "Bless you for helping me."

"Come on, then," I said. "We'll take our time going back."

"No. I know what I want. And this is it," she said, her voice stronger.

"Oh Ruthann," I said, taking her hand. "Please let's find another way."

"This is my life. Like I said, I know what I want."

I looked at her face, which bore an expression of anguish I'd never expected to see. "All right," I said, after a few long seconds. "If you're sure this is what you want, I'll honor your wishes as best I can."

"I have never been more sure of anything."

"What now?" I asked, letting go of her hand.

"You've done what I needed. Thank you more than you know," she said. She took one more step toward the edge of the river bank. Then with a burst of strength I didn't think she possessed, she whirled and launched herself out into the river, arms spread wide as if she were flying. She hit the water flat, with a huge splash and an indecipherable shout.

"Ruthann," I yelled, then froze for a few long seconds before limping as fast as I could toward the same rock where she'd rescued me. But the current had carried her out of reach. Her head bobbed above the water two or three times. Then she disappeared. I stood transfixed but she didn't reemerge.

I began to shiver, despite the fact the day wasn't that cold. I rubbed my hands together, trying futilely to warm them, while I stared at the water with a sense of unreality. The wind whistled past my ears. The shrill cry of a hawk broke my stasis. The river must have claimed Ruthann by now. It was what she wanted. But it was still a shock to think this woman I'd known all my life, with whom I'd had a tangled history, was gone forever.

I couldn't just walk away. Wanting to do something to acknowledge her passing. I turned to the most meaningful way I could find, music. Softly, I sang one of my favorite benedictions, one Ruthann and I had heard often through the years at church: "The Lord bless you and keep you, the Lord make his face to shine upon you, and give you peace."

Halfway through, tears began streaming down my face. When the last uncertain note died on the frosty air, I brushed away the tears and started back across the meadow to face the aftermath, my hip screaming with pain and tension. At the edge of the first street I came to, I stopped, leaning heavily on my cane, spent and hurting. I stood there for a minute, then hobbled up the street until I encountered a startled man, who raced to the fire station for a rescue crew when I told him Ruthann had fallen into the river.

Naomi, summoned by the firemen, came with her sons to take me to old Doc Bivens' office, where I said nothing about how things had happened. He fussed at me, then ordered me to bed. I slept for hours, too exhausted to even dream. When I awoke, Naomi came in and sat in a chair beside the bed.

"Feeling better?" she asked.

"A little."

"They found Ruthann's body," she said. She leaned forward in her chair. "What happened?"

"She lost her balance and fell in," I said. The image of her outflung body flashed in front of me. I hoped that she was greeting her dead husband and daughters in a new, painfree life.

Naomi stared into my eyes, her expression uncertain. "What were you two doing out there anyway? I don't understand this whole thing."

She was one of the few people who knew the full story of Ruthann and me. I was sure Kate didn't. I could see the doubt in Naomi's face as she waited for my answer.

"We wanted to have a picnic," I said.

Her expression lightened, as if I'd given her the answer she wanted, one she could accept. "A picnic. Sometimes you don't use good sense," she said.

"No denying that," I said. "Naomi, she wanted to tell me she was sorry for what happened when we were children, to ask me to forgive her."

"And...?"

"We both forgave each other."

"We could all use forgiveness," she said. "It's such a shame, though. Such a shame. Poor Kate. She'll be devastated. She really loved her grandma."

Kate came to me that afternoon while I rested at Naomi's house. Naomi showed her into the bedroom where I lay, exhausted emotionally and physically. Kate's eyes were red and swollen with crying.

"What happened?" she demanded. "Why did you all go all the way over there? She wasn't strong enough for that."

I thought of how Ruthann had asked me not to tell Kate the truth, and I lied, because choosing your words so someone believes something is true when it isn't is a lie of sorts. I was protecting myself in part. But I like to think a lot of my motivation was honoring Ruthann's last request.

"When she was a girl, she used to have something called a rain party. But as far as I know, she hadn't had one for years. Now she was old and sick. I knew what rain parties meant to her, so I suggested we have a rain party together," I said. "She asked to go to the river where we spent so much of our childhood, so I helped her do that. After the picnic, we were studying the river. She stood close to the edge of the bank and she..." I hesitated, searching for the right verb — "she went into the river, and the current swept her away downstream."

She looked at me with anguish.

"I wish you hadn't done that," she said. "Grandma would still be here. That's no way to die."

Kate looked away and grimaced. I could see a mental image of Ruthann's last moments struggling in the river forming in her mind.

"Don't remember her dying that way," I said quickly. "That was just a few seconds of her long life."

She nodded. "I know, but…"

"Maybe it would help a little if you thought of a happy memory of your grandmother."

"I guess." She was silent a moment. I could tell when she found one because the lines between her eyebrows smoothed out.

"Do you know the Elvis Presley song 'Blue Suede Shoes?'" she asked.

"I missed that one," I said.

"It came out last year. I liked that song and I sang it a lot, probably too much. One afternoon when I came home, Grandma had rolled out a bunch of sugar cookies and used a knife to cut them into the shape of shoes. Then she put blue food coloring on them and sprinkled grains of sugar so it looked rough like suede. Even Dad laughed at that. We all sat on the front porch that evening eating cookies, drinking lemonade and watching lightning bugs come out."

I realized there was a whole side to Ruthann I'd never known.

Kate's animation faded, to be replaced by sadness again. "Going that far from home for your picnic was still a bad idea," she said.

I looked down at the chenille bedspread, unable to disagree or agree.

"What did she want to tell you?" she asked. "She sent that letter and I could tell it was important to her. Did you ever find out?"

"Long ago, when we were girls, we had some disagreements," I said slowly. "She feared her health was fading and she wanted to make matters right between us. So did I. We'd known each other a long time, through good times and bad. In the end, we were at peace with each other."

"That's good then, I guess."

"Oh Kate," I said, reaching out my arms to her. "I know how hard this must be for you."

She let out a sob and fell to her knees in front of me. "I'll miss her so," she said.

"She had a long and useful life," I said, stroking her hair and feeling tears rise at her anguish. "And she loved you very much."

"I know," she said, her words muffled. "And I love her."

Perhaps it should have seemed hypocritical to be comforting Kate over something I had a hand in. There was some of that feeling, but it helped that I knew this was what Ruthann wanted. She'd specifically asked me to watch out for Kate, and I would. Even so, there would be a lot of sorting out for me to do later.

The next day, in a rickety wooden wheelchair Doc Bivens had found, I led a police officer as close as I could to the spot where Ruthann disappeared. I could see the checkered napkin still on the ground with a white and black lump on top of it, the remaining biscuit covered with ants.

He trudged over to it, then came back to where I waited. "Kate said something about y'all having a picnic," he said.

"It was a rain party, not just a picnic."

"A rain party, huh?" He shook his head. "If that don't beat all."

I could see him absorbing the idea that Ruthann and I were two eccentric old ladies in our dotage who decided to go eat biscuits in a field for some weird reason. Nonetheless, he questioned me, Kate and the neighbors with no result. With no witnesses, he finally declared the investigation closed.

Whatever Naomi suspected, she said nothing. I wanted to tell Mattie, but Ruthann was right: She couldn't keep a secret. I'd made the decision and I'd have to live with it.

After the funeral service, Doc Bivens, who'd tended to Ruthann and knew of her cancer, sidled over to me. He was near retirement age, a Santa Claus-looking man with a sizable girth, round cheeks and a short white beard. I tensed when he touched my arm. "Blessed are the merciful," he whispered, his tobacco-scented breath soft in my ear, and walked off, leaving me to wonder if he thought I'd been merciful or God should have mercy on my soul. Ruthann might have wanted desperately to die, but she couldn't have done it if I hadn't helped her get to the river. I hoped that was mercy.

Kate, urged by her father, returned to college, although she missed a week of classes, which gave me time to rest and recuperate before the trip back.

When she dropped me off at the nursing home, she kissed me on the cheek. "Let's stay in touch," she said. "Grandma would want that for her oldest friend."

If she only knew. Yet in the end, in a strange way, Ruthann and I had befriended each other.

"She definitely would want that," I said.

"I have some catching up at school to do, but maybe we can start piano lessons again later," she said.

"Count on me. For anything."

I resolved to funnel a little money to her anonymously, perhaps as a small music scholarship, so she wouldn't have to work so many hours. If she was like her grandmother, she wouldn't accept a direct gift. I'd promised Ruthann I'd watch out for her. But beyond that, I saw myself in Kate in her background and love of music. I would do what I could for her for her own sake.

Kate walked up the ramp of the nursing home with me, carrying my suitcase.

"Just set it inside the door," I said. "Someone can get it later."

She reached in her purse and pulled out a small package done up with brown paper and tape.

"I found this in Grandma's things," she said. "There was a note that said I should give it to you when you got back to the nursing home. So here it is."

She waited a moment to see if I would open it. Caution held me back. I examined it curiously, then slipped it into my pocketbook.

With a parting wave, she drove away and I stood in the entrance hall looking at the place with fresh eyes. My hip bothered me worse than when I left, and I'd been ordered to, as Naomi put it, "behave for a change" if I hoped to get well.

The medicinal smell in the air was as strong as ever. Beyond that, I imagined I could smell loneliness seeping into every crevice, an invisible presence. I thought of Ruthann. I wouldn't have made the same decision she did, swept away in a river to spare myself and others suffering. I wanted to be surrounded by people who cared about me at the end. It was up to me to do what I could to make that happen.

The television blared in the day room. Henry was seated in his usual armchair reading. I didn't see Alice anywhere. He looked up and smiled when he spotted me. I smiled warmly back. A flicker of something long dormant stirred in me as he stood and walked toward me. Who knew what was possible between us? Perhaps not a grand passion, but something.

He came over, picked up my suitcase and gave me his free arm. Reminded anew of the power of touch and with Kate's kiss still lingering on my cheek, I put my hand over his. He smiled at me again and we moved forward toward my room together.

"How was the trip?" he asked.

"Too much happened to tell about," I said. "Far too much."

I'd worn a blue dress today, instead of the black I'd adopted when I came here. Mrs. Atwood came toward us. She frowned at my more pronounced limp.

"Back safe if not sound, I see," she said.

I shrugged. "Yes, I overdid. But from now on I'll be a model resident."

She shook her head as if she doubted that. "One can hope."

"All right. Almost a model resident."

Her lips turned upward a tiny bit. Then she stepped back to inspect me, head cocked to one side judiciously. "That color goes well with your eyes," she said. "You should wear blue more often. Much better than that gloomy black."

She moved off and I looked around again at the scene. This was my new community, at least for now. I was tired of being an anthropologist observing the natives. Instead, I would think of myself as an immigrant to a new country. An immigrant would learn the ways. And an immigrant had the power to change the community bit by bit. I wondered if Mrs. Atwood liked to sing. Maybe a hymn sing for the residents would be a good start at making friends. I'd get to play the piano, something I'd never give up again. I was too tired to think about it now. But later, I promised myself.

After Henry left, I sat on the bed in my room and unwrapped the package Kate had given me. Inside was a battered tan book with a drawing of a whale and a sailing ship on the cover. I turned it over in wonder. It was a McGuffey's reader just like the one Ruthann tried to steal from me when I was in seventh grade. The brittle paper was yellowed with age, but still readable. I wondered how or when she'd acquired it and what she was trying to say. Perhaps it was even the same one I'd given Vernell as a goodbye gift when I left Felthame. I decided to take it as a confession and an apology.

No need for either, I thought. That was a long time ago.

Then I settled down and, more than sixty years later, plunged again into the story of what happened to Professor Wilson when he fell off the sailing ship in the night.

Questions for Discussion

1. Who is your favorite character? Why? Your least favorite? Why?
2. In what ways does the "accident" when Ruthann pushes Delia into the river alter Delia's life? Ruthann's life? The lives of their children?
3. What are some other examples in real life of actions reverberating through the years?
4. What motivated Ruthann to act as she did?
5. What is the role of the river in the novel?
6. Delia and Ruthann forgive each other in the end. How does this alter their relationship? What if they had not forgiven each other?
7. What does it mean to forgive someone? What are some ways in which a person can reach forgiveness of another person?
8. Are there things it is impossible to forgive?
9. Delia decides to honor Ruthann's dying request for assisted suicide. How do you feel about that decision?
10. Did Ruthann have the right to ask Delia to help her kill herself?
11. Why does Delia agree to Ruthann's final request?
12. Is assisted suicide ever acceptable?
13. How do you think the relationship between Ruthann's granddaughter Kate and Delia will unfold in the future?
14. What would happen if Kate knew the truth? Should Delia tell her someday?
15. Ruthann bullied Delia as a child? Why do people bully others and what is the best way to handle it?

CPSIA information can be obtained
at www.ICGtesting.com
Printed in the USA
LVHW081000291220
675315LV00016B/415